THE CURSE

ORIGIN OF THE VAMPIRES

KETHRIC WILCOX

✾ Created with Vellum

As always, to my Tiger for letting me create. To the fans of my first books who gave me the support and encouragement to keep writing. Thank you to my wonderful editor, Shannon, who turns my messy English into something legible. One last huge thank you goes to my beta reader and super promoter Lisa Cullinan, who lets me bounce crazy ideas off her via instant messaging.

PREFACE

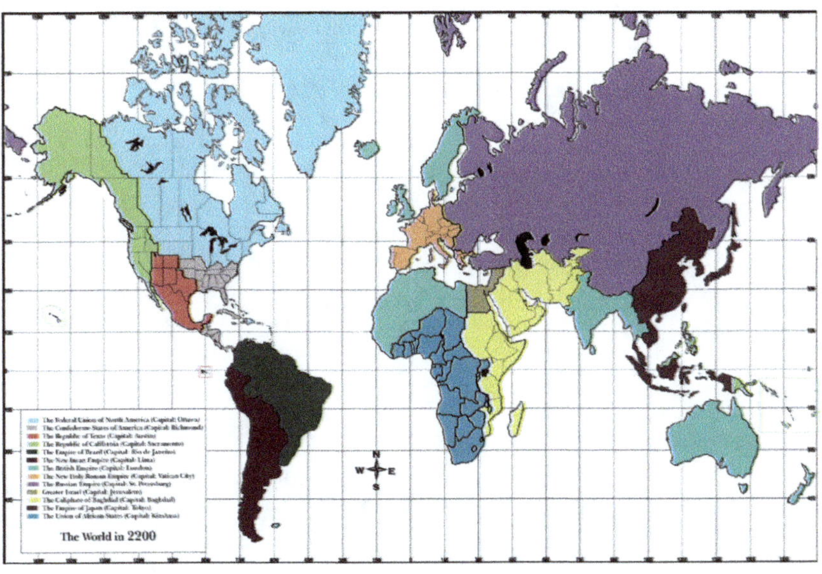

The world following the Upheaval and the Holy Accord

PROLOGUE

RICHARD ST. MARTIN SETS THE QUEST IN MOTION

"AND THE LORD COMMANDED ADAM, 'Go and fashion a knife to slay thy son, who is an abomination in my sight. The blade of the knife shall be a cubit in length of pure bronze. Fashion the handle and guard from cedar, and wrap the handle in leather made from a newborn calf. In the pommel set a ruby the size of the end of your thumb. When this blade is completed bring it to the Cave of Treasures and leave it at the entrance for three days. On the morning of the fourth day, take the blade from the Cave of Treasures and seek out thy son, the abomination, and slay him.'"

Gospel of El-Abel 2:1-5

An old journal sits open on the corner of a battle-scarred desk in the back of St. Martin's Antiques and Collectibles. Centered on the desktop lay his personal diary started several years ago. The diary's author glanced down at the current page of his life story.

March 5, 1992

I sat in the old house for two days after killing the being claiming to be Cain, son of Adam and Eve. Do biblical tales contain more than stories? Still can't decide whom to convince, myself here in the present or some time off in the future. The effects of Cain's curse started to take affect yesterday. In the course of lighting the fire, I found my Ruby magic tainted with Ebony magic, which possessed a strange sparkle. Faint stirrings of hunger manifested, and my canines elongated into fangs. Major magic awoke the moment my silver sword cleaved the vampire's head from his shoulders. Now to find out what becomes of my life or unlife.

The journal's author couldn't believe twenty-five years had passed since he'd written that entry. He didn't think the crazy old man was Cain, the first of his kind. The reality of his situation transformed everything his poor lost Susan had believed in, into the fiction the critics of Judeo-Christian beliefs claim. He wondered what the church would make of Cain's journal or any of the other ancient books in his private collection. He still couldn't figure out what to make of some of the passages directed at Cain's successor, in particular the one at the end of the journal; the man flipped to the last page of Cain's journal, which contained writing.

Under the full moon in the throne room of El-Abel, soak these last pages in blood from one of the grandchildren of Cain and reveal the deepest truth.

The man paused his reading when a text vibrated his phone. Pulling his phone out, he glanced at the message and decided to put himself to the test. He hit the phone number in the text and waited while the number rang.

"Kieran Belle, can I help you?"

"Mr. Belle, Richard St. Martin here. I'm a hunter, and understand your services as a tracker are for hire."

* * *

HISTORIANS DEBATE what events mark the collapse of the United States of America and Western democracy. Some argue for the contested elections in 2016, 2018, and 2020, which brought one-party rule to the American federal government. Others support the passage of indentured servitude laws to replace the banned death. The Third Russian Revolution of 2042, which ended the Russian Federation and restored the Russian Empire under a distant cousin of the czars rocked the American government. Most historians agree the declaration of intention to secede issued by California, Oregon, Washington, Hawaii, and Alaska in 2055 marked a defining moment in Western history. The stunning defeat of America's ruling party in the 2056 elections and rapid reforms prevented a second American Civil War.

The New Progressive Party (NPP) held the United States together until 2092. In the run-up to the elections of 2092, the NPP invited world religious leaders to attend a conference to promote an end to religious conflicts. History remembers the Fayetteville, Arkansas conference not for peace but for the terrorist attack, which sparked the Upheaval. To this day, those responsible for the six dirty bombs, which destroyed the city and killed the assembled religious leaders, remain anonymous. Sparked by the attack, radical eco-terrorists unleashed a dozen High-Altitude Electromagnetic Pulse (HEMP) devices across the globe. Chaos ensued as modern conveniences, electrical grids, and defense systems, low earth orbit satellites, and other sophisticated systems crashed.

A century of war exploded around the globe as progressive governments collapsed and new conservative nation states arose. The nations of North America dissolved, replaced by the Federal Union of North America, the Confederate States of America, the Republic of Texas, and the Republic of California. Continental Western Europe unified under the Catholic Church as the New Holy Roman Empire. By 2200, new nations settled into place with only a few minor border wars. In addition, the Catholic Church elected a new dynamic cardinal as Pope Francis III, to ensure no repeats of the Upheaval. Pope Francis forced the signing of the Holy Accord of 2204, banning the redevelopment of air and space technology. Travel restrictions became commonplace.

A Brief Overview of the late 21st through the early 23rd Century, Encyclopedia of the Confederacy, 13th Edition, published 2531, by the University of Havana Press.

* * *

RUSSIAN NEWS ACCOUNTS claim Richard St. Martin, the famous shifter hunter, died somewhere in the wilderness in early 2026. The entire team of hunters hired by the government vanished without a trace. The prime minister ordered an elaborate state funeral for the members of the hunting party. The St. Martin estate lingered in probate until a young man came forward with documents, which declared him St. Martin's heir. Witnesses at the time consider Seth Abelson, the man who inherited St. Martin's estate in 2030, an imposter.

At the time of St. Martin's recorded death, the Order of St. Hubert did not possess the power and authority enjoyed today. Founded to honor the patron saint of hunters and to train them, the Order serves as the law enforcement arm of Mother Church and the Empire. At the core, the members remain hunters.

The Upheaval enabled the Order's rise to prominence with the election of the Order's Cardinal/Grand Master to the Papal throne. Once relations between nations stabilized, law enforcement personnel received limited travel permits. After a century of chaos, rumors still circulated about St. Martin's collection of hunting trophies. Under Vatican instructions, the Order of St. Hubert formed a team and investigated the rumors. The chosen members discovered Richard St. Martin's secret library in Amsterdam, New York, Federal

Union of North America. In hopes of laying claim to this treasure, the Order dispatched an archival team to recover the contents of the library. Unknown forces killed both teams. The last authentic communication received by the Mother House of the Order came on January 25, 2211. Circumstances surrounding the event meant the Mother House acquired only one journal sent to inform the Order of the secrets St. Martin kept hidden. The Order received an incomplete copy, which leaves the leadership uncertain of the actual proof behind our agent's claims. Attached is a copy of the late Father Sebastian's cover letter for the records. Recovery of St. Martin's original journal remains one of the highest priorities for all members of the Order.

Alexander Le Roux

Knight-Archivist

Order of St. Hubert

Liege, Belgium, Holy Roman Empire

* * *

DECEMBER 10, 2210

Sorry not to call you by name, but by making and sending as many copies as possible, I am prevented from addressing those who receive these copies. By the time you receive this package, I am dead or worse. Do not trust any further communications from me. I beg you, take all precautions available to ensure these documents reach either my Grand Master or the Pope. Warn Mother Church an ancient enemy still exists. The Order counted Richard St. Martin, called Lord Hunter, as an ally. Now I fear we misplaced our trust. In the aftermath of Lord Hunter's death during the hunt for Celina Dyta, the Order did not possess the influence needed to claim his estate. The Upheaval and the wars, which followed the disaster, led to the Order becoming *influential enough to claim what the leadership believed belonged under church protection.*

After things settled down, travel resumed between the Holy Roman Empire and the Federal Union of North America. The Vatican dispatched my team to recover relics from Lord Hunter's last listed residence in Amsterdam, New York. What we found horrified us and challenged our faith in our Lord and Savior. The volumes contained in the St. Martin Museum of the Supernatural contain dangerous materials. The attached diary contains entries from a blasphemous tome purported to be the Journal of Cain. This journal's vague claims and twisted history challenge every tenant of faith. The author's claim of being the first-born son of Adam and Eve and the first vampire raises a specter of horror in everyone's hearts. Worse the book contains additional notes in the verified hand of Lord Hunter. Notes which claim one of his early kills as the vampire claiming to be Cain and receiving Cain's curse as foretold in the Bible.

I beseech you to pass this package on. Whatever the truth may be vampires started to come for the team and I alone remain, the last of the team as I write this. Warn Mother Church.

Father Sebastian Drummond,

A Priest-Scout

Order of St. Hubert of Lieges

* * *

IN HIS PENTHOUSE amid the ruins of Boston, Richard St. Martin stood staring out the windows. Behind him, one of his mortal servants admitted the cloaked form of Database, his spymaster.

"Master, we did as you required. The Order's team was destroyed before they communicated with their motherhouse. As you commanded, a false partial journal was sent to the Order with a letter from one member of the team. The agents scattered the partial copies as well as the one whole copy of the journal you prepared. We shall track and move the copies along as needed."

"Thank you, little spy. The whole journal must find its way into the hands of an academic, a religious scholar, or an archaeologist. The journal contains secrets I need revealed, starting with the location of El-Abel."

PART I

The Atlanta Theological and Archaeological and Conference of 2220

Chapter 1

A TALL REDHEADED man stood in the registration line for the conference. He spent months wading through reams of required paperwork in order to obtain permission for travel abroad. The documents allowed him passage from the University of Arizona in the Republic of Texas to Atlanta, Georgia in the Confederate States of America. The North American nations existed in an uneasy peace. Getting the permits to travel became easier after the conference invited him to submit a paper on his research on the earliest city-states of ancient Mesopotamia. Excitement gripped the archaeologist after discovering Professor Juan Di Vargas listed as a presenter. The professor was presenting his latest research on biblical theology surrounding the legendary city of Enoch. Much of his personal research into the region used Professor Juan Di Vargas' work as a base. The man hoped he might finagle a few moments of the professor's time to ask him some questions. After a thirty-minute wait, the line moved forward bringing the redhead to the table. He brushed back an escaped strand of long copper hair as he handed his paperwork to the registrar.

"Dr. Jeremiah Banks, Department of Archaeology at the University of Arizona in the Republic of Texas. I'm on the presenter list."

"Welcome, Dr. Banks. Yes, here you are." The man returned Jeremiah's paperwork. "This is your conference badge. Please make sure you keep the badge with you wherever you go. Now this bag contains all your conference materials, including a schedule of events. Should you require assistance in finding your way to events, please ask any member of the conference staff. Green badges and sashes identify all the staff, so please don't hesitate to ask for assistance. Any questions?"

"No, you've answered my questions for now."

After a quick nod of acknowledgment, the man sent Jeremiah on his way. The young doctor of archaeology headed back up to his room. The conference staff had left him enough time to get organized before the evening's reception. After he put away most of the papers, Jeremiah figured out what he was wearing for his first reception. He cursed silently after realizing he'd forgot to ask if Prof. Di Vargas checked in. He figured the staff wouldn't tell him and assumed he'd run into the professor during the conference.

* * *

ELSEWHERE IN THE HOTEL, Prof. Juan Di Vargas, Doctor of Ancient Theology at the University of Madrid, enjoyed a glass of wine before the opening banquet. He relaxed in his chair, sipped the wine, and read over the schedule of events. Two names caught his attention, one because of a rivalry in the field of ancient religions and the other because of the fascinating topic. The first belonged to Dr. Gerard Chevalier, a lecturer on theology at the University of Paris and a rival in Old Testament studies. The other name to pop out at him belonged to Dr. Jeremiah Banks. The young archaeologist discovered tablets, which provided clues later applied to break the secrets of the El-Isinian language. At the time of his discovery, the ink on Dr. Banks' PhD remained new, and he led his first private expedition. His alma marter gave him a teaching position and fast-tracked his path to tenure as well. Other universities made offers for him to teach at their schools, including the University of Madrid, hoping to gain the reflected glory of Dr. Banks' discovery. Disappointed the program didn't include a photograph of one of their key speakers, still Juan recalled that not long ago the Texans and Confederates had been at war. Perhaps the Texans had refused to provide Dr. Banks' image out of security concerns.

Based on the buzz, Juan decided to attend the man's lecture on those tablets. Setting down his program and wine glass, Juan crossed to the room's mirror, adjusted his suit and tie, and checked his hair as though getting ready for a date. For an ancient academic, he kept in decent shape. Juan refused to sit in the dark libraries of the university doing all his research in its stacks. He actually preferred to go out in the field and chase down leads on ancient scrolls or tablets. Sometimes, he thought he'd gone into the wrong field and should have chosen to be an archaeologist instead of a theology instructor. He did enjoy making Professor Chevalier look like a pompous idiot. With luck, he hoped to encounter Dr. Banks and spend time comparing notes on the ancient cultures of Mesopotamia.

Prof. Di Vargas walked down the corridor and rode the elevator downstairs to the conference's opening reception. In the hotel's opulent ballroom, several colleagues from various universities met him. They chatted about a variety of topics when a bright head of long, flowing copper hair caught Juan's attention. His eyes tracked the owner's progress across the room. At first glance, he mistook the person for a woman because of the length of the hair and the way the person glided as they moved. Juan let his vision scan down from the intriguing hair to the broad shoulders, defined chest, and tapered waist to the delicious looking ass and sturdy legs. What a stud, Juan thought as the redhead turned and Juan caught sight of the trimmed beard and pale skin. Quite a prize this one would be. He wondered if the red hair went further than the man's head. Juan took in the man's attire and noted the uncomfortable way he wore the tailored suit. The suit appeared not to be the man's style, as if someone else had him dress for the occasion. Juan guessed that the man didn't wear suits on a regular basis or at least not ones tailored to put him on display.

From behind the redhead, Juan spotted Prof. Susan O'Grady glide in and slip her arm through the young man's, giving the appearance she claimed him as her property. Juan glowered before returning his attention to the conversation around him. He dismissed the redhead as a mere ornament brought to make Prof. O'Grady appear more important than her colleagues.

* * *

ACROSS THE ROOM, the redhead reacted with surprise as a hand latched onto his arm. He found his former instructor, Prof. O'Grady, taking possession of his arm and his conversation with his old classmate, Dr. Eugene Lanister. The topic focused on the Republic of Texas' attempt to preserve the Alamo from further decay. Jeremiah wondered what the hell the woman was doing. Prof. O'Grady leaned on him in an unprofessional manner. Jeremiah tried to act as natural as possible. Dr. Lanister addressed a question to their former teacher.

"Prof. O'Grady, do you prefer an aggressive method or a more holistic approach to preserving the Alamo?"

The woman on Jeremiah's arm smiled at Eugene like a shark about to feed on a seal pup.

"Dr. Lanister, had you paid attention in class as an undergraduate, you wouldn't need to ask such a silly question. The proper method is holistic preservation of the archaeological site and keeping visitation to a minimum. Dr. Banks remains the better student. Come, Dr. Banks, let's introduce you around to some of the prominent attendees at this conference." Prof. O'Grady said.

Jeremiah extracted himself from Prof. O'Grady's grip on his arm and turned to face the woman.

"Thank you, but no thank you, Professor. I can manage to introduce myself, although by now most of the gathering thinks you hired some gigolo or dragged a grad student along to enhance your importance. Neither Eugene nor I are students anymore, Dr. O'Grady, so please show a little respect in the future." Jeremiah turned back to his classmate. "Hey, Eugene, let's catch up later in the conference. I've done enough socializing for the evening."

Jeremiah headed out of the ballroom, once again catching Juan's brief attention as he exited.

* * *

JUAN WATCHED the fascinating redhead stride out of the reception hall and noted that O'Grady didn't appear as stunning or as important without him on her arm. The rest of the evening passed with the usual boring whirl of academics trying to prove themselves to their colleagues and the few wives or husbands in attendance. As he made the rounds, Juan didn't run into anyone who recalled meeting Dr. Banks, nor did he cross paths with the man himself. Perhaps he hasn't arrived yet, or came late and went to his room for the evening. His lecture would come tomorrow afternoon, so it was best to try and catch him afterward.

* * *

BACK IN HIS ROOM, Jeremiah fumed. He had hoped for a chance introduction to Prof. Di Vargas, but O'Grady ruined the evening. Jeremiah couldn't believe how she insulted Eugene. Now he remembered why his friend changed specialties after the first semester of undergraduate classes. O'Grady's tenure, endowed chair, and stack of published works protected her from most formal complaints.

Jeremiah picked up his program schedule to make his list of lectures he wanted to attend around the slots where he either presented or participated on a panel discussion. He noted that Prof. Di Vargas' talk was scheduled early tomorrow morning, with an hour in between lectures. Jeremiah decided to catch him for a couple of questions before giving his lecturing. A knock on the door interrupted Jeremiah's thoughts. He crossed the room, answered the knock, and found a tipsy Eugene Lanister in the hall outside. Jeremiah seized the man before he collapsed in the hallway.

"Lanister, ye gods man, you're drunk. Come in here and sit down while I put on coffee."

"I didn't come for the coffee, Banks, but for the kind of comfort only another guy can give."

"What are you talking about, Lanister? Tell me, you aren't shit-faced because of O'Grady and her stupid comments. Ignore her, Eugene. She forgets your top rankings and how you changed specialties because of her crappy teaching methods. Hell, most students made sure not to take any more of her classes after the first semester."

"Yeah, so you went and got cozy with Dr. Adamson. The old man fawned over you and guided your career all the way to your doctoral thesis. Was he decent in bed? Not that skill matters. You're so fucking beautiful, any man would do whatever you wanted for a chance at time in your bed."

"What the fuck are you talking about? I never shared such an unhealthy association with Dr. Adamson. Hell, the man was a slave driver, and I almost quit school twice because of him."

"Oh, come on, Jere, you're one of those fucking liberal faggots who helped bring down the old order. I bet you're gagging to suck my cock. So why don't you—"

A vicious right hook to the jaw sent Lanister crashing to the floor, bleeding from a broken nose and missing teeth, and silenced him. Jeremiah picked up the man and carried him to the door, which he opened before tossing Lanister out into the hall.

"Don't ever call me Jere again, Eugene. No one calls me Jere. I suggest you check out in the morning. Go home before you embarrass yourself or are arrested in a foreign nation for unnatural acts or whatever they call two men fucking in the Confederacy."

Without giving Eugene a chance to pick himself up or speak, Jeremiah slammed his hotel room door shut in the man's face. Inside Jeremiah leaned against the door panting in anger and terror combined. How the hell did anyone ever figure out Adamson once made advances on him? Only by turning his mentor down several times did Jeremiah earn the man's respect and patronage. He wished Dr. Adamson had lived to enjoy his star student's graduation and the mounting of his first expedition. The man would be proud of what Jeremiah had accomplished. Dr. Banks pushed away from the door and stripped down to take a shower and rinse away the sweat of fear and anger. Jeremiah let the water wash over his athletic body while he tackled washing his long red hair. Once all the shampoo rinsed out of his hair, Jeremiah toweled off and slipped naked between the sheets. He tossed and turned for a while trying to adjust to the hotel bed, but later drifted off to sleep.

* * *

After the evening ended, Juan returned to his room, performed his usual routine, donned silk sleeping pants, and settled into read Dr. Banks' article on his Mesopotamian excavation. First, he skimmed the article for a picture of the archaeologist. There was one blurry black and white photo of a man working to clear one of the tablets. It was a shame a headshot didn't accompany the photos of the dig, tablets, and diagram of El-Isinian characters. Juan's rugged chest above the sheets sported a spray of black hair that matched his full head of thick black hair and beard all showed traces of silver. He laid the journal aside and turned out the lights, settling down to sleep.

* * *

Jeremiah surveyed his clothing choices for the conference and grimaced. He hated suits, but Dr. Sinclair, the dean of his department, and Mrs. Pike, the dean's secretary and sort of a second mother, both insisted he dress in professional academic attire.

"You're representing the University of Arizona and the Republic of Texas, Dr. Banks. Think of the university's reputation. Don't appear like you are fresh off the boat following months in the field," Jeremiah recalled Dr. Sinclair saying as he handed him his clearance to travel. During a visit to her house, Mrs. Pike said similar things before she called her late husband's tailor and made an appointment to fit Jeremiah for new suits. Suits made Jeremiah uncomfortable, he preferred sturdy field clothing, but Dr. Sinclair held firm, no wild field archaeologist attire. Resigned to his fate, Jeremiah gave into almost all the dean's requirements, but refused when the request came to cutting his long copper locks. Jeremiah brushed through his hair, twisted, and slid the length into a sapphire-encrusted leather tube to hold everything in check.

The Emir, who oversaw his dig on behalf of the caliph's government, gave him the hair binder as a gift. The man developed a fascination with Jeremiah's copper hair and its silky texture. With his hair under control, Jeremiah dressed to impress in a navy-blue suit with a subtle white pinstripe. Sapphire cufflinks and tie tack finished the ensemble. The cufflinks came as a second present from the emir after a night of admiring Jeremiah's body in all its naked glory. The combination of Jeremiah's pale skin and fiery chest hair and pubic region, plus the impressive prick and balls in their natural state, fascinated the noble. The emir never touched him or asked for contact; the man wanted to check if the red hair remained the same color all the way down.

All three pieces of jewelry helped to highlight his bright blue eyes. Jeremiah checked himself in the mirror before picking up his notes and slides for his lecture and heading down to breakfast. During the evening, the staff worked their magic, transforming the ballroom from reception hall into a dining room. A waiter led Jeremiah to his assigned table and seat right next to Prof. O'Grady. The rest of the table filled with other scholars from universities in the Republic of Texas. He found Dr. Lanister's vacant seat next to his and opposite Prof. O'Grady.

"Prof. O'Grady, I want to apologize for the rude comments last night at the reception."

"No, Dr. Banks, if anyone got out of line last night, I did, and should be doing the apologizing. Thank you for correcting my attitude towards Dr. Lanister. I spoke way out of line. I wanted to apologize to him in person, but the hotel informed me Dr. Lanister checked out late last night claiming illness and returned home."

"I'm sorry he departed. He stopped by my room last night reeking of alcohol, so I encouraged him to retire for the evening. I'm sorry to learn he caught something," came Jeremiah's reply as a waiter stopped and filled his coffee cup. "I wonder, are you familiar with Prof. Juan Di Vargas from the University of Madrid?"

"Only by reputation, Dr. Banks. I understand he's presenting today on how the story of the Flood developed in several early cultures," O'Grady remarked, signaling the waiter to take her plate. "Don't you present today as well, Dr. Banks?"

"Yes, about an hour after Prof. Di Vargas. I hope to catch a moment of his time between lectures. His latest paper mentioned the possibility of the biblical city of Enoch being in the Tigris-Euphrates Delta. I think Enoch might be part of the culture, which produced the tablets I found. I wish to compare research with him."

"Good luck in your endeavor. Di Vargas doesn't often deal with those who pursue the more physical aspects of their researches, at least according to his reputation. I can arrange for you to speak with a scholar of the period more open to using archaeology. Let me introduce you to Prof. Chevalier from the University of Paris."

She missed Jeremiah's grimace of distaste, which he hid behind a sip of coffee. Chevalier's research clashed with every line of the investigation he pursued while Di Vargas's headed in a similar direction from a different angle. Jeremiah wiped his hands with his napkin, picked up his notes and slides, and rose from the table.

"Thank you for the offer, Dr. O'Grady. Perhaps another time. Please excuse me. I need to make sure the media team receives enough time to arrange the presentation before lecturing. I'm confident we'll cross paths at dinner."

"I think they plan to mix things up tonight, but there will be other meetings during the conference. Such a pleasure to meet you again, Jeremiah, or I should say Dr. Banks. You stood out, one of my more promising students, and I'm proud of how well you blossomed under Adamson's direction." O'Grady offered Jeremiah her hand. "I'm eager for your lecture this afternoon."

Jeremiah shook her hand and left to track down the media team. He still needed to set up his slides before attending the lectures he wanted to listen to this morning.

* * *

FOR PROF. DI VARGAS the morning dragged as the clock ticked away to his presentation on the Flood and its impact on several ancient cultures. The time came to present. He rose from his seat and crossed to the podium while surveying the audience. He spotted the young redhead sitting in the third row. He figured the man to be one of O'Grady's grad students since he was attending lectures. Juan thought it was interesting how the man had chosen his lecture to attend. It seemed an odd choice for him when one considered that O'Grady sided with

Chevalier's camp on the argument of the Flood's impact on the cultures of the period. The conservative faction claimed God used the Flood as a way of resetting the world back to a pure state.

"Faiths and cultures still argue over the centuries of myths pertaining to the Flood. Did the gods use this as divine retribution for sin, a way for the gods to reduce the population, or an exaggerated cautionary tale about seasonal flooding occurring in the cradles of civilizations? The evidence contained within the Bible cancels the Judeo-Christian-Islamic idea of a divine cleansing. Based on lineage records in the preceding chapters of the Book of Genesis, Noah's family fails to be worthy of God's salvation offer. The Genesis account proclaims Noah a righteous man, yet his wife descends from the first murderer, Cain. The Flood story contains numerous contradictions. The writers claim the Flood destroyed the descendants of Cain and their wicked ways. A false claim, which requires us to forget Noah's children inherited Cain's heritage from their mother."

Juan took a sip of water and let his gaze drift over to the redhead and found him making notes and nodding his head in agreement.

"The authors and redactors of Genesis wish for us to believe the Flood served as a reset on the population of the earth. Why would God choose to save a family with direct descent from a person he condemned as the hope for a new breed of men free from the sins of the past?"

* * *

JEREMIAH TOOK lots of notes as he listened to Prof. Di Vargas lecture about how most of the accepted versions of the ancient Flood story didn't play out. As the professor reached the meat of his lecture detailing how ancient cultures recorded the rising rivers, weaving stories to caution future generations, Jeremiah's focus sharpened. Certain points the man made impacted on his research in the region.

The application of this theory led to his discovery of the minor outpost and the tablets, which unlocked El-Isinian. The professor's lecture contained hints about the city-states of the lower Tigris-Euphrates Delta. These hints matched some of the details contained in the tablets from El-Isin referring to a greater city-state. The section of the tablet with the name of the central city-state long ago suffered damage, leaving the team frustrated.

All too soon, Prof. Di Vargas wrapped up his lecture and left the stage. Jeremiah worked his way to where the man took questions, trying to move closer to ask a question regarding biblical references to the city of Enoch and its location.

A question in fluent Hebrew competed for a moment with the question of a local Baptist minister. Juan glanced up to find the speaker. The mysterious redhead continued past him with a stage-whispered comment about not ignoring questions from interested parties in Arabic before vanishing into the crowd. The redhead impressed Juan when he proved more than somebody's arm candy. A remarkable brain lurked in his handsome head. Now Juan wanted to catch up to someone to ask questions. The Baptist minister distracted Juan for a moment. After he broke free and surveyed the area, Juan realized the distraction allowed the redheaded man to vanish.

"*Maldición*," Juan muttered. Spotting a tall man with flame-red hair in a crowd of short, graying academics should've been easy.

First, the man had caught Juan's attention and then he disappeared. Di Vargas felt that with his luck, the redhead would be attending some boring lecture on ancient Judean pottery. Still he wanted to listen to what this Dr. Banks said about those tablets and the site where he found them. The notes in the journal article said the man tracked down the location based on something in one of Juan's papers. Juan passed one of the many tables arrayed with water, coffee, and other refreshments. He grabbed a piece of fruit and a bottle of water on his way to the room assigned for Dr. Banks' lecture. He found a seat at the front. A slideshow running on a loop showed an archaeological dig going on in what appeared to be a tributary valley of the Tigris river system.

Throughout the slideshow, Juan caught glimpses of the redheaded man among the workers on the site.

He wondered if the mysterious redhead had been a student working for Dr. Banks during his expedition. Juan didn't think the man had enough tenure to receive student assistants. It could be they'd shared a mentor and the redhead had volunteered. Juan couldn't decide which man he wanted to meet more, the redhead or the mysterious Dr. Banks.

The room filled, and establishing order took the conference organizers closing the doors and turning people away to keep the room from going beyond capacity. Dr. Banks' discovery astounded the archaeological community. The discovery of the first El-Isinian tablets took place in the ruins of the Assyrian capital Dur-Sharrukin around 1920. For the next two centuries, the mysterious language defied translation. After the slideshow ended, a distinguished man crossed to the podium.

"Ladies and gentlemen, I am given the pleasure of introducing one of the stars of this conference. Dr. Jeremiah Banks from the University of Arizona is new to our distinguished ranks, but deserves the praise heaped upon him. His discovery is changing many disciplines besides archaeology. So, without further embarrassing the young man, please welcome Dr. Jeremiah Banks."

Juan stood with all the other people gathered in the room to applaud the man who appeared on stage. Surprised, he almost fell back into his seat. The fascinating redhead headed to the podium and took the microphone from the man. Jeremiah waved for everyone to sit, his eyes raking the audience and locking on Juan. The professor experienced the full intensity of the man's brilliant blue eyes and caught the hint of a self-satisfied smirk in the man's smile. A smile, which reflected how overjoyed the man must have been since his appearance as the speaker surprised Juan. Once everyone settled back into his or her seats, Jeremiah nodded to the media crew and a new slide appeared on the screen. On the screen appeared one of the tablets from his find.

Jeremiah began his lecture with a string of words no one in the room understood, before repeating the phrase in English. "'On the sixth day after arriving in El-Isin, the merchants sent by the Great King of the Nile offered pottery in exchange for five slaves.' This translation is a rough approximation of what the opening verse of this tablet says. At this point, the pronunciation of El-Isinian remains pure guesswork. The team deciphered a dozen tablets, most being trade entries like this example. This next example held the real treasure from the site, a lexicon of El-Isinian into Sumerian-Akkadian. These lexicon tablets allowed the team to break the language used by the people of the site dubbed El-Isin. Based on other tablets discovered during the excavation, the site served as a trade outpost for the city-state of El-Abel."

Juan sat transfixed as Dr. Banks continued his lecture on the discovery of the tablets and the mysterious culture, which built and maintained the site. He caught the mention of his works a few times and sat fascinated by how the archaeologist employed his research. After the lecture finished, Juan's attention focused on Jeremiah gathering his notes and slides, while trying to answer questions from members of his audience swarming the stage. He remained in his seat until the crowds began to thin out and Dr. Banks headed towards him. The man moved with the grace of a cat on the hunt. Rugged and handsome, his square jaw softened by his copper beard, sapphire eyes gleamed with mirth as Juan locked gazes with him. Jeremiah stopped beside Juan's chair and extended his hand to the stunned professor.

"Since no one offered formal introductions, Professor Di Vargas, I'm Dr. Jeremiah Banks. I wish to discuss your findings regarding the lineage of Cain and the region where he built Enoch."

"Dr. Banks, I'm Professor Juan Di Vargas, and I must apologize for my earlier dismissal of your questions after my lecture this morning. It would be a pleasure to share my findings with you. Will you join me for lunch?" Juan held Jeremiah's hand beyond the time required to shake. "I'm not scheduled for any more talks today."

Juan's Spanish accent melted parts of Jeremiah's brain and sent the blood racing elsewhere. The man's hand radiated warmth and sent a tingle up Jeremiah's arm, making him reluctant to break the handshake.

"I would be honored to join you for lunch, however we'll have to watch the time. I'm part of the discussion panel at two on current trends in archaeology. Perhaps we can arrange to be seated together tonight."

"Did you want to attend any additional lectures before lunch, Dr. Banks?"

"None in particular. I would like to put my notes and slides back in my room if you don't mind. Shall we meet back in the lobby in half an hour?"

"If you don't mind, I'll walk with you to your room and we can talk on the way. I find after meeting you, I don't want to let you out of my sight."

Jeremiah blushed, turning almost as red as his hair. Juan smiled at the man's reaction and made a gesture for him to proceed. Jeremiah walked ahead, hoping to regain his composure. *Madre de Dios,* thought Jeremiah. At best, he and Juan had spent about five minutes together, and yet, there he stood crushing like a teenager. Once they reached the elevator, Jeremiah struggled to remember which floor held his room after the fleeting contact with Juan's body. The loss of mental clarity was strange because older men never excited him before. Something about the Spaniard made Jeremiah want to find out what lay under the man's suit. Behind Jeremiah, Juan admired the movement of the other man's ass beneath his suit. The Texan possessed everything Juan liked in a partner: a handsome appearance, a brilliant scholar, and, Juan suspected, a witty conversationalist once comfortable.

The one question Juan couldn't ask Jeremiah was if he was a virgin or an experienced player. Juan had to ponder if the man possessed a passion as fiery as his hair or if he was a shy and coy paramour awaiting seduction. For whatever reason, all he could think about was stripping him naked and making slow passionate love to him.

Intimate conversation proved difficult. With the return of slavery in the revived Confederate States of America, high-end hotels utilized elevator operators to improve their guests' stay. The presence of the slave made private conversations or other intimate matters wait for the privacy of a guest's room. He did stand closer than he needed to as they rode to Jeremiah's floor. Jeremiah cursed the Confederate decision reviving the tradition of elevator operators. He wanted to drag the Spaniard in for a searing kiss and experience the legendary passion of a Spanish lover. Jeremiah believed that with the way his luck ran, the man might be messing with him and he'd learn the professor had a wife and kids back home in Spain. Jeremiah didn't remember reading anything in Juan's biography about family and hoped it confirmed the man's status as a bachelor.

Many of the old Victorian terms, like confirmed bachelor, reappeared to help society mask practices deemed unnatural in polite conversations. The resurgence of these terms reached a high point following the succession of Empress Veronica to the British throne in 2096. Jeremiah came out of his thoughts as the elevator settled on his floor and the operator parted the doors. He managed to stop Juan from tipping the operator before they exited into the hallway leading to Jeremiah's room. At the door to his room, Jeremiah fumbled with the key trying to unlock the door. He enjoyed the sensation of Juan's body heat close against him as the man's hips pressed against his ass. The door opened, and Jeremiah found himself inside alone, Juan standing in the doorway. A puzzled expression crossed his face for a moment before he remembered his manners.

"Please come in, Professor Di Vargas." Jeremiah put away his slides and notes. "Sorry, we don't stand on such formality in the Republic at these kinds of events."

"Old world manners. At the University of Madrid, we wait for an invitation into a colleague's private space due to our combined suite of rooms often acting as office and living quarters." Juan closed the door behind him. "Please call me Juan. I think we can drop the formal titles."

"Only if you call me Jeremiah, I'll be honored to call you Juan." Jeremiah turned to find himself chest-to-chest with the handsome Spaniard. "I'm not sure how this works in Europe, but I want to kiss you, Juan."

"I hoped you would, Jeremiah, because I want to kiss you as well."

After the kiss, neither man cared which of them initiated the moment. After they broke, both of them panted and leaned in towards each other. Juan's hands cupped Jeremiah's ass, while Jeremiah's hands wrapped around Juan's waist. They molded into each other as Juan captured Jeremiah's lips once again. The Spaniard broke the kiss when Jeremiah fumbled trying to undo his belt.

"No need to rush anything, *mi muchacho hermoso*. We will spend plenty of time later exploring each other. For now, I want to enjoy how well you fit in my arms."

"*Mi muchacho hermoso*? So, you view me as your beautiful boy, *mi anciano*?" Jeremiah ran his hand over the man's chest. "Spanish is one of my languages, Juan."

"Yes, but your accent is horrible, Jeremiah."

"Sorry, I didn't grow up learning proper Castilian pronunciation. My

Mexican nanny thought only important people spoke English. She taught me Spanish, and at school, we learned the Mexican pronunciation as the Republic's second official language."

"I'll teach you proper pronunciation of some unusual endearments later." Juan's breath brushing Jeremiah's ear sent shivers down the younger man's spine. "For now, we should make sure we aren't too rumpled to appear in public."

The older man stepped back, breaking his embrace with Jeremiah, who found he yearned for the man's touch. He had never felt so desperate for physical contact. Jeremiah needed to control himself, or he'd never manage the rest of the day. Jeremiah pulled himself up to his full 6'2" height and checked to make sure his hair remained under control before adjusting and straightening his tie.

"I think I'm presentable again. Shall we go down to lunch?" Jeremiah removed a folder from his briefcase. "My notes for the panel. My departmental secretary warned me before I left the university to come here that Rev. Dr. Kenneth Coffin would be on the panel. He's a Southern Baptist minister with an enormous following who opposes using archaeology to dig into the biblical stories."

"I recall mention of him. He lectures in the same circles as my professional rival Professor Chevalier. I think fate intended we meet, Jeremiah. Interesting, how you appear to be developing the same circle of intellectual opponents. Come, we'll talk about some of the weak points of the reverend's arguments over lunch."

Though in Jeremiah's room, Juan ushered them out and made sure the door locked behind them. The pair made their way back to the elevator and waited for the operator to arrive on their floor. Juan took the folder from Jeremiah's hand and skimmed the topic notes and the list of panel members.

"I'm afraid my side of the debate is understaffed. Dr. Eugene Lanister left this morning to return home to the Republic. He claimed illness, but he came to my room drunk last night, and we argued about a touchy subject, which ended when I hit him. I shoved him out and told him he should go home if he couldn't behave."

"Perhaps, fortune is looking out for you and we can use this opening on the panel to our advantage."

"How is Dr. Lanister's departure an advantage? He's an expert in the field of comparative mythology."

Confused, Jeremiah blinked his bright sapphire eyes at Juan, causing the man's heart to race.

"Because this allows me to take his place. I'm no slouch in the comparative religion department. I didn't earn my chair by taking the simple theological path. This is the point where Rev. Coffin and Chevalier tear your friend Dr. Lanister apart." Juan's finger indicated a section of Jeremiah's notes.

Before Jeremiah replied, the arrival of the elevator interrupted their conversation; they entered and rode down in silence. Each man was wrapped in personal thoughts. Jeremiah reclaimed his notes from Juan and glanced at the theory revealed as the weak spot in his side's argument. He ignored many of Eugene's later papers as he toured with the El-Isinian tablets. What ran through Eugene's mind when he concocted this theory? The theory belonged to a madman. This panel was designed to be a nightmare and ruin both men's reputations as scholars and scientists when the trap point was raised. Unsure if he believed in guardian angels, Jeremiah felt someone was looking out for him by steering Juan in his direction. Jeremiah closed the folder when the elevator reached the ground floor and made sure he tipped the operator this time, letting Juan exit before him. The pair made their way to the dining room and found a table where they sat and talked while they ate. Once the waiter brought their lunch and drinks, Jeremiah glanced over at Juan and asked the question.

"Would you take Dr. Lanister's place on the panel? I'm convinced

Coffin and Chevalier designed this discussion to destroy Lanister's reputation. Due to the educational policies of the Republic of Texas, I'm obligated to defend Lanister's theory. My reputation becomes collateral damage when I don't turn on him and side with Coffin and Chevalier. What do I do, Professor Di Vargas?"

"By allowing me to take Dr. Lanister's place, his position won't be raised since attacking a theory when the author isn't available to defend the position is bad form. No, Chevalier must attack my most recent position paper on the location and importance of Enoch instead. Rev. Coffin will bolster Chevalier's attacks in hopes of tossing me from my chair at the University of Madrid."

"They're treading dangerous ground; the El-Isinian tablets supports the existence of a city-state in the region you and others argue as Enoch's location. El-Isin isn't the only outpost of this city-state referenced in the tablets. The tablets mention an outpost to the east of the central city called El-Kino. The directions are too vague to follow, but El-Kino is one of the targets of my current research. The focus of my research is locating the central city."

"I'm following your research because I think we're both looking for the same city along different tracks. I'm hoping to compare and share our research as we go along." Juan's deep voice conveyed more than a sharing of the investigation. "After meeting you, I'm hoping to entice you to the University of Madrid to teach and conduct research, Dr. Banks."

"Professor Di Vargas, please don't ruin a beautiful friendship with a sales pitch. Over the last two years, I've received so many offers my department's secretary, Mrs. Pike, goes through and removes job offers before sending letters on to me. I'm happy at the University of Arizona. Since they fund my work and control the access to the tablets, I can't continue my current research anywhere else."

Juan studied Jeremiah's face for a moment and noted the sadness dulling his eyes. He reached across the table and took Jeremiah's hand in his own for a brief moment. Not long enough to be assumed more than a gesture of friendship by those around them. Juan received a smile and a brightening of those beautiful eyes. The two men finished their lunch and made their way to the conference room, which would host the debate. Near the stage, they found the moderator fretting about the effect of Dr. Lanister's departure on the panel. He sighed when the esteemed Professor Di Vargas offered to take Dr. Lanister's place backed by the noted Dr. Banks.

Jeremiah choked on a laugh over his reputation getting Juan on the panel. He turned the laugh into a cough to cover his mirth. Juan stared at him, and Jeremiah's coughing fit continued. The moderator grew concerned until Dr. Banks pulled himself together and assured the man he was all right. Jeremiah excused himself to use the restroom. Juan followed him to make sure the archaeologist would be able to continue. After a splash of cold water on his face, Jeremiah regained self-control until he glanced up and caught Juan's determined scowl in the mirror. The Texan burst out laughing, grabbing the sink to keep from falling. Juan tried to remain grave, but soon his bass laugh joined Jeremiah's tenor laugh.

"I-I-I'm sorry," Jeremiah got out between laughs. "His saying my reputation holds greater importance is hilarious. The University of Arizona trumps the University of Madrid."

"I need to disabuse you of this strange notion later. Although I must say, I love hearing you laugh."

Jeremiah caught Juan's reflection in the mirror and smiled at the man. His smile conveyed a sassy almost childish glee in provoking the man to take a dominant role in whatever built between them. He glimpsed Juan moving closer and jerked upright as the man's strong right hand connected with his ass in a stinging spank. Juan moved over to the next sink to wash his face and hands. Jeremiah rubbed his ass for a moment to regain his composure and dry his face and hands. Before he escaped the restroom, Juan pinned him facing the door. The man's semi-hard cock pressed into his ass and forced Jeremiah to bite his lip to keep from moaning out loud. Juan's whispered words made Jeremiah almost draw blood as he bit down harder to keep his moan from escaping.

"After this panel finishes, I'm taking total control, my naughty little boy, and teaching you proper respect."

Chapter 2

EXHAUSTED JEREMIAH FOLLOWED **Juan back** to the man's room after the debate. His mind drifted out of focus until the door locked behind them. The click of the lock snapped Jeremiah's mind back into the here and now, as Juan's arms wrapped around him from behind, pulling him in tight against the man's hard body. Juan brushed Jeremiah's copper ponytail to one side and attacked the exposed pale skin with his lips and tongue, eliciting moans from the redhead. The Spaniard's fingers undid the buttons of Jeremiah's jacket and slipped in to rest on the firm abs beneath. Jeremiah's fingers traced over Juan's hands before turning to face the handsome older man.

The pair locked lips in a deep kiss, which melted Jeremiah into Juan's body as he locked his arms around Juan's waist. Juan's hands roamed across Jeremiah's back and up so the left hand cupped the nape of Jeremiah's neck. His right hand found the tube, which bound the copper hair. He slid the tube down the ponytail and freed the long locks of fiery hair. Sliding his fingers into Jeremiah's hair, he found the texture silky instead of coarse. Jeremiah moaned as Juan's fingers worked his scalp through his hair and nuzzled his beard into Juan's neck.

Shudders wracked Jeremiah's body as Juan found places on his scalp, which sent his mind reeling in pleasure. A finger traced the skin between his ear and head and drew a moan from deep within. No one Jeremiah ever dared to fuck did such things to him before. The fingers paused as they traced Jeremiah's face. A whimper escaped from Jeremiah when Juan released him, stepped back, and left him alone. A strong finger touched his lips when he opened them to speak.

"Shh, stay still for me. I want to admire you and take my time freeing you from those confining clothes. Can you be a patient boy and give me control?"

The younger man nodded to keep from begging. Juan knelt before him and lifted his left leg, resting Jeremiah's foot on his knee to remove the young man's dress boot. The sound of the zipper on the side of the boot stirred the imagination, and Jeremiah's prick thickened against his trousers. The boot tugged free and Juan's fingers caressed Jeremiah's foot before peeling off the dress sock. With shivers traveling from his toes to his balls, the young archaeologist almost fell. The older man caressed his bare foot, toying with the hair on the arch and up the ankle. Juan set the beautiful pale left foot down and repeated the process with Jeremiah's right foot. He preferred his lovers barefoot, as God intended man to be. Juan stood and moved behind the handsome young man. He slipped his hands into the neck of the suit jacket and slid the lapels over Jeremiah's pectorals before his hands moved back up and pulled the jacket off. He hung the coat on the back of a nearby chair to avoid wrinkles. Moving around Jeremiah, Di Vargas found the young man's eyes closed, blocking sight but letting touch, sound, and scent relay Juan's position.

Juan lifted the tie and removed the tie tack, placing the pin on the small table beside the bed, before he undid the knot of the tie and slipped the fabric off. The tie joined the jacket on the chair. With a step back, Juan admired Jeremiah in his crisp white shirt, suit trousers, and bare feet. The copper locks flowed around Jeremiah's face and over his shoulders, framing his pale face with fire. With a beard, Jeremiah appeared younger than his thirty years. How young would appear when clean-shaven, Juan wondered.

He moved in enough to cup the flame-bearded chin and run a finger over the sensual lips almost hidden within. Jeremiah shuddered and fought back a moan. The tip of his pink tongue escaped to lick the path Juan's finger traced after the man withdrew his touch again. Dark-skinned fingers lifted the pale right hand and undid the cuff link, which joined the tie tack on the nightstand. Juan rolled the right sleeve up Jeremiah's arm to the elbow, exposing a flame-haired forearm. He repeated the procedure on the left arm, also removing the ugly timepiece he found on the wrist. He was surprised Jeremiah stayed still; most of his lovers would give up and tear off their clothes before this point.

* * *

JEREMIAH COULDN'T BELIEVE he was standing still while Juan tortured him with the slow undressing. A typical encounter for him was so rushed; strip and go right to fucking. None of his past encounters lasted this long before. Jeremiah focused every ounce of control he possessed to remain in place as Juan started to undo the buttons on his shirt. Jeremiah paused, wondering if his pierced nipples would offend Juan or excite him. The crisp white shirt slipped off his shoulders as caressing hands traced his muscles all the way down to his wrists before the cloth vanished. The undershirt remained, keeping Jeremiah's torso hidden from the Spaniard's view. Jeremiah wondered what Juan would remove next: his undershirt or his trousers? He refused to open his eyes and locate Juan, despite the man going still again.

A finger traced over his length as body heat revealed Juan stood right behind him. Unable to hold back, Jeremiah moaned at the pleasure of

Juan's touch on his member through the fabric of the trousers and his boxer briefs. Those tender fingers erased his thoughts. His belt came loose. The clasp of his pants unfastened, and the sound and tugging of the zipper's decent followed. The weight of the belt took the trousers down his legs to pool at his ankles. He sensed Juan kneel in front of him again to lift each foot and remove his pants. Now left in his underwear, Jeremiah's boxer briefs grew sticky as his cock leaked precum. Juan's presence vanished.

Jeremiah experienced a moment of panic at the silence until he became aware of the rustle of clothes being removed followed by another noise. Sounds like someone sitting on one of the hotel's chairs.

"Turn around and show me your eyes, my beautiful one," Juan's deep voice commanded. "I want to gaze into those beautiful sapphire eyes.

Jeremiah did as instructed, blinked the room back into focus, and turned to find Juan seated, dressed only in a pair of silk boxers. The man's dark skin gleamed with sweat, which matted his chest hair to his torso. The man was so handsome, and Jeremiah wanted to feel their bodies pressed together.

"Take off the undershirt and reveal your chest, Jeremiah."

"Yes, sir."

He reached down, gripped the hem of the undershirt, and pushed up to reveal the treasure trail of bright red fur in reverse as the hair climbed his torso, fanning out to cover his chest. He couldn't gauge Juan's reaction when the sapphire studded piercings through his nipples appeared, but the man still stared at his chest as he freed himself from the undershirt.

Juan shifted in his seat to give his thickening cock room to expand as the nipple piercings appeared. He wondered if Jeremiah got the piercings for himself or to please a suitor. Juan envied the man who inspired those piercings, but he'd enjoy playing with them. Jeremiah was so beautiful and obedient. Like he was suppressing all his fire to try and prove himself to Juan. Soon, he'd go about unleashing the redhead's fire, because Juan wanted Jeremiah's passion more than his obedience.

Juan bent his legs and gestured for Jeremiah to lay himself across his lap.

"You need disciplining for thinking your reputation is the better one, boy. Stretch out facedown over my lap and prepare to be spanked as a naughty boy deserves."

"Yes, sir."

Jeremiah draped himself over Juan's sturdy legs.

"I deserve to be punished, sir."

Juan adjusted Jeremiah's position a bit before his right hand rose and fell against Jeremiah's ass with a mighty smack. Jeremiah stifled a cry of surprise at the power of the blow. An additional nine blows of equal power fell before Juan stopped and rubbed the firm cheeks to soothe them. He helped Jeremiah up and led him over to the king-sized bed. They kissed, and Jeremiah's passion reignited beneath the kiss. The redhead came alive again and held Juan tight. He allowed himself to fall backward on the bed, pulling the Spaniard down on top of him and grinding their cocks together.

Now came Juan's turn to moan and lose control as Jeremiah rolled them over and began kissing, licking, and nibbling his way down Juan's body. He teased and nibbled on first one nipple and switched to the other before working down to the prize hidden away in the silk boxers. Pale fingers slid beneath the waistband and tugged the fabric down to reveal lighter but still dark skin and a trimmed patch of pubic hair above the root of a thick shaft. Jeremiah nibbled and licked his way down the shaft, he kept trapped beneath the material of the boxers as he inched them down Juan's hips. He held Juan, panting and begging before he pulled the boxers down past the hooded head of the uncut cock beneath.

The foreskin drew back, exposing the head of Juan's dick as Jeremiah captured the cock in his warm, wet mouth. He let his tongue dance across the exposed slit, lapping up the first drop of Juan's precum. Juan's fingers locked into Jeremiah's hair as he slid deeper into the warm mouth and the tight throat beyond. Jeremiah swallowed his lover's entire shaft on the first go, burying his nose in Juan's pubic bush to inhale the scent of his Spanish lover. Soon, he established a rhythm, which drove Juan mad with a passion but kept him from reaching climax. Spanish curses and endearments flowed from Juan's mouth as Jeremiah worked over his shaft and paid extra attention to the sensitive head.

Spent, he pulled Jeremiah off and tossed him on his back. Reaching down Juan ripped the offending boxer briefs off his young playmate, revealing a patch of pubic hair as red as the rest of the man's body hair. The well-trimmed fur framed the base of an uncut cock as thick and long as his own. The hard, throbbing member leaked copious amounts of precum, and Juan lapped the fluid up before working on Jeremiah's cock and balls. The oral attention didn't take long before Jeremiah's orgasm exploded. Juan drank down the sweet load like drinking the ambrosia of the gods. Jeremiah lay panting on the bed, his red-furred chest rising and falling with every breath. Juan peered down at his lover's pale body against the dark material of the bedding. He was beautiful.

Juan stretched out beside Jeremiah and pulled the young man against him so his head lay on Juan's chest. He ran his fingers through the long silken red hair as Jeremiah recovered his breath.

"I want to be inside you, beautiful one," Juan suggested in Jeremiah's ear. "May I fuck you?"

"I think I like the idea, sir. The hesitation is because I've only topped, sir. This will be the first time on the receiving end."

"Please, dear one, let me be the first. I promise a pleasurable experience."

Jeremiah only nodded against Juan's chest, afraid to speak his desire aloud. He let the older man move them around so Juan ended up between his legs with his hard-on rubbing the area between his entrance and his balls. Juan managed to snag a bottle of lube from the bedside table without getting out of bed and took his time working on Jeremiah's asshole. Juan leaned forward and kissed Jeremiah while he worked his fingers into the opening to loosen the muscles. Soon, Di Vargas perceived Jeremiah relaxing. He reached down, slicked his cock, and pulled back the foreskin, before he placed the thick head against the loosened hole. Juan worked his cockhead past the muscle of Jeremiah's opening and paused inside before easing the rest of his thick nine inches into the virgin ass beneath him. Once his balls lay against Jeremiah's ass, Juan stopped to allow his partner to adjust to the sensation of a cock buried deep in his ass. He glanced down to find shining sapphire eyes gazing up at him with love blazing forth from them. Jeremiah reached up and pulled Juan down for a deep kiss before he moaned in the man's ear.

"Fuck me, Juan."

Juan kissed Jeremiah, lifted himself up, and began sliding out and back into his lover's ass. He built a rhythm, which increased in tempo, while making sure his cockhead stroked across Jeremiah's prostate, eliciting moans and whimpers of pleasure. As Juan reached the point of no return, he made certain Jeremiah reached the same peak of pleasure. In the moment he flooded Jeremiah's ass with his load, the other man's load exploded in volley after volley of cum. The copious load splattered across the redhead from chin to navel. Juan collapsed on top of his lover's heaving body, and they cuddled in the afterglow until Juan's dick deflated and slipped from Jeremiah's ass. Juan rose and went to the first half of the bathroom, which held the sink and a supply of hand towels. He sponged himself clean before bringing back a warm, damp washcloth to clean up Jeremiah. Running the cloth over Jeremiah proved a delight. The man released a sigh of contentment and regarded his friend with his bright blue eyes. Juan returned to the bed, and Jeremiah snuggled in, resting his head on the firm chest while running his fingers through Juan's chest hair, toying with the mixed silver and black strands. They drifted off to sleep.

Chapter 3

MUCH LATER IN the night Jeremiah awoke with a start, which woke Juan from his sleep.

"What's the matter, Jeremiah? Are you all right? It's safe here."

"No, it's not. If housekeeping comes in and finds us like this, the love between two people of the same sex is punishable with either hard labor or enslavement depending on where in the Confederacy an offender is caught. The state of Georgia is a little more liberal than most of the country, but they still hand out hefty indentured servitude sentences and fines here."

"Well, we'll make sure housekeeping doesn't catch us like this."

"I should return to my room. I long to stay and greet the sunrise."

"I wish this as well, my beautiful one." Juan laid a kiss on the nape of Jeremiah's neck. "I want to gaze on your sexy body painted with the colors of the rising sun. Can we take time to shower together before you run off?"

"Mmm, I wish, but we should save something for another time."

Jeremiah captured Juan's lips with a parting kiss. "Perhaps you'll come back to my room tonight?"

"I will, Jeremiah. Let's meet downstairs for breakfast and discuss schedules for the rest of the conference."

Jeremiah found his boxer briefs and the rest of his clothes and dressed in everything but his tie and jacket. Juan put on a robe and stole one last kiss before Jeremiah slipped out into the hallway headed for the stairs rather than risk the elevator. Juan slipped out of his robe and into pajamas to be decent when the hotel staff invaded his room. Jeremiah moved up the stairs to his room. He undressed, showered, and put on his sleepwear before crawling into the empty king-size bed. He tossed and turned. Sleep claimed him for perhaps an hour before the phone rang to wake him up. Dr. Banks prepared himself to face the day and picked up his program schedule to check which topics caught his attention. The schedule showed neither he nor Juan presented lectures today, so they would spend lots of time together.

Once Jeremiah arrived in the lobby outside the dining room, he found Juan conversing with a Catholic bishop. The topic must have been important because the men spoke Italian and the bishop gestured for emphasis. Jeremiah moved, allowing Juan to spot him, and waited for the doors to the dining room to open. Juan gestured him over and introduced him to the bishop.

"Bishop Romano was asking me to use my newfound friendship to convince the young Texan archaeologist to reconsider his rejection of the distinguished Alessandro Barsanti Chair of Archaeology."

"Perhaps His Grace forgets Señor Barsanti worked as an Egyptologist and the chair named in his honor is in Egyptology, not archaeology. Since I'm not an Egyptologist, I declined the offer, aside from other considerations, which affect my research."

Juan rattled off Jeremiah's explanation to the bishop in Italian. The prelate bowed his head to acknowledge his defeat and left the two academics to their own devices.

"I'm sorry, I promised not to make job offers, but His Grace is one of the men behind the funding at the university and I like to keep researching."

"Transfer to the University of Arizona; the religious studies department would go insane if they landed someone of your standing. There aren't any fancy-named chairs, but the dean's office is available. Prof. Juan Di Vargas, Dean of Religious Studies, University of Arizona, Republic of Texas has a nice sound."

"Not as beautiful as Professor Jeremiah Banks, Barsanti Chair of Egyptology, University of Madrid, Holy Roman Empire does. Take the Barsanti Chair and we'd be equal in the eyes of academic society."

"Let's not argue about standing in the academic community, Professor Di Vargas." Jeremiah leaned over and whispered in Juan's ear, "I rather fancy slinking off and making passionate love instead."

"I like the idea, beautiful one, but I'm required to attend Dr.— Sorry, Professor Martino's maiden lecture on the origins of the Gospel of John. She's the first to be awarded the Jane Dewar Schaberg Chair of New Testament Studies. Come with me?"

"Okay-y." Jeremiah hesitated in agreeing. "Fair warning though, the field is beyond my understanding. Too modern for me."

The doors of the dining room opened, and wait staff escorted people to tables. Juan and Jeremiah found themselves seated with a pair of scholars from the Federal Union of North America, renowned specialists in European Folklore and Mythology. They settled into an interesting discussion over breakfast before Juan and Jeremiah excused themselves to attend Professor Martino's lecture. The pair spent the day together, often talking about their research or engaging in conversations with other scholars with similar pursuits. Lost in conversation was how they spent the rest of the conference when not lecturing or participating in panel discussions. In the evenings, they alternated rooms for passionate lovemaking. Juan expressed surprise when on their last night together Jeremiah led him into the bathroom of his suite, and he caught the view out of a floor-to-ceiling window over the vast park surrounding the hotel. He stared at Jeremiah with concern when his lover began undoing the buttons of his shirt from behind as they faced the window.

"Isn't this one of those dangerous things we shouldn't be doing, Jeremiah?" His shirt slid off his body. "What happens if someone spots us?"

"Relax, my love," Jeremiah whispered in his lover's ear. "The glass is one way. We can enjoy the view without being viewed in return. This is the tenth floor and the nearest building with a similar height is over a mile away on the other side of the hotel. Using this room is as close as possible to making love in the outdoors. Somehow, it doesn't seem possible to lure you out on a dig to share a tent in the wilderness of Mesopotamia."

"Well, the comforts of a hotel in Damascus or Baghdad would be preferable to a cot in the desert. Ask again someday and perhaps the answer will change."

"Count on it. I wish for more time together, Juan."

"I do too, Jeremiah. You found a place in my heart I didn't think to ever fill. To be closer instead of separated by miles of ocean is what I wish for, but we made our choices back at the beginning of this romance. We will exchange letters until we arrange to meet someplace."

"Letters are poor substitutes for kisses and caresses. For now, let's enjoy each other and forget about the rest of the world." With a deft hand, Jeremiah unfastened Juan's pants and allowed them to drop to the floor. "Come on, you're almost naked and I'm not. Someone's not paying equal attention to the details."

After a long session of lovemaking and showering, they collapsed in Jeremiah's bed to enjoy one last long cuddle session. Jeremiah's head rested on Juan's chest. Still, the time came to part, and Jeremiah sat in silent observation as Juan dressed. They kissed one last time at the door before Juan slipped out to return to his rooms. With a sigh, Jeremiah began packing to be ready for the porter to take his luggage to the station for the train ride back to Tucson.

PART II

The Quest for Enoch Begins

RICHARD'S JOURNAL

Now Adam made love with his wife Eve, and she became pregnant and gave birth to Cain. The woman said, "I created a man as the Lord did!" She gave birth to his brother Abel. Abel took care of the flocks, while Cain cultivated the ground.

At the designated time, Cain brought some of the fruit of the ground for an offering to the Lord. But Abel brought some of the firstborn of his flock, including the fattest of them. Abel pleased the Lord with his offering, but Cain and his offering did not please the Lord. So, Cain became enraged, and his expression downcast.

The Lord spoke to Cain, "Why are you angry, and why is your expression downcast? Did I not say do what is right, and all shall be fine? But fail to do what is right, and sin crouches at the door. Sin desires to dominate, but sin must be subdued."

Cain said to his brother Abel, "Let's go out to the field." While in the field, Cain attacked his brother Abel and killed him.

The Lord spoke to Cain, asking, "Where is Abel?"

And he replied, "A better question is, am I my brother's guardian?"

But the Lord said, "What did you do? The voice of Abel's blood cries out to me from the ground! So now, I banish Cain from the ground, which opened and received Abel's blood from the hand of Cain. When cultivating the ground no longer yields the best, Cain shall be a homeless wanderer on the earth."

Cain spoke to the Lord, saying, "My punishment is beyond enduring! My Lord drives me off the land today, and I must hide from your presence. I am made a homeless wanderer on the earth; whoever finds me shall kill me."

But the Lord told him, "This I decree, whoever kills Cain suffers Cain's Curse sevenfold."

The Lord put a unique mark on Cain so no one who found him would strike him down. So, Cain went out from the presence of the Lord and lived in the land of Nod, east of Eden.

Genesis 4: 1-15

* * *

January 9, 1999

Every trail I try following regarding the origins of the curse laid on me with the destruction of the most recent target leads back to this account in the Bible. The vampire who called himself Cain left journals and religious passages from books long hidden from religious scholars, with mysterious clues to an ancient city and hidden meanings behind the stories contained in the Book of Genesis. After gathering what I believe are the passages holding vital clues into one journal, let word spread of the existence of the book, and waited for the text to land in the hands of an expert scholar.

* * *

December 12, 2210

The Russians announced my death a hundred and thirty years ago, but I think the report got lost in the mess of the Upheaval. Somewhere an archivist for the Order of St. Hubert discovered a clipping or a printout of my obituary. They sent a team to my old antique shop and home five nights ago to secure artifacts from my hunting days. In his report last night, Database mentioned the destruction of the majority of the team during the raid by the small vampire court I placed several years ago. They let a couple of the team escape to follow back to their safe house. My agents waited until after the group's scribe finished writing his letter to the motherhouse of the Order before moving in and finishing off the team. Those agents sent out copies of the letter, the complete original, and dozens of incomplete copies of the journal. Now, I wait to discover where the complete journal ends up.

Chapter 4

March 15, 2223

Dr. Jeremiah Banks

Department of Archeology

University of Arizona

The Republic of Texas

Dear Dr. Banks:

Last month, an unexpected death left me in possession of a strange journal. I believe the information contained within might interest you. I have continued to follow your career since we met at the conference in Atlanta in 2220. Your search for the lost cities of ancient Mesopotamia is reaching a point where our research paths are crossing once again. I am tracking the origin of several ancient myths. The entries in this document contain unusual accounts and strange biblical narratives, which are bizarre. Further research is required to establish whether the tales contain truth or more myths. I believe we may find the answers we seek in the Tigris-Euphrates Delta.

I remember you found my theory on the origin of the worship of the ancient proto-Sumerian god Yahweh to be of interest. If these pages are believable, someone claiming to be Cain, the first-born son of the mythical Adam and Eve, wrote them. Some of his declarations I find far-fetched, such as all the magic and the actual existence of angels. The author also claims he died and returned in a half-living state. I am more interested in his talk about the early worship of Yahweh and the creation of a city-state called El-Abel.

I'm hoping you wish to renew our acquaintance and pursue this as a joint project. I seek to secure a source of funding from a patron, which will cover my half of this venture should you wish to join me. Enclosed with this letter is a copy of the journal in my possession.

With Respect,

Juan Di Vargas

Professor of Ancient Theology

University of Madrid

Province of Spain

Holy Roman Empire

Professor Di Vargas double-checked his letter to make sure he didn't give the censors at the Holy Postal Service anything, which might be used to prevent his further communications with his American colleague. He smiled as he remembered the redheaded archaeologist from the Conference of Theology and Archaeology.

The invitation to the conference provided Juan with his first chance to transit overseas since his teens. The trip in his teens to the Holy Land provided the spark, which lit his passion for studying the theological development of ancient Judaism and early Christianity. Along the way, Juan discovered his other passion, the bodies of men. In the ultra-conservative post-Upheaval era, his second passion remained a secret, which he currently shared only with the fiery Texan. Before Jeremiah, he'd had a series of discrete affairs, but something about the Texan made Juan wish to settle. Modern Europe resembled a strange mix of Medieval Europe in the Age of Charlemagne and the Victorian Era. The missing element is a secular crowned head of state.

In the aftermath of the Upheaval and the wars that followed, the Church rose to dominate Western Europe. A series of strong pontiffs created a new Holy Roman Empire with Vatican City as its capital and the Pope as the new political head. The Vatican reversed the civil rights gains made by minority groups in the century prior to the Upheaval. Canon law ruled the land, and the Order of St. Hubert became the means of enforcing the law. The Church established harsh penalties for those caught in homosexual acts. Men like Juan had to be careful not to draw official attention to his preferences in bed partners. Di Vargas sighed as he sealed the envelope addressed to the handsome American professor. He hoped Jeremiah would be as discreet in his reply. Di Vargas recalled the Republic of Texas, another of the successor nations to the shattered United States. It was ultra-conservative, but from what Jeremiah told him, not as repressive as the Holy Roman Empire.

The contents of the package represented enough mystery to lure Jeremiah to Madrid. Once he arrived, further discussions would follow. Perhaps the young archaeologist would wish to renew more than their academic affiliation. Juan wanted him researching by his side and back in his bed. They would need to be careful; conditions in the Empire were different than they were in the Americas. They'd avoided trouble three years ago while in the conservative Confederate States of America. Although, Juan thought the easy time in Atlanta came more from the color of their skin. The Confederate authorities seemed to prefer hassling the delegates from the Union of African States.

Juan sealed the package and hoped that Jeremiah would be cautious when he replied. This isn't one of our private letters, beautiful boy.

Professor Di Vargas picked up the package and left his office, heading for the campus mailroom to send the letter on a slow journey across the Atlantic by ship. After the political situation settled following years of war, the Holy Father in Rome called a conference of world leaders. Held in Venice, the conference produced the Holy Accord of 2204, wherein all nations agreed to ban planes, rockets, and airships to prevent a second Upheaval. Subsequent to the devastation of the Upheaval and the wars, the nations clawed their way back to the age of steam power and early diesel. The cargo lines expanded to handle the increased shipping traffic around the world. The loss of air traffic meant journeys, which used to take days or hours, now took weeks. Land transportation slowed as the industry retooled factories to produce vehicles designed to survive another EMP attack. The modern governments also held back advancement of transportation as a means of controlling their populations and the spread of radical ideas.

Di Vargas laughed as he remembered the photo Jeremiah included in his last Christmas card. The dashing redhead seated on a horse as he rode back to campus from a dig in the Arizona desert. Much of the world regressed to using horse-drawn carts or walking. High society in the Confederate States of America and the Republic of Texas made the use of horse-drawn carriages a status symbol as part of their return to the glories of the past. A long journey took planning and making sure all the proper paperwork was processed to cross borders. Most people took one of the few trains over long distances. The university clock struck the hour as Professor Di Vargas emerged from the mailroom and realized he needed to return to his office and grab his lecture notes. He was due in class in twenty minutes to present a lecture on the early church.

CAIN'S ACCOUNT FROM THE STOLEN JOURNAL OF RICHARD ST. MARTIN

To my successor:

My heartfelt condolences, noble hunter. Understand I regret being the cause of you losing your mortal life. You read this journal because I failed to convince you killing me would be the worst thing to do. The Curse inflicted upon me by my family's pathetic little god transformed you into the most influential member of your new family. In my place, you reign as Lord of all Vampires.

I'm sure I introduced myself when you broke into my home intent on slaying me, but I reintroduce myself here so perhaps the knowledge I impart to you in this journal can be absorbed. I am Cain: son of Adam, the first man, and Eve, the second woman, and elder brother to both Abel and Seth. I am the first vampire. Heed my warnings and read this book for here is the origin of the vampires. The Curse laid on me for striking down my evil and twisted brother.

I cannot call you by name in this letter. I can't guess which of several hunters claimed my Curse. Signs and portents show me potential futures, so I am aware you are coming for me. I made vague notes about following the comings and goings of mortals, for no one has ever survived long enough to track me to my doorstep. Condolences once again, noble hunter. You read this because you sent me to my final death and received the Curse of Cain in my place. Take this advice to heart, my successor, surround yourself with loyal servants and heed their warnings when you grow ancient. Because you are reading this letter means either I failed to heed my wisdom or grew so tired of existence I let you cut me down and allowed the curse to put you in my place. My apologies for failing to convince you to stay your hand and spare you from my fate.

Cain

First-born son of Adam

* * *

January 5, 2005

The above letter is believed to be a fabrication created by a deranged mind by many scholars and members of the clergy. I'm sure because I showed the document to several of them after the letter came into my possession along with Cain's curse, house, and library. I tried to determine if my years of hunting vampires drove me insane. The reality of vampirism is undeniable, but did I inherit the curse from the biblical Cain? Having met vampires old enough to remember the pyramids as construction projects, I believe divine-level magic transferred the curse to me from the source. I'm sure sometime in the future someone will read these entries and think I'm a raving lunatic.

Richard St. Martin

Chapter 5

APRIL 30, 2223

Professor Juan Di Vargas

Department of Theology

University of Madrid

Province of Spain

Holy Roman Empire

Dear Professor Di Vargas:

I am pleased at receiving your letter of March 15, containing your offer to share the spoils of your research coup. I do remember you from the Atlanta conference. Are you still fond of Confederate whiskey and silk sheets?

My schedule so far prevents me from doing more than skimming this journal, but the mentions of this unknown city-state of El-Abel caught my attention. After highlighting several passages, I brought this to the attention of my department's dean. Although I also discount the magic and talk of angels and vampires, the historical details match up with several other sources, including some additional translations of the El-Isinian tablets. Did we find the missing piece in our search? I believe I will receive funding before the middle of May. I do worry about the opinions of some of my colleagues and the politics here in the Republic of Texas. The government will saddle me with a political overseer, both to keep me in line and to make sure the Caliphate of Baghdad doesn't act uppity about infidels digging up their country.

I'm making sure my part of the expedition is equipped with plenty of underwater equipment based on my regional knowledge and analysis of the journal. The pages' location for El-Abel may now be beneath the waters of the Persian Gulf. I will write again as soon as all my clearances and travel arrangements are approved. Should we meet in Spain, or perhaps Damascus would be a better location? Please inform me of your arrangements.

With respect,

Jeremiah Banks

Professor of Archeology

University of Arizona

Republic of Texas

Jeremiah sealed and addressed the envelop to Juan before realizing the mistake of mentioning silk sheets.

¡Maldito Sea! Juan mentioned people read his mail before delivering his letters. Jeremiah felt like an idiot. He shredded the letter, wrote a new version leaving out the dangerous reference, and put the envelope on the department secretary's desk for mailing. Jeremiah remained more interested in pursuing the leads Juan's package contained regarding a lost city in ancient Mesopotamia than in dealing with the current political climate in Europe. Juan had caught his attention with this strange book.

The clock on Jeremiah's desk chimed the half hour, reminding him of his meeting with the head of his department regarding the funding needed to mount an exploration in Southern Mesopotamia, a region long held under the control of the Caliphate of Baghdad. Juan suggested meeting in Madrid. During his walk to the dean's office, Jeremiah tried pushing the memories of the older Spanish professor of ancient theology out of his mind. The trick didn't help as his mind replayed the man's thick accent while they lay next to each other after an evening of lovemaking. Jeremiah wanted to stay with Juan. The problem was the love between two men was illegal in most nations. He supposed they might find employment in the Republic of California where almost everything was legal.

Jeremiah gave his mind a quick shake as he reached the outer door to the dean's office to focus on his presentation. He needed the dean's backing to move forward in getting the university's support for a dig. Dr. Banks straightened his suit jacket and made sure his long hair remained bound behind his head and not running wild. He entered the outer office to be greeted by the clacking of an ancient typewriter and caught the attention of the dean's secretary. The matron guarding the inner sanctum of the dean's office glanced up and smiled at him.

"Dr. Banks, to what do we owe the pleasure of this visit? Did you come to take me out for a wild night of passion?"

Jeremiah blushed at her outrageous flirtation and stammered out. "M-Mrs. Pike! I hope Dean Sinclair hasn't forgotten we are meeting to discuss my request for funding."

"Of course not, Dr. Banks." Mrs. Pike laughed. "I enjoy watching certain young redheaded professors blush the same color as their hair. Wait a moment, sweetie. I'll tell the dean you're here."

The ample figure of Mrs. Pike rose from behind her desk. The rumor around campus said she gave up a promising movie career after meeting Dr. Pike. She chose to settle down and become a wife, mother, and secretary. She was a handsome woman now; how stunning did she appear in her youth? Jeremiah appreciated her mature beauty, though women held no attraction for him. She enjoyed teasing him ever since his days as an undergraduate student and adopted him as something of a surrogate son. Dr. Pike passed away a few years back, but Mrs. Pike soldiered on, moving out of the president's residence and into a small house off campus. Jeremiah helped her move and settle in. They still met for dinner once a week, when Jeremiah's schedule allowed.

"Go on in now, dear."

"Thank you."

He entered the dean's office. Jeremiah needed to convince Dr. Sinclair the book contained valuable and unique information lost in antiquity. He stopped short when he discovered a third person in the office besides himself and the dean.

"Dr. Banks, I believe you're acquainted with Representative Beauregard Beaumont, the local member of Congress," Dr. Sinclair, the Dean of the Department of Archaeology, said.

"Yes, sir. Representative Beaumont, a pleasure to meet you again." Jeremiah extended his hand to the politician. "I believe we met at the congressional hearing on the restoration of the Alamo last year."

"Yes, Dr. Banks. You made quite an impression on the committee. So, when Dr. Sinclair mentioned this project you wanted to pursue to further research into the history of the Bible, the committee decided someone should come and listen to your proposal in person."

"T-Thank you, sir. I'm trying to prove the existence of the city of Enoch. A colleague at the University of Madrid shared a copy of an old journal containing references to the city."

"You think you found Enoch?" Dr. Sinclair asked.

"You'll forgive me, I'm not familiar with Enoch." said Beaumont. "What's the significance of this city?"

"Enoch is regarded as the first city ever built. The Book of Genesis says Cain built Enoch after he murdered Abel and God banished him to the land of Nod. He named the city for his first-born son," Jeremiah explained. "Cain and his family lived in Enoch for many generations until Cain's many times removed great-grandson killed him by accident."

"Thank you for the Bible lesson, Dr. Banks. I'm not as up on the Old Testament as I should be."

"What does this book say about the city, Dr. Banks?" Dr. Sinclair asked.

"Well, first off, the author calls the location by a different name. In this journal, Enoch is called El-Abel. Although the author still calls the place the city of Cain, he states the city isn't the first. The author quotes a text referred to as the Gospel of Cain: 'Father Cain returned to the land of his birth and decided to take a hand in governing a city-state. He gathered the brightest of his brother Seth's descendants as his ministers and city officials and established the city-state of El-Abel to the south of Ur along the coast.' Which would put El-Abel between the outpost at El-Isin and the possible location of the trading center at El-Kino."

"A location which still puts the city in the territory claimed by the Caliphate of Baghdad. Dangerous territory, son," Rep. Beaumont commented.

"Yes, sir, the location is dangerous. Part of the danger is because Enoch or El-Abel lies inside the caliphate; the other part is because the actual site may be underwater. The water levels of the Persian Gulf are higher and further inland now than when Enoch existed."

"This sounds like an expensive undertaking. How much are we talking about?"

"To finance a search, receive the permits from the caliphate, pay the workers, rent the ship and underwater equipment, somewhere around five million Republic red backs. My colleague in Madrid says the University of Madrid is willing to finance his half, but most of his search is in the libraries of Baghdad and Damascus."

"Who is this colleague, Dr. Banks?" asked Rep. Beaumont.

"Professor Juan Di Vargas." Jeremiah tried to keep his voice steady. "The—"

"University of Madrid's Ancient Theology Department. He holds the Ferdinand II Chair for Biblical Studies," Dr. Sinclair cut Jeremiah off. "I'm sure if the Republic made the funding available perhaps the Holy Father in Rome's government might also move to match the Republic's funding. I believe His Grace the Papal Legate is in Tucson for the opening of the Hopi exhibition. I happen to possess an extra ticket and an opening at my table; perhaps you would join me, Representative Beaumont. We can present Dr. Banks' proposal together on behalf of the university and the Republic."

"Sounds like an excellent suggestion, Dr. Sinclair. Of course."

"Wouldn't it be helpful if I attended to answer questions for His Grace?" Jeremiah attempted to interject.

"We must send a representative of the Republic along with Dr. Banks to manage our investment and assist in dealing with the caliph's agents."

"I'm quite capable of managing the funding and dealing with the agents of the caliph," Jeremiah offered.

The conversation between Beaumont and Sinclair continued about how to approach the Papal Legate, with both men forgetting Jeremiah's presence. Defeated, Jeremiah slipped out of the office to be confronted by Mrs. Pike.

"Took over your plans, didn't they, Dr. Banks? Leave the politicking to the professionals and do your planning for the real work."

"I think you're right, Mrs. Pike. I'm headed back to my office to grab my notes for my next lecture period. Would you do me a favor and lock these away in the dean's safe until I can come back for them?" Jeremiah held up his folder with the copies of the journal pages inside. "I lack the time to put them in my office safe, and I don't want to take them with me to class."

"Don't worry about them, Doctor. I'll lock them up for you."

Chapter 6

THE SETTING SUN turned the remaining glass in the old Hancock Building a brilliant orange. The city struggled to recover from the damage done during the Upheaval, and the reorganized government of the Federal Union of North America spent its money fortifying the borders with the other new nations on the continent. Adam FitzCaine, owner of the local hotspot Dante's Inferno gazed out of his office window over the remains of the city of Boston, Massachusetts. The vista below was overlaid with his memories of the city in its heyday before the Upheaval. He flexed, trying to pop loose a tight spot between his shoulder blades, before reaching up to run his long fingers over his short graying hair. He adjusted the jacket of his tailored suit. Adam turned as someone knocked on his office door.

"Come in. This better be important. I told Stan not to disturb me."

"Mr. FitzCaine, I'm Father Nathan. Her Eminence, Cardinal Joan of El-Abel, sent me with word on Lord Hunter's stolen journal."

"Let me guess, another one of the infernal copies surfaced someplace."

"Given the details we received from our agent in Madrid, Her Eminence believes the original surfaced."

"What details did you receive, Priest?"

"Our brother at the University of Madrid received the privilege of being among the select members of the theology staff present when Professor Juan Di Vargas showed a rare book to the Master of the School of Theology. He glimpsed a few odd pages in the bundle written in what he believed to be the blue ink of one of Lord Hunter's ballpoint pens."

"What? Are you sure?" Adam moved with such speed the poor cleric screamed in surprise when the man grabbed him by the lapels of his suit coat and lifted him from the floor. "Is this intelligence accurate, Priest? Pray to the Lord Hunter this isn't a waste of his time."

"By the blood of Cain and Lord Hunter, I swear this is the truth." The man fumbled for the cross at his waist. "I received the knowledge direct from the priest who witnessed the professor displaying the book. Her Eminence sent me to Madrid straight from her service."

Adam dropped the monk and returned to his spot in front of the window. Once the priest picked himself up, Adam turned back to face him. His dark eyes smoldered with repressed anger. The priest cowered from him, holding tight to the blood-red crucifix like a talisman. Adam laughed at the fear showing on the man's face.

"Relax, Father. You're safe from me, for now. Let yourself out." Adam waited until the monk reached the door before adding, "If you value your life, Father Nathan, forget what happened in this office tonight."

The priest nodded and fled the room. Adam crossed to a bookcase opposite his desk and tilted Dante's *Paradise*, his private joke. The bookcase slid aside to reveal an elevator into which he stepped. As Adam turned and pressed the button, which would take him up to the

Lord Hunter's secret levels, his gaze fixed on his reflection and the glamor of mortality faded. He grinned as his eyes changed from bright green back to his darker blue.

Adam's hair grew in length until reaching the middle of his back. Its color changed from black to light brown, and his fangs descended. The appearance of middle age faded away, replaced with the glow of youth. As Adam continued to gaze at the reflection, he slipped back into the recesses of the man who created him when he needed a public persona. The glamor vanished and Richard St. Martin stepped out of the elevator on his floor. Two young men dressed as monks bowed to him as he came towards them. The elder of the two spoke first. "How may we be of service to you, Lord Hunter?"

"Are any of your court joining you tonight, Lord Slayer?" from the second youth.

"Contact your abbot. I need internal verification on a report delivered from your Cult," Richard directed the first youth.

"Yes, Lord Hunter."

"Go and inform Database and Armand that I need their services tonight," he addressed the second youth.

"Yes, Lord Slayer."

The power to mesmerize still amazed Richard. His ability kept these two young monks from hearing what the other said. One youth he programmed to answer only things Lord Hunter directed toward the mortal world, while the other only responded to things Lord Slayer addressed to the supernatural world. Though he pondered his condition often, Richard remained amazed he retained his sanity after close to three centuries, as his titles evolved to become separate personas.

The mortal members of both the Cult of Cain and the Brotherhood of the Crimson Hand addressed him as Lord Hunter, the title given to him a half-century before the Upheaval by the Emperor of all the Russias. All the vampires, except Database, called him Lord Slayer out of respect for the number of elder vampires killed. The spy proved a particular case; the little Barghest Clan vampire first met him a few days after Richard's transformation. The teen vampire—Richard chuckled at the thought since Database was over 4,000 years old—tried to follow Richard, hoping to collect information on him.

"Master, you sent for me?"

"Yes, my little spy. For you and Armand, a task for both of you."

"Sorry for the delay in answering, My Lord. How may I be of service?"

Both vampires bowed to Richard, rising to face the man who saved them several times from destruction. They served as his left and right hands, acting in the supernatural world while he dealt with the mortal world. He cherished both of them while marveling at their differences. Armand the peacock strutted around in the latest of fashions and often modeled for select designers. Database shrouded his appearance in a jacket with an oversized hood, which kept his face hidden in deep shadow. Only once in the three centuries of their association did he allow Richard to glimpse the beautiful face the shadows hid. The curse on his clan's bloodline brought out the beauty of his soul, transforming his once-twisted body into a work of art. The curse laid by Cain on the founder of the clan brought out the truth of the soul, foul or beautiful. The thought of rewarding them with his own blood often crossed his mind. Fear of the changes, which might happen, kept him from following through.

"I received news from Adam."

Both vampires stiffened at the mention of his mortal persona. Despite being Richard's closest advisors, Database and Armand lacked the knowledge of Adam FitzCaine being an alternate persona for Richard.

"A report reached him claiming the Cult of Cain discovered my stolen journal. I need to verify this information through channels other than the Cult."

"Of course, Master. Allow me to check my network and discover what is passing among the clans."

"What do you wish me to do, My Lord?"

"I want you to make sure the discovery of my missing journal doesn't reach certain parties among the clans. I also want to ensure the mortals in possession of my journal come to no harm. From the report Adam gave me, the recovered sections are from the intact original journal, which contains information left to me by Cain, including the location of El-Abel."

"My Lord, is leaving such information with mortals wise? What if they give up those sections to the Order of St. Hubert or another of the enforcement agencies?"

"The man with the book is the type of person I wanted investigating the contents, a professor of theology in Spain. Being too open with the information invites the Church to destroy him before he can help us. The Order would burn him as a heretic. No, I'm more worried the Izcacus Clan attempting to gain control of them."

Armand shuddered at the mention of the Izcacus Clan for their slaughter of his actual clan's founder to gain his power. Before he spoke further, Database spoke up first.

"Master, what about the rumors the Primordial Bellabarisruk of the Bel-Kino Clan woke from languor? The fact he seeks any knowledge of those searching for the location of lost El-Abel is well documented."

"From what I read in Cain's notes on the different clans, Bellabarisruk possess the location of El-Abel since he lived in the city before its destruction in the Flood. The notes mention Bellabarisruk believes himself the city's appointed guardian. Yet, I take your warning to heart, Database. I need both mortal and vampire guards we can trust watching over this professor and whomever he confides his find too. I'll trust you two to figure out the vampire watchers. I'll use both the Cult and the Brotherhood. If this professor goes exploring, he'll end up in Muslim lands where the Brotherhood operates. I need all the information you can find for me on this professor."

"I'll talk with Adam and arrange to acquire the details from him, My Lord."

The clear clipped tone to Armand's rich Italian baritone rang in Richard's ears.

"My friends, please tell me why dealing with Adam is a problem for both of you? He's loyal and serves the vital function of giving us a mortal to deal with humans. Remember, he came up with the idea of creating a nightclub as neutral territory where the clans can meet with mages, shifters, and humans without violence. It made our lives easier."

"I'm worried you trust him too much, My Lord."

"You let him closer than either of the last mortals you used before in this role. Did you mesmerize him to be so trusting of him, Master?"

"No, Adam isn't mesmerized to be loyal. Only with freewill does he do the job I need him to do. Mesmerizing him to be loyal only leaves me with another mindless servant like the boys in the hall. I trust Adam because he's earned my trust. I wish you would learn to trust him, both of you, but for now, I'm asking you to work with him for my sake."

"I'll talk with him, My Lord. Will he be on club duty tonight?"

"No, he mentioned taking the night off and letting Henry gain some experience handling the club alone. Leave him a note and I'm sure he'll make sure all the anti-sun precautions are in place so you can visit him in his office tomorrow."

Armand and Database said their goodbyes and left to start their assigned tasks. Richard crossed his apartment to enter his personal office and check messages. Perhaps someone would seek to hire Lord Hunter to handle a shifter problem or an out-of-control mage.

Chapter 7

Professor Di Vargas stood before the Rector and Council of the University of Madrid to make his proposal. He couldn't remember being this nervous about requesting funding or making a speech. He didn't think he was this nervous when making his inaugural address after being awarded the chair. He'd been so full of himself twenty-five years ago, the youngest scholar to ever win the Ferdinand II Chair for Biblical Studies. Well, now he needed to channel the pompous young professor for this presentation. Juan drew himself up to his full height and coughed for attention from the Rector, the Council, as well as the Papal representative, and his supporting clergy.

"Rector, Your Grace, and Councilors, thank you for taking time from your busy schedules to consider my request for funding. I realize this isn't the proper time of the year to be seeking expedition funding, but I believe this research cannot wait for better timing."

"Professor Di Vargas, you brought this university an enormous amount of prestige over the years, and we realize research breakthroughs don't always adhere to fiscal planning calendars. Please present your request and what you can of your research for consideration."

"Thank you, Rector. As you are aware, I came into possession of a mysterious journal. One rumor mentions the members of the Order of St. Hubert attempted to recovered from the collection of the late Richard St. Martin, referred to as Lord Hunter—"

"I'm sorry to interrupt Professor Di Vargas," the Papal representative interjected. "Why didn't you turn a relic of the blessed Lord Hunter over to the Order of St. Hubert? They handle all items concerning famous hunters."

"In part because I believe, Your Grace, the Order of St. Hubert possesses a copy of this particular journal. The copy I obtained contains a cover letter from a member of the Order stating a number of copies exist so one would reach the Order and the Holy Father. Should I be mistaken, I will, of course, make my copy available to members of the Order to study," Juan answered before resuming his presentation. "This journal contains entries and notes by St. Martin, which lead me to believe he gathered the other entries together for personal reasons. The author of the majority of the journal claims to be Cain, the son of Adam and Eve. This author states his intention in writing these passages is to give a real account of the events surrounding the first mortal family. Under normal circumstances, I would chalk this journal up to the writings of a madman. Except my colleague, Dr. Jeremiah Banks of the University of Arizona's Department of Archaeology, and I discovered several passages which provide details of ancient cultures of biblical significance. This journal also contains references to what Dr. Banks and I believe to be the biblical city of Enoch. "

"Why would Lord Hunter possess such a journal, Professor?" the Papal representative asked.

"As mentioned, between the individual journal entries, Your Grace, are a few notes made by Lord Hunter regarding information on hunting and slaying a creature referred to as a vampire. I'm only familiar with the Bram Stoker novel and theatre vampires, Your Grace. The journal accounts show Richard St. Martin believed these creatures existed and needed to be hunted, much like shifters."

"So, what are you requesting funding for Professor Di Vargas?" one of the Council members asked.

"Dr. Banks and I are proposing a joint research and archaeological expedition to Southern Mesopotamia to search for the city of Enoch and proof of the lineage of Cain."

"Where is Dr. Banks, Professor Di Vargas? Shouldn't he be here with you making your case for funding?"

"Rector, Dr. Banks is organizing his half of the expedition, which his university and the Republic of Texas agreed to fund together. The desired outcome is our university matching the amount they put forward."

"How much did they make available to Dr. Banks?"

"The University of Arizona put up one and a half million Republic red backs and the Republic's government gave an additional three and a half million red backs."

"You're asking the university to fund you with the equivalent of six million papal ducats?" the shocked treasurer struggled not to choke on the amount as she spoke. "We can't justify such a level of funding, Professor Di Vargas. Based on normal funding levels, the best the university can provide is around half a million ducats."

"Perhaps, you can persuade the Holy Father in Rome to assist in financing the expedition for the glory of the Empire, Your Grace. Does His Holiness wish to be outshone by an upstart nation like the Republic of Texas?"

"Of course, His Holiness wouldn't wish such a thing, Professor Di Vargas." The Papal representative growled at the thought of such a petty nation getting the lion's share of the credit. "I will transfer the funds from the Vatican accounts. The Empire will support your entire half of the expedition as well as ease your way with the caliph's government. You will take a Papal observer as part of your team to ensure a proper accounting of His Holiness' funds."

"Thank you, Your Grace. A slot remains reserved for your choice of an observer in my half of the expedition." Prof. Di Vargas bowed in appreciation. "His Holiness' observer will share the duties for bookkeeping and as liaison with a counterpart from the Republic of Texas on Dr. Banks' half of the team."

The meeting adjourned with handshakes. Professor Di Vargas left wondering if his research topic sparked the Papal representative's offer of funding or the threat of the Republic of Texas receiving all the glory. In truth, he believed the latter. Funded by the Texans and the Empire, the expedition possessed the means to stay in the field for close to a year and half. He also surmised his university would add their half million ducats to the pile to make sure of being included as a sponsor of the expedition. His mind wandered to thoughts of Jeremiah unrelated to the journey. He loved the contrast between Jeremiah's pale skin and flame-red hair. The archaeologist had appeared groomed to perfection the last time, but what was he like now?

VAMPIRE INTERLUDE: A MONTH BEFORE DEPARTURE OF THE BANKS EXPEDITION

Flashes of tanned flesh drew many eyes to the ripped figure intruding into their company uninvited. A purple silk bandana did its best to keep his midnight hair away from his chiseled face and kohl-rimmed eyes. The red brocade jacket swinging open showed off his toned physique, while his jeans clung to his lower body like a second skin. Dark-brown leather boots completed the outlandish garb. Shock ran through the fashionably dressed patrons, disrupting their enjoyment of heretical entertainments offered on the sixth circle of Dante's Inferno as the first mate of the pirate ship *Sunniva Mare* passed between them. He glided between the wealthy patrons, heading straight for the private table reserved for the club's owner, Adam FitzCaine. Along the way to invade FitzCaine's private space, the man swiped a bottle of expensive rum from a passing serving tray and a startled server. The server started to complain until his eyes locked with the dashing pirate's eyes.

"Marcus, go fetch the exclusive and take a bottle to the mayor's table with the house's compliments. We'll talk in my office after your shift ends." A cold voice broke the spell of the dark man's eyes.

The young blond server fled to fulfill his new mission, aware of his boss's displeasure with his performance.

"You sure can kill the mood, FitzCaine. I don't recall seeing a blond so pale in three or four centuries. Imagine his pale beauty spread out naked on black silk sheets."

"Marcus is off-limits, Shadow. The boy is under Lord Hunter's protection and mine."

"The boy must be unique to warrant so much protection."

"Not your business, Shadow. Your personal membership doesn't let you pass the third circle, so what are you doing down here in the sixth?"

"Searching the place for you. The captain lent me her membership pass, which allows access down to the eight level."

"I'm aware of how far down Laverna Salacia's pass permits her to venture into my club. So why are you here instead of the lady?"

"The captain wants a meeting with your boss. She's picked up on some things he'll want to know."

"He's not my boss. What kind of information does the Queen of Pirates hold for Mr. St. Martin? He'll want some hint of whether he should give her time or not."

"The captain says to tell him the information is about the book."

A brief flash of irritation crossed FitzCaine's face. He schooled his expression before addressing the pirate messenger.

"I'll pass along her request when I meet with him later tonight."

"Are you sure I can't obtain a little sample of young Marcus?"

"You wouldn't survive to enjoy your sample, Shadow. Attempt to take one and final death claims you."

"Either you or Lord Slayer shall hunt me down and kill me."

"Only if you survived the moment your fangs pierced his flesh. The boy is a descendant of the House of Beauty and is gifted. I understand Silver magic is fatal to vampires." Adam's smile revealed the sharp canines, which made his mortal patrons believe him a vampire and confused the hell out of the undead because they sensed his blood pumping.

Shadow took in Adam's smile and blanched as far as his condition allowed. Adam reached across the table and plucked the bottle of rum from his grasp.

"Your visitor time on Laverna's membership is expired. Time for you to depart, handsome Shadow. Tell the Queen of Pirates the Lord of all Vampires will be in touch."

Chapter 8

JEREMIAH STOOD on the dock in the Port of Galveston, watching his equipment get loaded aboard the cargo/passenger ship, which would carry his part of the expedition to the Port of Valencia in Spain. He wore clothes of leather and denim, and ran his hand through his short red hair. After a year delay for military service, he was finally able to get his expedition underway and let his hair start to grow back.

The arrival of an official Republic of Texas limo drew his attention away from the loading. Jeremiah stood unimpressed, though cars of any type remained rare enough to catch the interest of the dockworkers. He shouted at them to return to loading his equipment as he crossed the dock to meet the arriving dignitaries. The public security personnel emerged from the vehicle, followed by the tall, lean figure of Rep. Beauregard Beaumont and a statuesque blonde woman dressed in what must have been one of the latest fashions from London. Jeremiah forced himself to acknowledge being underdressed for the company. The arrival of a steam-powered car marked with the University of Arizona's emblem offered some hope. Until he espied three young people emerge ahead of the Dean of the Department of Archaeology.

Groaning, Jeremiah recognized the three as graduate students assigned to Dr. Hezekiah Sampson. Jeremiah wondered if his expedition was expanding to include teaching sessions. Well, so much for the daydreams of renewing more than his academic relationship with Juan. He guessed the fickle winds of fate decided otherwise. Jeremiah sighed. It was incredible how much he still missed the elder man's touch after three years. The things Juan taught him about his own body during the few days they'd spent together, nobody else could replicate.

"Dr. Banks," Dean Sinclair called out across the dock. "We're glad we caught you here. We meant to handle the introductions at your hotel, but the clerk said you left before dawn to come here."

"Dr. Sinclair, Rep. Beaumont." Jeremiah shook hands with the two men as he ushered them back from the active loading. "My apologies, Prof. Adamson drummed into me as a graduate student to always be on hand when your equipment is loaded for an expedition." Jeremiah turned and shouted, "Be careful with those crates; what's inside them is worth more than all our lives combined." Turning back, he said, "I'm sorry this is a bad time for interruptions. Can this wait until I return to the hotel this evening?"

"No, Dr. Banks, I'm afraid not. Rep. Beaumont needs to return to Austin. He wants to make his introduction in person," Dr. Sinclair said.

"Sorry to interrupt your preparations, Dr. Banks, but I wanted to introduce the Committee's selection for observer and accountant for your expedition. Dr. Jeremiah Banks, this is Miss Eunice Beaumont. Eunice, this is Dr. Jeremiah Banks, the young professor of archaeology I told you about," Rep. Beaumont said.

Jeremiah wiped his hand on his pant leg before extending to shake with Miss Beaumont. She regarded him like someone out in the field for six months without a bath, before taking his hand for a brief shake.

"Miss Beaumont, an honor to welcome you as a member of this expedition. Is everything you need packed? We sail in the morning."

"No need to worry about me, Mr. Banks. I packed everything and my baggage is ready to be loaded. I'm a certified public accountant, and I also speak fluent Arabic, Hebrew, and enough Persian to manage."

"My name is Dr. Banks, Miss Beaumont, and I'm not worried about your language or mathematical skills; those aren't a problem. Forgive sounding sexist, and me for being blunt, but your gender is the problem when dealing with the caliph's agents, the local workers, and medical personnel in the caliphate. I need someone to whom Muslims listen. Despite the fact we're in the 23rd century, the attitude of the caliphate remains mired in the 13th century. I'm sorry, but you won't do as my government representative."

Miss Beaumont's right brow arched as her face transformed into an icy mask. Her hands came to rest on her hips.

"Too bad for you, Mr. Banks, I'm the government representative assigned to your mission."

"A last reminder, Miss Beaumont, the name is *Dr.* Banks, and if you can't show me the courtesy of using my correct form of address, I shudder to think how you might insult our hosts in the caliphate. Enough dangers are involved in this venture without you insulting some member of the caliph's government and getting us executed. Rep. Beaumont, I suggest you take this young woman back with you to Austin and send someone else or send me the authority to negotiate on behalf of the Republic."

"Sorry, the president chose my niece as the government's representative. If she doesn't go with you, the Republic's withdraws backing and revokes all travel documents."

"Oh for... I should expect nothing less than nepotism to be at work. Lucky for us, once we reach Spain, Professor Di Vargas becomes the expedition's leader and the Empire's representative handles the major negotiations. Be in the hotel lobby with your bag at four tomorrow morning, Miss Beaumont." Jeremiah turned his attention to the three graduate students. "Now, Dr. Sinclair, who are these three?"

Jeremiah turned his attention to the group he'd first assumed to be three young men based on their clothing. Only on closer inspection did he realize the third young man was actually a young woman. He gave her a few points for wearing practical field clothing. All three were dressed as if they'd expected to mount horses and ride off to the desert. From beneath her Stetson, the young woman smiled at him, while her companions attempted to mask their looks of disappointment.

"These are Dr. Sampson's doctoral candidates in Native American Studies. Because Dr. Sampson suffered an accident a few days ago, their planned expedition is cancelled. In view of the fact that not going into the field would hurt their semester, Dr. Sampson asked they be attached to your expedition. Let me present Ms. Quillion Post, Mr. Macejah Puap, and Mr. Theophisus Polzin." Dr. Sinclair indicated each student in turn. "This is Dr. Jeremiah Banks, professor of archaeology and the man who discovered the key to El-Isinian. He's your mentor on this expedition."

"Well, I'm sorry about Dr. Sampson. I bet you're disappointed to be forced on a journey to the Middle East instead of out into the tribal lands. I'll try to make your time engaging, and I suspect you'll come to love the ancient Middle East. Like, I instructed Miss Beaumont, be ready by at four tomorrow morning."

* * *

After the two-week crossing from the Port of Galveston, the bustling Port of Valencia came into view, much to Jeremiah's relief. The calm sea made the voyage pleasant enough, but part of the company drove Jeremiah mad. The three archaeology grad students the university dumped on him didn't pose a significant problem. No, the member of the expedition he wanted to do harm to remained the representative from the Republic's President. The students, while useless now, showed potential. The woman from the committee was a different story, one which made Jeremiah contemplate a variety of accidents occurring at sea. Miss Eunice Beaumont, of the Phoenix Beaumonts, proved as snobbish as her introduction made her sound. A niece of Representative Beauregard Beaumont, she got the observer position by family connections, although she possessed certification as an accountant and a skill for stretching the value of a red back.

Miss Beaumont should've been someone he wanted to respect; instead she either ignored him or insulted him following their introduction. After two weeks at sea, she still refused to address him as Dr. Banks. The woman's attitude left his grad students correcting her every time she called him Mr. Banks. He hoped for her to be courteous to Professor Di Vargas and the Papal representative. *Buona fortuna*. He hoped Juan was waiting at the dock when they arrived.

The call of the deck crew to the longshoremen drew Jeremiah from his pleasant memories of Juan and back to reality. Time to make sure everyone packed and made ready for transfer to the Papal vessel, which would take them to Tel Aviv in Greater Israel.

VAMPIRE INTERLUDE:
PRIMORDIAL RISING

Two members of the Bel-Kino clan met in an ancient and crumbling crypt, long forgotten in the French countryside, to consult over current events and the possible need to awaken their clan's founder.

"Do you believe we're making a wise choice to wake Lord Bellabarisruk over a mere rumor?"

"The master left firm instructions regarding what to wake him for, and rumors of anyone searching for El-Abel is high on the list."

"You do understand the amount of work you're dumping on my shoulders to prepare for his awakening?"

"Planning and arranging the ritual for his awakening should be the least of your worries. Consider what he'll do to me for authorizing waking him should these rumors prove false. I'm giving you warning while I make sure our lord and master doesn't hand me my head."

"The sad fact is we realize he will hand you your head in the literal sense."

"Yes, so I'll use the three months you'll need to prepare everything for the ritual and make sure facts lie behind these rumors."

* * *

Three months later.

The torches flickered and hissed as the procession moved down the rough-hewn corridor towards the massive chamber at the end. The members of the procession split as they entered the room as those carrying torches used them to light the braziers before racking them in holders around the outer wall. The participants shoved three struggling naked teens to the center of the room and forced them to kneel. Their chains rattled against the stone floor. In the heart of the room stood a bier carved from the finest marble and resting on top lay the desiccated body of a man in blood-red robes and heavy gold jewelry.

The members of the procession knelt facing the sarcophagus except those guarding the three naked youths. With everyone kneeling, they began to chant in a strange and ancient language. Only the repetition of what must've been a name caught on the ears of the chained youths. Bellabarisruk was the only word any of them understood. The chant contained a hypnotic effect, lulling the young men out of their terror until the guard on the youth in the center whipped a vicious knife across the throat of his captive. Blood sprayed over the other youths as the guard lifted his victim up and over the figure on the bier, letting the blood flow down and into the mouth of the corpse. By the time the youth's heart shuddered to a stop from blood loss the figure on the bier showed signs of reviving.

The creature sat up on the sarcophagus and surveyed those gathered in his resting place. His eyes fell on the two remaining captives, and he gestured for the youth on the right to be brought to him. The guard behind the youth lifted him to his feet and dragged the young man to his doom. The living corpse on the bier reached out and gripped the chains holding the youth and pulled him in tight. The creature's canines extended into wicked fangs, which sank into the teen's throat. The boy struggled for a few minutes before euphoria and blood loss overwhelmed him. He slumped against the creature as he grew weaker, until the monster feeding on him withdrew and cast him aside. The young man died before he hit the floor. The ancient vampire descended from the bier and crossed to the massive stone throne carved in the wall beyond the bier. The group moved to kneel before the throne, while the guard brought the final youth forward and forced him to his knees beside the throne. Terror and shock registered on the teen's face. He whimpered and cowered as the monster rested a hand on his head and stroked his hair.

"Why do you disturb my rest?"

"Master Bellabarisruk, in your instructions before you entered languor you requested to be awoken should any word of ancient El-Abel be found."

Irritated at being awoken from his long sleep, Bellabarisruk yanked his servant closer. "I gather some mention of El-Abel reached you."

"More than a word, Master Bellabarisruk. Some of our agents report an archaeological expedition is being sent to locate the city based on information discovered in a journal believed to be from the collection of the Lord Slayer."

"Whom are you talking about? What information on El-Abel does this journal contain?"

"M-my Lord." The servant struggled to draw air to continue speaking until the primordial relaxed his grip. "The information gleaned from the Barghest clan indicates the pages contain information written by Cain about the city's exact location."

"Cain's journals? How did this Lord Slayer acquire them? If you don't possess an answer, find out!" Bellabarisruk hurled the lesser vampire across the crypt to smash into the bier in the center of the chamber.

The leader of the ceremony assisted his compatriot to rise so the man could finish imparting all the information he'd gathered to their master.

"According to a source who espied some of the copies, Master Bellabarisruk, Lord Slayer earned his title by slaying Father Cain. I brought a copy of one of the entries where he admits as much." The minion limped across the chamber and handed the paper to his master. "Should this be the truth, the Lord Slayer isn't a mortal but one of us."

December 10, 2001

No language possesses sufficient words to curse my stupidity. I struggle with believing what I read in this old journal. I sensed the darkness take hold of me at the exact moment my silver blade cleaved Cain's head from his shoulders. The blessed Goddess and her consort caught part of my prayers for salvation. I kept chasing down these monsters learning every way possible to kill vampires, though they aren't my natural targets. I started as a hunter of shifters, apprenticed to my mentor at the age of ten. I doomed myself, and my questions still go unanswered as to why they chose my dearest Sarah. I kept reading and re-reading this journal, hundreds of times over the last two years, trying to take Cain's warnings and lessons to heart.

My powers are greater than Cain's. I need only fear the touch of sunlight in the purest form at dawn; running water doesn't hamper my abilities. Only devout faith can prevent my passing a threshold. I do not cast reflections on mirrors backed with silver, but at least technology caught up to where I appear in photographs and on video. Thanks to this journal, I realize how pointless searching for a way to remove this curse is. No point in wasting the time. Since I am now Lord of all Vampires, I must build up a court to control the scattered vampire lords around the world.

I cannot guess what the future holds for me. I only remember the vows I made to myself. Do not feed on a human and do not create another vampire. I'm not sure why I'm making these notes, as I plan to lock this journal away along with my journals of my life to this point. The shock value of this journal on those of faith is staggering. I pity whoever reads these words beside me.

Richard St. Martin, Lord Slayer

"Who is this Lord Slayer or Richard St. Martin? How did he find Father Cain, never mind manage to kill him? I won't tolerate interference in my duty to guard El-Abel from outsiders. Should Richard St. Martin cross my path, I will put an end to the infant upstart."

The ancient vampire rose to his feet and seized the chain around the chest of the last mortal in the room. The monster lifted the youth as though the boy weighed nothing. Terror-filled eyes locked on the calm eyes of the monster. Bellabarisruk laughed at the kid's expression and dragged him in for a kiss tinged with the blood of his fallen friends. The youth sagged as the kiss broke only for the vampire to sink his fangs into his neck. A scream tore its way out of his throat before the euphoric effect of being bitten took complete hold of him. The boy pulled himself tighter to his killer. The ancient vampire discarded the lifeless husk when he finished.

"Arrange for us to venture to Mesopotamia to await our intrepid archaeologist and his team. What is the name of the regional ruler?"

"Based on the last report, My Lord, Hassam el-Mohammed rules the region."

"Contact him and tell him to prepare his vassals to assist us. They are to keep an eye on this archaeologist but not to interfere unless another vampire faction interferes."

"Arrangements will take some time to make, My Lord. Much changed after you entered languor."

Bellabarisruk waved the concern off and, touching a hidden stud on his throne's arm, vanished backward into the wall.

Chapter 9

PROFESSOR DI VARGAS waited in the passenger receiving area, trying to keep his excitement contained. Behind him stood Father Raymond Dupuis, Knight-Diplomat of the Order of St. Hubert, his Papal watchdog, or government liaison as the formal documents called him. Juan caught his reflection in the glass and straightened up to his full height, putting himself into teaching mode to tamp down the joy of seeing Jeremiah again. The whole show needed to be done as protocol dictated: the standard quick pecks to the cheeks, and not the soul-baring lip lock Juan wanted plant on Jeremiah. Juan tried to remember he would gain personal time with Jeremiah once the formalities were over. Di Vargas' attention shifted to a flash of red out at the top of the gangway from the ship.

Schooling his features, he moved as close to the entry as the customs officials would allow. The doors opened, and a statuesque blonde woman emerged followed by a dark-haired young lady, who appeared to be a graduate student. Juan tried to remember if Jeremiah mentioned bringing graduate students in his last letter or not. The blonde woman paused only long enough to let the customs official check her papers before she breezed past him and headed straight for Father Dupuis. The young brunette appeared embarrassed as the other woman blew right past the man she should greet first according to Dr. Banks' instructions. She went to the distinguished gentleman, who must've been Professor Di Vargas since he matched Dr. Banks' description to a T.

"Professor Di Vargas, Dr. Banks sends his apologies for not coming ashore and greeting you. He said you understand his need to make sure none of the equipment shifted or sustained damaged when we docked."

"Thank you, young lady, I do indeed understand. My apologies for not greeting you by name, but I can't recall if Dr. Banks mentioned the names of the rest of his part of the expedition in our last letters," Prof. Di Vargas said.

"I doubt he got the chance, Professor. The university dumped three of us on him at the last moment. I'm Quillion Post, a graduate student at the University of Arizona." Quillion offered her hand to shake. "Our regular mentor suffered an accident and broke both legs. We packed for his expedition into the Arizona desert so the university dumped us on Dr. Banks."

"A pleasure to meet you, Ms. Post," Prof. Di Vargas said, taking her hand and kissing the back in the traditional manner. He regarded her blush as he let go. "I'm sorry about your mentor's accident, but I trust your learning will continue with Dr. Banks."

"Thank you, Professor. Dr. Banks is fantastic. I think I learned more in the last two weeks about practical archaeology than over the last two years." Quillion leaned closer and whispered in Juan's ear, "Please don't think me forward, but I believe Dr. Banks is fond of you, and I hope the feelings are mutual, but please be careful, spies are everywhere."

Juan's mind reeled in shock at this young woman's observations and his eyes narrowed their focus to Quillion's face for a moment before he masked his reaction. "Thank you. I believe between us, Dr. Banks and I can show you some of the wonders of shared research across disciplines. I will let you return to assisting Dr. Banks with the equipment check."

"I wish. Better to be checking equipment than keeping an eye on the ice queen."

"I must assume she's not a chosen member of Dr. Banks' team." Di Vargas peered at the blonde woman with questioning eyes. "Is she the government liaison for the Republic of Texas?"

"Yes-s-s." Quillion's voice carried the venom of a thousand vipers. "Her cousin is the president and her uncle is the representative from the district, which includes the university. Dr. Banks tried to object, but they told him to take her or go back to the university because otherwise he would find his funding and travel papers revoked. She's wealthy and rude. Ms. Eunice Beaumont of the Phoenix Beaumonts. Since the moment they introduced her to Dr. Banks, she's been a bitch. Keeps calling him *Mr.* Banks instead of *Dr.* and she addresses us like servants."

Juan gave Quillion a sympathetic smile of understanding. "Thank you for the warning." Juan filed the information away; the Beaumont woman would bear watching as a threat to Jeremiah.

* * *

FATHER RAYMOND DUPUIS regarded the blonde woman breezing past Professor Di Vargas and headed his way. His superiors both in the Order and in the diplomatic department warned him of the Republic of Texas' blunder in their choice of a representative. These are the hazards of nepotism in foreign governments, and it was his luck to be selected to deal with this woman. Father Dupuis made sure to pull and read her file for himself. Ms. Eunice Beaumont was well connected back home, so well connected her past indiscretions, including bearing a child by a father of color, remained hidden from public knowledge. The report on her described a genius in mathematics, accounting, and a smattering of languages. Father Dupuis noted Latin, the unofficial-official language of the Holy Roman Empire, wasn't listed among her languages. So, while fluent in many languages, including both official languages of the Texan Republic, Father Dupuis decided to keep her one step removed. The Papal watchdog called one of his monastic assistants forward to act as buffer and translator.

"Brother Colum, we will be testing your Latin and Spanish, and perhaps English as well today, as I forgot how to speak the Republic of Texas' official languages."

"*Sì, naturalmente, Padre Dupuis, che era piuttosto scortese ignorare il professor Di Vargas.*" The young monk's comment about her rudeness toward Professor Di Vargas rolled off in his native Italian, before switching to English. "The woman deserves to be shown all the proper courtesies due to a foreign diplomat of such finesse."

"Take your place before me and let us find out if you are ready for more advanced training."

Brother Colum blocked Eunice Beaumont's path as she approached the Papal delegation.

"*Señorita Beaumont, esto es un honor de dar la bienvenida a usted de parte del Santo Padre en Roma.* I am Brother Colum aide to Father Raymond Dupuis, the Holy Father's representative. Please forgive his use of my little skills as a translator. Father Dupuis is not yet up to speed on his assigned duties regarding the Americas and isn't familiar with your languages."

The man's European accent forced Eunice to take a moment to figure out what he said. A moment later, she caught up and realized he held out his hand for her papers.

She handed them over and replied, "Please tell Father Dupuis I'm honored to meet him and greet him on behalf of the President of the Republic of Texas."

After handing over the documents to Father Dupuis, Brother Colum muttered a few unflattering phrases about the Texan representative and her lack of proper protocol. Dupuis nodded and skimmed over her papers. The priest found them all in order, but he made a mental note, reminding himself the Empire retained the right to refuse her as the Republic's representative. The decision meant to be based on if she proved unfit in the eyes of the Holy Father's representative. So far, her lack of diplomatic training showed. First, he must speak with Dr. Banks and Professor Di Vargas before dismissing her.

"Dismiss her; no wait, find out where Dr. Banks is, although if I understand archaeologists, he's down checking his equipment. I want to listen to how she talks about the doctor," Dupuis told Colum in Latin. "The Holy Father empowered me to leave her behind in the Empire if she's too much to deal with."

Colum nodded, mumbled a reply in Latin, and handed Eunice back her papers. In Spanish, he asked her where Dr. Banks was.

"Mr. Banks is down in the ship's hold checking his equipment. I told him such matters should wait until we made our proper introductions." Eunice did not attempt to disguise her contempt. "He insisted the equipment took priority over introductions and Father Dupuis and Professor Di Vargas would understand the delay while he checked to make sure nothing shifted during our voyage."

"Thank you, Señorita Beaumont. Father Dupuis arranged for porters to take your baggage to the finest hotel in Valencia, and a carriage waits to take you, so you may relax and refresh yourself before dinner this evening. Is the young lady talking to Professor Di Vargas your traveling companion?"

"Heavens no, the poor child, with her delusions of being a scientist someday. She's a graduate student and Mr. Banks' responsibility, whereas the expedition's finances and diplomatic relations are my responsibility."

Without realizing her mistake, Miss Beaumont sealed her fate. The disrespect she showed the others in her party went beyond words in any language, and Brother Colum didn't need to translate for his superior. Father Dupuis waved her off in the direction of the waiting carriage, and his other attendant monk went with her to give the driver directions to the hotel he chose. When they left, he instructed Colum to tell the porters where to deliver Miss Beaumont's baggage. The young monk gave an impish grin and scurried away to carry out the instructions. Father Dupuis joined Prof. Di Vargas and the young woman with whom he spoke. With introductions made, Father Dupuis led them past the customs officials and out across the gangway. The ship's captain turned over the shift to his first officer and went out to meet the party at the foot of his gangway.

"Greetings, Father. How can I help the Holy Father's agents?"

"Greetings and blessings to you, Captain. I'm looking for Dr. Banks and the rest of his party."

"Ah, the youth with the fiery spirit and the hair to match. You'll find them down in hold three, Father. I kept telling him nothing shifted during the voyage, but he insisted on checking for himself." The captain's response contained a mix of annoyance and respect. "I can't blame the lad though, Father. I've seen the manifest for myself and almost fainted from the price tags on some of the cargo. I'm not sure the ship's insurance policy is enough to replace the equipment if we lose any."

"Don't worry, my son. The Holy Father and the President of Texas stand surety on this cargo, and I believe your ship as well. Let me make sure the Holy Father's insurance extends to your ship and crew before we sail."

"Bless you, Father, and bless His Holiness as well. The information will set my ship's crew at ease knowing His Holiness thinks of his humble flock."

* * *

DOWN IN THE hold while everything else happened, Dr. Jeremiah Banks and the remaining two of his graduate students went over each crate, inspecting for damage. The captain continued insisting nothing shifted or suffered damage. The first field lesson Jeremiah's mentor drilled into him: always check the status of your equipment for yourself before offloading. Now he tried to drum the lesson into the graduate students he found himself overseeing. He needed to make this up to Quillion later. Jeremiah experienced a little guilt assigning her to keep an eye on Miss Beaumont and to deliver his message to Professor Di Vargas. He had to keep thinking of him as an academic advisor and not a lover or they'd land in jail. He thought Quillion might have figured out Prof. Di Vargas and his relationship was more than a professional one. He wasn't sure about these two. Jeremiah glanced in the direction of the two male grad students. He couldn't decide whether they were sincere about archaeology or if they didn't possess a passion for the ancient Middle East.

* * *

FURTHER DOWN THE HOLD, Theophisus Polzin, who preferred the name Theo, and his partner in crime Macejah "Mace" Puap followed their new mentor's directions. The pair made sure every strap remained as tight as when they left port in Texas. Both resented reassignment to Dr. Banks' expedition to the Middle East when their specialty centered on ancient Native American studies. Nevertheless, like their fellow student Quillion, they fell in love with Dr. Banks' passion for his subject. The trio developed a defensive reflex around Miss Beaumont. Theo glanced down the hold to where Dr. Banks inspected a crate, which contained the scuba gear. Turning back to his work, Theo caught Mace grinning at him like an idiot. Given the fact sounds carried like mad in the hold, his fellow student mouthed the words, "The Doc is hot, isn't he?"

Theo only nodded in agreement. Both had developed something of a crush on their redheaded teacher and to relieve the pressure started their little affair. Quillion caught on within a couple of days to the change in the boys' friendship, and didn't take long to figure out why the bromance developed. She helped them keep their secret by flirting with both of them in front of Miss Beaumont. The guys, with Quillion's assistance, figured out Dr. Banks' affections belonged to someone else: Professor Di Vargas. The bond between the two men was one of the reasons they all referred to their mentor as Dr. Banks rather than as a professor, which passed as the norm in Texas universities. Mace gestured for him to focus on the crates.

"Dr. Banks, this stack is as secure as when we left Galveston. I'm moving on to the next row of boxes," Theo called out.

"This stack is locked down tight, Doc," Mace called out. "I'm almost to the end of my row."

"Excellent, Mr. Polzin. Mr. Puap, a little more respect please. Keep working, we're almost finished. Only a couple of crates to check before we join Ms. Post and Miss Beaumont on shore."

"Have you ever been to Valencia before, Dr. Banks?" Theo asked.

"A few times but never for an extended stay, Mr. Polzin. We'll spend a few days here while Professor Di Vargas' party settles on board. You're free to explore the city for a day or so before we sail for Tel Aviv."

"Why am I certain you won't be exploring the city, Dr. Banks?"

"Because, Mr. Puap, I must meet with Prof. Di Vargas, Miss Beaumont, and the Papal representative to review the goals of the expedition and our needs once we arrive in the caliphate."

"Shouldn't we be with you, Dr. Banks? Dr. Sampson took us with him to his meetings with the Navajo and Hopi elders."

"I figured on sparing you the boring meetings, Mr. Polzin."

"But, Dr. Banks, how do we keep up with what's expected of us if you leave us on the sidelines?"

Jeremiah straightened up to his full 6' 2" height and stared down the ship's hold at the two young men standing in the aisle between the crates. He glimpsed the slight telltale signs of two men in a sexual relationship and hoped he kept his less obvious. Mace stood behind and a bit to the left of Theo with his right hand placed on the other man's shoulder. Some might think the gesture a sign of friendship, and perhaps this was all they shared, but their closeness made Jeremiah a little concerned. He frowned at the two students, but they played the contact off as joking around.

"Tell me how many languages you each speak and read."

Mace answered Dr. Banks' question first. "I speak six, understand four more, and can read all ten. Those are in addition to English and Spanish."

"I speak seven, understand five more, and can read and write all twelve. Add in Russian, English, and Spanish for a total of fifteen."

"Are any of those languages, Latin, Arabic, Hebrew, Italian, or Greek?"

"No, sir," came the reply in unison. "We focused on Native American languages because of our field of study."

"To be of assistance to me in meetings, you need at least one of those five tongues, and I prefer you speak all five, as we often switch between them. You need to pick up at least a smattering of Arabic to help me as more than extra hands in the field. I understand you guys didn't want to come on this expedition because this isn't your field of study and I'm not your designated mentor."

"Hey, Doc, cheer up. We're willing to learn and work hard. You might not be Dr. Sampson, but to be honest, you're way more entertaining. I don't think any of us, including Quillion, thought anyone made these old dusty Middle Eastern cultures anything but boring. Aside from which, we're not leaving you alone with the ice queen," Mace said.

"We'll talk more after I meet with Prof. Di Vargas and the Papal representative. I believe the captain is correct about our equipment being in the same shape as when we left Galveston, so let's go topside and ashore."

* * *

JUAN SPOTTED a flash of copper-bright hair as Jeremiah and his other two students emerged from the cargo hold. He managed not to gasp aloud at how savagely short the copper hair now was. He was still as beautiful as Juan remembered, but what made him cut his hair so brutally short? He noted Jeremiah was perhaps in better physical shape than he'd been four years ago. Juan let his glace take in the two young men behind Jeremiah. Both were physically impressive and could easily be models for recruiting posters for either the Imperial military or for the Order. Juan blinked himself back into the present as Jeremiah came close enough to touch.

* * *

"PROFESSOR DI VARGAS, what a pleasure to meet you in person again." Jeremiah drew close enough for the traditional cheek kisses. "I trust we didn't keep you waiting too long."

"Not too long, Dr. Banks. I enjoyed the pleasure of chatting with your charming student, Ms. Post. Let me introduce you to His Holiness' representative, Father Raymond Dupuis. Father Dupuis, this is my colleague from the Republic of Texas, Dr. Jeremiah Banks."

"Father Dupuis, an honor to meet you. Please convey our thanks to His Holiness for his blessing and backing of this expedition."

"Such is my pleasure, Dr. Banks. Now who are these two young men behind you?"

"Allow me to present my graduate students. You met Ms. Quillion Post earlier, and these fine gentlemen are Mr. Theophisus Polzin and Mr. Macejah Puap. The school commandeered them from another colleague's expedition when the poor man broke both legs. Their actual field of study is Native American archaeology. Gentlemen, this is Father Dupuis, he represents the Pope's government and will assist Miss Beaumont in easing our way through the bureaucracy of the caliphate."

"My assistants should be back by now," Father Dupuis said. "Are your bags ready for the porters to collect?"

"They are, Father, although I'm not sure where Miss Beaumont vanished to," Jeremiah replied.

"I sent Miss Beaumont on ahead to the hotel. I wish a frank discussion with you and Prof. Di Vargas about the Republic's representative. Would you and the professor join me? Your students may ride with my assistants in the second coach."

"Excellent, Father Dupuis, but if you will, please direct your driver to this address for myself and Dr. Banks. I arranged to take a house for the week with Dr. Banks as my guest. We need to discuss a number of topics, and the privacy of a house allows us to keep late hours when we lose ourselves in conversations and research."

A young monk arrived, drawing Father Dupuis' attention from the professor and the archaeologist. Jeremiah caught Juan's eye, and they stepped away to give the priest a bit of privacy while gaining some as well.

Jeremiah wished he could drag Juan in for a proper kiss and to feel his solid body against his own. There would be time for that once they got back to the house and settled in. At least, Jeremiah hoped Juan wanted to resume that aspect of their relationship. He wasn't sure he could bear being so close to him and not being wrapped in his arms.

* * *

Juan's thoughts were running along the same track as Jeremiah, only he had a little more daring as he voiced his welcome and part of his concern.

"I hope not to be too forward by stealing you away from the rest of the expedition to stay with me. Four years passed with miles between us, and I'm not sure if you still thought the same way about me as I do about you." Juan swallowed against his nerves. "Perhaps one of your graduate students is more than he or she appears."

Jeremiah throttled the anger, which the suggestion engendered. "Juan Di Vargas, don't be an idiot," he hissed. "I worried about having time for us on this expedition. I'm glad you found us a place away from the crowd. I missed you so much. What about servants?"

"The house comes with a cook to prepare meals for us, but she stays in her part of the house. A service comes to clean when we leave for Tel Aviv, and we send our laundry out for cleaning. Let us rejoin the others for now."

Once on land, the team split between the two carriages, Father Dupuis, Juan, Jeremiah, and Brother Colum in the first carriage; Quillion, Mace, Theo, and Brother Tobias the other of Dupuis' assistants in the second carriage. They made their way to the hotel the Empire reserved for them before Dupuis' carriage took Juan, Jeremiah, and Brother Colum off to the house Juan rented for the week. Dupuis loaned Colum to the two academics as a messenger and guide. Juan wanted to protest the service as unnecessary, but Jeremiah accepted the young monk's service before his partner objected. They arrived at the house and were greeted by the agent of the owner who handed over the keys and made introductions to the cook. Brother Colum took one of the rooms in the servant's quarters to help him keep his vows. Juan led Jeremiah upstairs to the second floor where they each chose rooms to keep up appearances. As Jeremiah unpacked his suit for dinner at the hotel with the rest of the expedition, someone knocked on his door. Expecting to find Juan outside his door, he was surprised to find Brother Colum instead.

"I'm sorry to intrude, Dr. Banks. I promise to make myself as scarce as possible. I'm instructed by my superiors to give you this and ask you to destroy the paper after sharing the contents with Prof. Di Vargas."

Jeremiah took the sealed letter, and Colum turned and left, sandaled feet slapping down the tiled hall. Jeremiah crossed the corridor and knocked on Juan's door. He slipped inside the room and closed the door by leaning back. Juan pressed against him in a deep kiss. Jeremiah let the kiss linger, enjoying the press of Juan's lips. Their passion for each other remained unchanged despite the three years since their last kiss. After Juan broke away to drag Jeremiah into the room, he caught the concern on his young lover's face.

"What's the matter, my beautiful one? You act like we've been discovered instead of having privacy."

"I can't help thinking Father Dupuis suspects something, which is why he gave us Brother Colum."

"Why did you accept the monk's service if you think he's here to spy for Dupuis?"

"Because turning down his service as you wanted would confirm

Dupuis' suspicions. Unless you wish to be sitting in a jail cell waiting for the Inquisition or whatever group the Church uses to extract confessions of immorality out of prisoners."

"The Order of St. Hubert handles such things these days. The Holy Father didn't think reviving the separate Inquisitors to be a wise idea. We'll be extra discreet, my love."

"Well, we possess the missive Colum gave me. He told me to share this with you and destroy afterwards. Does his warning sound ominous or am I being paranoid, Juan?"

"Before we deal with this mysterious correspondence delivered by the young monk, tell me what happened to your beautiful long hair."

"Mandatory military service to the Republic. Two years after high school and then permanent listing with the reserves. We're all assigned numbers and report for duty when called. Bad luck mine came up for reservist service, resulting in the mandatory military hairstyle and the yearlong delay in getting the expedition underway. Are you disappointed you won't be able to run your fingers through my hair like you did in Atlanta?"

"The length of your hair doesn't matter, beautiful boy. What counts is having you here, and I'll prove how much later. For now, let's read what's in the note."

Jeremiah leaned in and stole a quick kiss for courage before breaking the seal. They found a beautiful handwritten note.

Dr. Banks and Prof. Di Vargas,

Either Brother Colum or Brother Tobias delivered this message to you at my behest. I am Cardinal Joan IX of El-Abel, and I lead the Cult of Cain. We are mentioned in the journal in your possession. Please forgive the mysterious method of delivering this message. Do not worry about Brother Colum or Brother Tobias; they work for me and will take any confidences with them to the grave. This message is a warning.

The tome in your possession contains dangerous information. Many seek to stop you from continuing the quest for the city you call Enoch. Lord Hunter ordered me to put you under the protection of my people. Both Tobias and Colum are more than they appear. They are knight-protectors in our order and assigned as bodyguards to each of you.

Leave both Father Dupuis and Miss Beaumont behind in Valencia, as they are working for agencies wishing you to fail. Father Dupuis is empowered to dismiss Miss Beaumont from the expedition; make use of his authority. Tobias is to make sure Father Dupuis passes his power as the Holy Father's representative on to another of our choosing. Do not worry about your funding, Dr. Banks. The agents in the Republic are at work reminding the president she owes some favors, which are now due. Those who take over your protection in the lands of the caliph where my people cannot go are to deliver another message when you reach Tel Aviv. For now, destroy this message by fire; the brief cloud of blue smoke informs my closest agent you read the message. Enjoy the time together without fear. The cook works for me, and the house is mine.

In the name of Cain

Joan IX

Cardinal of El-Abel

Cult of Cain

* * *

Jeremiah and Juan stared at each other with fear in their eyes. Who was this mysterious Cardinal Joan? Juan crossed the room to where his briefcase sat holding the journal, which started this whole quest. He met Jeremiah at the chairs before the fireplace, laid the pages down on the lanterloo table, and opened the book between them.

"Here's what we want."

Jeremiah plucked the page from the table and read aloud. "'I wandered alone for many centuries, exploring the world and studying the different settlements created by mortals. I spent many hours observing them as they worshiped their various gods and went about their daily routines. Sometimes I interacted with them as a passing merchant, trading goods and information. Other times I settled into a community to study magic techniques. A few times, I found myself worshiped as a dark god when I revealed my true nature. I maintained two cults as servants over my long existence. The Cult of Cain, which developed during my extended stay among the nomads of the Asian steppes. Due to my dark appetites, the nomads thought of me as Komur Han and gave their third-born sons to my service. After a few centuries, I grew bored and moved on, but my cult remained and became influential within the clans, until I called them to the West to infiltrate the followers of the crucified Christ.'"

"Ah, here's another passage," Juan declared. "'I was next visited by leaders of my beloved Cult of Cain, who told me of a rival cult among the Muslim forces in the land of my birth. They called themselves the Brotherhood of the Crimson Hand, and the Islamic world feared their assassins. The leader of my western cultist took the title of Abbot of El-Abel to honor my lost city. He brought forward a young man of Armenian ancestry, a member of this Brotherhood who was captured in a raid on the Islamic camp outside of Jerusalem. He is a warrior. Despite the chains, his fierce spirit fights against my cultists. I bade him sit with me, and he showed no fear despite the corpses piled around me and the blood covering my face. I bid him relate to me the story his people told of me and why they chose to worship me. I included his tale for you so you may read and weave yourself into the story if you wish to keep the Brotherhood as servants.'"

"This entry contains a passage referring to the Cult of Cain and El-Abel." Jeremiah read the section, "'I also strengthened the faith of the Cult of Cain by giving the Abbot of El-Abel a promotion. Go forth and be my Bishop of El-Abel, I said to him before giving him a gift. No, my successor, I didn't make him into a vampire, I gave him a jug filled with my blood and instructions to dole out one drop at a time as a relic. The cultists to this day keep the tradition. I would advise you, my successor, to do the same to keep the cultists loyal to you. The Cult's loyalty may come in handy.'"

Juan stood and grabbed the bottle of Confederate whiskey he'd placed earlier along with two glasses. He poured two generous fingers into both glasses. Jeremiah snatched the glass from Juan's hand and gulped the contents down in one swallow. He held the glass up for Juan to refill.

"Do you think we can find any way to prove this?" Jeremiah asked. "Notes follow some of these passages from Lord Hunter who believes he's somehow Cain's mysterious successor. This Cardinal Joan implies she works for Lord Hunter and he's still alive. The thought a secret society of assassins is guarding us is disturbing, *mi corazón*."

"Your heart, am I? My beautiful one, I'm flattered." Juan kissed Jeremiah. "Yes, the news is disturbing, but I think we need to take every precaution. Let's do as Cardinal Joan says and destroy the note, so perhaps Brother Colum can be enticed to tell us more about the real order he belongs to."

"As a precaution, we should make a copy of this message as insurance against the Cult of Cain." Jeremiah grabbed the whiskey bottle and poured more into both their glasses. "Better for someone to discover what is going on if things go south on us. I'll transcribe this into El-Isinian so no one can decipher the contents by accident."

Juan snatched the bottle out of Jeremiah's reach. He placed a clean sheet of stationary in front of Jeremiah and handed him a pen and ink. As Jeremiah translated the message into the mysterious El-Isinian, Juan put away the journal pages and the whiskey. Jeremiah regarded his translation before taking the original message, wadding the paper up, and tossing the ball into the fire. The fire flared for a moment before a puff of blue smoke went up the flue. When the inked dried, Jeremiah folded his copy of the message and tucked note into his jacket pocket. Now they waited for events to unfold.

VAMPIRE INTERLUDE:
RICHARD AND THE QUEEN OF
PIRATES

The light of the full moon reflected off waves in the harbor as Richard walked down the old wharf. Docked at the end bobbed the flagship of Laverna Salacia's pirate fleet. In a former life, the littoral combat ship belonged to the United States Navy; now she served as to promote piracy instead of ending the practice. Laverna Salacia was a primordial, a clan founder, and inspired two Roman goddesses. The ancients of the vampire world often perceived Richard as insignificant because of their vast ages. Database's briefing on the Queen of Pirates mentioned her receiving the gift from Nina-Ishtar, the legendary Queen of Vampires and daughter of Cain. Many among her crew ranged in ages from centuries to millennia older than Richard, but all showed him courtesy on their captain's orders.

Waiting at the top of the gangway stood Laverna's stunning first officer, Eder Ganix Itzal, the Basque crewman most called by the English translation of his name, Handsome John Shadow. The vampire swept Richard an exaggerated bow, doffing his tri-corn hat from his head to reveal the purple bandana holding back his long midnight locks.

"Greetings, Lord Slayer. On behalf of my captain, I bid you welcome aboard the *Sunniva Mare*."

"Permission to come aboard?"

"Permission granted, Lord Slayer."

Richard walked up the gangway until he stood beside John Shadow. The first officer led him up to the command deck of the frigate and into the presence of Laverna Salacia. The pirate queen presented a striking figure, dressed in shades of red and gold. Her natural dark skin tones, hair, and eyes added to the mystery of her being. She gestured for Richard to take the seat across the desk from her, and gold jewelry flashed on her wrist.

"Thank you for agreeing to meet with me, Lord Slayer."

"The honor is mine, Laverna Salacia. Those of your rank prefer to send minions to meet with me or one of my agents. I'm amused at the name you gave your flagship. *Sunniva Mare*, the sun-gifted sea. How long since you last experienced the sun reflecting off the water?"

"Around the time you took Grandfather's life and rank, Lord Slayer. My mortal lover filmed a sunrise and a sunset over the ocean for me. Nevertheless, we're not here to discuss things we'll never experience again in person. I received word from my spies. The Bel-Kino plan to revive Bellabarisruk to thwart your plans to find El-Abel."

"Thank you, this information confirms my sources. Bellabarisruk entered languor before my transformation, so he's never acknowledged me."

"I doubt he would support you. When the mage-lord Noah unleashed the forces, which destroyed our parents' kingdom, Bellabarisruk claims Grandfather charged him to lead our kind."

"Noah, as in the guy in the Old Testament who built the giant boat to carry all the animals to safety?"

"Do not believe all you read in the holy books of any religion, Lord Slayer. Long ago, Rome worshiped me as two goddesses. The number of cults and religions which sprang up around Grandfather would amaze you."

"His journals advised only worrying about keeping control of two of his cults."

"The Cult of Cain and the Brotherhood of the Crimson Hand? Both are efficient and influential in places where the oldest of us dare not venture."

"So, his journals revealed. Tell me, Laverna Salacia, what might I do to persuade you to take me to El-Abel?"

"The journey to El-Abel is a quest laid on you by Grandfather. When you need me, I will come to El-Abel."

With a sudden swiftness, Richard avoided an attack, which almost removed his hand. Laverna Salacia held up a silver-bladed dagger, stained with blood. Glancing down, Richard inspected the gash along the back of his hand. The pirate queen remained seated as Richard glared at her. Confident no retaliation would follow her attack on him, she drew the dagger across her hand. From a drawer, she removed a signet ring, on which she dripped the mingled blood. The clear stone darkened while absorbing the blood.

"Apologies, Lord Slayer, but the nature of the stone's magic requires the blood of the recipient be drawn in a sneak attack."

"A summoning ring? Cain's journal mentioned one, but not much detail on its nature."

"Because only the one exists. The mage who developed the spell belonged to my cult in ancient Rome during Nero's reign. Our numbers taxed the mortal population, threatening to reveal our existence. Grandfather ordered the Cult of Cain to hunt us down and thin the herd."

"What happened to the mage?"

"He took a silver spear meant for me. The mage came to my base of operations on the riverfront to offer the ring and to make others in exchange for the gift of Cain."

"He wanted to give up his magic to become a vampire?"

"No, he did not ask for himself but for a young slave boy owned by a cruel and influential master. This ring is one of a kind; any mage across the ages who tried to duplicate the spell failed."

"So, what do I need to activate the magic?"

"Think of me and our blood will call to me regardless of the distance. Now, perhaps you'd like a tour of the *Sunniva Mare*?"

"It would be a good to know what strength and weapons you bring to my cause, Laverna Salacia."

"I think you'll be pleasantly surprised, Lord Hunter."

Chapter 10

After the trio of Theo, Mace, and Quillion settled into their rooms, they met in the sitting room of the boys' suite to discuss plans to protect Dr. Banks and Prof. Di Vargas.

"I hope Doc and the professor work the excited schoolboy out of their system while we're here," Mace said.

"Mace you really should show Dr. Banks more respect. Besides, the bromance between you and Theo is evident to anyone who takes more than a passing look at you two."

"WHAT?" Mace and Theo exclaimed together.

"Dial down the constant body contact. Dr. Banks and Prof. Di Vargas are discrete in comparison."

Mace and Theo locked eyes across the table. Fear and panic overwhelmed their control, and they acted more like little boys than college students. Quillion took pity on them.

"Sit on the couch. I've known you both since Dr. Sampson chose us to mentor. Something has changed in your relationship since we met Dr. Banks. I gather more is going on besides a couple guys getting their rocks off. Whatever's happening is none of my business, but you're suffering from something.

Mace took the lead in replying to Quillion's suspicion about them suffering. With a deep breath, he replied, "We're not sure what's going on, Quill. A number of things have changed since we boarded the ship. Theo and I both discovered we were developing a crush on Dr. Banks and figured maybe it was better to help each other out instead of making fools of ourselves by trying to hit on him."

"So, what else changed besides a relationship developing beyond a jack-off session or two?" Quillion chuckled over their discomfort. "I've heard rumors mage blood runs in both your families." The glances between them only confirmed the rumors.

"Yes, we use magic. Before we boarded the ship, we'd both barely qualify as hedge witches. Now we might qualify as full witches. There are also a few physical changes as well," Mace said.

"The elders wept when my talent turned out to be feeble as well." Theo leaned against Mace, ignoring Quillion's expression. "However, something changed in the last couple of weeks. I used to consider myself lucky to manage chilling a glass on a hot day. Since Mace and I started being together, my magic grows stronger every week. I froze then thawed a glass of water yesterday." Pride reflected in Theo's voice as he admitted his success.

Quillion looked at both of her fellow students and realized Theo's dark blue eyes appeared at least a shade lighter. Nowhere near as bright as Dr. Banks' sapphire eyes, but lighter. Glancing at Mace, she noted his brown eyes were developing a greenish cast beyond the tint, which most would call hazel. Theo relaxed as Mace wrapped his arm around his shoulder and pulled him closer. Quill coughed in disapproval, but realized Theo didn't care what the world thought; he belonged in

Mace's arms. Quillion wished someone would think the same way about her. She had to refocus as Mace was explaining the growth of his own magic.

"The rhythms of life—like people's heartbeats and breathing patterns—are getting easier to read," Mace said. "For instance, Theo's heart is hammering. He's worried. Relax and breathe, my friend. I think Quillion is onto something. I can almost grasp the connection. The plants in the ship's galley became healthier over the last couple of days; plus, I caught the thyme and sage whispering to each other," Mace said. "Prior to this trip, meeting Dr. Banks, I never picked up plant speech."

"What I don't understand is why this is happening now. We've been around each other for the last two years," Theo said.

"I may be the cause of the changes." Quillion blushed in shame.

"In what way, Quill?" Mace asked.

"On occasion in my family a Gold mage is born, and my parents suspect I inherited the trait. In our line, the ability isn't something we can control and the magic acts more as a catalyst for change. It enhances powers or strong emotions."

"So, Theo and I are attracted to each other, because your magic enhanced our powers?" Mace asked.

"As I said, my family's magic enhances strong emotions as well as powers. At a guess, you feel more for each other than you've admitted to either yourselves or each other. I'm sorry, it was never my intention to cause you distress." Quillion rose as she fought back tears.

Theo got off the couch and blocked her exit for a moment. "Don't apologize, Quill. I suspect Mace and I have danced around our true desires for the last two years. Maybe he and I should discuss the matter further in private."

Theo handed Quillion his handkerchief. She gathered her courage and dabbed at her eyes to dry the tears before they could spill. "I'll knock on the way down to meet for dinner."

Chapter 11

THE SOUNDS OF MUSIC, conversations, clinking glasses, clanking plates, and silverware, and the rattle of bottles overwhelmed Armand as he exited the elevator on the third floor of Dante's Inferno, searching for Adam FitzCaine. Gregori, the floor manager on duty, crossed the floor, meeting Armand near the edge of the dance floor.

"Master Armand, Mr. FitzCaine said you planned on joining him this evening, and he's reserved a private table. Please follow."

"Thank you, Gregori. Congratulations on the promotion to being the floor manager, although I'm not sure how you keep your beautiful body working the third circle."

"Thank you, Master Armand. One thing I'm not is a glutton for food. I am infamous for my gluttony for sex, however. They speak the truth when they say I fucked my way into the management of this floor." Gregori gave Armand a lecherous leer, which spoke volumes. "I'm available should you require personal attention, Master Armand."

"Your contract doesn't allow for the types of personal care I need and desire, Gregori." At Gregori's beautiful pout, Armand said, "Should you wish to indenture yourself, perhaps we can discuss the terms of a contract of servitude."

"No matter how much I enjoy teasing you, Master Armand, we both understand I'm too busy to be what you desire from an indentured servant. Besides, I'm not your preferred blood type. I'm an ordinary type O."

"Alas, so right. I do enjoy our little games though."

"This is Mr. FitzCaine's table, Master Armand. He should be with you in a few minutes. He needed to deal with a small complaint on the sixth circle."

"I can only imagine. Which of our beloved clergy members is having problems giving into his heresy?"

"The clergy member in question is Bishop Hollister from the New Reform Episcopal Church."

Adam FitzCaine slipped into the seat across from Armand. "Gregori, a bottle of my reserve and whatever, or whomever, Master Armand is having."

"Ha, funny as ever Adam." Armand's voice lacked any trace of amusement. "I'm here on Richard's business, not for pleasure. For what I need, a meeting in your office is sufficient."

"I can't figure out why you don't like me, Master Armand. Richard trusts me, despite the fact I refuse the gift when he offers. I don't desire to live forever. You better than anyone understand I'm not the first mortal included in Richard's life and plans. However, since you're in a hurry to be away from my club and presence, here's the information Richard wants regarding the intrepid adventurers and what they can access."

Adam slid a thick envelope across the table to Armand. The handsome vampire grabbed the packet and stood. He made a curt bow to Adam before striding back to the elevator. Adam sat watching the club members stuffing themselves on delicious foods and expensive alcohol, and the sight turned his stomach. He motioned Gregori to take the bottle of wine he ordered back to the cellar, before making his way to his private elevator and heading up to Richard's private suite. Adam gazed at his reflection in the polished doors of the elevator and sighed. The glamor of mortality faded away, and Adam's personality disappeared back into the recesses of Richard's mind as the vampire emerged. Richard wondered if he should retain more of his own personality when he became Adam. The charade was proving harder to maintain, because something in Adam's character annoyed both of them, yet neither wanted to tell him what they didn't like about Adam. He arrived to find Armand pacing a path into the Berber carpet of his suite's sitting room. On the coffee table rested the packet handed to Armand a few moments ago.

"My Lord, disturbing news regarding the professor from Spain in possession of the journal pages. He corresponds with an archaeologist colleague in the Republic of Texas."

"What can you tell me about this archaeologist?" Richard settled down on the sofa. "Stop pacing, Armand, before you ruin the carpet. I don't believe anything can be that disturbing."

"My Lord, the archaeologist in question—a Dr. Jeremiah Banks— discovered the key to decipher El-Isinian. His familiarity with the concept of El-Abel's existence borders on dangerous."

"So, they stand a decent chance of finding El-Abel."

"Master, they stand an excellent chance of finding El-Abel. Dr. Banks made his famous discovery in the outpost town of El-Isin, which handled trade to El-Abel coming from Egypt and points in the west, or so my sire once told me."

"Why do you both view this as a disaster in the making?"

"Several of the primordials put agents into play, the most numerous belong to Bellabarisruk and Izcacus, Master. Their actions forced the Order of St. Hubert's active involvement, and Cardinal Joan XI added members of the Cult of Cain as part of the expedition."

"Cardinal Joan and the Cult of Cain, I ordered into action, as I also gave instructions to the Imam Ali and the Brotherhood of the Crimson Hand to assist the two cultists once the expedition reaches Damascus." Richard sighed. "You both warned me Bellabarisruk would stick his nose into this project. Let me deal with him when he gets in the way. As for Izcacus, we must address his clan as well, and I think the best way to deal with them is to use the Order of St. Hubert to keep them busy. So, my little spy, if you possess any information on Izcacus' clan in Europe, send the intelligence to someone near one of the Order's houses. Let us see how the Order of St. Hubert honors their patron on the hunt."

VAMPIRE INTERLUDE: A TRAP
FOR THE IZCACUS

The tiny outpost of the Order of St. Jerome, patron of librarians and archivists, in the forest outside of Viseu de Sus in the Romanian Province of the Russian Empire was burning. On the hillside above the burning outpost, Brother Wadim listened to his brothers' screams as they perished in the fire. The young scribe's tears rolled down his cheeks as he sent a silent prayer to heaven for the mercy of his brothers' souls. Behind him stood the architect of the horror below, a vampire dressed in the costume of the Magyar raiders of centuries past.

"I asked a simple question of your brothers, little monk, and did not receive the answer I require. I give you a chance to respond to the same question."

"You refuse to accept the truth, demon."

"Where is the copy of Lord Hunter's journal that your little community received?"

Brother Wadim pointed to the burning buildings. A snarl tore from the vampire's throat.

"The journal you sought lay in plain sight on a table in the library. By now the book is a pile of ash."

The young monk died the instant the vampire's sharp nails ripped out his throat. Three new Magyar warriors joined their cursing leader around the body of the young monk.

"Lord Izcacus will not be pleased with the failure to find the upstart's journal."

"We can use the blood from this pathetic excuse for a monk and force his spirit to reveal the truth."

One of the vampires knelt beside the cooling corpse and placed a wooden bowl beneath the gaping wound in his throat. A small amount of blood collected in the container to which the warrior-shaman added exotic herbs and powders. He traced symbols long thought lost. A pale figure twisting in agony appeared over the dead monk, the black opening of its mouth gaping in a scream, which started silent before shattering the quiet of the night. Brother Wadim's spirit hovered before the circle of vampires.

"Why do you torture me?"

"Tell us, where is the journal of Lord Hunter."

"I told you in life. What you sought lay on a table before your eyes in the library."

"Tell us the truth, spirit, or I will torture the information out of you."

"The truth, monster, is the brave brothers you murdered tonight acted as bait in a trap," a mortal voice replied from outside the circle.

The leader of the vampires witnessed his brethren cut down by silver swords wielded by hunter-knights of the Order of St. Hubert. He turned to flee and ran straight into the tip of the silver spear held by one of the knight's squire. The vampire crumbled as the head of the spear pierced his heart. From the shadows, another knight of the Order emerged, dressed in a flowing cassock with a purple stole around his neck. The priest-knight made the sign of the cross over all the gathered members of the Order before closing to stand before the spirit of Brother Wadim.

"I am Father Dragomir, a priest-knight and exorcist. Who are you, my son?"

"For this mission, Brother Wadim, a monk-scribe of the Order of St. Jerome. Outside of this mission, the chosen agent of Lord Hunter and Her Excellency Cardinal Joan IX of El-Abel."

Gasps arose from the gathered knights and squires. The priest-knight uttered a prayer.

"A pity the Order thought I needed help to free my spirit from the bindings of the Izcacus' spell, but I require no assistance. For the record, Lord Hunter's journal was never here."

The spirit vanished, and the corpse of Brother Wadim burst into flame.

Chapter 12

THE MEMBERS of the expedition waited in the hotel bar for an additional coach. Due to formal dress, they required additional space for the ride to the archbishop's palace. The archbishop's formal reception offered a chance to receive a final blessing of the journey from the Holy Father's representative in Valencia. Theo and Mace wore almost matching formal wear from one of the better tailors in Tucson. Miss Beaumont arrived overdressed in a gown from one of the Paris fashion houses. The surprise of the evening came when Quillion descended the stairs in a dress of dark black silk trimmed with gold and pearls, her hair in an elaborate coiffure, with gold-and-pearl earrings to match the necklace around her throat. Despite being a more conservative design than Miss Beaumont's gown, Quillion's dress proved no less stunning. Jeremiah chuckled as both Mace and Theo jostled each other to be the one to escort her to dinner. Juan tried to contain a laugh at the boys' expense.

Leaning close to Jeremiah, he whispered, "I thought you told me they desired each other, my love. They appear crazy for Ms. Post."

"I thought I glimpsed signs of attraction between them, but I guess I made a mistake. I pray she can keep them in line," Jeremiah muttered. "I would rather only worry about us."

"Perhaps you should escort Miss Beaumont to the reception this evening, Jeremiah."

Jeremiah snarled at him in disgust before realizing doing so made sense. He resigned himself and adjusted the sapphire waistcoat beneath the black jacket of his formal tails. He crossed the room and made a precise old-world style bow to Miss Beaumont.

"Miss Beaumont, would you allow me the pleasure of being your escort for the evening?"

"Color me surprised to be asked, Mr. Banks, since you made clear you despise me and wish for someone else to fill my part of your expedition."

Jeremiah ground his anger down and swallowed some of his pride.

"Miss Beaumont, please accept my apologies for not attempting to fix our working relationship sooner. I'm not sure where the problem originated, but let's put the past behind us and move forward. I read over what the government released of your dossier, and I'm impressed with your skills in languages and mathematical abilities. My concerns focus on the lack of diplomatic skills beyond some minor dealings with the Confederacy and the Republic of California. The Caliphate of Baghdad serves as a dangerous training ground for a neophyte in Middle Eastern diplomacy. They are hostile towards women in diplomatic circles. The officials at the caliph's court examine body language and speech for the slightest of missteps to turn into diplomatic incidents. Their automatic hostility towards women raised my primary concern about your appointment."

"Why, Mr. Banks. Did you practice this little speech in front of a mirror or while you wallowed in your perversions with Prof. Di Vargas? Did you somehow believe the Republic didn't suspect you of being a pervert? The expedition serves a purpose to the president and her agenda regarding the caliphate. As for why I dislike you on a personal level aside from your disgusting sexual habits, it's simple. You came back from your last student expedition and my half-brother didn't. So, no, Mr. Banks, I won't accept your apology nor will I require your services as an escort this evening."

Jeremiah's vision flashed red. His greatest secret almost escaped control save for the timely intervention of Quillion. With a quiet hand on his arm, she calmed the storm brewing inside of the fiery archaeologist. A silent flash of gold sparked in her hazel eyes as she slipped her arm into the proper position.

"Excuse the interruption, Dr. Banks, but I find myself without a proper escort for the evening. Since Miss Beaumont declined your services, perhaps you would be so kind."

"To escort a real lady to dinner would be a privilege, Ms. Post." Jeremiah glared at Miss Beaumont as he spoke before turning his attention to his student. "Why don't we join Prof. Di Vargas and Father Dupuis for an aperitif? I believe this evening calls for a glass of champagne before we dine."

Jeremiah led Quillion across the floor to where Juan stood deep in conversation with Father Dupuis. The cleric paused the conversation as Jeremiah and Quillion arrived, and the American archaeologist snagged a pair of champagne glasses from a passing tray with such force the tray almost unbalanced. Jeremiah apologized to the waiter as he handed one of the glasses to Quillion. The server explained about the tray being for a private party, not for regular guests, so Jeremiah released Quillion and took the waiter aside.

"What year and vineyard is this champagne from?"

"The vintage is a 2100 Moët & Chandon Impérial Brut, *Señor*."

"Is this the best in the hotel's cellar?" Jeremiah sipped from his glass.

"Not a bad vintage, but isn't the party involved celebrating something important?"

"A wedding engagement, sir, and on their limited budget, this is the best they can afford. The hotel's supply of this vintage is limited."

"Do you stock a Philopponnat Clos des Goisses, 1989?"

"*Si Señor*, but it's expensive and beyond the means of the wedding party."

"Go and fetch every bottle as my present to the happy couple. Do not open the bottles until you are with the party. When they ask you, tell them Miss Eunice Beaumont of the Republic of Texas offers this so the happy couple may toast their future. Tell the cellarer to deliver the bill to the young blonde woman wearing the red dress over by the bar." Jeremiah pointed to Miss Beaumont. "The lady will argue she did no such thing because she's modest about her vast wealth. If she gives the cellarer too much trouble, he should remind her she's dining with the archbishop, who wouldn't take kindly to having to rescue a foreign woman from the local police."

Jeremiah slipped the man a huge tip to cover the tray of champagne and bribes for the waiter and the cellarer. He scooped up the tray and returned to his party, joined by Mace and Theo. He handed the serving tray to Mace and swiped a new glass for himself. Juan and Father Dupuis stared at him, waiting for an explanation.

"Dr. Banks, what did you do?"

"Made a happy couple jubilant, I hope." Jeremiah's attempt to appear innocent turned into an epic failure under their withering gazes. "Attempting to make Miss Beaumont's evening miserable and expensive. Let's find out how creative an accountant she is."

"Doc, you pulled a stunt worthy of me. I can't believe you did something so evil."

"Do not encourage his bad behavior, Mr. Puap. He's a teacher and should provide a better example." Juan switched to full professor mode. "Behavior like this in my class would draw a caning as the punishment for pulling such a stunt."

Jeremiah blushed, knowing Juan's statement hid a second meaning and he would receive an actual punishment when they returned to their rented house this evening. The arrival of the additional coach spared him further embarrassment. He escorted Quillion out to the coach and helped her aboard. As he started to step up, Theo tapped him on the shoulder.

"Excuse me, Dr. Banks, but tonight the duty of escorting Quillion is mine."

"Ms. Post asked me to accompany her this evening since, by appearances, you and Mr. Puap couldn't decide which of you would be her escort. Are you telling me you've come to a decision?"

"Yes, sir. Tonight, if Quillion is willing, I am to act as her escort, and for the next formal event, Mr. Puap will escort her."

"The decision is once again Ms. Post's."

"I believe since I asked for an escort before witnesses, Dr. Banks, you should continue as my companion for the evening. Mr. Polzin may escort me home tonight."

"Do we agree, Mr. Polzin?"

"Of course, sir."

With a nod, Jeremiah pulled himself up into the coach, taking the seat next to Quillion. Theo and Mace followed, filling the coach. Jeremiah tried not to stare at Juan climbing into the next coach with Brother Tobias. This left Father Dupuis to travel with Miss Beaumont and Brother Colum, and Lord, one only guessed at what the woman would say to the priest. He caught the worried expressions on his students' faces.

"I'm sorry I dragged you across the ocean on a quest doomed by petty vindictiveness, and I made a mess by acting like an errant student."

"Hey, Doc, don't worry about the prank. We might do something worse to her than sticking her with a bill for fancy champagne." Mace laughed the matter off. "She's always rude to you, and from what Quill says, Father Dupuis isn't fond of her. He uses the little monk as a translator and pretends he doesn't speak any language Miss Beaumont speaks."

"Well, perhaps she won't confide in Father Dupuis. She worries me, but I shouldn't burden you with my problems. I'm supposed to be here for you to confide in."

"Dr. Banks, you can trust us. We've got as much to lose as you do if Miss Beaumont goes off the deep end. Mace and I must confess we're more than we appear." Theo's Slavic accent was thicker than usual, revealing his nervousness. "I think you guessed part of our situation."

"Here is not the place to talk about such things, Mr. Polzin. Tomorrow, I'll send Brother Colum and the coach to fetch all three of you and bring you back to the house Prof. Di Vargas rented for the week, and we can all talk. Tonight, we must all be cautious. Should Miss Beaumont decide to reveal things she's privy to, the evening will be interesting, to say the least."

"Doc, we understand and we've got your back," Mace said. "Who cares if supporting you means hard labor?"

"I appreciate your support, Mr. Puap. We'll anticipate the only hard labor being our excavations should we find Enoch or El-Abel, as our source called the city in his journal."

"What is the difference, Dr. Banks? You mentioned a couple of times how the writer of your source material calls the city El-Abel or the City of Cain. Are they the same city or two separate cities?"

"An excellent question, Ms. Post. I'm afraid until we find more clues we need to keep both lines of research open. Prof. Di Vargas is tracking the location as Enoch through his biblical research path. We will search for the city as El-Abel through archaeological methods and use the tablets I translated from El-Isinian as our guide. Consider this, we possess knowledge of the outposts called El-Isin and El-Kino. Based on the notes in the journal, El-Abel is located south of Ur on the coast of the Persian Gulf. Each of the outposts is located about three days journey from El-Abel." Jeremiah slipped into lecture mode. "The author of the journal wrote, 'I returned to the land of my birth and decided to take a hand in governing a city-state. I gathered the brightest of my brother Seth's descendants as my ministers and city officials and established the city-state of El-Abel to the south of Ur along the coast of what is now the Persian Gulf. The farmlands proved fertile and my people prospered by farming and fishing the waters of the gulf. Trade flourished with our sister city-states. I established an influential center of learning to draw the brightest students to my service.' Therefore, we're looking for a major cultural center. Of course, the coast of the Persian Gulf changed from the days when El-Abel existed."

Jeremiah glanced at his students who raised their hands in surrender. The laughter filled the coach as Dr. Banks caught the professor tone in his voice. The trio enjoyed experiencing his almost manic moments of excitement about the target of the expedition. Though they each thought of questions they wanted to ask, they agreed to wait and ask them with Prof. Di Vargas present to answer the biblical aspects of the expedition. The coach's arrival at the palatial archbishop's residence saved them from further lecturing by Dr. Banks. Theo and Mace exited the carriage and helped Dr. Banks and Quillion down. Jeremiah took Quillion's arm and escorted her up the stairs to the entrance of the residence. Father Dupuis with Brother Colum's help assisted Miss Beaumont from their coach and up to the entrance, and Juan along with

Brother Tobias joined them to complete the party as the archbishop's priest-secretary arrived to greet them. The middle-aged priest stood on the stairs as though he was about to deliver a homily.

"His Grace, the Archbishop of Valencia, welcomes you to his home. I'm Father Raphael, His Grace's secretary, and household manager. Please follow me, His Grace awaits in the drawing room."

The gathering followed the priest to the elegant drawing room, where a pair of monks presented trays of champagne and hors d'oeuvre. After imbibing more alcohol than he should, Jeremiah asked one of the serving monks to switch his drink to water instead. The monk nodded and whisked off to fill Jeremiah's request. Quillion smiled up at Dr. Banks' choice.

"A wise choice, Dr. Banks. I think too much alcohol flowed this evening."

"Yes, I don't handle copious amounts of alcohol well. I figure better to stop now and preserve what's left of my battered dignity."

Before Quillion replied, the serving monk returned with Jeremiah's water in an elegant crystal glass. The Archbishop of Valencia entered the room as Jeremiah lifted his glass to take a sip, forcing him to abort his action. His Grace greeted everyone and allowed them to approach to make obeisance, by kissing his ring in the case of Father Dupuis and Brothers Tobias and Colum. Jeremiah followed the process as Juan also bowed and kissed the prelate's ring. This open acknowledgement Juan gave of church's authority surprised Jeremiah, but the archbishop held the power to prevent their expedition leaving the harbor. Jeremiah nodded to Mace and Theo to make sure they corralled Miss Beaumont, as he escorted Quillion forward to greet the archbishop. The priest-secretary whispered information into His Grace's ear, and the prelate turned his hand to shake instead of having his ring kissed. Father Dupuis presented Jeremiah to the archbishop.

"Your Grace, I am honored to present to you Dr. Jeremiah Banks of the

University of Arizona in the Republic of Texas. Dr. Banks is the co-leader of the expedition along with Prof. Di Vargas."

Taking the archbishop's hand in a brief but formal handshake, Jeremiah made a slight bow to the high church official.

"Your Grace, an honor and a privilege to make your acquaintance. Allow me to introduce the rest of my party; this is Miss Eunice Beaumont, our liaison on behalf of the Republic of Texas; and these are my graduate students, Ms. Quillion Post, Mr. Macejah Puap, and from the Russian Empire, Mr. Theophisus Polzin. We are grateful for the assistance the Holy Father in Rome offered in making this expedition possible. I understand you and His Grace of Madrid provided instrumental assistance in arranging Prof. Di Vargas' funding."

"You are too kind to note our minor involvement in persuading His Eminence to assist your expedition, Dr. Banks. His Holiness is impressed with your discoveries regarding the ancient language of this mysterious civilization and the usefulness to Prof. Di Vargas' quest for the biblical Enoch."

"The expeditionary team hopes we can discover the truth of Enoch or El-Abel, Your Grace."

"We expect regular reports of your expedition's progress, Dr. Banks."

The doors to the next room opened, revealing the episcopal dining room, and a priest called them to the table. Jeremiah escorted Quillion into the dining room and to her seat at one end of the table before continuing to his place along the left side of the table. He found himself seated next to Juan and opposite Miss Beaumont, with Father Dupuis beside her. She glared across the table at him like she wanted to set him ablaze. Under the guise of draping his napkin across his lap, Juan reached over and gripped Jeremiah's leg to keep him from reacting to Miss Beaumont's glare. Jeremiah's cock started to stiffen and he nudged Juan's hand away as he smiled back across the table at the woman he despised. Frost met fire across the table, and Miss Beaumont turned away first. Beside Jeremiah, in the chair between him and the archbishop, sat an elderly bishop, and across from the bishop was an older woman in a nun's habit. Father Dupuis surprised Miss Beaumont by making the introductions in fluent Spanish.

"Miss Beaumont, Dr. Banks, and Prof. Di Vargas, allow me to introduce His Excellency, Bishop Benedicto of Utiel, and Reverend Mother Superior Prudencia of the Convent of Ayora."

Jeremiah and Juan made pleasant replies to the introductions, and while Miss Beaumont spoke courteous, she remained distant and aloof towards the religious guests. The evening dragged on as Jeremiah engaged in small talk with Benedicto and Prudencia during the meal. Despite talking of his favorite topic, his mood failed to lighten. The evening ended early when the needs of a wealthy patron of the church called the archbishop away. The household staff escorted the expedition members out of the residence to their waiting coaches. The Rev. Mother Prudencia stopped Brother Colum and whispered something to him. Quillion, Theo, Mace, and Brother Tobias climbed into one coach; Father Dupuis and Miss Beaumont into the second coach; Jeremiah and Juan, along with Brother Colum, settled into the third coach. The expression on Juan's face didn't boded well for Jeremiah.

"Brother Colum, would you be so kind as to ride up top with the driver and direct him the long way back to the house via the shore road."

"Of course, Professor." Colum swung out and climbed to sit beside the driver.

"What do you think he meant?" Jeremiah asked, hoping to delay his punishment.

"You acted like a child this evening." Juan's deep voice made Jeremiah shiver. "When we get home, you will be punished for this behavior."

Jeremiah blushed as red as his hair, knowing how much he disappointed Juan.

"Do you remember what you promised in your last Christmas letter, my beautiful but naughty boy?"

"Yes, sir. I promised to submit myself to your discipline and your mentoring should we ever be together again. I promised never to do anything, which would embarrass you or place us in danger of discovery. I'm sorry, sir. I failed to live up to the promise not to embarrass you, and I'm afraid we are in danger of being discovered."

"Also, what did I say your punishment would be for embarrassing me?"

"Ten hard swats to each ass cheek sir," came Jeremiah's weak reply. "Plus, I must count each one and thank you for them, sir."

"Good, prepare yourself."

* * *

THE MONK ATTEMPTED to push aside thoughts of the professor punishing the archaeologist. After four years of separation, no one can blame them for ignoring this beautiful ride while they reconnected to the other half of their soul. Such a shame the world returned to an era where love such as theirs was a crime in most nations.

Her Excellency would send a message tonight once the removal of Father Dupuis and the Beaumont woman from the picture was accomplished. Colum still couldn't believe Cardinal Joan had come to the archbishop's dinner acting as a mere mother superior.

When the coach turned away from the shoreline and headed back towards the rented house, Colum rapped on the roof to signal the couple inside their time was short. He caught a grunt from within and took the sound for acknowledgment of his signal. The coach turned and headed for the house when Colum sat upright as the message hit him via magic.

The carriage carrying Dupuis and the Beaumont woman was destroyed. He couldn't tell if they survived or not. There were too many attackers and some were vampires. He doubted either of them would live out the night, whether or not they arrived at a hospital.

"Are the professor and the doctor secured?"

"Secured. And the doctor's students?" Colum sent back his mental response.

Do not worry about them; they are safe for now. Do not tell Dr. Banks and Prof. Di Vargas what happened. We will need their natural reactions full of shock.

Colum acknowledged the order and let his shoulders relax. The authorities wouldn't come to talk to the professor and the doctor before late morning. Let them enjoy their peace and pleasure tonight. Colum grimaced as his lustful thoughts fixated on the lovers.

Chapter 13

BROTHER TOBIAS SAT in silence beside the driver of the coach carrying Dr. Banks' graduate students. The trio extended an invitation for him to sit inside with them, but he declined. He listened to them banter about the evening and how rude Miss Beaumont continued to be toward Dr. Banks. Theo, the young Russian, repeated several of his comments when the others didn't understand. Under the influence of the vast amounts of champagne and wine Theo consumed this evening, his accent became thicker and he slurred his words. Tobias pictured the handsome blond leaning against Quillion, perhaps attempting to slip his hand into her lap. A strict Dominican upbringing left Brother Tobias with a narrow worldview, which his training with the Cult of Cain failed to breech. The actual scene inside the carriage would shock him.

Theo sprawled across the carriage seat with his head in Mace's lap, gazing up with lust and alcohol-fogged eyes. Mace ran the fingers of one hand through the blond locks, while the other hand played with the cravat around Theo's neck. Across from them, Quillion sat watching with amusement. Theo started humming a tune from his homeland, and the vibrations of his body affected Mace's body. His cock grew hard, and his balls tightened with a massive load. Mace missed his chance at any relief because Dr. Banks insisted on checking the equipment before coming ashore. Add in unpacking at the hotel, followed by dressing for and attending the formal dinner, and now Theo's humming vibrating his body, and everything edged him closer and closer to exploding in his pants. Without Quillion sharing the carriage with them, Theo might be taking care of his hard cock. Theo moved in his lap, turning to face him, his hot breath now adding to the misery Mace experienced.

"God, I want his breath on my naked cock instead of trapped like this. Theo, you're beautiful, but you're killing me," Mace thought.

"I'm sorry, moye serdce. Slip your cock out. I'll suck you to a mind-blowing orgasm, and Quill will never find out," Theo thought back at Mace.

Surprise and shock hit Mace. *"What did you call me? How are you in my head?"* he thought, gazing down at the blond head so close to his cock. Quillion stared out the window of the coach trying to give them privacy.

"Moye serdce, my heart in Russian, this is how I think of you. That we can communicate by thought proves there's more happening than Quill's magic enhancing our emotions. I think her magic has created a link between us fueled by our emotions. The only other magicians who communicate like this are those bound by Silver magic. Do you want me to sit up since I can tell you don't want to engage in sex in front of Quill?" Theo's thoughts echoed in Mace's head.

"Please, if you can manage to sit up, Theo, the situation isn't fair to Quill," Mace thought back at Theo.

With a groan, Theo sat up and almost fell off the bench. Mace held him, keeping him steady in an upright position. Quill turned back to face them again.

"I should have ridden with Father Dupuis and the ice queen. Make sure you put out the 'Do not disturb' sign tonight."

A sudden change of pressure followed by a horrible crashing sound and the screams of injured horses interrupted Mace's reply. Their coach jerked as the driver fought to control his team. Mace pushed on the door, but Brother Tobias slammed the door shut with an order to stay in the coach and keep the door shut. All three students wondered which coach had crashed.

THE JOURNAL OF CAIN

"And Yahweh of the Mist, deprived of a higher place among the Elohim, departed their company. With the stolen knowledge of creation, He established a high place for himself. In this holy place, Yahweh created a host of angels to serve Him. Then Yahweh created a garden centered on the twin trees of knowledge and life. Within the garden, He brought forth Adam, a man, and Eve, a woman of his own creation, and set them above all his other creations. Now in this time many angels dwelled in the villages near to the sacred garden. They had congress with mortals and brought forth children of semi-divine power.

Now, Adam and Eve also bore children of power. Their sons they named Cain, Abel, and Seth. Each brother had a twin sister, and all the children of Adam and Eve possessed the gift of magic. The children of magic befriended the children of angels and Yahweh grew jealous of their joy. The Lord did order His angels to destroy their children and return to the high place. But Lucifer, called the Morning Star, raised his sword and his people in rebellion against the Lord. The war for heaven split the children of Adam into three factions, Cain of the dark magic did side with Lucifer's rebellion, Seth of the light magic did choose the side of the Lord, and Abel the gentle did seek a path to peace. The Lord is a jealous deity and He opposed all attempts at peace. Heaven's civil war became Earth's first war between mages. Cain used his darkest magic to twist first the children of angels into the shapes of the beasts before settling the magic on mortals. Seth wove spells to defend and spells to bind. Both raised armies to do battle at their command."

Ham 2:1-17

INTERLUDE: WHAT BROTHER TOBIAS SAW

After slamming the door to the students' carriage shut and ordering them to stay inside, Brother Tobias raced back towards the coach carrying Father Dupuis and the Beaumont woman. As he rounded the corner, he slid to a halt, reaching for a weapon he did not carry. Vampires swarmed the wreckage of the carriage as his fellow cultist fought to keep them back. Bodies lay scattered across the street, where cultists had fallen, torn apart by fangs and claws.

None of them were armed with silver. No one considered one of the vampire clans would make a try for either Dupuis or the woman. They would all be torn apart. Holy Mother, why did Tobias listen to Colum and leave his weapons behind?

Into the middle of the horror unfolding before him, Tobias spotted a pair of figures move in from opposite sides of the street. The pair became a blur as they sped across the distance to the ruined carriage. Flashes of silver appeared, and where silver flashed a vampire vanished. Some of the vampires turned from their focus on the carriage and the cultists to battle back against the new foe. The battle began moving back towards where Tobias crouched, watching. When the severed head of a vampire crashed down in front of the barrel he hid behind, Tobias made his escape. As he jumped on the back of the carriage containing the students, the driver made as though to flee the scene.

"Stay put. Moving will only attract unwanted attention. The local authorities will respond, and then we can return to the hotel," Tobias said to the driver.

When he received a grunt of acknowledgement from the driver, Tobias sent a mental message to Colum alerting him to the situation.

Tobias climbed up to the seat beside the driver. He hoped that his plan would work, failure could mean death for them all.

Chapter 14

THE COACH CARRYING Jeremiah and Juan drew to a halt in the yard of their rented house. The pair exited the coach and went inside, leaving Brother Colum and the driver to tend to the horses. Juan stopped Jeremiah in the entry hall, and picked up the silk cloth he'd placed on the small table earlier in the day. He wrapped the cloth over Jeremiah's eyes as he whispered for trust in his lover's ear. Jeremiah nodded his head as Juan's powerful body pressed against him from behind. Juan guided Jeremiah along the hallway and down a flight of stairs. He stopped just outside the doorway to a secluded room in the basement of the house.

"Your punishment for your poor behavior will start in a few moments. I discovered this little room the other day and it seems designed for punishing misbehaving archaeologists." Juan put his finger against Jeremiah's lips when the younger man attempted to speak. "You do not have permission to speak. You will remain silent unless I ask you a direct question. Do you understand?"

"Yes, sir."

He led Jeremiah inside a stone-walled room. From a hook in the center of the ceiling hung a pair of manacles attached to a chain, which could be adjusted by a winch set in the wall. The floor hosted a pair of chains, each ending with a leg iron. Along one wall hung an array of whips, floggers, and other devices to torture or tease a submissive. Juan led Jeremiah to the center of the room

"Strip!" Juan ordered.

Jeremiah began to undress, carefully folding his suit and placing it on the floor. When he was naked, Juan came and locked the manacles to his wrists and the shackles to his ankles. He crossed to the winch and turned it to raise Jeremiah's arms above his head, before adjusting the controls for the shackles on Jeremiah's ankles to spread his legs. Juan walked behind his lover and delivered a hard slap to Jeremiah's firm ass.

"I'm going to begin your punishment now. You will not make a sound and you do not have permission to cum," Juan said as he crossed to the wall of implements and selected a wooden paddle.

* * *

JEREMIAH FROZE as panic threatened to overwhelm his reason when he felt Juan lock the cuffs around his wrists and ankles. The heat of this room made his mind flashback to the jungles of Belize, where he served out his mandatory reservist duty to the Republic. The shackles brought back the memories of being captured by the Confederates and held as a spy. The Republic chose him for a mission to investigate a set of ruins, which straddled the Republic-Confederate border between Mexico and Belize. The Belizeans held him prisoner for a month before the interrogation sessions began. Over the course of two months, they'd tried to break him, the scientists and guards, to gain confessions of espionage.

The sting of the paddle on his bare ass unleashed the memories of his torture. The Belizeans began by shaving off his flowing copper hair, which the Republic had let him keep as part of his mission cover. Then came the beatings with fists to loosen him up. Question after question hammered at his mind while blow after blow hammered at his body. As the nominal leader of his team, Jeremiah was forced to watch the sadistic guards repeatedly rape the few female members of the team.

Sweat poured off of Jeremiah, caused by the combined heat of the room and the memories of the steaming jungle. He'd lost track of Juan and the paddle as the memories carried him back to the prison camp in Belize. He'd held out against his tormentors until the day they decided to start using hot pokers on his flesh. Acting on pure survival instincts, Jeremiah unleashed his magic at full strength. The room's temperature plunged to below freezing. The heated pokers exploded as the metal went from red hot to frozen, sending shards into the nearby guards. In the next instant, deadly ice daggers exploded from the air around Jeremiah. The flying ice killed everyone around him as the cold made his shackles brittle enough to shatter.

* * *

JUAN FELT the room growing colder as he applied the paddle to Jeremiah's ass. When he stopped to check Jeremiah for damage, he found his lover's skin to be cool to the touch and the red of the paddling fading quickly. He reached up to unfasten the cuffs from Jeremiah's wrists and found the locks covered in ice.

"Jeremiah, what's going on?"

"I should have told you about last year." Jeremiah wept tears of ice. "My magic is about to escape my control, Juan. Please get out of here."

"I'm sorry, my love, but I'm not leaving you."

Juan watched as ice ran up the chain holding Jeremiah arms above his head and was shocked when with a firm tug Jeremiah shattered the links. The actions repeated themselves with each leg. Jeremiah turned to face him, and his sapphire eyes were sparkling pools. Jeremiah took a step in Juan's direction and collapsed into a heap. The normal temperature of the room began to return as Juan picked up his lover and headed back to their bedrooms. With tenderness, Juan tucked Jeremiah into the bed before slipping in beside him. Before sleep claimed him, Juan vowed to let Jeremiah decide when or if to tell him about his magic and what happened to him the previous year.

VAMPIRE INTERLUDE: THE CAPTURE OF MISS BEAUMONT

Eunice Beaumont was not a happy woman as she rode across from her Imperial counterpart. The priest had treated her no better than the perverted archaeologist. The time had come to do away with the man who'd ruined her brother's budding career. She could make use of the priest's connections to the Order of St. Hubert to have both Banks and Di Vargas arrested for their perversions.

"Father Dupuis, I think we should have a frank discussion about Mr. Banks and Prof. Di Vargas."

"Ah, I wondered when you'd dare to broach that subject with me, Mademoiselle Beaumont. What complaint do you have with these fine gentlemen?" the priest asked.

"Fine gentlemen? Please don't make me laugh, Father. They are sexual deviants, lovers of men. They should be arrested and removed from this expedition and their materials given to respectable authorities in the field."

"Mademoiselle Beaumont, Prof. Juan Di Vargas is a scholar of impeccable reputation and the acknowledged expert in Ancient and

Medieval Theology. The reports passed to me from His Holiness make no mention of any deviant behavior. As for Dr. Banks, our reports on him show a young man of remarkable promise. What proof do you offer to back these claims of sexual perversion?" Dupuis demanded.

Miss Beaumont's reply was lost as the air in the coach suddenly vanished and then returned with such force the vehicle exploded. Both passengers slammed into the ground and were pelted by the falling debris. Eunice heard her own screams of agony mix with those of the wounded horses. Then came the sounds of combat. A momentary lull in the fighting gave someone above them the chance to rip away the debris pinning them to the pavement. Before Eunice could draw breath to scream at the horrid face in front of her, a fist slammed into her gut, driving what little air she had from her lungs. She felt herself being flung over her captor's shoulder like a sack of potatoes at the county fair. She thought she heard someone call out orders to burn the remains of the coach, but she couldn't be sure before her captor ripped open a sewer cover and dropped her down the shaft to the foul water below.

Chapter 15

After a lazy morning, Juan and Jeremiah sat beside the pool going over notes taken from the journal pages. Juan read a passage out loud.

Cain took a wife, from the people of a foreign god, who bore him Enoch, for whom he named the city he built. As did his father, Enoch took a foreign wife and of this union is born Irad, and Irad fathered Mehujael, the father of Methuselah of the long life. Methuselah fathered Lamech. Lamech married two women, one named Adah and the other Zillah. Adah birthed Jabal, father of those who live in tents and raise livestock. His brother, Jubal, fathered all who play stringed instruments and pipes. Zillah also bore a son, Tubal-Cain, who forged all kinds of bronze and iron. Tubal-Cain's sister bore the name Naamah." Juan's deep voice made Jeremiah's blood race when he read the scripture. "This passage mirrors the phrasing from the Old Testament and forms the basis for my argument against the Flood being sent to wash clean the world from sin.

"Before I read the counter passage from this journal, explain the basis for your argument from your passage of Scripture," Jeremiah said.

"The argument is based on two sources, the Genesis Rabba midrash and the 11th Century Jewish commentator Rashi, naming Naamah as Noah's wife. If God is purging the world of sin, Naamah and her children should perish in the Flood, leaving Noah alone. Naamah is the seventh generation in descent from Cain the first murderer."

Jeremiah paused in thought for a moment before reading the counter passage from Cain's journal.

Of course, this entire lineage attributed to me is fiction. In truth, this line might be descended from Abel. Seth and his scribes assigned this family to me to hide his guilt in my death. When I revealed this truth to him, despair claimed him until I taught him the lineage of Cain.

Jeremiah added, "The journal seems to be recording a conversation between Cain and a member of the Brotherhood of the Crimson Hand. The author switches here to quote the Gospel of Cain, Chapter 10, verses 1 to 8."

Hear now the actual lineage of Cain, the First Victim and Father of Vampires. In the nights after Cain returned to the lands of Adam, he founded the city of El-Abel in honor of his brother Abel, whom he loved. After many years of single rule, he chose five leaders from among the Children of Seth and granted to them the Gift of Cain so they might rule with him.

For many years, the five ruled beside Cain in peace, but Cain left one day to visit an ally. Two of the five raised their hands against the rule of Cain and did imprison their brothers and sister. Father Cain erased them from history. The remaining three: Bel-Sarra, the mighty general of El-Abel, who granted the Gift of Cain unto Lamasthu, Howahkan, and Sigrún. Sharru-Kino, god-king of El-Abel, who granted the Gift of Cain unto Bellabarisruk, Parlathán the cursed, and Kamadia; and Nina-Ishtar, beloved consort and wise counselor of Sharru-Kino, who gave the Gift of Cain unto Immertun, Astryiah, and Laverna Salacia. From these chosen nine are the clans of vampires descended.

"So, our question is which lineage is the correct one to pursue."

"I don't think our research paths converged as much as we thought. Your biblical research still focuses on the line leading to Noah's wife regardless of whether she descended from Cain or Abel. My archaeological research still focuses on locating the mysterious city between El-Isin and El-Kino, which may be El-Abel or Enoch. I need a break. Come take a swim with me and let this sit for a bit."

Juan paid attention as Jeremiah stood and stripped off his shirt and pushed down his shorts to reveal a form-fitting Speedo. He marveled at the gleaming copper hair over the pale skin of Jeremiah's chest, arms, and legs. Though he missed the long, flowing copper locks, the brutal short hair suited him well and gave the younger man the air of maturity missing in Atlanta. Watching Jeremiah's graceful dive into the water, Juan found himself adjusting his thickening cock. He grabbed a pair of towels and laid them out by the lounge chairs on the pool deck. Between them, he placed a tube of high SPF sunblock to rub on to Jeremiah when he emerged from the pool.

Under the Mediterranean sun, Jeremiah's fair skin would burn. Juan unbuttoned and laid his shirt on the chair before stripping off his slacks to reveal his square-cut swim trunks. A loud wolf whistle caught him by surprise, and he almost fell into the pool, much to Jeremiah's amusement. Juan stern glare made Jeremiah blush and disappear beneath the water as Juan sat on the lip of the pool with his legs dangling into the water. Jeremiah surfaced between Juan's legs and rested his arms on his lover's knees as he gazed up into his coal dark eyes. Sapphire eyes twinkled in the sunlight, along with the dazzling smile Jeremiah flashed as he gazed up at the man who captured his heart.

"Your bright eyes never cease to fascinate me, beautiful boy. This, I imagine, is what gazing into the clear ocean against white sand beaches would be like. I'll go blind from gazing at your beauty."

"Well, I don't want you going blind, so I guess I should hide my beauty under lots of clothes from now on. Or I will buy you a pair of sunglasses."

Juan's hands came down on top of Jeremiah's head and pushed him under the water—something, which proved a mistake, as Jeremiah latched on to his ankles and yanked Juan into the pool. Juan broke the surface sputtering as he gasped for air. Jeremiah surfaced out of easy reach and laughed, a sound Juan missed hearing. Juan launched himself at Jeremiah, and they dodged and chased each other around the pool for a while before Juan grew winded. Jeremiah surfaced right behind Juan in the shallow end of the pool and wrapped his arms around the man as he snuggled against his broad back.

"You're not breathing hard, my love." Juan noted as his breathing slowed to match Jeremiah's breathing rhythm. "Is this part of your magic?"

"Yes, I'm sorry, it's not fair of me to play water tag with you when my magic lets me draw oxygen from the water."

"Let's dry off and cover you in sunscreen before your skin turns the color of your hair." Juan tried to move to the edge of the stairs leading out of the pool. "My love, we can cuddle once we're out of the pool."

Juan wobbled as his balance shifted and only remained upright because Jeremiah was holding on to him. They rose out of the water and moved toward the edge of the pool. Glancing down, Juan found the water almost solid beneath them and moving them up and out of the pool. The water receded after depositing them on the deck near their lounge chairs. Jeremiah let go of Juan long enough for the older man to turn around, watching the water return to the pool, including the water clinging to his skin and soaking his trunks. He and Jeremiah stood dry as his lover drew him in for a kiss.

"I don't work magic on this scale often, so here's hoping you're impressed."

"Why keep your talent hidden, Jeremiah? Such an ability would be an asset."

"Magic is more of a liability, my heart. Should the Republic learn I hold this kind of power, I'll never teach in a classroom or venture out on an archaeological dig again. I'll become a permanent part of the military, forced to use my powers against the enemies of the Republic. So, I learned a long time ago to control my abilities and hide them away. I'm using them now to burn off the excess power I acquired in the past couple of weeks."

"How much extra power are you carrying?"

"Stand behind me and direct your attention to the pool."

Jeremiah stood still and focused on the pool. The water rose and began to take on the form of a man mounted on a seahorse. Once the man took on Juan's image, stylized like a hero of old, Jeremiah shifted his magic and froze the water into a giant ice sculpture. He sagged into Juan's embraced as the power left him.

"A lot of extra power," Jeremiah whispered as Juan settled them both down on one of the lounge chairs. "I hope we aren't expecting company for at least an hour."

"Rest and let me care for you, beautiful one. The sculpture is incredible and beautiful. Is this how you regard me, Jeremiah?"

"As a hero of old? Well, I do picture you as a crusader at times; perhaps I should cast you as Don Quixote instead of Poseidon. I think I inflated your ego."

Jeremiah snuggled into Juan's embrace and soon slept as Juan rubbed the sunblock into his exposed skin. Juan regarded the ice sculpture Jeremiah created, amazed by the detail crafted from the water. He dozed off as his breathing came into sync with the sleeping Jeremiah.

* * *

THE SOUND of shattering glass startled both men into wakefulness. Jeremiah sprang to his feet in a defensive stance between the noise and Juan. Sapphire glowed around his hands. Juan glanced in the direction of the crash and found Brother Colum staring at the ice sculpture, a tray dangling in one hand. At his feet were the remains of two glasses and a bowl of fruit. Juan stood and placed a calming hand on Jeremiah's shoulder. Calmed by Juan's touch, the glow of magic surrounding Jeremiah faded as he became aware of Colum disturbing them.

"Professor, Doctor, my apologies for disturbing you. I thought perhaps you might like some light refreshment. I-I didn't expect to find the pool frozen over in such a fashion."

"My apologies, Brother Colum, I drifted off before I restored the water to its proper form. I trust you'll keep this event to yourself."

"I-I-I, of course, Dr. Banks. No one briefed me on your possession of magic; such information isn't in your dossier."

"Best for everyone my possessing magic remain unknown, Brother Colum. I'm of no use to anyone locked in the chains the Republic."

"Your secret is safe with me, Dr. Banks."

Brother Colum and Juan stared in awe as Jeremiah made a gesture and the ice returned to liquid. Jeremiah sagged again, still not recovered from his earlier grand display. Juan eased him back down on the lounge.

"I'll clean up this mess, Brother Colum, if you'll go fetch Dr. Banks a glass of fruit juice."

The young monk nodded and fled the pool area. Juan found a broom and dustpan in the pool house and used them to clean up the broken glass and splattered fruit. He glanced at Jeremiah on occasion to check on his lover. Fatigued from the use of magic, the man dozed on the lounge chair. Brother Colum returned with a new tray of drinks and fruit, twitching enough to make the items dance.

"What's the matter, Brother Colum?"

"I'm informed the local authorities are on their way here to speak with both of you. A horrible accident occurred last night involving Father Dupuis and Miss Beaumont's coach."

Shock hit Juan, rocking him back for a moment. "What happened?"

"I don't have any details, Professor. I was just given a warning that the authorities are coming here to interview Dr. Banks."

"Jere...Dr. Banks isn't in any condition to deal with visitors."

"The authorities are concerned because Miss Beaumont is a foreign diplomat and part of Dr. Banks' expedition. I'm told her injuries are life threatening."

Juan swore under his breath as he regarded the prone form of Jeremiah. He turned back to Brother Colum. "Help me dress him. A bathing suit isn't proper attire for an interrogation. Put the tray down, Colum. Jeremiah, you need to rouse yourself. Visitors are expected soon."

"W-what, visitors? Why are they visiting?" Jeremiah rose to face Juan. "What's going on Juan, um, Prof. Di Vargas?"

"You can use each other's Christian names in front of me. My assignment is to guard you both and your secrets are my secrets. I promise to take them to the grave with me if needed."

Jeremiah and Juan nodded to each other, confirming to the other a comfort with taking the young monk into their confidence. Jeremiah reached out and dragged the young monk forward. Colum clutched Jeremiah's clothes to his breast like a talisman. Jeremiah gave the monk a gentle hug before prying his clothes from his hands.

"We realize you're in a tight position, Colum. Your instructions require protecting us at all cost while reporting everything you learn about us to your superiors, don't they?"

"Yes," came the whispered reply as Colum shuddered, drawing close to despair. Juan embraced him from behind as Jeremiah hugged him from the front. The young monk latched on Jeremiah as sobs wracked his body.

"Colum, we can make things easier on you, but we need a little information first so we can decide how much to share with you. Do you agree to help us?"

Pulling back and wiping his eyes on the sleeve of his robe, Colum nodded his assent.

"Whom do you report to, Colum?"

"For the Order or the Cult?"

"Let's start with the Order, although I suspect Father Dupuis as your contact."

"Yes, he was. The report I received last night said he died in the accident. No one has informed me of who his replacement is."

"And in the Cult?"

"To Her Eminence, Cardinal Joan IX."

Jeremiah bent over to pull his cargo shorts back on, and Juan caught Colum's eyes fixed on Jeremiah's firm ass and the movement of his muscles beneath the skin. He leaned close to the monk and whispered in his ear to make sure Jeremiah didn't eavesdrop.

"He possesses a beautiful ass, doesn't he?"

"Yes, he's stunning. I-I—"

"Relax, Colum, your secret is safe with us. I assume you took a vow of chastity."

"When I gave my vows to the Order, but my actual oaths belong to the Cult of Cain, and they do not require chastity; in fact, the condition is discouraged. My primary vow is not to interfere in an existing relationship, yours and Dr. Banks' in particular."

"But you want to explore Jeremiah's body and worship his cock and ass. Don't you? Admit the desire, Colum."

"Yes, sir. Dr. Banks is exotic. I never met an actual red-haired person before."

"Help us through this interrogation, Colum, and I'll ask Jeremiah if he wants a third to join us in bed tonight."

Juan released Brother Colum when Jeremiah turned to face them as he pulled on his shirt. Jeremiah quirked his head to the side, looking a question at Juan and Colum before moving back to join them. He caught the lust on Colum's face before the young monk regained his composure and he guessed what Juan did while he dressed. Juan walked over to where his clothes lay on the chair by their research notes. Jeremiah took hold of Colum's shoulders and turned him to face Juan as the older man got dressed.

"I can guess what Juan's up to, Colum. He's put the vow of chastity to the test with his teasing, hasn't he?"

"I didn't make an actual vow of chastity, Dr. Banks. I swore all my real pledges to the Cult of Cain. My vows to the Order are part of my cover."

"Well, I can guess he will ask me if I mind another joining us in bed tonight, provided we're not sitting in a jail cell. He's such a good-looking man, in such fantastic shape for an older man. Don't you think?" Jeremiah let his breath tease Colum's ear. "I remember the first time he undressed in front of me."

"Please say yes to his request, Dr. Banks. I promise I'll do everything to prevent trouble with the authorities." Lust turned Colum's breath ragged. "I'll do whatever is required so long as the plan doesn't require me to go against the Cult of Cain."

"No need to beg yet, Colum. Tell Her Eminence about my magic as long as she understands the information must not enter any written record until after I'm long dead." Jeremiah's hand glided down Colum's back to cup his right ass cheek through the thick monastic robe. "I think she'll welcome the information."

"Oh, yes, sir. We need to go set things up to retain the advantage in the interrogation." Colum hesitated before pulling away from Jeremiah's touch. "I think meeting them in the formal parlor would be best."

"I believe we're better off meeting them out here by the pool. Better to appear casual and unknowing. Colum, go and greet them when they arrive and bring them out here. Dr. Banks and I will meet them poolside."

"Professor, one of the men who comes is sure to be a member of the Order's Law Enforcement Division on behalf of the Empire, because of Miss Beaumont's status. A formal setting is required when dealing with such a personage," Colum explained. "Dress in your suits and be engaged in research in the study if you won't use the parlor."

"I think we should listen to Colum's advice, Juan. He's our inside man for information on the Order," Jeremiah cut off Juan's counter reply. "My guess is some flunky from the Republic's consulate will be along with this officer to keep him from violating my rights under international law. Let's go dress for company."

Brother Colum escaped once he regained his composure. He never meant to let his desires for the two men to show. Cardinal Joan would be cross with him, despite the men's invitation to join them. He doubted telling her Jeremiah was a Sapphire magician would soften her anger. She'd forbidden his getting involved with them. He had to hope her punishment wasn't too severe. Colum took up a station near the front door preparing for the authority's arrival.

VAMPIRE INTERLUDE: THE VALENCIAN COURT

"The court of his Excellency the Grand Duke Estavan Acosta Castellano of Valencia is now open to those who bring petitions."

On the carved marble throne, the ancient Spanish vampire lord sat surveying his court. The strangers mingled among his courtiers. Foreign vampires come to pay nominal homage to the area's ruler before spending any time in his territory. One small group of strangers caught his attention. A tall, dark Italian vampire leaned toward a shorter vamp, wrapped in the concealing robes favored by members of the Barghest Clan. They exchanged information behind the back of a beautiful, dark-skinned, young vampire. The duke regarded the beautiful vampire, gasped when he realized while the man appeared young and beautiful, he was of incredible age and of the same generation as himself. His chamberlain rapped his staff as the trio moved forward to present themselves to the Lord of Valencia.

"My Lord, a personal envoy from His Unholiness, Lord Slayer. I present Armand Silvestro of the Bel-Kino clan." The chamberlain gestured to the tall Italian vampire. "Database of the Barghest clan." He indicated the figure wearing the dark concealing hooded jacket.

"Abel Adamson of the Lorelei clan." He indicated the beautiful youth. "They bring a request from the Lord of all Vampires."

"Except for Lord Adamson, I am familiar with these visitors by reputation. How does an elder of such vast age escape the attention of the courts, Lord Adamson?"

"I spent many years in languor, Your Grace. His Unholiness woke me himself to request my service for this task. This is why the courts are unfamiliar with me."

"What does His Unholiness require of our small court?"

"Listen to the words of His Unholiness, Lord Slayer." Abel turned toward the shrouded vampire in his party. "Database give us Lord Slayer's words in his voice."

"Estavan of Valencia, in your city a party of explorers prepares to proceed to the city of Cain. No harm is to come to this party or the spies planted on them by the agents of the church. Should any harm befall them brought by vampiric hands, my judgment will be as swift as well as violent. These three are empowered by me with authority to carry out my High Justice."

The gathered vampires trembled in fear. Under orders from the primordial founder of his clan, Castellano dispatched agents to attack the political watchdogs of the expedition. The entire situation was beyond his control. The duke realized, forces beyond his control, maneuvered him between the titanic powers of the primordials and the Lord of all Vampires. They gawked as their leader descended from his throne to kneel before the trio. Bloody sweat marred the pale features of the ancient vampire.

"My Lords, I beg grace from His Unholiness. Not four hours ago agents of this court went to ambush the priest and the foreign woman on their return from the archbishop's palace. I received a direct commanded to dispatch them from the founder of my clan."

"Bellabarisruk came to this court, Duke Castellano. How long did he stay?"

"Will His Unholiness spare my court?"

"Answer Lord Adamson's question," Armand said in his Italian-accented baritone voice. "Bellabarisruk does not command here."

"Like His Unholiness, he sent a messenger. The mortal came from the Cult of Cain. He bore written directions under Bellabarisruk's personal seal, a device I'm familiar with since I served at his old court in my youth."

"Where are these directions and the cultist who delivered them?"

"Destroyed per Lord Bellabarisruk's command, I drank the mortal's life."

Terror stirred the vampires of the court. Final death waited to claim them if they remained in the hall. One of the courtiers broke for the door only to find the shrouded vampire blocking the way. The first courtiers to reach the door retreated in shock; no vampire possessed the ability to move so fast. Other courtiers refused to cower before a single enemy.

"Rush him; he's only one Barghest. The little monster can't stop us."

The hidden figure drifted past them, transforming several vampires into piles of ash by severing their heads from their bodies in a blur of silver. By the throne, Abel and Armand seized Estavan and settled him on the stairs out of the path of frightened vampires. In front of the primary exit of the hall, a whirling dervish of a figure dispatched monster after monster. When the rush faltered and broke before him, the vampire let his glamour fade and strode towards the throne. He climbed the steps and sat upon the throne. The man callously sprawled on the precious marble. One leg draped over an arm of the chair while his silver sword rested point down before him, with one hand resting on the cross-guard. The vampire's long dark hair flowed over his forward shoulder. He was dressed in a white hoodie, jeans, and sneakers. Dark eyes gleamed as he surveyed the cowering court of vampires before him, in particular the kneeling Grand Duke. He smiled, revealing impressive fangs.

"Forgive my deception, Duke Castellano, but since Bellabarisruk's agents visited, I couldn't be sure of a happy reception."

"Should I recognize who you are, *espuma juvenil*?"

"Youthful scum? Wow, a new insult. Database, make a note of this one for me. A lord should be more careful in his choice of which guests he grants favors to, Duke Castellano."

The young man sprawled on the throne noted the dawning comprehension on the ancient vampire's face when the nightmare on his throne called the beautiful youth Database. The illusion of beauty faded to reveal a figure wrapped in a jacket with a hood, which shrouded his face. More bloody sweat appeared to mar the pale face of the Grand Duke of Valencia.

"I gather you figured out how deep the hole is." Richard gave a wry chuckle. "Yes, Castellano, I am who you think I am, and the answer to the earlier question about grace is no."

The faint breath whispered over Castellano, who found himself in a firm grip he couldn't break despite his ancient status.

No vampire of such youth could hold him like this; he couldn't be more than a century old. Were the rumors true?

"I can almost read your thoughts, my dear duke," came the silky whisper of a tenor voice in his ear. "I am Lord Slayer, Cain's successor and Lord of all Vampires. You possess information I need, and there's only one way I'm sure to learn what I need. The mortal's blood adds a tang to your sweat. Most are unaware a human's last memories lingered in the vampire who consumed the mortal. By feeding on the vampire, I can extract those mortal memories."

"Please, My Lord, I can tell you everything. The cultist babbled and begged for his life."

"I'm sure he did; he was mortal. Don't forget the members of the Cult of Cain are under my protection. For his death alone you earned death at my hand; for the other crimes committed, death would be slow and painful, but I need information more than I need to make an example."

Estavan Castellano tensed at the sharp pain and sagged from overwhelming euphoria he last experienced the night his sire took his mortality and gave him the Gift of Cain. Memories flowed from the Lord of Valencia into Richard from both the ancient vampire and his last victim. A struggle ensued to separate the human memories from the vampire's own. Castellano sagged in Richard's grip as he decayed into final death. Richard pulled his fangs free and the ancient Spanish vampire became a pile of dust at his feet.

"Master, did you discover what is needed?"

"Yes, I did. The poor monk, they coerced him into delivering the message and into giving up his life. Bellabarisruk ordered his death, but others are also involved in the plots to remove the priest and the woman from Texas from the archaeologist's party."

"My Lord," Armand interrupted. "What of the rest of the Valencian court?"

Richard turned and surveyed the remaining vampires, and with a gesture, Ebony magic flowed around the room like a scythe. When the magic faded, only Richard, Armand, and Database remained.

"Thank you, my friends. Database my dear, the portrayal of Abel was masterful."

"He would drive a stake through my heart for such a poor performance, Master."

"We should be going, My Lord. I don't think we can rescue either the priest or the Texan woman."

"I think we might salvage the party by moving with haste. The coaches carrying most of the party pass by here soon. We can intercept them and Bellabarisruk's team of assassins. A member of the Cult of Cain is in the party. We can use him to ensure Dr. Banks' grad students aren't involved."

The trio of vampire left the empty hall and made their way out to a place where they maintained surveillance for the mortal party while checking for the immortal attackers. Database faded into the shadows seeking the vampires. Richard and Armand took places across the street from one another alert for activity. The heavy clopping of hooves and the grind of wheels soon echoed down the road as a figure darted out to place a small canister in the center of the road.

Chapter 16

FATHER LUTHER KASSMEYER, a knight-inspector for the law enforcement arm of the Order of St. Hubert, stood before his superior in the Order. The Bishop, Fabrizio Fabbri, handed over his commands regarding the "accident," which seemed to have claimed the lives of Father Dupuis and Miss Beaumont. The imposing German inspector scowled as the senior Italian bishop directed him to collect the local and national police files on the case and bring them back to the Order's headquarters in the city.

"Do you understand the instructions, Father Kassmeyer?"

"Yes, Your Eminence, I am to gather all the files on the accident and bring them here, before conveying information about the accident to the Republic of Texas' consulate and returning here."

"No solo investigating, Father Kassmeyer. This order comes straight from the Holy Father."

"Yes, Your Eminence." Bowing over the man's hand, Father Kassmeyer kissed his ring.

* * *

THE SPANISH POLICE returned the shocked American trio to their hotel after brief questioning. Their concerns passed on to the knight-inspector from the Order of St. Hubert, who arrived at headquarters about an hour after the inspector leading the initial investigation got back from meeting with the coroner.

"Apologies, Inspector, I'll need all files on this incident," the knight-inspector said.

"We've only started our investigation, Father Kassmeyer."

"I understand, Inspector. However, a person of diplomatic standing is one of the victims, which places the inquiry into the jurisdiction of the Order of St. Hubert. We are facing a possible international incident, as Miss Beaumont is a relative of the President of the Republic of Texas."

"What of the investigation into Father Dupuis' death?"

"Father Dupuis was a member of the Order and the Holy Father's designated envoy. We will require his files as well. The Provincial Police's involvement is over inspector. We thank you for the diligence in this matter, but we'll take the case from here."

The inspector and his senior sergeant viewed the knight-inspector departure with relief while fuming in silence at the high-handedness of what amounted to the Empire's police force. They went into the inspector's office and, behind the closed doors, gave vent to their feelings.

"We can handle this investigation with the finesse required to deal with prickly diplomats. The paper pushers from the Republic of Texas are some of the easiest foreign officials. Why did the Order jump on this so fast, Inspector?"

"At a guess, they're grandstanding sergeant Miss Beaumont isn't the usual VIP; she is influential and connected in the halls of power in the

Republic of Texas. No, I'm more concerned with what they're trying to cover up with regards to Father Dupuis's death. No one murders a minor priest of the Order acting as a Papal envoy for some archaeological excavation. Shouldn't we be the one's questioning Dr. Banks and Prof. Di Vargas instead of a member of the Order? Understand this sergeant, the knight-inspector won't allow Dr. Banks to call on the consulate staff for a representative."

"Well, sir, one avenue of investigation remains open to us. The driver of the coach also died in the accident."

"Tread with care, sergeant, we don't want to find ourselves in an inquisitor's chair."

Chapter 17

With Brother Colum's warning, Juan and Jeremiah dressed in appropriate attire and were ready when the representative from the Consulate for the Republic of Texas arrived with a knight-inspector from the Order in tow. Brother Colum led the consulate representative and the inspector into the study where Dr. Banks and Prof. Di Vargas waited, poring over research notes. The sound of the door opening drew the men's attention, and both noted the scowling face of the tall, muscular man wearing the black leather uniform of the Order of St. Hubert. This man hated roadblocks to the performance of his duty, they surmised. Given the smug expression the man from the consulate wore, Jeremiah guessed who blocked the inspector.

"Dr. Banks, Prof. Di Vargas, forgive the interruption of the important work on behalf of the Republic and the Empire. We came with some disturbing news and a couple of questions, which need to be asked for formality's sake."

Jeremiah held up his hand and interrupted the man. "Excuse me, sir, but back home in Arizona, we introduce ourselves before launching into conversations or interrogations." Jeremiah's Texas drawl flavored his Spanish. "I'm Dr. Jeremiah Banks of the University of Arizona, and this is my colleague Prof. Juan Di Vargas of the University of Madrid."

Jeremiah caught the faintest hint of a smirk on the face of the inspector before giving his full attention to the man from the consulate.

"My apologies, Dr. Banks. Roger Garland, associate Consul for the Republic of Texas, and my grim friend here is Father Luther Kassmeyer, a knight-inspector with the Order of St. Hubert," the short man from Texas said.

"Thank you, Mr. Garland. Please sit, gentlemen. You indicated the news is unsettling. I hope everything back home is all right."

"Back home, things are fine, Dr. Banks. This matter concerns an accident part of your party suffered on the way back to their hotel from the archbishop's residence last night."

"Dear Lord, what about my students? Are they, all right?"

The inspector leaned forward at Jeremiah's concern, but Juan detected the lack of comfort in the gesture. Both Jeremiah and Mr. Garland spoke in the Mexican-flavored Spanish of the Texan Republic, so when Father Kassmeyer spoke, his German-accented English proved a shocking contrast.

"Your students are safe, Herr Doctor. The victims of the accident are Father Dupuis and Fräulein Beaumont."

"Since Mr. Garland said the news is grievous," Juan cut in before Jeremiah spoke, "I assume one or both of them suffered traumatic injuries."

"The medics pronounced them dead at the scene, Prof. Di Vargas," Mr. Garland replied before Kassmeyer stole any more of the conversation. "This came as a shocking blow to the Consul, and he wired the news back home to our government. Miss Beaumont's family is upset. The president is considering cancelling the expedition."

"WHAT?" Jeremiah caught everyone off guard. "Sorry, this sounds callous, but Miss Beaumont isn't a vital part of the expedition. In fact, she proved an embarrassment to her position. I'm sorry for her family's loss. Please send my condolences to the president. Tragic as her death is, I fail to view this as a reason to cancel the expedition."

"Dr. Banks! What a horrible thing to say," Mr. Garland said.

"Yet the doctor makes a point, Herr Garland. I'm sure another agent of the Holy Father in Rome is being assigned to fill Father Dupuis's place. Why not fill Fräulein Beaumont's position, Mr. Garland?"

Jeremiah and Juan regarded each other for a brief moment, a glance, which revealed how uncomfortable they were with the inspector's immediate support.

"Forgive me, Father Kassmeyer, but this must be more than a mere accident; the victims are government officials. If the matter is only a tragic accident, I'm sure the local police, or perhaps the Spanish National Police, would handle the matter instead of an inspector from the Order."

"Correct, Prof. Di Vargas. We believe Father Dupuis and Fräulein Beaumont were the intended targets of an assassination since the attackers allowed the carriage carrying Dr. Banks' students to pass unmolested. The question remains as to why your carriage did not accompany the others returning from the archbishop's residence."

Before either Juan or Jeremiah reacted to the sudden shift in the conversation, Brother Colum slipped out unnoticed and returned with a man in a black cassock trimmed with episcopal purple.

"Father Kassmeyer, your instructions said to convey the news of Miss Beaumont's death to the Consulate for the Republic of Texas and return to headquarters. Yet, I find you here questioning Dr. Banks and Prof. Di Vargas like suspects in a murder investigation. Go back to our headquarters now and trade places with one of the monastic brothers on kitchen duty, as well as switching rooms with him for the next week as part of your penance for insubordination. You are dismissed."

Father Kassmeyer rose from his seat, bowed, and kissed the episcopal ring before departing. Mr. Garland half rose from his seat as the inspector left in a rush. The bishop waved him back into the chair before claiming the empty seat. Brother Colum bowed to both Jeremiah and Juan.

"Forgive me for leaving you to Father Kassmeyer's indelicate handling; I feared he exceeded his authority and sent word for reinforcements with authority. Please allow me to introduce His Eminence, Bishop Fabrizio Fabbri of the Order of St. Hubert."

"Your Eminence, a pleasure to make your acquaintance." Juan spoke on behalf of himself and Jeremiah. The Texan was still trying to regain his composure. "I'm sure in the regular course of his duties, Father Kassmeyer is an able investigator."

"The truth is he's one of the best, Prof. Di Vargas. Sadly, he knows how highly we regard him, which causes him to forget himself in his pride. The locals don't consider either you or Dr. Banks of being involved in the deaths of Father Dupuis and Miss Beaumont. Under different circumstances, I would allow Father Kassmeyer to proceed, as he deemed appropriate. Your students assured us, while you aren't friends with Miss Beaumont, you're more likely to annoy her with kindness or major bar tabs than to seek a way to kill her. Prof. Di Vargas' reputation puts him beyond reproach as well. So now the question is who will be the new watchdogs on behalf of our respective governments."

"The process will take weeks, first for the Republic to decide on a new representative and second for their choice to arrive unless they chose someone located in Europe or the Caliphate." Jeremiah groaned. "If the foreign affairs committee gave me back the authority from my last expedition, Miss Beaumont's untimely death wouldn't cause a delay."

"A negative attitude won't help the case, Dr. Banks. I must report this conversation to the Consul before he wires the government his report and informs them of your reaction to Miss Beaumont's death," Mr. Garland said.

"We're not revealing any state secrets, and I never hid my resentment of and objection to Miss Beaumont's presence on this expedition. The foreign affairs committee is aware I dislike any delays in moving on to at least Damascus where Prof. Di Vargas can begin his research based on our new materials. How long does the Consul think the legislature will take before they either transfer diplomatic authority to me or send someone to deal with the caliph's agents?" Jeremiah spat as he rose and moved to the sideboard, which held glasses and a bottle of Madeira wine. He poured himself a drink before asking, "Would anyone else like a glass?"

"I will take one, Dr. Banks," answered the bishop.

Both Juan and Mr. Garland declined, and Jeremiah poured a glass for the bishop, which Brother Colum collected and delivered to the man. Colum whispered a message to the bishop before withdrawing.

"While we wait for the Republic's gears to grind, we also must wait for a new appointment from His Holiness to represent the Empire."

"Here we are fortunate His Holiness believes in backup plans, Prof Di Vargas. Should everyone agree, I will take Father Dupuis' place. As his superior, the Vatican authorized me to take up his responsibilities and duties. Should we fail to agree, we will send a message to Rome asking the Holy Father to appoint someone else."

"Won't we be taking you away the parishes under your jurisdiction, Bishop Fabbri?"

"I serve no fixed jurisdiction, Dr. Banks. My duties are overseeing the various branches of the Order to make sure they are complying with the rules. The Vicar-General will appoint another to cover my responsibilities here in Europe if you decide to include me on the expedition."

Jeremiah glanced at Juan, who nodded. "Welcome to our team, Your Eminence," Jeremiah said.

"Please, my son, Father Fabbri will do. I fear we will trip over titles if we worry about all the Your Eminences and such once we arrive in the lands of the caliph."

They all shook hands. Jeremiah and Juan invited the bishop to stay and join them for a light supper. Mr. Garland returned to the consulate and reported back so the gears of government might begin their slow movement. Colum took instructions to the cooks preparing the meal and set an additional place at the table.

"I am something of a student of the past myself, and I would be honored to learn more about your discoveries."

Jeremiah led them all over to the table where research notes lay spread out on top of a map of the Middle East. The bishop noted two strange markers, one on each side of the Tigris-Euphrates Delta where the rivers met above the Persian Gulf. The names written on the map didn't mean anything to him. He pointed to the sites on the map.

"I never read of either of these places; are they modern cities?"

"No, Father. They're quite ancient. El-Isin and El-Kino are outposts of the city, which is the subject of our search. What we aren't certain of is if we are searching for the city under the name of Enoch or El-Abel." Jeremiah shook his head before taking pity on the bewildered bishop. "We are of different opinions based on conflicting source materials. Professor Di Vargas prefers Enoch, given the biblical sources. However, I prefer El-Abel based on the archeological evidence discovered by my team in El-Isin. The conflict arises because the Bible and El-Isinian tablets refer to the place as the City of Cain, hence our conundrum over the name."

Juan standing behind the Bishop grinned as his lover slipped into lecture mode. Now he understood why the three young students didn't complain about the mentorship of someone in a different field of archaeology. Granted, the topic tended to be confusing, but Jeremiah Banks simplified the narrative to meet his audience. His young archaeologist brought the bishop up to speed and the man now asked the proper questions. About the time Jeremiah was ramping up the level of discussion beyond a first-year student, Brother Colum arrived to announce dinner was ready in the dining room. The young monk couldn't help but get caught up in Dr. Banks' passion for his subject, but he couldn't be sure if it was his infatuation with the redhead or something deeper to the mystery the man sought to unravel.

Chapter 18

MACE AND THEO stood in their hotel room staring at each other wearing only their trousers. Emerald and Sapphire magic twined between the two young men. Theo swayed on his bare feet, still affected by the massive amount of alcohol consumed earlier in the evening.

"Are you sure this is the best way to sober me up, Mace?" Theo's accent was making his words hard to understand. "Hard enough to stand let alone pull magic."

"This forces you to concentrate, and drawing magic will speed the removal of alcohol from your bloodstream. The process is aided by you being a Sapphire witch. With my Emerald magic helping, you should be sober in a few more minutes."

"After what happened tonight, being drunk is an advantage."

"Quillion matched you drink for drink this evening, and she doesn't possess a controllable magic. I bet Dr. Banks can be sober in less than a heartbeat if he needs to be."

"H-he doesn't do magic," Theo's words slurred. "If he possessed magic, I doubt Miss Beaumont would have been rude to him."

"I think the doc is hiding mage-level talent. Fear is the reason why I kept it hidden and insisted you do the same thing when you arrived for school."

"I am a citizen of the Russian Empire; your little Republic wouldn't dare to drag me off to some secret laboratory."

"You're a student with no political connections back home, Theo. The Republic can make people vanish faster than a glass of vodka. They send a letter to the folks back home, in which they state the accompanying box contains the ashes of their loved one and explaining the tragic accident." Mace let the drawl he hated slip into his voice. "I will not lose another loved one."

Their magic snapped together and engulfed them as Theo reached out, pulling Mace into his embrace. Mace's confidence slipped away as Theo's lips captured his in a deep kiss. Mace didn't want to lose Theo. He vowed he wouldn't let anyone take him away, as they did to his uncle. He would fight with everything to keep Theo by this side. Mace lost himself in Theo's kiss but broke the connection when Theo slipped a hand into the back of his trousers to cup his ass.

"Not so fast my friend. I'm aware of the bond growing between us, but I'm not ready to go all the way while we're under the influence of alcohol. Let's clean up and go to bed. Dr. Banks and Prof. Di Vargas will likely give us work to do in the morning."

"You're right. I shouldn't push when you're not ready." Theo headed to the bathroom to try and finish sobering up with a hot shower. "Any aspirin around? I don't want to wake with a killer headache."

"In my kit, over on the counter," Mace called back as he rummaged for sleepwear.

"Are you saving this for a momentous occasion, *moye serdce*?" Theo leaned against the doorframe in his boxers, holding up a tube of lube. "You pack prepared, but shy away from following through. Does the idea of being on the receiving end frighten you?"

Mace blushed crimson at being caught. He tried to glare at Theo, but his blush made the Russian laugh at him and deepened his blush.

"I guess I didn't want to be the first to receive," Mace admitted. "I'm afraid of how painful getting fucked is reported to be."

Theo crossed the room and took Mace in his arms. He kissed him and ran his hands up and down Mace's back trying to ease his lover's fears.

"This is new for both of us, but if we go slow, neither of us needs to experience pain. To make you comfortable, you can make love to me first. You understand you're safe with me, Mace. I won't hurt you or let anyone hurt you."

"You do understand this goes both ways, Theo. I'll do everything in my power to make sure you're never hurt."

Rather than say anything, Theo kissed Mace, but broke off when his stomach revolted from all the alcohol consumed. He raced for the bathroom, and Mace listened to the sounds of violent retching. How sexy. He hoped it taught him to moderate how much he drank. The whole evening had become a nightmare. Mace hoped Quill was holding up. Though, he still couldn't believe Miss Beaumont and Father Dupuis were both dead. From the comments by the local police, their carriage had been reduced to splinters, but Mace found it strange they didn't experience an explosion. Could it have had something to do with the sudden pressure change? Did someone hit the coach with magic?

VAMPIRE INTERLUDE: PRIMORDIAL PLOTS

Bellabarisruk sat on his marble throne in the massive tomb, which served as his base of operations for countless millennia. His court gathered to pay him homage. A disturbance at the rear of the hall caught his attention as his agents dragged in two mortals, both suffering with severe injuries.

"I thought my orders clear were clear: don't harm the mortals! These mortals are finding breathing difficult. Why are my servants, incapable of capturing a pair of mortals?"

"My Lord, our ambush turned into an ambush. We came under attack by two parties, one of which consisted of a pair of ancient vampires of the fifth generation."

"I fail to comprehend who or what caused a half-dozen warriors to fail the simple task of destroying two fifth-generation vampires. You're all at least sixth generation and at minimum a thousand years old."

"Considering the speed, he moved at and the use of a long silver sword, we believe the other attacker to be Seth Adamson, a mortal who claims the title of Lord Hunter. When we went out, My Lord, our force numbered twenty. We're the only survivors."

"No mortal hunter is so skilled. All the information given to me since I awoke from languor leads me to conclude this Lord Hunter is the pathetic hunter who claimed he dispatched my grandsire Cain. Am I misinformed?"

"My Lord, you slept for a long time. The hunter you speak of is long dead. Richard St. Martin died while hunting the Barghest crone, Celina Dyta. The reports of his claim of killing Cain are but one rumor among many surrounding him."

"Go and finish what I sent you to do. Fix the woman, turn her, and let her feed on the priest."

Bellabarisruk rose from his throne and left the hall for his private quarters.

Chapter 19

Throughout dinner with Bishop Fabbri, Jeremiah remained in instructor mode. The teacher in him sought to avoid dealing with the impact of Miss Beaumont's death. Resentment filled him when thinking about the woman, her political connections back home, and how despite being dead, she still messed with his expedition. The previous Papal watchdog, Father Dupuis, he tolerated because the priest kept his questions to a minimum. The bishop insisted on poking his nose into aspects of his and Juan's research, though his education left him inadequate to understand. Perhaps Jeremiah would be lucky and the bishop would stay behind in Damascus with Juan rather than venture out into the desert. *Putain l'enfer Ce qu'est use mauvaise pensée*, Jeremiah cursed in thought. I hate the idea of leaving Juan behind in Damascus regardless of Brother Tobias staying behind to play bodyguard. The problem was once everyone was in Damascus the research diverges into two separate paths. Jeremiah snapped to attention when Juan spoke.

"I'm sorry, my mind wandered off on a tangent, Father Fabbri. What did you ask?" Jeremiah said.

"I inquired about the possibility of seeing these journal pages you both referenced," the bishop said.

Jeremiah and Juan exchanged glances across the table and almost in unison told the bishop no. They gave the man points, because he remained calm despite the rejection of his offer. Not long afterward, he made his goodbyes and left to return to the Order's headquarters. Juan led Jeremiah back into the study, closed the door behind them, and locked the doors. Jeremiah glanced at the bottle of port on the sideboard and decided to ignore the alcohol. He crossed to the wingback chairs and nestled into one of them. He waited while Juan settled himself.

"From the way the evening went, I expect to be summoned to the dean's office. I still can't believe the woman is dead, and the German priest thinks we're somehow involved," Jeremiah said, watching Juan set down his glass of port. "What do you make of Bishop Fabbri?"

"I think he's another spy trying to gain access to the journal pages, although I believe he works for the Cult of Cain," Juan said. "Did you spot Colum whispering something to him when he delivered the glass of wine?"

"No, I missed their exchange. Do you think Colum tried to receive orders or to pass a message on to his superior?"

"I believe he gave the bishop instructions from the head of their order. Remember Colum mentioned he reports straight to Cardinal Joan."

"Do you think Colum is interested in us, or is he pretending to be seduced so we grant him access to the journal pages?"

Juan surveyed his lover before taking a sip from his glass. He let the port sit on his tongue for a moment, then swallowed as he thought about Jeremiah's question. The professor studied the man and discovered a slight flush to Jeremiah's skin. He wanted the little monk. Juan wondered if Jeremiah wanted to fulfill a fantasy, or if something else drove his desire. Was Juan too old? Juan smiled as Jeremiah began to fidget like a schoolboy under his gaze.

"Why do you want Brother Colum, my love? Am I not enough for you?"

Jeremiah grinned at Juan. He rose from his chair and seated himself in Juan's lap before whispering in his ear, "Don't tell me you never wanted to corrupt a man of the cloth? True, he won't be breaking a vow of chastity, but the naughty little fantasy runs through my brain." Jeremiah let his breath tease Juan's ear for a moment. "And for the record, you're perfect for me."

To prove his words, Jeremiah locked Juan into a kiss, which went from a tease to a full lip lock with dueling tongues. The redhead ground his ass against Juan's crotch until the man hardened beneath him. In a moment, Juan seized control of their session, and Jeremiah found himself on his back on the floor with Juan's weight pinning him to the oriental carpet. Hard cocks rubbed against each other through the barriers of their trousers. Jeremiah reached to slip his hands beneath Juan's jacket, but the older man caught his wrists and locked his hands above his head. Juan lifted himself up enough to break their kiss and lock eyes with Jeremiah. Lust, love, and desire blew out Jeremiah's pupils so only the faintest trace of the bright sapphire irises remained. His lips swelled from their kisses, and a soft whimper escaped his throat at the break in their kissing. Jeremiah's hips bucked against Juan's when the man stopped grinding their cocks together.

"Go to our bedroom and prepare yourself for me, beautiful boy, while I tell Brother Colum to secure the house for the evening before he joins us."

Jeremiah shivered with lust at the thought of the young monk joining in their play tonight. He snatched a brief kiss as he rose from the floor.

"Thank you, sir. Please don't be long." Jeremiah left the study.

Jeremiah's step possessed their missing bounce as he went to the bedroom he shared with Juan. Once inside the room, he undressed and hung his suit in the closet. He placed his shirt, undershirt, socks, and boxers in the laundry hamper before entering the en suite bathroom to clean and prepare for Juan's arrival. When he was clean inside and out, he padded back into the bedroom and knelt beside the bed, head bowed and hands behind his back.

* * *

JUAN FOUND Brother Colum on his way back to his room in the servants' quarters. The young monk turned at the sound of footsteps behind him. The expressionless face didn't give anything away, but his body radiated the tenseness of someone prepared to attack. The sight of Juan standing in the hallway helped him relax a bit.

"How may I be of service, Prof. Di Vargas?"

Juan closed the distance between them and lifted Colum's chin so the monk was gazing into his eyes.

"Time to fulfill two fantasies at once. For you, Colum, a chance to explore a true redhead and for Jeremiah, a chance to pretend he's corrupting a member of the cloth."

"What about you, sir?" Colum' voice was a bare whisper. "What fantasy will be fulfilled for you?"

"No fantasy fulfillment for me, little monk. I wish Jeremiah to be happy. Prove to me you're worthy of a place in both our hearts and as something besides a sexual plaything."

"I seek to be worthy of your hearts, sir."

"Secure the house before you come and join us in my bedroom. And, Colum, understand if you break his heart, I'll never forgive you."

"I understand, sir."

"Jeremiah is extraordinary because his heart possesses the capacity to love on many levels." Juan headed upstairs to the bedroom he shared with Jeremiah.

Colum checked every door and window before making his way up to join the men he discovered he was falling in love with. He knocked on the door and Juan's gruff voice called for him to enter. Stepping past the door, he gasped at the sight of the good-looking redheaded man on his knees worshiping the thick cock of his older lover. Jeremiah's pale skin gleamed in the candlelight, which lit the room. Colum bit back a moan as Jeremiah dragged his lips back along the length of Juan's cock, which was not only thick but long as well. The young monk marveled at the difference between Jeremiah's pale skin and Juan's darker flesh. He stood transfixed as Jeremiah rose from his knees at a mere gesture from Juan, bringing his copper-haired pubic region into view along with the impressive cock and balls.

Juan turned around and stepped behind Jeremiah so Colum possessed an unobstructed view of the red-furred, pale body. The young monk stood frozen a few feet inside the room. The Spaniard whispered something in Jeremiah's ear and, after leaning back for a quick kiss, Jeremiah approached. Colum trembled as the naked man moved towards him. This experience happened as though he stood outside his own body as Jeremiah touched his cheek with his calloused hand. The hand slid around behind his head and pulled him close for a kiss. Emotional fireworks exploded at the touch of Jeremiah's soft lips against his own. Colum started to faint. The monk sagged into the other man's strong arms.

"Little monk, is everything all right?" the magnificent baritone voice deepened in concern. "Did we move too fast?"

"I'll be all right, Dr. Banks. I want to please you both, but I'm afraid of disappointing you."

"For all the bravado, you're a virgin, aren't you, little monk?" The redhead led Colum over to the bed. "You never expected an invitation for you to join us."

"I'm not sure what I thought or if I was thinking. Something drew me to both of you from the moment I met each of you. I should forget about this and go."

Jeremiah held him fast, keeping Colum in place on the bed.

"Juan can be intimidating, and I'm betting his jealous side gave some dire warnings about not breaking my heart tonight." Jeremiah peered over Colum's bowed head to his lover. "Am I right?"

Colum nodded and curled into Jeremiah's chest. Jeremiah slipped the hood of Colum's cassock off his head to reveal the beautiful golden hair beneath. A small shaven circle at the crown of Colum's head gave the only indication of the youth's membership in holy orders. Jeremiah placed a kiss on the tonsure as he ran his hands over Colum's back and arms.

"Well, Juan, how should we proceed?"

"I think we both need to cuddle with our young friend here until he's comfortable with both of us." Juan spoke to his lover, before addressing Colum. "I'm sorry I came off as so gruff, Colum. I never expected Jeremiah would want to add a third to our relationship so early. I let my jealousy interfere."

"I'm the one who should apologize for intruding on this relationship. You two don't spend much time together, and I'm getting in the way." Colum was sobbing against Jeremiah.

"Nonsense, Colum. I'm the one who asked Juan to include you for a selfish reason. I didn't consider your feelings and obligations before making you uncomfortable."

"I want to be here with both of you." Colum glanced up with tear-streaked emerald eyes. "But this is wrong, and I'm breaking my vow and orders from Her Excellency. Please let me go."

Colum shrugged his way loose from Jeremiah's warm embrace and adjusted his cassock. He considered both Jeremiah and Juan one last time before fleeing the room, tears pouring down his face. Jeremiah started to rise to go after the young monk, but Juan stopped him. Tears flowed down his own face as Juan pulled him tight against him.

"Let him go so he can figure out what he wants for himself, my love. Believe me, I understand how you hold him in your loving heart, and I don't begrudge you because I did the same. Should he change his mind, we'll keep a place for him in our hearts and in our home," Juan said.

Jeremiah turned so he was facing Juan and buried his face in his lover's chest. He let Juan wrap him in his strong arms and lead him back towards the bed. Their evening of wild and kinky sex forgotten, Jeremiah clung tight to Juan for a moment longer before dropping to his knees in total submission to the older man.

"Forgive me, sir, I ruined the evening's pleasure. I should be punished." Jeremiah's dejected voice tore at Juan's heart. "Should you not want me in your bed anymore, I understand and accept, but I hope we can continue our professional relationship."

Juan dropped to his knees in front of Jeremiah and lifted his lover's face to lock gazes with him. The beautiful sapphire eyes stood out red-rimmed against the blotchy mess of his pale skin. Sorrow took a toll on Jeremiah's appearance. He brushed away the tears and stroked the younger man's face. Juan drew Jeremiah in and brushed a light kiss across his lips.

"Jeremiah, I don't think this sir-boy routine is what we want our actual relationship to be. We can keep role play in reserve for the occasional night, but I prefer a more romantic relationship." Juan brushed another kiss across Jeremiah's lips. "What I want is the strong capable man I met in Atlanta."

"A romantic relationship is what I want, too. While I do like submitting on occasion, you're right. A Dom-sub relationship isn't what we need full time." Jeremiah reached out and pulled Juan down for another kiss. "What I want is for you to make love to me, reclaim all my heart for yourself."

Juan stood and drew Jeremiah up after him. He turned Jeremiah so his back pressed against Juan's chest before turning them to face the full-length mirror. Juan nuzzled into Jeremiah's neck while letting his hands roam over the hard, defined body before him. Jeremiah began to relax and his head drifted back to rest on Juan's shoulder.

"My beautiful one, I want your attention on us while I make love to this incredible body. Focus on the interplay between our bodies, but float on the experience," Juan whispered in Jeremiah's ear.

Jeremiah shivered as Juan's words caressed his skin of his neck. He forced himself to experience the sensations as Juan's hands wandered from his shoulders down across his chest to cup his pectorals and tease his nipples. Jeremiah moaned as Juan's fingers closed on and tugged the sensitive buds capping his pectorals. He leaned his head to the right as Juan's mouth laid claim to his neck. Juan's tongue licked its way up from his collarbone to a spot behind his ear. The spot happened to be one of the most sensitive of his erogenous zones. Jeremiah shivered as he remembered Juan's first exploration of his body and the man's discovery of all the spots, which made him tick.

Juan didn't forget any of them, Jeremiah discovered to his delight. His dark hands played across Jeremiah's pale body and through the copper hair covering most of his chest, teasing all the places above the waist and setting Jeremiah ablaze. His massive cock rose to the thick full length, the foreskin retracting on its own. Pre-cum moistened the exposed head of his prick before Juan's hands wandered down to cup his sack and caressed the length from base to tip. The movements smeared the moisture back down the shaft as Juan's hand moved back down to the base. Behind him, the rigid length of Juan's cock pressed into the crack of his ass. Jeremiah reached his hands back to grip Juan's firm ass and pull his lover closer to him, rubbing his ass against Juan's cock and using his lover's pre-cum to moisten his crack.

Juan's moan joined Jeremiah's moans, as his lover became an active part of their lovemaking. Jeremiah twisted, breaking free of Juan's grip, and locked their lips together as his hand slipped down to grasp his lover's dark cock. Jeremiah drew back when their kiss broke. For a moment, their gazes followed the other's hand stroking their cock. Jeremiah pulled Juan back towards the bed until the back of his knees hit the frame of the bed. He let himself collapse on the bed, pulling Juan down on top of him. His lover's cock slid across his hole as Juan settled his weight to pin him to the bed. They resumed their kissing and stroking each other's bodies, raising their passions higher and higher.

"I want you inside me. I need you to reclaim me, Juan. Please fuck me now."

"I love hearing you beg, my beautiful one," Juan's husky voice whispered.

Juan reached over to the nightstand and retrieved the lube with one hand while stroking Jeremiah's thick cock with the other. With a brief popping sound, he flipped the lid of the tube open. He squirted some into the crack of Jeremiah's ass and let his fingers sweep up from below to catch the lube. Juan teased his lover's hole open with a gentle working of his fingers in and out of his partner's ass. Juan focused on stretching Jeremiah opening and massaging his prostrate. Soon the redhead lost all powers of speech. His whimpers and moans, along with the flood of precum pouring from the slit of his cock, told Juan to sheathe his cock in Jeremiah's ass. The Spaniard lifted his lover's sturdy legs up on his shoulders, pressed the head of his cock against the opening to Jeremiah's ass, and pushed in, plunging deep. Jeremiah cried out in mixed pleasure and pain as Juan buried his thick cock balls deep in his ass on the first thrust.

"Oh God, how I need this. Fuck me, Juan. Make me yours forever."

Juan leaned forward to kiss Jeremiah, pushing his lover's legs back toward his chest, lifting the redhead's hips so Juan's meaty cockhead hit Jeremiah's magic spot again and again. The pace increased as Juan fucked Jeremiah until his thick cock flexed and erupted without being touched, bathing the gorgeous copper fur of his chest with his load. Jeremiah's ass clenched tight around Juan's cock, milking his load from his balls to paint the inside of Jeremiah's guts. They stayed locked together until Juan's cock deflated and slipped from Jeremiah's ass.

Jeremiah kissed Juan once more before using his superior strength to roll his lover off him and on the bed. Once out from underneath his lover, he rose and went into the bathroom to clean up. He planned to wet a cloth to clean Juan. He found his lover standing behind him while waiting for the water to warm. Juan's muscular and hairy arms wrapped around him, drawing him back against his lover's chest. He relaxed against Juan, basking in the man's love. This man was incredible. Despite the physical distance, he kept them together after the conference where they met. From the moment, Jeremiah set eyes on Juan again their time apart vanished. Jeremiah knew he was safe in Juan's arms because Juan loved him. Jeremiah turned in Juan's embrace and stared straight into his lover's eyes.

"I love you, Juan."

Juan's dark eyes widened at Jeremiah's declaration but softened as his pupils expanded in renewed lust for the good-looking man in his arms.

"I love you too, Jeremiah." Juan drew him into another kiss.

When they stopped kissing, Jeremiah scrutinized the giant tub, and a wicked gleam lit up his sapphire eyes. He slipped from Juan's embrace and set the bath to filling, adding in a foaming gel. Taking the lead this time, he drew Juan into the tub with him. Jeremiah settled into the water first and drew Juan down between his legs so his back rested on Jeremiah's chest with his head on his shoulder. He let his hands run from the water level up Juan's chest, running his hand up and through the mixture of charcoal and gunmetal hair on his lover's chest. His caress became firmer and more like a massage as Juan relaxed against him and let the warm water soothe them both.

* * *

DOWN IN THE SERVANTS' wing of the house, Brother Colum was in his room on his knees praying to both Cain and God, begging for guidance. His cassock was shrugged off his shoulders and hanging from his waist as he worked a heavy leather flogger against his back as tears flowed.

"Forgive me, Ancient Cain and Holy Father, for my sins are many. I allowed myself to follow my heart into temptation. I vowed to my superiors not to interfere with the relationship of my charges, but my heart draws me to them. Guide me back to the path I should walk. Harden my heart so the pain of love, which cannot be mine, may not burden me. Please take from me this desire to love these men whose hearts belongs to each other. Send me a sign I am still in your favor."

Colum set down the flogger on the little altar table he'd established and kissed his blood-red cross before rising and stripping off his cassock to reveal his well-honed body. He was all lean muscle; training scars crisscrossed his arms and legs. His uncircumcised cock stood at rigid attention, the hood drawn back revealing the dripping head, as he stood naked in the center of his room. Hazel eyes red-rimmed and bloodshot from his crying, the monk tried to ignore his hard cock. Despite his efforts to push the memory of Jeremiah's gentle embrace and Juan's rough voice out of his mind, he found himself fantasizing about giving into his desires.

The monk was desperate for both men to make love to him. Colum took his hard cock in his hand and began to stroke himself while dreaming of being in their bed. He wondered what textures he would experience running his fingers through the hair on their chests. He imagined Juan's hair was soft and silky, while Jeremiah's was wiry and coarse. Jeremiah's hands were so gentle and still firm. He suspected Jeremiah caressed a lover with a gentle coaxing towards orgasm, while Juan might stroke a lover in a demanding manner, controlling when they spent. Would they fuck him at the same time, pass him back and forth, or stuff him from both ends? The memory of Jeremiah's lips on his drove Colum to orgasm. When he came down from his orgasm, Colum cleaned up his mess and sponged down his body before curling into a ball on his little cot and crying himself to sleep.

Chapter 20

A FEW DAYS LATER, Brothers Colum and Tobias directed the loading of their charges aboard the ship, which would carry them to the port of Tel Aviv in Greater Israel. In Tel Aviv, the expedition would transfer to a train to travel to Damascus. They would await final permission from the caliph's government before loading equipment on half-track cargo haulers. Once everyone boarded and with the equipment loaded, Tobias headed up to the ship's command deck and gave the captain his orders. With everyone else occupied, Colum slipped below to the cargo hold and began searching for anything out of the ordinary. In the far corner of the hold, well away from the reach of sunlight, he found three figures in cloaks, two stretched out appearing to be asleep. The third vanished before Colum tracked his movements.

"Who are you, little monk?" came a voice from behind.

Colum stilled as the tip of a sword touched his back. Given the man's speed, Colum feared not being able to move fast enough to avoid a fatal or disabling blow from the weapon.

"I'm Brother Colum of the Order of St. Hubert, assigned as an aide to Bishop Fabbri on the expedition of Prof. Di Vargas and Dr. Banks."

"I sense more to you, Brother Colum. You bare a talisman of power. I think you serve someone other than the hunter saint. Yes, I recognize the scent. You bear a scarlet cross somewhere on your person, which contains a drop of my blood within a small vial hidden in the back of the cross."

"Lord Slayer?"

"Not today, little monk. I'm on a hunt myself. Lord Hunter is how you should address me." Richard moved around to face Colum.

"Lord Hunter, are you my sign from Ancient Cain and God? Command me, I am your servant." Colum dropped to the floor of the hold to kneel before Richard.

"Stand up, little monk. What is your rank within Cain's cult?"

"I am both a knight-protector and a knight-hunter, Lord Hunter, in direct service to Her Unholiness Cardinal Joan IX."

"Two others of the Cult are aboard this vessel. I will assume the other monk holds a rank similar to yours. What of the other?"

"His Excellency, Bishop Fabbri's actual position is Seneschal of the Order of St. Hubert, but he is claiming to be Master and Commander of the Regional Spanish Commandery of the Order. He is a Judicial Vicar of the Cult of Cain."

"Interesting how one of the Cult is so high in the Order. I wonder what the Holy Father in Rome would do if someone told him they only need a few words to turn his little holy army against him." Richard spoke, thinking out loud. "Give me the cross, Brother Colum."

Colum reached inside his robes and pulled out a cross made of jasper, which he kissed before handing the relic over to Richard. The man popped the lock on the back and revealed the hidden vial with its holy drop of blood within. Richard slipped the bottle out of the cross and handed the cross back to Colum. He uncapped the bottle and sniffed the contents. The scent of his blood rose from the vial. He let his fangs descend and bit his own wrist. Black shining blood welled up from the wound, and Richard let enough drip into almost fill the vial, leaving only enough room for the cap to go back on. He recapped the bottle and handed the whole thing back to a stunned Colum.

"From today, Brother Colum, you serve me," Richard said after sealing his wound with a lick of his tongue.

"Are you ordained?"

"No, Lord Hunter. I did not experience a calling toward the ordained priesthood."

"Well, you are now called to my priesthood. When you can slip away from your duties, come here in the evening hours and my associates, or I will train you in your new responsibilities, Vicar Colum."

"I live to serve, Lord Hunter."

"You will defend Dr. Banks and Prof. Di Vargas with your life, little monk."

"I'm not worthy of such a task, My Lord. My heart conflicts between duty and desire where they are concerned."

"You desire to be their lover. I assume you're under orders or took a vow not to become involved in their relationship." Richard's tone was more statement than a question.

"I made such a vow, but now my heart is in conflict with my mind." Colum was almost in tears.

"Should I choose another, Vicar Colum, or can you adhere to my commands?"

"Command me, Lord Hunter." Colum glanced into the dark blue eyes staring down at him.

"Guard them with your life. Let nothing separate you from them. We will give you additional clues you can slip them during the dig, which will lead to El-Abel. When you go back on deck, suggest to Brother Tobias he come down here so I may judge him for myself. I have an assignment of equal importance for him."

"All will be as you command, Lord Hunter."

THE JOURNAL OF CAIN

"Behold, the beloved son, and brother, cursed so the Lord, your God might reign supreme. I do not understand what I am, but I demand my brother suffer for what he wrought upon me."

And Adam raised his hand swathed in divine Gold magic. Thus, Adam spoke unto the thing, which was once his son, saying, "For thou art cursed beyond any man. In the name of God who gave me life, I banish thee from these lands never to walk in these hills until the end of days."

Therefore, did Adam's magic flashed over the accursed and blasted him out of the holy valley. Burned, the lost son of Adam rose and faced the entrance to the valley. The lost one cursed his brother's future, saying, "This is my promise to the surviving son of Adam, so long as thou dwell in the valley of Our Father, thou art safe. Cross into the world of men and thy life is forfeit. I am thy brother no longer for by thy treachery did I become the Master of Darkness. Fear my wrath for I will come to thee before the end of days."

Gospel of Cain 8:20-30

* * *

I included the following passages of Cain's introspective in this journal, because he went on about some of his powers and weaknesses. I have to guess that another power heard my plea as the Curse claimed me, for I do not share most of the limits Cain had.

Richard St. Martin

* * *

June 2, 1995

When I turned to leave, a bolt tipped with silver struck me in the arm. The pain was intense, and my arm started to wither before the healing effect of the life force I'd recently consumed repaired the damage. An important lesson learned. Silver could harm me. Today was a day of discovery. I ran before my brother decided to use his Silver magic, and found I moved faster than anyone did. Soon I reached the hills far from the villages I once tended as a healer. I took up residence in a cave overlooking the villages and began to test the limits of my new abilities. I fed on cattle when the hunger took me. After a time, 1 mastered sensing the rising beast of hunger within me and to slake the thirst before being overwhelmed. Once, I discovered the limits of my speed and strength, I turned to mastering the new magic within me.

To master the twisted magic took many years. The years of trial and error led to many discoveries. The new magic allows me to shape change, become mist, blend with shadow, merge with the earth, and control the minds of mortals. My skin burns in the light of the sun, forcing me to move at night.

Should I attempt to cross pure, running water, I find myself blocked. Stir up silt and I can cross. I cannot enter a religious building when a true believer attends. A person with faith will prevent me from entering a dwelling unless I receive an invitation. Wood numbs whatever part of my body is pierced; silver causes my body to desiccate because of its relationship to the magic of my creation, and I cannot abide the touch of gold. This is only a guess, but I surmise a weapon of silver or gold piercing my heart or taking my head will dispatch me. I worry I cannot die a final death or perhaps I fear what will happen to the one who succeeds in killing me. The curse is a living thing, which will pass to the one who slays me.

PART III

Greater Israel and the Caliphate of Baghdad

Chapter 21

DR. JEREMIAH BANKS paced the balcony of his hotel suite in Damascus. His party arrived in Greater Israel a week ago, and all their equipment sat in a storage facility as they waited for the caliph's governmental representative to make an appearance. Juan spent much of his time away from the suite, either urging Bishop Fabbri to keep visiting the caliphate's consulate or visiting the library of Damascus. Jeremiah's angry frustration drove Juan into avoiding him. Brother Colum acted distant and formal with them since the disastrous invitation to be part of their relationship; Theo, Mace, and Quillion only dealt with him when they all met for dinner.

The city of El-Abel taunted Jeremiah because he couldn't go out into the field and do actual field work. Why did everyone insist on preventing him from engaging in the challenge the city presented? Being cooped up in the hotel drove him mad, and no one back home answered his telegrams urging a replacement for the late Miss Eunice Beaumont. They told him to remain in Damascus, refusing to grant him the diplomatic status to deal with the caliphate's agents as he'd had on the previous expedition. A knock on the door to his suite stopped

Jeremiah's pacing. Halfway across the room the door exploded open, and three men in desert attire burst into the chamber, wicked-looking knives in their hands.

"Time to die, infidel," the leader shouted. "You will not desecrate our lands."

Survival instinct took over, and Jeremiah shouted and lashed out with Sapphire magic. He flung a blast of ice daggers at his attackers. The men possessed an unnatural speed, allowing two of them to dodge the wicked ice blades. The third took one dagger to the shoulder and another on the side, but bit back his scream of pain to join the attack. The explosion and Jeremiah's shout brought both Colum and Tobias from the next suite. Tobias stumbled, caught unaware as Jeremiah raised a shield of ice to fend off the blade of his nearest attacker. Colum ignored Jeremiah and launched himself into the injured attacker, bringing him to the floor and driving the man's own dagger into his chest. With a brief glance, Colum spotted the man's red palm.

"By Cain and the Lord Slayer, stop. Dr. Banks is the man you're supposed to be assigned to protect."

The second attacker whirled back to face Colum and Tobias, his curved blade gleaming in the light. Colum and Tobias met him barehanded in a fighter's crouches. Behind him, the first attacker continued his assault on Jeremiah's defenses.

"Our orders are to prevent him from exposing El-Abel to the world. The secrets of Father Cain must be maintained," the assassin said.

"Who issued those commands?" Tobias demanded.

"The Imam Abd-el-Basir gave us our instructions."

A quick glance passed between Colum and Tobias, ending any further discussion and launching them both forward in a blistering whirlwind of striking hands and feet. The attacker went down. Jeremiah screamed in pain as a dagger found an opening. Colum delivered a swift leg strike, shattering his opponent's knee, matched by Tobias catching and breaking the man's knife-wielding arm. Tobias swiped the curved blade from the man's numb fingers and across his throat, while Colum launched himself at the man attacking Jeremiah. Colum caught the edge of the blast of ice, which tore through Jeremiah's attacker's chest. Tobias stepped past both Colum and the fallen attacker to grab up Dr. Banks. Stronger than his small, lithe form would suggest, Tobias cradled Dr. Banks and whisked him from the suite. He raced down the hall to the room his male charges occupied and kicked the door. Theo whipped the door open to find the young monk holding a bleeding Dr. Banks in his arms. Tobias tossed Jeremiah into Theo's arms, before whirling to race back down the hall.

"He needs medical attention. A stab wound in the right shoulder."

The monk vanished back into Dr. Banks' room as Theo called for Mace to find Quillion and the first aid kit. Tobias reentered Dr. Banks' suite to find Colum sitting up amid the wreckage and the bodies. Puddles formed where Dr. Banks' ice melted. Water soaked one side of Colum's robe. Tobias took in the condition of the room and realized they couldn't hide everything from the authorities. He contemplated his fellow cultist and wondered why he didn't tell him about Dr. Banks being a mage. Colum always shared relevant information with him before. He pushed questions about his friend and fellow cultist aside.

"We need to dispose of this man's body before the authorizes arrive. We lack an explanation for the hole in his chest," Tobias said.

"Let's use the empty crate in Jeremiah's sitting room. We can stuff the body in the crate and dump everything in the back alley." Colum didn't realize his slip in using Dr. Banks' first name. "We'll deal with the final disposal of body after the authorities are dealt with."

"When this is over, you and I need to talk Brother Colum," Tobias said.

Colum focused on his fellow cultist for a moment, perplexed by his comment before realizing Jeremiah used magic in front of others when his file said he didn't possess magic. This whole situation was a disaster, Colum thought. He had called Dr. Banks by his given name while talking with Tobias. Damn, now Tobias would report him to Her Excellency, and she'd remove him from this assignment. Now he'd never be near Jeremiah or Juan again. Colum knew he couldn't let his superiors remove him from this assignment. The real question here was why the members of the Brotherhood were carrying out orders to attack and kill Dr. Banks. Colum pulled himself from his thoughts and returned his focus to Tobias and their situation.

"We'll talk when this is done. Let's dispose of this one before the authorities arrive," Colum said.

Together, they entered Dr. Banks' sitting room and found the empty crate. Colum figured the man used the box to help try and focus his energies. He spent an afternoon watching Jere...Dr. Banks pretending to pack artifacts into the crate. The repetition served as part of a mental exercise, and he suspected a way for the archaeologist to forget Colum's presence in the room. The young monk couldn't blame the archaeologist for treating him as part of the furniture. He would focus on protecting them and not how much he yearned for them to take him in their arms. He shook his head when he caught Tobias staring at him. Colum slammed away his rambling thoughts and focused on the task, grabbing half of the crate as Tobias picked up his side. Together, they carried the box out into the central room of the suite and dumped the body of the assassin into the crate. The mystery remained as to why their Islamic counterparts from the Brotherhood of the Crimson Hand received directions to kill Dr. Banks. Colum double-checked the crate to make sure nothing remained to tie the corpse back to the expedition before the two cultists carried the box across the hall to their suite and crammed everything into the bathroom. They crossed back to Dr. Banks' suite in time to intercept the man and his students before they entered. Colum noted Mace helping the pallid form of Dr. Banks upright. Jeremiah's shirt was half gone, and a huge bandage swathed the man's shoulder. He needed to sit and let a real doctor check his wound. Tobias took charge before Colum spoke.

"Better for everyone, Dr. Banks, if you and your students didn't enter the room. The authorities must be summoned, and this scene's hard to explain with all the water around the room and nothing to explain why."

"I can remove the water, Brother Tobias," Jeremiah said.

"Doc, you're in no shape to work magic. Let me clean this mess," Theo said.

Jeremiah noted how thick Theo's Russian accent was, revealing the young man's nervous state. Theo stepped forward, caught sight of the bodies and the destruction within, and blanched. Mace shifted his grip on Dr. Banks and reached toward Theo, but his friend was beyond his grasp. Theo straightened his shoulders and raised his hands. He whispered in Russian, and a dull blue glow surrounded him before flowing outwards to collect the moisture in the room. Theo continued chanting, directing the water to flow outwards toward the balcony to pour into the gutters and drain away. The cleanup finished a moment before a voice called out in Hebrew, telling them to stay put. Jeremiah turned his head to find members of Damascus' police force coming down the hallway. He tried to pull away from Mace to stand on his own, but the grad student wouldn't let go of him.

"Stay put, Doc. Too much movement and you'll start bleeding again," Mace whispered.

"We received reports of an explosion and a fight on this floor. Who are you people?" the lead officer asked in Hebrew. "Who is in charge here?"

"I'm Dr. Jeremiah Banks from the Republic of Texas, and I'm in charge of this group. I'm also the person who was attacked by armed assassins," Jeremiah fired back in rapid Hebrew. "For the benefit of my students and these two monks, do any of you speak English or Spanish?"

"I speak English, Dr. Banks. Your Hebrew is excellent by the way."

"Thank you, Officer...?" Jeremiah started to address the man. "I'm sorry I didn't learn your name, and I need to sit."

"My apologies, Dr. Banks, for failing to note your injuries. Let me send a man to find a medic while we wait for the crime scene unit to arrive. We can find a room close by so you can sit."

"Our room is a few doors down the hall. The first aid kit is out from trying to stop Dr. Banks' bleeding," Theo said. The young Ukrainian took charge as he came to support Jeremiah, who sagged despite Mace's assistance. "We're down here."

Theo and Mace carried Dr. Banks between them back to their suite. They settled him into a chair, and Quillion checked his bandages to make sure they kept the pressure on the wound to stop the bleeding. Mace stayed by Dr. Banks after Quillion moved away as the officer addressed their teacher.

"First off, Dr. Banks, allow me to introduce myself. I'm Sub-Inspector Yonatan Pensak of the Israeli Police. I lead this investigation for now. These officers are taking your associates aside for questioning while I interview you."

"Understandable, Sub-Inspector. For the record, let me remind you I'm the only one of those present who speaks Hebrew."

"Are any other members of your party not present, Dr. Banks?"

"Yes, my co-leader, Prof. Juan Di Vargas, and Bishop Fabrizio Fabbri, our envoy from the Holy Father in Rome."

The sub-inspector issued orders to his men, and they each escorted one of the other party members out of the room for separate interviews. He returned his attention to Jeremiah.

"Dr. Banks, I thought you said you came from the Republic of Texas," Pensak said.

"I did, as did my grad students. This is a joint archaeological expedition funded by the Republic of Texas and the Holy Roman Empire. I can't direct you to the Republic's envoy, as she died in an accident in Spain on the way here. The Republic hasn't replied to my requests for a new one or to appoint me to the position," Jeremiah said.

"Would you like someone from the Republic's consulate to be present during questioning, Dr. Banks?"

"Perhaps such representation would be wise, Sub-Inspector. I don't want to hamper your investigation, but this expedition is under government oversight, and since His Excellency isn't available to provide at least Rome's protection, I prefer counsel from the Republic be available to my students. I ask you to halt your questioning until the bishop returns or a representative of the Republic arrives to cover our legal rights. You may investigate the crime scene and perhaps be kind enough as to ask the hotel manager to find me a new suite of rooms."

"Of course, Dr. Banks. Give me a moment for my men to end their questioning."

Chapter 22

Professor Di Vargas and Bishop Fabbri arrived back at the hotel before Sub-Inspector Pensak, and his men began questioning Jeremiah and the rest of the party. The bishop held a folder of papers from the Republic of Texas' consulate. He pulled the sub-inspector aside and their conversation started escalating into an argument until Dr. Banks interrupted the heated Hebrew with a plea in English.

"Excellency, Sub-Inspector, bickering over jurisdiction between the Israeli Police and the Order won't move us along. I'm a citizen of the Republic of Texas, as are Mr. Puap and Ms. Post, while Mr. Polzin is a national of the Russian Empire under my authority as his graduate advisor. Given I am the victim of this attack, and since this is Israeli territory, I suggest you let Sub-Inspector Pensak and his men handle the investigation."

"You're not an average citizen of the Republic, Dr. Banks. If His Excellency would be so kind as to turn over the portfolio, you'll find the Republic named you envoy and ambassador-at-large."

Juan took the folder from the bishop and handed the documents to Jeremiah, who glanced through the paperwork contained within. He frowned before closing the folder. Looking up at the sub-inspector, he drew himself up as best as possible with his wounds.

"I'm sorry, Sub-Inspector Pensak, but I must ask you and your men to depart and leave behind all the evidence gathered, as well as statements and notes taken. As the Republic's ambassador, this suite is my embassy and therefore the sovereign territory of the Republic of Texas and off-limits to local police."

"Please show me your documents, Dr. Banks."

"Of course, Sub-Inspector Pensak." Jeremiah turned over the portfolio. "You will find all the documents in order, appointing me an ambassador-at-large on behalf of the Republic of Texas and the president's personal envoy to His Islamic Majesty, the Caliph of Baghdad."

"My apologies, Ambassador Banks, my men shall withdraw and turn over to you all the items requested for the security of the Republic of Texas to deal with. If we may be of any assistance in their investigation, Ambassador, please contact me." Pensak handed over his business card.

"Thank you, Sub-Inspector. I'm sorry to inconvenience your men this way."

"No apologies are necessary, Ambassador Banks."

When the Israeli policemen left, Jeremiah sank down into his chair and passed out. Mace and Theo moved to his side to check on him.

"Your Excellency, would you come with me to assist in asking the hotel manager to fetch a doctor? I'm afraid my Hebrew isn't up to the task." Quillion drew the bishop from the room.

"Oh, of course, my dear. I don't do well around the sight of blood." Fabbri allowed Quillion to lead him out of the suite.

"We should deal with our other problem while Mace, Theo, and Prof. Di Vargas tend to Dr. Banks," Colum said to Brother Tobias. "We can talk about other matters while we clean up the debris."

Tobias nodded and followed Colum in silence from Dr. Banks' suite to theirs. Once in their suite, Tobias rounded on his fellow cultist.

"You violated your vow to Her Eminence. You vowed no involvement in whatever relationship Dr. Banks and Prof. Di Vargas share. You're involved with at least Dr. Banks on more than a professional level," Tobias gave a blunt assessment. "I don't understand how you kept this from her so long, but you need to end your involvement, or I will be forced to report your failure to Her."

"I ended any chance of things becoming physical. I can't help what is still in my heart. I perform the penance laid on me for my sins by guarding them both. Did you ever go down into the cargo hold while we sailed from Valencia to Tel Aviv?"

"No, and I can't fathom why going down to the hold would matter. You're hiding valuable information from Cardinal Joan. How long did you hide the information about Dr. Banks' magic?"

"I learned about his magic the morning after Miss Beaumont and Father Dupuis 'accident.' I know the Cult failed in its mission to eliminate the threat they posed," Colum snapped. "For the record, Her Eminence received the information about Dr. Banks' magic with his permission in my report."

"How did you work out the Cult didn't kill Miss Beaumont and Father Dupuis?"

"If you went to the cargo hold like I told you to and spoken with him, you wouldn't need to ask. He stayed, along with his companions the Barghest and the Bel-Kino."

"I still don't believe he traveled as a stowaway on our ship or he spoke with you."

"He did more than talk to me, Tobias." Colum took his red cross out from beneath his robes. "He and his companions trained me to take my unholy vows, to serve him as a priest. He also did this."

Colum opened the back of his cross and removed the full vial from the back. Tobias' jaw fell open in awe as he gazed on the full bottle of the holiest substance as far as the Cult of Cain was concerned. The full vial of the Lord of all Vampires' blood was the only thing that convinced Tobias Colum was telling the truth. No cultist would disturb the contents of the vial inside their cross.

"I'm sorry I doubted you, my brother." Tobias dropped to his knees before Colum. "You are blessed by the Lord Slayer. How may I serve you?"

"My blessing comes from Lord Hunter, for he said he was on the hunt when he took me into his direct service and made me a Vicar-trainee. We need to act as though nothing changed between us, my brother. His Unholiness doesn't trust Bishop Fabbri's loyalty to the Cult given his real status within the Order. You must continue to make our reports to Her Eminence, but she mustn't find out he's involved or how I'm no longer hers to command. Dr. Banks and Professor Di Vargas must be our total focus, by his order."

"I'm yours to command, brother."

"Stay with Prof. Di Vargas when we split up. I will be part of Dr. Banks' expedition into the desert, though I pass beyond the border between Cult and Brotherhood. The professor shouldn't draw as much attention as Dr. Banks, but since the Brotherhood faces divided loyalty, keep him under observation. Do not trust the bishop out of your sight. Ask Her Eminence for assistance."

"What about you? You'll be out in the desert alone where the Brotherhood holds the advantage."

"As we've seen, Dr. Banks isn't defenseless. Theo holds the same power, if not as high, and I suspect Mace is hiding similar secrets, although not Sapphire magic."

"What of Ms. Post? Do you think she hides a magical talent?"

"I don't believe so, brother. She picks up languages with ease, but she may possess an eidetic or photographic memory. You care for her, don't you?"

"She possesses certain charms, but I'm not sure she returns my affections. She plays a part for the young men, but she's more their sister than a potential partner. I suspect they made an arrangement to cover the men's actual relationship."

"Tobias, do you think they're like Dr. Banks and Prof. Di Vargas?"

"Perhaps. We should fix our little problem before the assassin starts to rot."

* * *

Across the hall in the remains of Jeremiah and Juan's suite, Mace and Theo worked on trying to control the bleeding wound in Dr. Banks' shoulder. Juan stood behind his lover's chair with a hand on his uninjured shoulder to keep him in place should he regain consciousness. The two graduate students regarded each other and decided to reveal their secrets to Prof. Di Vargas.

"We think you should be aware, Professor, Dr. Banks isn't the only one with magic. We both possess the gift, and if you don't mind, I think I can heal some of the damage he's suffered," Mace offered.

"You can work magic? Can you heal him? Please, do what you can for him. I'm not sure a doctor will arrive soon enough."

Mace knelt beside Jeremiah's chair. With care, he slipped one hand behind the man's shoulder and placed the other on the front. An emerald light flared around his hands, and Jeremiah let out a pained groan as blood vessels began to knit followed by the sliced muscle tissue. Dr. Banks' Sapphire magic rose to join Mace's Emerald magic as the older man blinked back into awareness.

"Easy, Doc. You lost a lot of blood and used a lot of power during the fight. Let me do the work; my magic is better suited to the task," Mace said.

"A hidden talent, Mr. Puap. Is this why the native nations welcomed you?"

"In part, sir. Their primary reason was because I stopped a grave robber from pillaging the burial site of a shaman."

"Thank you, Mace. I think we should leave something for the doctor Ms. Post went to fetch. We don't need the bishop asking too many questions."

"Yes, sir," Mace and Theo responded together.

"Since the management doesn't seem in a hurry to send anyone up to check on us, I'll go and speak to the manager about getting us a new suite. The ambassador of the Republic of Texas staying in a destroyed suite won't do," Juan said.

"Thank you, my love." Jeremiah said. "Humor me though and take Theo with you. I don't want any of us going anywhere alone."

"I'm quite capable of taking care of myself, but I understand the need for caution, beautiful one. Come along, Mr. Polzin."

Theo cast a glance at Mace to make sure his partner would be fine on his own with Dr. Banks. Mace's smile reassured him, and Theo followed Prof. Di Vargas out of the ruined suite.

"So, is Ms. Post aware you two love each other?" Jeremiah surprised Mace with his question.

"Yes, sir. She keeps pushing us together. I didn't want to rush things, and Theo is patient and understanding with my decision."

"Don't let things go too long, Mr. Puap. He might not wait forever."

"I won't, sir. Why don't you use our first names instead of always being so formal, Doc?"

"I keep things formal around outsiders so they will treat you with respect, Mace. Using your given names, in particular Quillion's, would show a familiarity, which makes people wonder which of you is sleeping with me or if I'm getting some action off all you in exchange for your position on my expedition. Trust me, I went through those questioning glances during my doctoral process. I don't want any of you to share my experience"

Before Mace replied, Quillion and Bishop Fabbri returned with a doctor in tow to examine Jeremiah's shoulder.

* * *

DOWNSTAIRS in the hotel's lobby, Theo kept an eye out for trouble. Over at the front desk, Prof. Di Vargas used considerable charm and dire warnings of the Republic of Texas' response should Ambassador Banks not receive a new suite. He admired the way the Spaniard took care of the American archaeologist not only as a colleague, but also as a lover. The love between the two men was undeniable. They did a remarkable job of hiding their love from those only aware of their professional association. Theo admired, respected, and loved both of these men. He only hoped his own budding relationship with Mace would become as tight as what he witnessed between those two men. Prof. Di Vargas' voice rose and grew angrier as Theo listened. Theo's Hebrew was horrible, so most of the conversation escaped him, but by the volume of the professor's and the manager's voices, perhaps he should lend some assistance. Listening closer, he caught the Russian accent to the manager's words. Theo caught the manager's attention and rattled off a quick burst of Russian, letting his native accent grow thick. The manager blanched and changed his tone with Prof. Di Vargas, handing him the keys to the hotel's presidential suite while calling for the bellhops to attend to the professor's requests.

With everything in hand, Prof. Di Vargas drew Theo aside for a private chat.

"What did you say to the man, Mr. Polzin?"

"I mentioned something about possible reactions should His Most Russian Majesty learn of Ambassador Banks' horrible treatment. And how his reaction might affect the climate for business back home." Theo tried to suppress his accent again.

"Sounds like a threat at his family back in Russia." Juan's tone of disapproval caused Theo to cringe. "Dr. Banks won't like the use of threats to receive what should come from respect for his position with the Republic of Texas."

"The Republic of Texas is a new nation, Professor, and while I don't approve of threats based on religion or any other reason, those of the Jewish faith from back home fear the bad old days of pogroms will return." Theo kept his voice hushed to avoid eavesdroppers. "The fear of the Imperial Secret Police keeps everyone in line. Russia is an old power and fear of its forces run deep in people whose families left long ago."

"I don't favor threats either, but since this gets Dr. Banks into better quarters with more security, I'm all for keeping a secret between us, Mr. Polzin."

"What I don't understand is why all the attacks on this expedition appear to be focused on the Republic of Texas side. Don't take this wrong, I don't wish for you or Bishop Fabbri or the annoying monks to be attacked."

"The situation is a mystery to me as well, Mr. Polzin. Given I'm the one who put this expedition together, you would think they would come after me. Forced to guess, I think, Dr. Banks' reputation draws more attention than my own. Let's resettle him in his new suite before we sit and discuss plans for the next phase of our expedition."

VAMPIRE INTERLUDE:
RECLAIMING THE
BROTHERHOOD

Richard stood in the desert surrounding the plateau where the ruins of
the fortress of Masada stood. He stood shirtless and barefoot, wearing
only jeans, and he wore a crucifix around his neck. Richard gathered
his long hair in one hand to let the tiny breeze blow across his back and
shoulders. The temperature didn't bother him, nor did the noonday sun.
Why those he met thought these things would hamper him remained a
mystery. If they'd asked to meet him at dawn or for him to wear a
pentacle or other pagan symbol, that would bother him. Around the
time his patience wore thin, a knot of camel-mounted men arrived
dressed in the desert robes of the Brotherhood of the Crimson Hand.
Once they dismounted, an elder and two assistants approached to greet
him. He noted the wicked daggers they carried along with the wooden
stakes they attempted to conceal from him. Did the Brotherhood think
they could kill him with those toys? The daggers were steel and wood
didn't slow Richard down. The elder nodded his head as though
greeting an equal. Richard didn't acknowledge the man, instead
addressing one of the assistants.

"Why did the leaders of your brotherhood demand this meeting and these conditions?"

"They do not believe you are who you say you are, Lord Hunter," the elder answered.

"I did not address this dog of the desert; if this one speaks again without my consent, kill him. Now answer my question, youth of the sands."

"Master of Darkness, the elders of the Brotherhood are in disagreement over your claim to be Father Cain's successor. They seek proof you aren't some mortal hunter seeking glory he does not deserve." The youth knelt before Richard. "We are the faction which aims for peace between our brothers."

Richard nodded in acknowledgment of the youth's bow of respect. The elder was livid the half-naked man ignored him. The older assassin became convinced a mortal stood before him, as no one of the lineage of Cain survived in sunlight. He drew his dagger and made to rush Richard. Ebony magic rose at Richard's command, and his silver, longsword appeared in his hand. He parried the elder's blade before reversing to remove the man's knife hand. The man dropped, trying to staunch the bleeding. Ruby magic flared around the stump of his wrist, cauterizing the wound.

"Be gone, dog of the desert." The young assistant spit on the wounded elder. "Remember Lord Hunter spared your miserable existence, but your name shall be forever cursed by the Brotherhood for your actions here today."

The youth kicked the former elder to drive him into the desert. Afterwards he turned and dropped to his knees. He bowed his head to touch the sand. Richard tapped his shoulder with the point of his sword, signaling the youth to rise. He sat on his heels gazing up at Richard.

"Master of Darkness, how may I serve?"

"Tell me your name and rank, son of the sands."

"I am Zan, Master. I am an apprentice protector."

"As of today, you are no longer Zan. I give you a new name, Azim abn Alssashra. After we meet with the Brotherhood's elders, a mission waits for you and one other."

"I live to serve, Master. May I introduce my fellow apprentice?"

"Please do."

Now renamed, Azim signaled for his companion to approach. The other youth knelt and bowed his head to the sand.

"Master of Darkness, this is Fahim, an apprentice scholar."

"Rise, Fahim. I can use your skills as a researcher. Wisdom and might working together make a stronger team."

"Master of Darkness, we are but lowly apprentices," Fahim rose to sit on his heels like Azim. "Our words will not be heeded by the elders. With the loss of our master, we shall be considered outcasts as well."

"You both carry a symbol of the Brotherhood containing a drop of blood your elders claim comes from Father Cain; bring the symbol out so you may discover the truth of this claim."

Both young men drew out a pendant in the shape of a crescent moon carved from pure alabaster. Richard held out his hands and the youths placed their talismans in the hand closest to him. Both pendants crumbled into dust in Richard's hands.

Azim and Fahim threw themselves face down on the sands in despair. Richard knelt beside the distraught pair and touched the youths once on the head, once on the back of the neck, and once at the base of their spine. They lifted themselves to the deep bow of respect position. Richard commanded them to rise.

"Master of Darkness, why are we not worthy of Father Cain's blessing?" Azim remained bowed in respect. "Our former master chose us as the best candidates for the protectors. Where did we fail, My Lord?"

"Neither of you failed, Azim. Your former master played you both false. Now you serve me, and the most trusted of my advisors will train you. Rise, Azim, and begin your service."

"I am not worthy, Master of Darkness," Azim protested. "Better for you to slay me and leave my corpse to the vultures."

"I find worth, Azim," Richard said. "I shall shape the warrior and weapon I need, as I shape Fahim into the scholar and spy I need. You are more than my apprentices; you serve as my instruments for a critical task. For now, lead me to the meeting place of the elders so I may speak with them."

Both youths bowed before rising and preparing the camels for the trek back to the Brotherhood's encampment. Richard returned his sword to the pocket dimension he hid things in and drew forth clothes and shoes to wear. Azim helped Richard mount the camel, which once belonged to the elder, before helping Fahim mount and mounting his own. Taking the lead, Azim escorted the small procession across the desert for several hours, pausing only twice, so that Fahim and he could dismount and pray facing Mecca. Richard sat impassive while they carried out their prayers. After close to two centuries of vampiric existence, Richard found many things leading him to believe the power behind three faiths, existed as something less than the all-powerful deity they believed in. At best, Yahweh remained the minor little rain god who originated in Sumer, and despite somewhere around three billion worshipers, the little godling didn't grow omnipotent. No, if anything, Yahweh grew weaker because the three faiths fought with each other and with themselves over their own beliefs. Few places existed where the godling's power intruded without a priest or caretaker with real faith dwelling within.

* * *

After hours of riding, the trio arrived at the camp around an oasis used by the elders of the Brotherhood as their base of operations. Azim dismounted his camel before coming to assist Richard and Fahim in dismounting. With a twist of magic, Richard opened a tiny pocket dimension, a trick learned a few years ago. From inside, he pulled a dark-blue hooded cloak, which he wrapped around himself. Azim and Fahim guided him to the center of the camp and to the fire where the elders sat eating the evening meal. The watchman at the outer edge of the elders' circle halted the trio.

"Zan, why do you bring a cloaked stranger in place of your master?"

"I am Zan no longer, but Azim abn Alssashra. I bring my true master before the elders, as you required of me. Kneel before the Master of Darkness." Azim's voice carried authority. "All should kneel before Lord Hunter."

The chief elder rose, his rage written upon his face as he confronted Azim and Fahim.

"You dare bring an imposter before this council? Where is your proper master, who we sent to dispatch this mortal fool?"

"If the desert is crueler than I am, he is food for the vultures. Otherwise, the old fool is beginning a long wandering exile. Who dares to question my authority?"

"I am Hakim abn Al-Hamid, Chief Elder of the Brotherhood of the Crimson Hand. Who questions my authority?"

"I am Richard St. Martin, Lord Hunter, Lord Slayer, Lord of all Vampires, the Slayer of Cain, and Master of Darkness. Be as your name, Hakim abn Al-Hamid, a wise servant of the praised, kneel and acknowledge your master."

"What proof is offered to back the claim, stranger? What becomes of me if I kneel before you and you prove false?"

"Better to ask what happens if you fail to kneel before me and I prove to be true. One among your number gave Azim abn Alssashra and Fahim false talismans of Father Cain. Contact with my flesh destroyed the false vessels. Who is the dispenser of the talismans of Father Cain among the Brotherhood?"

"Qasim abn Rashid is the giver of the talismans."

"Bring him forth to be judged."

"You do not command here."

Richard stripped away the cloak and revealed his face in the firelight. His eyes turned solid black, and his fangs descended. Rage at the constant questioning of his identity twisted his handsome face into a frightening visage. Both Azim and Fahim flung themselves to the ground in the deep bow of respect and submission at Richard's feet.

"I grow tired of being questioned, Chief Elder. I sense the vampires hidden within the camp, who whisper folly in the ears of those who advise. Bring me the children of Bellabarisruk. Their master chooses to oppose me and, for his folly, they must die."

Four vampires moved into the light of the campfire and faced Richard across its flames. He sensed their vast ages. The primordial sent compelling agents to make sure of his influence within the Brotherhood. They stared at the infant vampire who dared to challenge their ancient master.

"I am Caius Remus Gaullicus, Envoy of Lord Bellabarisruk to the Brotherhood of the Crimson Hand. In our master's name, greetings, hunter."

"The ancient Roman diplomat who once served the senate of the early Republic. You received the Gift of Cain from Solon of Thebes, the third chosen of Bellabarisruk. Where does the primordial hide, Roman?"

"Well, you're an educated imposter but an infant in comparison to the youngest of this party. Give up the quest for Father Cain's holy city. The city belongs to likes of Lord Bellabarisruk."

"I am Cain's successor and lord of our kind, Caius Remus Gaullicus. Kneel and swear allegiance to me and be spared, or continue to oppose me and be destroyed."

The four vampires didn't speak; they instead launched themselves across the fire to attack Richard in mass. Richard whipped his cloak around the first one to reach him, shoving the monster backward into the fire. The cloak caught fire, turning into a fierce blaze. The trapped vampire screamed as silver chains hidden in the lining grew hot and burned into her skin. Caius swiped at Richard with clawed hands and scored along his shoulder. Richard struck back, and his fist slammed into Caius' ribcage, sending bone splinters into the man's heart and lungs. A shattered rib cage might keep him out of the fight for a few minutes. Richard need to move these four away from the camp. Kicking the nearest of the two remaining opponents, Richard made a break for the outer edge of the encampment with his last opponent close on his heels.

"Escape is impossible, infant," the woman called out.

Richard whirled to face her, his longsword gleaming silver in the night. She managed to stop before impaling herself on the blade by a narrow margin.

"I'm not trying to escape, only find a little more space to fight in. Now who are you? A wild guess says you're Melissa of Pisa. Am I correct? Armand spoke well of you. He'll be disappointed to learn you chose to side against us."

"No, My Lord, he won't be. I also wanted space to deal one on one. We need to make this convincing if I'm to continue serving as an agent in Bellabarisruk's court. Please be careful when striking me with your silver sword."

Richard produced a dagger from his sleeve and plunged the blade into her chest close to her heart but missing anything which would cause her demise. Melissa fell to the sands and didn't move. Richard staggered as Caius and the other two vampires collided with him. Grabbing the recovering burn victim, Richard wrenched her around in front of him and sank his fangs into her neck. He drew two mouthfuls of her blood and she crumbled into dust. Caius stepped back and let the other male of the group attack Richard. He dodged many of Richard's blows, but a few landed and left burning marks behind as the silver of the blade met the Ebony magic of the vampire's blood. The silver decelerated vampiric healing abilities, and the ancient monster began to slow and tire as he continued his attempts to penetrate Richard's defenses. In time, Richard wore the man down and cleaved his head from his shoulders.

"Run back to Bellabarisruk, Caius, and take this message to him. Tell him to come and face me in person. Lord Slayer is tired of dealing with the flunkies."

"Time to die, pitiful excuse for a vampire."

The elder leaped towards Richard and cast a handful of powder into his face. Richard screamed as the silver dust burned his skin, but managed to keep the dust from his eyes. The beast within him escaped his rigid control, and he snatched Caius out of the air as the elder made another leap to attack. With a snarl of defiance, Richard plunged his fangs into the neck of his foe and drank away his life and memories. Visions of the lair of Bellabarisruk flooded his sight along with the dark rituals used to bring the primordial back from his languor. Richard mastered his beast and held Caius a heartbeat from final death until he pulled all the details of Bellabarisruk's plans from his beaten foe. Caius crumbled into dust as Richard drew the last of his life force out of him. Richard moved back to where Melissa lay and pulled the dagger from her chest.

"Melissa of Pisa, carry my message. Take this blade with as proof you escaped my attack on Caius' party. Give my message to Bellabarisruk along with word of how I deal high justice. What I do is forbidden to our kind, save Father Cain and myself. Let him understand the fate which awaits him."

"I obey, Lord Slayer."

Richard perceived the faint tread of feet over sand approaching him from the direction of the camp and turned to find Azim and Fahim kneeling before him. The pair bowed their heads to the sand before rising to sit on their heels.

"Master of Darkness, the elders wish an audience with the successor of Father Cain," Fahim said.

"The time for meetings is past. Take them these commands before rejoining me with enough supplies to sustain two people for the weeklong crossing of the desert to Damascus," Richard said. "Any followers who reject me as Cain's heir are to be executed and their apprentices brought back for a re-evaluation of loyalty. Protect the members of the expedition to find El-Abel at all costs. Destroy any agent or vampire not working to support my goal. You are to be given two empty alabaster talismans of the Brotherhood."

Fahim bowed, rose, and returned to the elders to do his new master's bidding. Azim remained on the ground before Richard, waiting for acknowledgement. Richard fought down the beast within him and took time before realizing Azim remained before him.

"What would you ask from me, son of the desert?"

"To understand what you want from us, Master."

"I chose you to augment my protection of the archaeologist and the theologian searching for lost El-Abel. I worry my agent is distracted by physical lusts towards these men."

"Forgive my asking questions, Master, but this agent in place is my Christian counterpart from Father Cain's western cult, is he not?"

"Yes, Azim. He is Brother Colum to the worldly, who views only a monk of the Order of St. Hubert. Like you, he is a protector. My spies in Damascus tell me he helped deal with lost members of the Brotherhood. He and the other agent, Brother Tobias, are members of the Cult of Cain sent by the leader of the Cult."

"He is a lover of his own sex, Master?"

"So, my agent informs me, Azim. Considering both cover religions preach against those who love their own sex, tell me if you will face difficulty working with this young man."

"Does the cultist possess your trust in all things aside from the direction of his physical lust, Master?"

"Yes, Azim. Colum is under my personal protection and tutelage. Understand the two learned men leading this expedition are lovers and their relationship is not to be questioned regardless of what any religion teaches."

"Master, I must confess, I am also a lover of men."

"Is Fahim your lover, Azim?"

"No, Master. You exiled the one who awoke my understanding of physical love. I did not choose this relationship with him, but went along to remain in training to fulfill my calling."

"Rise, Azim. Whom you love or are physical with is your choice. My orders will never force you to do anything against your will. I have many places where you may serve if this mission is objectionable."

"Master of Darkness, nothing you order me to do will be against my desire, for my desire is to serve you in all things. Command me, Master, and I will obey."

As they spoke, Fahim returned to where they waited. Richard decided to test Azim, fearful of the boy developing into a fanatic.

"If you would serve me in all things, Azim, bind and bring Fahim to me so I may feed."

Fahim paled as he listened to Richard's command but surrendered to whatever fate lay in store for him. He bared his own throat and approached Richard.

"No need for my brother to bind me, Master. Command and I will give my life force over." Fahim knelt before Richard. "Do you prefer to draw from the throat or the wrist, Master?"

Azim stood behind Fahim with a quivering dagger in his trembling hand, fearing an order to open Fahim's veins. Disgust crossed Richard's face at the thought of mortal blood. He spotted the alabaster crescents in Fahim's outstretched hand and snatched them from him.

"You would give up your life to preserve mine, wouldn't you? What inspires such faith in me? I'm a century and a half old as a vampire. Around the time I turned twenty-two, vampires killed the one I loved and I ended up like this."

"From what few stories our elders told us, Master, you never give into the monster dwelling within all Father Cain's children. We offer our lives to show we accept the promise never to take them nor inflict the Gift of Cain on us." Fahim spoke for himself and Azim. "Our Brotherhood's founding premise is of Father Cain as the victim, not Abel or Seth. We are dedicated to avenging the wrong done to Father Cain; now Azim and I dedicate ourselves to avenging the wrongs done to Richard St. Martin."

Bloody tears flowed from Richard's eyes at the loyalty he somehow inspired. He raised the alabaster crescents to his right eye and let each talisman collect his tears. Richard returned the talismans and both young men kissed them before putting them on and hiding them beneath their robes. The two members of the Brotherhood bowed their heads to the sand in acknowledgment of their oaths to Richard.

"Enough, our journey must be underway. Dr. Banks' expedition may find a way around the delays my agents put in his path. I want you included in his party before they leave for Baghdad," Richard said.

Fahim and Azim rose, leading him to the camels loaded while everything else was going on. The elders stood nearby but did not approach the trio. Richard acknowledged their presence and the offering of the camels and supplies. The elders knelt and bowed their heads to the sand, affirming their oaths to him as leader of the Brotherhood. The trio mounted their camels and set out for Damascus.

Chapter 23

AFTER SETTLING into his new suite and recovering from his injury for a couple of days, Jeremiah decided he needed to present his students with some of the background materials that served as the basis for the expedition. With Juan's help, he laid out copies of the journal pages, translations from the El-Isin tablets, and copies of both his and Juan's latest papers on the subject of Enoch/El-Abel. He sent messages to the suites his students occupied, instructing them to come to his room and to bring their field kits for inspection. A knock on the door announced the arrival of his students. Juan answered the door and admitted the trio burdened by field kits.

"Set the kits down and come to the table."

"Dr. Banks, what is the reason to review our kits?

"Ms. Post, I want to make sure each of you is kitted out for working around artifacts, which are thousands of years old. Unlike Native American sites, the location of our excavation's only protection over the millennia is time forgot about the place. In fact, I worry about El-Isin since my last expedition revealed its location to the world. The

University of Baghdad took over the site after my group departed on behalf of the caliph's government."

"But you're worried about looters slipping in and damaging the site searching for gold and other items they can sell on the black market."

"Yes, Mr. Polzin, the possibility is my greatest worry. Prof. Di Vargas and I also wish to show you how our independent research crosses with each other. A note of caution, one of our sources of information is odd and perhaps the work of a madman."

"Is the source the mysterious journal?" At the expression on Dr. Banks' face, Mace threw up his hands in surrender. "In my defense, the bishop and those annoying monks of his are loud when they argue."

"And you happened to be in the hallway outside their suite as they argued. The innocent schoolboy act doesn't fool anyone, Mace."

"Not fair, Quill. Fabbri raged at Colum for hiding the fact this party contains mages unregistered by the Empire or the Republic loud enough to record back in Rome."

"The professor and I will deal with Bishop Fabbri later, Mr. Puap. To answer your question, yes, the source is the mysterious journal. The primary author of the journal claims to be Cain, the son of Adam and Eve. The secondary author is Richard St. Martin, a famous hunter from the twenty-first century."

"Dr. Banks, St. Martin is a well-documented historical figure, so what in his journals makes you question the authenticity of the source?"

"Both authors make an odd claim, which we will go into after I check over your field kits. Mr. Puap, let's start with yours. Bring your pack here to the table, and we'll begin by discussing your packing skills."

With a grunt, Mace lifted his kit to the table and waited for his mentor's critique.

"Please, remember we packed for an expedition to the Arizona desert, not the wilds of the Middle East, sir."

"The essential tools in your kits are the same whether you're digging in Arizona or the jungles of the Brazilian Empire. The rest of your gear may well change based on climate, expected soil conditions, or the demands of the leader. Establish a solid base and be flexible with the rest of your equipment."

"Perhaps you should show them your personal equipment first, Dr. Banks."

"I'll demonstrate my kit after I check what they packed in theirs, Prof. Di Vargas."

While walking around the table, Jeremiah examined the packing of Mace's field kit. Everything appeared rolled tight and sealed against desert conditions. Poking a few worn places, Jeremiah determined the wear came from prolonged use rather than from carelessness with the equipment.

"Open your kit for me please, Mr. Puap."

Unsnapping a few clips, Mace opened his bag to reveal his tools packed with care and order. The tools showed the same wear from use as the rest of the kit.

"Your equipment appears in decent order, Mr. Puap, and I didn't find any items missing or tools in need of replacement. Pack everything back up, and we will move to Mr. Polzin's kit."

THE JOURNAL OF CAIN

I wandered alone for many centuries exploring the world and studying the different settlements created by mortals. I spent many hours observing them as they worshiped their various gods and went about their daily routines. Sometimes I interacted with them as a passing merchant, trading goods and information. Other times I settled into a community to study magic techniques. A few times, I found myself worshiped as a dark god when I revealed my true nature. I maintained two cults as servants over my long existence. The Cult of Cain developed during my extended stay among the nomads of the Asian steppes. Due to my dark appetites, the nomads thought of me as Komur Han and gave their third-born sons to my service. After a few centuries, I grew bored and moved on. My cult remained and became influential within the clans, until I called them to the West to infiltrate the followers of the crucified Christ.

I returned to the land of my birth and decided to take a hand in governing a city-state. I gathered the brightest of my brother Seth's descendants as my ministers and city officials. To the south of Ur, about five days journey from the coast, I established El-Abel. The lands are fertile and my people prospered by farming and trading. Trade flourished with our sister city-states. I established a center of learning to draw the brightest students to my service. After about a century of rule, my people realized I didn't age. The people worshiped me as a god-king. The long rule alone reminded me of my vowed curse on Seth's descendants. I chose five of the brightest and most loyal of my ministers, and I drained each near to death before feeding them my curse-tainted blood. At the end of three days, my ministers arose transformed. Thus, I created the second generation of vampires. Over the next couple of centuries, El-Abel flourished until my children fell to squabbling amongst themselves. I visited a neighboring ruler to receive his submission to the god-king of El-Abel. When I returned, I found the streets of El-Abel running red with the blood of my people. From the palace, two of my children ruled the city while their three siblings lay paralyzed by wooden stakes in the crypt below my palace.

I took my place upon my throne and called the paired rulers before me to face judgment.

"Why did you raise your hands against your brothers and sisters?"

"Father Cain, they sought to turn the city against you and to overthrow your wise rule. We attempted to preserve all you built up. We guarded your throne, as you required of all your children."

"I gifted the five of you to rule together as a family. I will acquire the tale of this revolt from my other children as well. Bring them before me."

The wooden stakes were removed from their hearts. After a few moments, they awoke and knelt before me. I questioned them and forced the answers from them under compulsion. I reviewed the battle for control of El-Abel between siblings. Those who wished to rule the city and create more of our kind and those who sought to uphold my rule. The two children who conspired against me, I executed by driving a silver spike through their brains. My remaining children witnessed their brothers' bodies dry up and became dust. I did this as an example of the penalty for betraying me. To my surviving children, Bel-Sarra, Sharru-Kino, and Nina-Ishtar, I gave what their brothers tried to take by betrayal. Wise Sharru-Kino, I placed on the throne as the new god-king of El-Abel, with Bel-Sarra as his general and Nina-Ishtar as his consort and vizier. Another gift I gave to my children, permission to transform three mortals each into vampires to serve in their court.

They must bring me their candidates for approval before they converted them. After installing Sharru-Kino as my successor, and making sure of his acceptance by the people of El-Abel and by my allied kings, I left heading west to visit the lands of Egypt and the great kings of other lands. I wandered for many centuries.

Through our connection, my chosen found me to present their candidates. A few I rejected, concerned about creating power-mad monsters. Many, I rejected as too weak or naive to hold the vast powers of our kind. The search took almost a thousand years before my children presented their final candidates and transformed them with my blessings.

INTERLUDE: TRANSLATIONS FROM THE EL-ISIAN TABLETS

Translation of tablet 1-25A17

In the (missing symbols) Sharru-Kino El-Abel ordered the construction of four great outposts to conduct trade with our neighbors. Westward towards the lands of (damaged symbol) rose El-Isin and to the East among our brothers of Sumer rose El-Kino. Northward on the border with Nineveh rose (tablet broken here).

* * *

Translation of tablet 2-13G95

Purchased from (damaged symbols) ten slaves captured from Nineveh. The slaves will form part of this season's tribute to El-Abel in place of those chosen from among the children of El-Isin.

* * *

Translation of tablet 9-01P09

A group of strange priests arrived from the lands of the Nile. They bring fine cloth, pottery, and strange customs. They speak of many gods and of their great king. (Symbols appear to be deliberately chipped away) speaks of a warning not to come to El-Isin from the village headman at (more deliberately damaged symbols). Lord Parlathán came to guide the strangers to El-Abel to meet with Sharru-Kino of the eternal reign.

Chapter 24

THREE SETS of eyes glanced up at Jeremiah from the page before them. The expressions ranged from disbelief to excitement. The trio started talking over each other, trying to attract Jeremiah or Juan's attention. Raising his hand, Jeremiah silenced their chatter.

"Before you start asking questions, let me give you a little background on the tablets that make up our understanding of the El-Isinian language," Jeremiah said.

"Dr. Banks, didn't your first solo expedition find the tablets that serve as the Rosetta stone for the language?" Quillion asked.

"Yes, Ms. Post, but my tablets were not the first ones discovered," Jeremiah said before slipping into lecture mode, as the trio called it. "El-Isinian script was first discovered on small alabaster slabs in the ruins of the Assyrian capital Dur-Sharrukin, near the ruins of Mosul in 1843, by Paul-Émile Botta, the French consul. The strange symbols and characters matched no known languages in the region. The slabs got lost amid the grandeur, Botta sent back to the Louvre and were later sold to languish in a random collectors' hands before being sold in

2003 to the University of Arizona, where there were occasional attempts to translate them."

"Were you one of the people who attempted to translate them, Doctor?"

"I found them in a storage container while searching for a topic for my doctoral thesis. It was also around that time I discovered Professor Di Vargas' papers and the topic of my thesis came to me, Mr. Puap."

"Do any other civilizations record contact with El-Abel and those who ruled the city?" Quillion asked.

"Outside of one tablet found in the ruins of the library at Ur, no major civilization beyond the Sumerians makes mention of El-Abel. Mr. Polzin, your question."

"The tablets from El-Isin mention trade with Egypt and the Egyptians are noted for their records, so why hasn't anyone found mention of El-Abel in Egypt?"

"Excellent question," Juan said. "Some Egyptologists, after reviewing Dr. Banks' papers and the translations of the tablets, suggest the deliberate removal of references to El-Abel or Enoch around the time of the Twelfth Dynasty."

Their discussion went on late into the evening until Juan finally called a halt to it. "We'll discuss the topic more in the coming days. Now I think it's time for everyone to seek their beds and get some sleep."

Chapter 25

Juan lay on the bed watching Jeremiah pace like a cat in a cage. The young archaeologist grew frustrated with the lack of communication from the caliph's government. Eager to go to the desert and start digging for answers to the puzzle discovered in both the journal and the ancient tablets, Jeremiah couldn't tolerate the delays. Juan enjoyed the play of sunlight on Jeremiah's pale body and red hair as he paced in his underwear.

"Come back to bed, my beautiful one. You're wearing out the carpet with all this pacing," Juan said in his thick come-hither voice. "Making love is a better way to take your mind off the lack of communication from the caliph."

"I'm sorry, Juan. The situation is beyond frustrating at this point. I don't understand why after approving the expedition before I left Tucson, the caliph and his government decided to halt the entire project." Jeremiah slumped down on the bed next to Juan. "I love your distractions, but I don't think I'm in the mood now."

Jeremiah let Juan draw him back against his chest and wrap him in his strong arms, while his lover nuzzled his neck.

"As much as I enjoy making love to you, the distraction in my plan for today is different."

"What are you thinking?" Jeremiah's back arched like a cat as Juan's lips hit a spot on his neck. "Mmm, I love when you hit the spot."

"Come with me to the library. I want to show you a couple of promising passages I discovered," Juan murmured as he teased the spot, making Jeremiah purr. "I found a mention of Enoch in a non-biblical text, but I think the author tried to cover up El-Abel in his writings."

"WHAT? You found a non-biblical reference to Enoch. What is this text? When was the document written and in what language?"

Juan laughed at the sudden excitement in his lover. He stood and captured the bouncing redhead in a hug. Jeremiah kissed Juan before breaking away to find clothes for both of them. From the depths of the closet, he called out to Juan.

"You aren't answering my questions, old man. What is this text you're teasing me with?"

"You're asking for a spanking, little boy," Juan mock growled. "The text is in hieratic from around the time of the Twelfth Dynasty, written by a priest called Khons."

Jeremiah emerged from the closet dressed in a lightweight linen suit carrying a similar suit for Juan.

"Khons is a name associated with an ancient mummy cult from around the time of Pharaoh Rameses XII. Do you think the two are connected?"

"I don't think so, unless this Khons was a mage with immense power,"

Juan said as he dressed. "Khons may be a common name or priests took the name when they rose to a new rank."

"Let's accept the fact that we're both men of science using a journal written by someone most people would believe was insane. Perhaps we should face the idea that we're deliberately ignoring the possibility vampires do exist, Juan. What if this Khons is a vampire and built himself a cult of followers and worshipers to hide his activities?"

"Perhaps we ruled out the supernatural, because we refuse to be unscientific, love. Let us discuss the matter after you read this text. We'll be able to discover a lead."

They left their suite at the hotel and made their way down to the lobby where they met a subdued-looking Brother Colum, who added himself to their little party. In silence, the young monk followed along, alert to the hustle and bustle of the city around the trio. Colum stopped listening to their academic conversation since they didn't include him. His attention focused more to their surroundings than on Dr. Banks and Prof. Di Vargas' conversation so he missed the question Dr. Banks asked him. Dr. Banks touched his shoulder, and only then did Colum realize the man wanted his attention. He blinked and focused, looking up into those sapphire blue eyes that haunted his dreams.

"Brother Colum, I realize you think you're obligated to guard us, but to be part of this little trip, pay some attention to us, as well as the city. Prof. Di Vargas asked you a question."

"I'm sorry, Dr. Banks, Prof. Di Vargas. What did you ask about?"

"We are wondering if the Cult of Cain holds any knowledge on someone called Khons."

"Why do you ask?" Colum focused his gaze on Prof. Di Vargas. "Did you find something in your research professor?"

"I found a text which may mention Enoch written in Twelfth Dynasty hieratic; the text is attributed to Khons, a priest of Anubis."

Colum grabbed both men and ushered them down a side alley. The monk's reaction startled both of them before they found their balance enough to stop him dragging them further from their destination.

"Colum, stop!" Jeremiah ordered. "Tell us what this about."

"The Khons you mentioned is an ancient and dangerous vampire. He belongs to the Barghest Clan and his spies are everywhere. Don't draw his attention. You're both important and your quest attracts threatening attention."

Juan understood how much Jeremiah wanted to bring the young monk into a hug. His lover held back, afraid of causing the younger man additional emotional distress. He caught Jeremiah's beautiful eyes and nodded, giving him permission to embrace Colum. Jeremiah's hand reached out and drew the monk in against him for a moment before restoring the distance between them.

"Colum, listen to me." Jeremiah lifted Colum's bowed head until their eyes met. "We're as careful as we can be, but archaeology these days involves risks greater than those faced by the Egyptologists before the Upheaval. We realize we're attracting the attention of dangerous people. We're counting on you and Tobias to help keep us out of avoidable troubles, but we can't become paranoid about monsters in the shadows."

Colum straightened and attempted to retreat into his guardian persona, but Jeremiah shook his head.

"Stop it, Colum, the distance you put between us hurts. We like your openness. We understand your feelings for us, which conflict with your vows. We respect how you appreciate our relationship." Jeremiah locked his fierce sapphire eyes on Colum's hazel ones. "Your heart is safe with us, Colum. We miss the shy and playful Colum, because he is our friend."

"I never went away, Jeremiah. I can't be close to either of you and not want to touch you. I won't disrupt what you share with Juan because what I want conflicts with my vows. I miss being friends with both of you, Jeremiah." Colum fought back his tears. "I still must honor my vows of obedience and stay apart from your relationship."

"We respect and understand your feelings, Colum. Should you choose to join us, we reserved a place in our hearts for you."

"Out of respect for your relationship is why I distance myself. Your relationship existed before I came on the scene and you'll be a couple after my recall to my other duties. Your relationship is what's important."

"What's important is lunch and a date with a dusty tome," Jeremiah tried to lighten the mood. "I'm not speaking for anyone else, but I'm starving, and Juan promised me a distraction from wondering why the caliph's representative won't talk to me."

Both Juan and Colum laughed as Jeremiah's stomach gave a loud growl. With a sigh, Jeremiah joined the laughter. Juan pulled them together for a moment, making sure to trap the shorter Colum between him and Jeremiah in the brief hug. The moment they exchanged over Colum's head delayed any further discussion. When Juan released them, Colum scooted out from between the two men and led them to a small hidden restaurant off the little alley. He whispered a few words to the server, and the man returned with a huge platter of local foods and drinks. Both of his charges gawked at the food and drinks in disbelief before digging in.

"How did you find out about this place, Colum?" Juan asked for both himself and Jeremiah. "I come to Damascus often, and I never find places like this."

"A cousin of a brother in the Cult owns the place. We use the restaurant as something of a message drop and location to lose a tail if need be. I passed on the information about the possible involvement of the Barghest Clan and a warning to be extra vigilant. They also passed me word about the delay you're experiencing, Dr. Banks. The delay is because of a radical change in the government. The word is the old caliph died in his sleep around the time we set sail from Valencia to Tel Aviv. Reports are a new, much younger caliph occupies the throne."

"Dynastic politics, ugh," Jeremiah grunted before taking another drink. "Any word on who became the new caliph?"

"Based on our limited resources, he goes by the name Makhdoom ibn Pervaiz ibn Sad."

"Quite a pretentious mouthful; protocol will make things worse by trying to add on all the traditional titles. Any idea what name he used before assuming the caliph's throne?"

"Sorry, no. The new caliph's ascension caught everyone by surprise. Our resources are limited inside the caliphate; perhaps if we can make contact with members of the Brotherhood not trying to kill you, we can find out."

They finished their meal in quiet conversation, and Colum covered the bill with a brief blessing for the household. Colum led them out a different way and got them back on course for the vast library. He deemed the burden in his soul lighter despite the lingering conflict between love and duty. The barriers between him and his charges vanished, and he returned to being himself. The trip to the library didn't take long. Once inside, Prof. Di Vargas took the lead, requesting a private reading room and access to a scroll called the *Wadjet Khakaure*. Juan told both Jeremiah and Colum the manuscript was discovered in the pyramid of Senusret III, a late Twelfth Dynasty pharaoh. The scrolls name comes from the lunar eye Horus amulet, called a *Wadjet*, which sealed the scroll shut tomb, and the pharaoh's Horus name Khakaure. The sealing amulet, in Juan's opinion, led the discoverer to misname the manuscript, which contained a priestly text on Anubis. He finished describing the manuscript as the librarian in charge of the ancient scrolls arrived to lead them back to the archival viewing booth.

"The scroll is unrolled to the section you requested Prof. Di Vargas. Please ring the bell if you need to view other passages and a member of my staff will change the viewing area for you."

"Thank you. Be sure if either Dr. Banks or I need any further assistance, your staff will be summoned."

"Dr. Jeremiah Banks, the archaeologist who deciphered El-Isinian?" The man glanced from Juan to Jeremiah while ignoring Brother Colum.

"Well, I didn't decipher them alone, but my discovery of the El-Isin tablets made the work of deciphering the language possible."

"Such an honor to meet you, Dr. Banks. We've followed your papers in the journals. Please inform us if we can be of further service," the librarian said before walking away to tend to other business.

Jeremiah shook his head before taking a seat in front of the archival case holding the ancient papyrus scroll. The hieratic characters proved well preserved and easy to read. Jeremiah found the passages Juan spoke of and began to work his way through the text. The text read from right to left across the scroll in the pattern set by the Twelfth Dynasty. This method replaced the older style of reading top to bottom in columns. Documents written prior to the Twelfth Dynasty used the older style.

"I, Khons, a priest of Anubis, am chosen by Khakaure to be part of the trade delegation to the city of our newest trading partner. The trade between the Land of Egypt and the Land of Sumer flourishes, but this city-state is new and influential. The god-king they serve is unfamiliar, but our messengers refer to him as Cain El-Abel. We are to bring our trade goods to an outpost established by Cain three days travel from our border with the Lands of Sumer."

"I think he's talking about El-Isin. We found a lot of Egyptian artifacts on the site. In addition, he mentions Cain by name and city. The standard practice is to reference the rulers of city-states in this manner. We insert 'of' between the nouns, making the name read Cain of El-Abel."

"Keep reading." Juan pointed to a different section of the text. "This is where he talks about Enoch."

Jeremiah bent over the case again and began reading the ancient scroll. Several minutes passed before he began to read aloud.

"We traveled four more days, then planned for and arrived at a small trading outpost belonging to Enoch, son of Abel al-Adam. Enoch isn't the place we seek and the inhabitants here urge us not to continue on to El-Abel, for a terrible darkness dwells within. The folk here are strange. They speak of only a single god and of a monstrous evil dwelling in the place we seek. We shall push on, for Great King Khakaure commanded us to reach the outpost city of Cain El-Abel and establish a trade route."

"This sounds like Enoch and El-Abel are two separate places, Juan. Raising a question about the lineages recorded in the Bible and validating the journal's entry, which says Enoch might be the son of Abel, son of Adam and Eve."

"The author of the journal isn't sure if the biblical lineage attributed to Cain might instead belong to Abel since he only suspected Abel's bride was with child at the time of his death. This sound like Enoch is a separate place from El-Abel. I'll keep digging here once you're on your way to Baghdad."

"We'll discuss plans later. I think we need to return to the hotel and bring the rest of our people up to speed. I need to write to His Islamic Majesty and hope direct appeal speeds things up."

Juan summoned a librarian to return the scroll to its place in archival storage. Once the librarian took the manuscript away, they left the library and made their way back to the hotel.

VAMPIRE INTERLUDE:
DARKNESS PLOTS AGAINST
THE LIGHT

Bellabarisruk sat upon his marble throne in the ancient tomb listening to his clan's leaders. The primordial grew disinterested in the majority of the information until the agent of the Grand Duke of Baghdad reported in.

"Ancient One, Grand Duke Omar Ghazi of Baghdad says he stalled the expedition of the archaeologist by creating a succession crisis in the Caliphate of Baghdad. The mortal elders are in conclave holding discussions on the choices for a successor. My Lord ensured a considerable delay before a consensus can be reached to enthrone a new caliph."

"Now, I shall move my court to Baghdad, so I may be in a place to deal with the archaeologist. How is our guest faring?"

"The woman survived the granting of the Gift of Cain and joined our ranks, Ancient One. The priest's faith turned out to be weak, and she overwhelmed him and consumed his life force."

"We will bring her with us, for her appearance will give us the element of surprise when we move to destroy the archaeologist and his party."

"What of the religious scholar with the copy of Father Cain's journal, Ancient One?"

"Send a group to capture him. We will use him to force the archaeologist to surrender. Once we secure El-Abel, we'll kill them both," Bellabarisruk said.

Chapter 26

JEREMIAH STOOD WRAPPED in Juan's arms on the balcony of their suite overlooking Damascus. Juan's embrace was as much to restrain Jeremiah as to show his affection. Juan used his body to contain his lover and partner, trying to absorb some of the tension. Earlier, Jeremiah discussed the division of the expedition into his archaeology team and Juan's research team. The plan required leaving both Bother Colum and Brother Tobias behind to protect Juan and Bishop Fabbri. Based on his orders requiring him to protect Jeremiah at all cost, Colum objected to remaining in Damascus. Fear of Colum undergoing his first sexual experience in the form of rape drove Jeremiah's decision to leave the young monk behind. Jeremiah shared some of his experiences as a grad student in the caliphate with Juan. During his doctoral fieldwork, Jeremiah overheard an argument between his field mentor, Dr. Henderson, and the regional emir over access to the dig site. The emir threatened to withdraw permission to excavate if Dr. Henderson didn't offer up additional compensation. Instead of demanding an audience with the caliph, Dr. Henderson caved into the emir's demands and offered up his top graduate student's virginity as compensation. Memories of listening to the repeated sexual abuse of his fellow student at the hands of the emir's guards still inflicted the occasional nightmare on Jeremiah.

His first solo expedition fared better with the prince of the region, an older man with a curiosity about Jeremiah's red hair and how far the color went. In his quest to discover the answers, the prince gave gifts of beautiful jewelry for Jeremiah to display his body for him but never touched him. Juan shared Jeremiah's fear of possible problems for the young people under his protection. The caliph's court and the expedition held a number of hidden dangers. Juan wrapped himself tighter around Jeremiah, offering security and protection.

"Thank you for trying to take my mind off Colum, the others, and what might happen once we're in the caliphate, my love. Thank you." Jeremiah leaned back against his lover. "I wish for the option of leaving them all behind here with you and going alone. My traveling alone negates the reason Mace, Theo, and Quillion are here. Colum won't listen to me either because he loves us for whatever reason or because of some hidden set of orders."

"And what of me, my beautiful one? Would you take me with you, or are you glad I'm staying here in Damascus?"

"The truth is, for selfish reasons, I'm glad you're staying here in Damascus' relative safety. The outcome of this expedition is too important. What I want to say is we should give up and go spend the rest of our lives on a beach someplace far away." Jeremiah sighed, leaning into Juan. "All I want is to be with you somewhere crazy people aren't trying to kill us."

"How bad do you think the situation is for them?"

"Quillion is the safest because no Muslim man wants to be defiled by a Western woman. The troublesome part is Tobias, Mace, Theo, and Colum, who are attractive young men and the lure of their virginity or seeming virginity makes them a temptation." Jeremiah snapped upright at his last statement. "Oh, bright mother, I didn't think to ask if any of them bear any tattoos. If they do, they must remain here."

"Why do tattoos matter? They're art."

"Stop thinking with the Western attitude, Professor. Tattoos in the caliphate are a sign of slavery."

"Dear Lord, how barbaric. We better find out for sure. I can find plenty for them to do if they must remain here with me."

They went back into their suite and Jeremiah picked up the voice pipe and blew to attract the front desk's attention before removing the whistle on his end and listening for the clerk on duty. A tinny voice responded.

"Front desk, how may we help the ambassador?"

"This is Dr. Banks. Would you please contact my students in rooms 506 and 508, as well as the young monks traveling with us in 509, and ask them to come up to my suite?"

"Of course, Ambassador. I'll make the arrangements for you at once."

"Thank you; disconnecting now." Jeremiah racked the speaking tube and replaced the whistle in the end. "They should be up in a few minutes."

"Relax, you're doing everything you can to protect them." Juan wrapped his lover into a hug. "Relax, my love. Worst case, I go with you and leave your students to carry out my research since I don't bare any tattoos and I'm too old to be attractive to horny guards or emirs."

"You're perfect and a beautiful specimen of manhood. I bet on fighting off the palace guard to keep you. I still find how well we fit together hard to believe and our three years apart didn't lessen our feelings toward one another."

"I like the idea of you fighting off the palace guard to protect me, because I think the same way about you." Juan pressed a kiss to Jeremiah's forehead. "I'm still surprised you gave me a chance after I blew you off as an overeager grad student at the conference. Imagine my shock from finding out the guy I'd dismissed as a plaything was one of the principal speakers for the event."

"I chased after you for your mind and never figured the intelligence came wrapped in such a sexy package."

"When I first spotted you at the reception, I figured Professor O'Grady brought a boy toy for the conference. I didn't realize such an amazing body hid a brilliant mind. I found all my focus on the beautiful cascade of copper hair, the thick beard, how uncomfortable you appeared in the suit, and how well the fabric accented your ass."

"Well, by the time I come back from the desert, the hair will be longer and the beard will be back but out of control. I'll be mistaken for some Old Testament prophet." Jeremiah laughed as he turned his face and locked eyes with Juan. "Think you can still love the wild desert hermit?"

"You realize I love you no matter your appearance. I don't care about the hair, my beautiful one." Juan's mouth captured Jeremiah's in a deep kiss.

A knock at the door broke their moment. Juan let go of Jeremiah and crossed the suite to answer the knock after checking through the peephole. He admitted Mace, Theo, and Quillion. He showed them into the suite's sitting room where Jeremiah was waiting. A second knock a few minutes later announced the arrival of Colum and Tobias to join the gathering. Once seated, Jeremiah spoke to everyone.

"I received a reply from the caliph. His Islamic Majesty agrees to allow us to enter the caliphate and proceed to Baghdad. Therefore, it's time to divide up into those remaining here in Greater Israel with Prof. Di Vargas and those who will travel with me to Baghdad and to the dig site at El-Isin." Jeremiah raised his hand to forestall comment. "I must ask an important question before we divide up the group. Do any of you sport any tattoos?"

Mace, Tobias, and Colum raised their hands to indicate they possessed tattoos. Theo and Quillion both appeared puzzled.

"What's so important about whether anyone is sporting tattoos, Doc?"

"In the caliphate, tattoos are a symbol of being a slave, Mr. Polzin"

"Well, they're crazy, Doc. What difference does some ink make?"

"The difference is between being free to move about and direct the workers on the dig and being someone expected to serve anyone at any time in any way. Before you ask, Mr. Puap, yes, my meaning includes sexual service, as well as anything else."

Jeremiah concentrated on all three young men as his words sank in, and they blanched in fear.

"Brother Tobias is staying here with Prof. Di Vargas and Bishop Fabbri. I think you and Brother Colum should do the same, Mr. Puap."

"I won't be credited for field work if I stay and do library research, Dr. Banks."

"I'm under orders to stay with you and protect you, Dr. Banks."

"I can't risk having either of you with us. If your tattoos are discovered, the repercussions threaten the safety of the whole party," Jeremiah pointed out. "The possibility of winding up dead for daring to give orders to free men, getting gang raped, or worse, can't be mitigated."

"What if their tattoos are in places no one will ever find them?" Juan offered. "They might be able to avoid detection."

"The showers for men are communal; the tattoos will be seen."

"Perhaps, Ms. Post should return to her room while Brother Colum and

Mr. Puap show you where their tattoos are," Juan suggested. "This way we can find out how much ink we're dealing with."

Mace brightened at the possibility of getting to go into the desert. Quillion rose from her seat and headed for the door of the suite. Juan nudged Brother Tobias in her direction as an escort to maintain Jeremiah's no one travels alone rule. When the pair departed, Jeremiah got severe.

"Both of you strip and show me where your tattoos are."

Both Mace and Colum blinked at Dr. Banks' order before they recovered and did as requested. Colum removed his cassock revealing his lithe, muscular body to the room full of men. On his left breast was small crimson cross. Mace also stripped naked, revealing a biblical passage on his upper thigh near his thick cock and heavy balls. Theo fought to remain seated as Dr. Banks rose from his chair and moved closer to both of the naked men. His hands started poking and prodding Mace as though judging him for a horse sale. Those long, strong fingers traced the tattoo before cupping Mace's cock and balls. Theo fought to hold his temper in check and keep his magic under control. Dr. Banks cast a glance over his shoulder at Theo as the man's Sapphire magic rose before Jeremiah released Mace's manhood. He noted Theo relaxing his stance until he moved around behind Mace and bent him over, forcing him to grab the chair for balance. Sapphire magic burst into life around Theo's hands.

"Control your magic, Mr. Polzin. This is a bigger problem. If you can't exercise caution regarding your relationship and keep your magic a secret, you become a threat to the expedition. Your relationship would be easy to exploit given Mr. Puap's status as a slave if he comes with us."

Mace straightened up and turned to face Dr. Banks. "I can make the tattoo go away using my magic to absorb the ink into my body."

"If you can do a permanent removal, you may join us, Mr. Puap."

Emerald magic flickered around Mace's leg, and the tattoo faded and vanished. He reached out and touched Colum's chest, and the young monk's tattoo disappeared.

"Now Brother Colum and I can both travel with you, Doc. Can we dress now, or would you like to fondle us some more?"

"Put your clothes back on. Mr. Puap and Mr. Polzin, I suggest you settle the issue of your relationship. If you haven't already made love, do so soon; it is better to be each other's first lover. Neither of you want to experience your first time as an unwilling partner. Trust me, the possibility exists depending on the caliph's whims."

Chastised, Mace and Colum dressed before Mace and Theo departed to their room. Colum remained with Jeremiah and Juan, looking lost and confused.

"What about me?"

"You pose a dangerous challenge, Colum, as a non-Muslim religious person, with or without the tattoo. If you insist on going with us, lose the religious garb and dress like Mr. Puap and Mr. Polzin. You must blend in as my personal secretary."

"You're concerned about Mace's and Theo's appearance attracting unwanted attention. Do I not fit this category as well?"

"Yes, you do, which is my other concern. We'll hope nobody pays attention to you, little monk."

"I don't own the proper clothes to pass as a personal secretary."

"We'll fix the problem of clothes tomorrow. Why don't you head back to your room for now?" Jeremiah showed the young monk out. "Prof. Di Vargas and I need to discuss some things."

Disappointed and confused, Colum left the ambassadorial suite and returned to the room he shared with Tobias. Jeremiah and Juan stood facing each other, both with stern expressions on their faces. Neither moved nor said anything for several minutes before Juan spoke.

"I didn't realize you possessed such a mean streak, Jeremiah. Did you need to embarrass both Mace and Colum in such a fashion?"

"Our lives are on the line in so many different ways, Juan. Yes, I needed to do what I did to Mr. Puap and to Brother Colum, and before you ask, yes, Ms. Post would receive the same treatment if she bore any tattoos." Jeremiah held up his hand before Juan said anything more. "I sensed something between Mace and Theo a while ago, and a budding, but as of yet unconsummated, bond between witches is a dangerous thing for not only both of them but for us as well. You caught Theo's reactions when I fondled Mace. Imagine what his reaction would be like when Mace was being gang raped by the palace guards or, worse, the workers he supervises on the dig site. Once they complete their bond, they can access each other's emotions as well as the other's magic. As they are now, they pose a threat to each other and leave me unable to act to defend either of them."

"What of Brother Colum? He isn't a mage. He's not one of your students. He's here as a guard and spy, with orders to report everything we do back to some shadow organization."

Jeremiah cringed while his lover shuddered with his efforts to control his rage and hurt. He started to move towards Juan to take the older man in his arms, but Juan held up his hand to stop him.

"Not now, Jeremiah. I'm not sure I find comfort in your arms when I'm not sure I know who you are now. I plan to find Bishop Fabbri and go to the library for a while. I need time to figure things out."

Juan walked past Jeremiah well out of arm's reach to prevent his lover reaching out and drawing him in. He didn't slam the door behind him, but the soft click resounded like a dirge for the comfortable relationship between him and Jeremiah. Juan walked to the stairs and went down to the sixth floor to the bishop's rooms. Juan knew he shouldn't doubt Jeremiah's love. He'd learned his lover possessed a protective streak a kilometer across. Yes, Jeremiah was trying to protect his part of the expedition in a dangerous situation, but not knowing where the danger is coming from put everyone on edge. Juan needed to clear his head and decide where his own heart lay.

* * *

ONCE THE DOOR closed behind Juan, Jeremiah crashed to his knees, his heart in agony. Soft sobs escaped as tears began to leak from his eyes as deep conflicting emotions raged through him. Fear and anger over thoughts of Juan breaking off both their romantic and professional relationships left Jeremiah reeling in self-doubt. The major conflict raged over his intense love for Juan, and the nagging desire to shelter his students and the infuriating monk from the evils of the world. Could they both be his?

Jeremiah picked himself up off the floor and went into the master bath where he stripped off and sank himself into a scalding bath trying to erase his pain. He drifted off and was still in the tub when an anxious Juan returned to their suite.

"Wake up, my beautiful boy, time for a frank discussion." Juan shook Jeremiah's shoulder.

Jeremiah sat up, startled out of his dreamlike state. Water splashed everywhere, soaking Juan's suit and most of the linens in the bathroom. With blind desperation, Jeremiah grabbed Juan and drew him in for a kiss, in part for reassurance of Juan's physical presence and the rest out of love. Juan kissed back and let Jeremiah soak his suit, needing the reassurance of their love as much as the younger man. Only when Juan shivered from the ice-cold water of the bath did Jeremiah break their kiss.

"I'm sorry I forget you don't share my tolerance for the cold. Let me empty the tub and dry off; afterwards, we can talk, Juan. I promise to listen to everything you say to me."

"Let me go dry off and change clothes."

Jeremiah emptied the tub, dried off, and wrapped himself in one of the robes the hotel provided before padding barefoot out into the master bedroom where Juan pulled on dry pants. His muscles flexed and rippled beneath his skin, causing Jeremiah's cock to harden as his breath caught in his throat. He stood transfixed at the sight of the man he loved. Was Jeremiah about to lose Juan? Would Juan tell him they were best working as professional colleagues, that their relationship shouldn't go any further? Jeremiah found himself frozen in place, and a shiver of panic flowed down his spine.

Juan turned to find Jeremiah standing in place with fear on his face. He realized that Jeremiah was thinking he was about to tell him their relationship is finished. Everything revolved around the little monk. All their most recent arguments center on including or excluding Brother Colum in their relationship as a lover. Truth be told, the situation was Juan's fault because he'd been the one to invite Colum to join them back in Valencia. The little monk confessed how much their open relationship awed and intimidated him. Colum' emotions started running wild when he'd first found them together back in Valencia. The boy admitted he loved them both and couldn't decide which of them he wanted to take his virginity. Colum vowed never to touch Jeremiah unless Juan was present. Juan knew he was trying to fool himself into thinking all he wanted was Jeremiah to himself when he wanted Colum as well. He loved Jeremiah, and he could never let him go; Jeremiah could fuck the blasted little monk in front of the Caliph and his court.

"Relax, Jeremiah." Juan stretched out his hand and stroked Jeremiah's cheek. "I love you no matter what. Colum and I spoke downstairs. I think I better understand what makes our little monk so frustrating. Our conversation also helped me grasp what sorts of problems await you at the court of the caliph. You fear what happened to your fellow student happening to Colum or your students. We can work through whatever we need to protect Brother Colum, Mace, Theo, and Quillion. I won't lose you by being overprotective of our relationship, so relax, my love, and be mine."

"I love you so much, Juan. I couldn't live with myself if I lost you because I let a stupid fantasy come between us. I would give myself over to the caliph's guards before I lose you."

"Well, I don't think you need to do anything so drastic, my love. One last book remains, and I can find the text here in Damascus, and I owe our little monk a thank you for putting me on to the path." Juan pulled back from the tight embrace he shared with Jeremiah to find a puzzled expression on his lover's face. "He's embarrassed. Colum thought his reluctance tore us apart and wished a flood like Noah's would sweep him away. Colum's comment made me recall a mention of an ancient book of biblical wisdom purported to be written by a son of Noah not long after his father's passing."

"W-wait, what? I'm lost. Are you looking for a copy of the Book of Ham?" Jeremiah blinked in confusion, trying to process Juan's comments. His lover returned his confused glance before nodding. "You don't need to dig through the Damascus Library. My copy is in my luggage."

"Your copy of the Book of Ham? How is this possible?" Juan gazed into Jeremiah's sapphire eyes. "Where did you find this copy?"

"I did a year abroad during my master's study. I stayed in Jerusalem learning Hebrew and Aramaic. My professor made me copy old text to practice writing Hebrew. I don't think he realized what book he gave me to copy since he taught language, not religious studies." Jeremiah walked over to one of his steamer trunks. He dug into the stack of books and came up with a leather-bound notebook, which he handed to

Juan. "I hope you can read the text. I'm afraid my penmanship isn't neat in any language."

"I can't believe you hand copied the Book of Ham as an exercise in writing Hebrew. Well, this makes my last bit of research easier." Juan drew Jeremiah in and kissed him. "You never cease to amaze me, Dr. Banks."

Juan settled into a chair and opened Jeremiah's notebook copy of the Book of Ham. He frowned and squinted at the handwritten Hebrew characters. Jeremiah sighed, waiting for the inevitable comments on his miserable handwriting. Juan got up and sat down next to Jeremiah on the love seat.

"I think the light is bad. Perhaps over here will be better." Juan stole a kiss from his lover. "At least company exists here; the chair is lonely."

"The flirting and flattery can lead you to lots of places, Professor Di Vargas." Jeremiah's reclining pose in the loveseat displayed his board hairy chest. "Go ahead and admit you can't read my handwriting. I think bad handwriting is the only reason I keep this notebook. Nobody can figure out what I wrote and they overlook my scribbles."

"Why do I think you're leading me on with this copy, Jeremiah?"

"Why, Professor, what are you implying?" Jeremiah cocked an eyebrow at Juan. "I do keep a better copy hidden away in my portable library. What are you looking for in the text?"

"Confirmation that Noah's wife's family descended from Cain."

"Back to the argument evil and sin didn't wash away with the Flood, I gather. Here, give me the notebook. I can find the passage you're looking for faster." Jeremiah took back the notebook and flipped through to a page near the middle. A calloused finger traced from right to left across the page until he found the passage they needed.

"A reading from the Book of Ham, Chapter 18, Verses 19 to 46." Jeremiah intoned in his best priest impression.

"Father's God is upset with him for arguing about saving his family from the Flood. Once I found him arguing with the air over the little altar he kept near the rafts we used for trading up and down the river. I listened to the air curse mother's heritage as descended from the first murderer, Cain. 'Her lineage is as cursed as yours is blessed,' the mysterious voice said. And father spoke, 'Yes, you reminded me often enough. Naamah was born the sister of Tubal-Cain the forger of all kinds of bronze and iron. Tubal-Cain was born the son of Zillah; second wife of Lamech the son of Methuselah, the long-lived. How Methuselah was the son of Mehujael, the son of Irad, born to Enoch, son of Cain, who murdered his brother Abel, and for whom Cain named his city. I learned her lineage as I learned mine from the priests, who pass along the story, which makes you appear in the best light.' Father's frankness with God baffled me for many years after my exile. Enlightenment came to me from one claiming to be Cain. From him, I learned how Dark Lilith turned her back on Father's God and Adam. How Eve brought condemnation down on herself and Adam for eating a piece of fruit meant to make a minor god omnipotent. How the war between the semi-divine children of God destroyed the sons of Adam and drove righteousness out of all the lands."

Jeremiah set down the notebook glancing over at Juan. His lover pondered, trying to take in all the new information. Re-reading this passage from the Book of Ham reminded Jeremiah of the passage out of scroll he and Juan read earlier. He rose and crossed the room to pull out his map of the area around his dig site at El-Isin. Jeremiah laid the map out and leaned over, searching for references he was recalling mentioned in the scroll. A touch on his ass caused Jeremiah to jump.

Juan laughed before sliding his hand up under the robe Jeremiah was wearing and letting his finger slide up the crack of his lover's ass to brush over his hole. Jeremiah leaned back against Juan and moaned as his lover teased his opening. Juan's other hand wrapped around Jeremiah's waist to slip between the flaps of the robe and caress his throbbing cock. The archaeologist braced himself against the table as Juan proceeded to remove the robe covering Jeremiah's athletic body. Juan pressed his hard cock still trapped in his trousers against Jeremiah's ass and listened to his lover moan in desperation to fucked.

"Please, Juan, fuck me. I need you inside me. I need you to take charge because I'm spinning out of control."

"You're adrift, my love. Let me in and I will anchor you in this storm of emotions."

Jeremiah listened to the sound of Juan's zipper lowering followed by the heat of Juan's cockhead push against the opening to his ass. The thick cock pushed its way into the tight confines of Jeremiah's ass until Juan's balls touched his own. Jeremiah moaned as the head of Juan's cock brushed over his prostrate, sending tingles of pleasure into his cock. Once Jeremiah adjusted to his cock, Juan began to fuck his lover, not with gentle lovemaking strokes but with a hard and forceful pounding. After only a few strokes, Jeremiah thrust his ass back to match the rhythm of Juan's thrusts.

The older man gripped the redhead's waist with bruising force as they slammed into each other. He longed to be able to grab Jeremiah by the hair, but with the long length gone, he settled for leaning in and sinking his teeth into the man's shoulder. Jeremiah cried out in mixed passion and pain and exploded in orgasm. His ass clamped down on Juan's cock and pulled the older man over into orgasm as well. They pulled apart, breathing hard. Jeremiah became aware of Juan's load starting to drip down his leg and clenched his ass to keep from getting any on the Persian carpet below them. He took Juan's hand and led him into the bathroom. Jeremiah stripped Juan of his clothes before pulling him into the shower where they kissed while cleaning each other up from their sex.

"I think I figured out Enoch's location. What surprises me is how close to El-Isin Enoch is," Jeremiah said as Juan scrubbed his back. "Khons mentioned stopping in Enoch before continuing on to El-Isin because they got lost in the desert on the way."

"So where do you think Enoch is?"

"Khons mentions a small village outside of El-Isin's territory to the northwest at an oasis about two days travel at caravan speed."

"Which means Enoch is the wrong direction to also be El-Abel."

"Yes, two separate locations for us to chart and explore."

"You sound like you expect me to come with you into the caliphate and beyond." Juan turned around and Jeremiah washed his back. "Are you asking me to go with you?"

"Yes, Juan. I want you to follow me into the desert and share a tent with me. I want you where I can find you and keep you safe." Jeremiah leaned against Juan's back and wrapped his arms around the older man. "I believe we discussed this three years ago in Atlanta. I said I might ask you to come to the desert with me someday."

"Yes, my love, we discussed you dragging me out to the desert," Juan said, leaning his head against the tiled wall of the shower. "Actual fieldwork is beyond my skillset, but to set your mind at ease, I shall brave the desert. The only problem I foresee is that I don't own desert clothing."

"We visit the outfitters tomorrow. I can make sure everyone gets outfitted for the wilderness, including Bishop Fabbri," Jeremiah said as he stepped out of the shower to grab a towel. "Shut off the water, love, and let's go to bed. Tomorrow is a long day."

INTERLUDE: BECOMING A BEL-KINO

Miss Eunice Beaumont stared at herself in the full-length mirror. Her reflection possessed an odd color because of the mirror's bronze backing instead of the traditional silver. She didn't recognize the ugly woman in the mirror. The once beautiful dress from a Paris fashion house hung in rags on her in a filthy mess. Her beautiful blonde hair hung in tragic tangles around her head. Her face was caked with dirt and blood. No one should appear like this; her appearance was criminal. She felt anger rising alongside confusion over her situation. Somewhere between the destruction of the carriage and this moment, unspeakable horrors had upended her world. Miss Beaumont, for the first time in her life, wasn't sure where to direct her outrage. At first the monsters that captured her seemed the appropriate target for her hatred. However, after careful consideration, she knew that Jeremiah Banks was the real cause of her current conditions, just as he'd been responsible for the disappearance of her stepbrother several years ago. The arrival of the monster, which cursed her with this existence, interrupted her pity party.

"The master wishes to meet with you. We arranged for delivery of your belongings. Alice is here to help you clean up and be ready."

A beautiful young woman entered Eunice's rooms, pulling a rack on which hung several of the designer gowns and a few outfits of business attire. Her captors delivered a trunk with her undergarments and accessories as well. Eunice listened to the beating of Alice's heart and her hunger grew, causing her fangs to descend. The monster detected this, too.

"No eating the help, Miss Beaumont. Alice is the only servant we'll provide until you prove your worth. If you kill her, she will not be replaced and you will fend for yourself."

With all her remarkable self-control, Eunice forced down her hunger and drew in her fangs. Alice moved about the small suite, setting up a small makeup table and the items needed to fix a lady's hair. She walked into the bath and began filling the tub, adding in scented oils.

"If you will excuse us, Master, the mistress needs privacy to be ready to meet Lord Bellabarisruk."

An hour later, Alice settled Eunice in front of the vanity and began to work on her hair, brushing out the tangles until the strands lay flat. With the knots removed, Alice started to weave an elaborate style of ringlets framing Eunice's face. The serving woman took up the various makeup tools and went to work on Eunice's face. When she finished with hair and makeup, Alice helped Miss Beaumont into undergarments and a gown of russet silk and ivory lace. Dark leather ankle boots completed the ensemble. Alice moved a full-length mirror over to let Miss Beaumont survey the results. With all the grace of her upbringing, Eunice glanced at herself in the mirror and was pleased with the results.

"Now, My Lady, you're fittingly attired as a member of the Bel-Kino clan. Lord Bellabarisruk will be delighted when he meets you."

"Alice, what can you tell me about this Bel-Kino clan and Lord Bellabarisruk? I find myself at a disadvantage."

Chapter 27

After several days of travel from Damascus to Baghdad, the expedition arrived at the palace of the caliph. Guards and servants escorted them to their quarters within the palace complex. The members of the expedition received several unique sets of rooms. Jeremiah and Juan's chambers featured luxurious rooms tiled in white marble with gold veins. The bed's expanse, draped in sapphire-blue silk, was enough to hold four people in comfort. The last time Jeremiah visited the palace, his room held a cot and his packs. Two young male servants came to help them bathe and dress for dinner with the caliph and his advisors. When the servants began to undress Juan, Jeremiah barked out a sharp order in fluent Arabic dismissing them. His sapphire eyes blazed with jealousy and possessiveness, and the two young men turned and fled the suite. Juan glanced over at Jeremiah and smiled as he became aware of his lover's refusal to let another touch him.

"Come here, my beautiful boy," Juan said, arms outstretched to receive Jeremiah in an embrace. "I'm honored you're so brave in defense of my virtue, dear one."

"I remember the way they treated me the last time I visited this palace, beloved. I won't allow you to be dealt with as a piece of meat to satisfy the lust of those who condemn everything about us. Not while they indulge themselves behind their walls."

Juan wrapped Jeremiah in his strong arms, and the two men held each other for several moments before Juan drew back, slipped his hands under the shoulders of Jeremiah's jacket, and pushed the garment off his shoulders. Sapphire eyes blinked in momentary confusion before allowing his lover to continue divesting him of his clothes as he did during their initial affair. Juan admired the healthy body revealed before him. The past three years added more definition to the man's muscles and the red fur added to the definition. Gone was the longhaired boy, mistaken as some aging academic's boy toy grad student. Juan smiled at the memory of his surprise at discovering the truth. Jeremiah Banks was more than his distinctive beauty; he possessed a towering intellect and deciphered a language when others failed. Jeremiah cocked his head in question as Juan stared at his naked body and scrutinized his lover as Juan pulled back to the present.

"*Bei ricordi spero, il mio amore?*"

"*Molto dolci ricordi, amore mio.*" Juan's beautiful accent wrapped each word. "We must work on your accents; your Texan drawl infects so many of the languages you speak."

"So, what memories did you recall, *amore mio?*" Jeremiah worked loose the knot of Juan's tie. "I do think I can guess, though."

The memory brought an impish smile to Jeremiah's face, something Juan missed.

"I remembered our brief time in Atlanta when you let me undress you before we made slow and passionate love," Juan said.

"I recall you needed to slow me down or our first time wouldn't be so memorable," Jeremiah said. "I never showed much patience during sexual encounters before I met you, because both parties remained so nervous about getting caught."

Jeremiah removed Juan's jacket and shirt, revealing the muscular chest covered in more silver hair than dark hair. The mix was still as intriguing to Jeremiah as three years ago when they did this for the first time. His fingers stroked through the thick mat of hair on his lover's chest to find one of the dark nipples, which capped the firm pectorals. The rough callous on his fingertip rubbed across the sensitive nub and brought a swift intake of breath from his lover. Juan's hands rose and cupped Jeremiah's face, bringing his love close enough to kiss. When they broke apart to breathe, Juan stroked his left hand from Jeremiah's face to the center of his chest to rest over the younger man's heart.

"You learned a lot of patience, *amore mio*."

"Patience is hard won, *il mio cuore*," Jeremiah murmured as he rested his head on the older man's shoulder. "You're more than an ocean away, neither of our governments tend to give tourism visas, and I feared you went home to a wife you never mentioned."

"I hope the first of my private letters put to rest the thought of a Senora Di Vargas waiting back in Spain," Juan said. "I worried about you moving on to someone closer and younger."

Jeremiah released the clasp of Juan's belt and unfastened his suit pants, letting them fall to the floor.

"After everything you showed me in Atlanta, I realized none of my peers are capable of being the partner you became in those few days we shared." Jeremiah sank to his knees to remove Juan's shoes, socks, and pants. "The only one who might have filled the strange emptiness I experienced was the man who mentored my academic career."

Tears brimmed in Jeremiah's eyes, which Juan brushed away with his thumbs. The touch turned into a caress of his lover's face. Jeremiah pressed his face against Juan's firm abdomen and let the tears flow for a moment as he remembered the kindly professor. Dr. Adamson made sure no hint of scandal ever touched Jeremiah's academic career.

"I'm sure he's proud of your accomplishments." Juan ran his fingers through the soft copper hair. "I'll enjoy meeting the man."

"I wish meeting him remained possible, because I think Dr. Adamson would approve of you." Jeremiah glanced up at Juan. "About a week before I presented my doctoral thesis, Professor Adamson suffered a heart attack and died. He didn't survive to share in my graduation or my first discoveries."

"I'm sorry, my bright one," Juan said. "I'm sure Dr. Adamson would be proud of you."

Jeremiah slipped Juan's boxers off before standing. Leading his lover to the enormous bed, Jeremiah lay down, spreading himself across the silk coverings and offering his body to Juan.

"Make love to me, Juan," Jeremiah said. "This will be one of the few chances we share a real bed."

"Do you often make love in the desert?" Juan pressed himself to Jeremiah's body.

"Make love, nothing so special. I don't consider the desert romantic. The last sexual encounter in the desert left me thinking myself a whore for sucking off some guardsmen." The memories made Jeremiah grimace. "I sacrificed my dignity to save the son of one of my workers from rape. The poor kid spilled the dirty water from doing the dishes on one of the emir's men's boots by accident."

"Each night we will make passionate love, so the desert holds only pleasant memories for you," Juan said, settling his ass against Jeremiah's hard cock. "Now, I want you inside of me; later I will make slow passionate love to you until your brain explodes as your cock erupts."

"I'll hold you to your promise, lover," Jeremiah said.

Jeremiah's hands clamped down on Juan's ass and spread the firm cheeks apart so his cock found the entrance. Juan shifted his position until the head of Jeremiah's cock lined up with his hole and sat back, taking his lover's thick cock in one motion to move past the burn of taking him dry. Once seated in Jeremiah's lap with his partner's cock buried to the base in his ass, he reconsidered the wisdom of his choice. He wasn't a young man anymore; this hurt a lot more than he remember. Jeremiah remained beneath him, not moving as those sapphire eyes burned into his plain, brown eyes.

Juan cursed himself for an idiot, he'd hurt himself trying to make Jeremiah forget his worries. Not the smartest of moves, Juan realized; now his lover was worried about hurting him when he should be finding pleasure. When Juan started to bounce, Jeremiah clamped his grip on Juan's waist to still the man. A cooling sensation began to spread around his burning hole, and the pain began to subside. Juan relaxed as the moisture developing in his ass eased the burning sensation of being stuffed full of Jeremiah's long, thick cock. He stared down at his lover in puzzlement.

"I'm not allowing you to hurt yourself, Juan," Jeremiah said. "This is supposed to be about pleasure, not pain. Relax, my love, we can take our time."

Jeremiah pulled Juan down so the older man lay on top of him, still impaled on his cock. He drew Juan's face down and they kissed with a passion as Jeremiah stroked his hands over Juan's body. Juan sighed and settled along Jeremiah's body, molding them together. Contentment settled over the lovers, and they drifted into a pleasant doze until Jeremiah's cock softened and slipped out of Juan's ass. Juan sought to move to bring back Jeremiah's erection, but his lover stopped him.

"I'm content with you here in my arms, Juan," Jeremiah whispered. "Being together like this shows me I'm loved and protected."

"I think when this is over we should find someplace where we can bask in each other's presence, far away from the rest of the world. I'm willing to retire from teaching."

"The University of Hawaii in the Republic of California never closed their job offer. I would need to find a different line of research to pursue since my current school owns the rights to all my most recent work. Would you come with me to Hawaii, Juan?"

"I'm following you into a desert wasteland, Jeremiah. Do you think I wouldn't follow you to a tropical paradise?" Juan pulled far enough away to gaze at Jeremiah's earnest face. "I'll follow you wherever you want to go."

"Well, for starters, you should come with me into the bath, because once we're in the desert, a sponge bath is the best on offer. After a bath, I'll show you how to dress for the court of our host," Jeremiah said.

The lovers padded into the huge bathing chamber, and Jeremiah acted as servant to bathe Juan. Juan took the sponge away from Jeremiah when his lover moved to wash himself. Once cleaned up and dried off, Jeremiah showed Juan how the various layers of Islamic garb went together and helped him wrap the thick sash around his waist. Juan slipped into the jacket and Jeremiah placed the turban on Juan's head to complete the outfit. Juan's outfit was layers of maroon and cream silk, which complimented his dark complexion. Jeremiah rushed to don his outfit of sapphire and silver silk. The outfit drew attention to Jeremiah's brilliant sapphire eyes. After dressing, Jeremiah rang for the servants to return to guide them to the caliph's presence.

* * *

ELSEWHERE IN THE palace of the caliph, Bishop Fabbri along with Brothers Colum and Tobias found their accommodations as Spartan as a monk's quarters in a monastery. Colum discovered their door locked, with a guard stationed in the hall. Tobias stopped the bishop from raising a protest of their treatment.

"Don't protest, Your Grace. All you will succeed in doing is damaging Dr. Banks' expedition. The original plan didn't call for us cross into the caliphate, so we cannot expect a warm welcome," Tobias said.

"I am the Holy Father's Ambassador," Fabbri started.

"Here, we're all infidels and heretics. We are not considered a part of the expedition," Tobias interrupted. "The caliph is within his rights to execute us as spies. Keep your thoughts private, Your Grace, and let Dr. Banks or Professor Di Vargas handle the matter. For now, I suggest we all avail ourselves of the limited facilities to clean up and dress for a state dinner."

* * *

QUILLION FOUND herself in a private suite attached to the caliph's harem, a place which didn't leave her comfortable in her accommodations. She laid out her outfit for the dinner later in the evening and found her personal products for bathing when a light knock on the door leading to the harem interrupted her. Turning to the door, she bid the knocker enter. The door opened on silent hinges, revealing a young woman in pale-yellow silk bearing a tray of oils and perfumes. Her dress was of a different style and fabric from what Quillion glimpsed on the other ladies of the harem.

"I am Abal Dayyan Zidan, Mistress," the young woman said in halting English. "I am assigned to assist you while you are a guest of His Islamic Majesty."

"I'm Quillion Post, a student of Dr. Jeremiah Banks. A pleasure to meet you, Abal Dayyan Zidan," Quillion said in halting Arabic.

"An honor knowing the lady speaks the holy tongue, but if she accepts a word of advice from a lowly slave, she will keep the knowledge to herself," Abal said. "Show wisdom and allow one's opponents to underestimate one's value."

"I'll keep your wisdom in mind, Abal. Thank you for your advice," Quillion said. "Tell me why your dress is different from the other ladies of the court."

"I'm not a noble of the court, Mistress, although under different circumstances, I would rank highest save only for the caliph's first wife," Abal said. "My father—may Allah grant his soul mercy—sold me to settle a massive debt. This is why I don't share in my brother's blessed fortune. Alas, Mistress, I am as you view me, a humble slave."

"Can your brother not redeem you now since his fortune is improved?" Quillion asked.

"Perhaps if my master chose to allow such a thing," Abal said. "I bear my master's mark of ownership, so no one will ever treat me as anything but a slave."

"Your master tattooed you. In the West, such a tattoo would be meaningless," Quillion, said.

"Mistress, I am not in the West, and I am not free. Now we need to prepare you for your appearance before His Islamic Majesty and the court. Ah, someone made sure you possessed an outfit approved for foreign ladies." Abal arranged the dress and its attendant veil out on Quillion's bed. "Did your mentor also provide you with gloves to cover your hands?"

"Yes, the box on the top of my trunk contains the gloves and shoes." Quillion strained to unhook the buttons on the back of her dress. "I do not understand why proper fashion must always be some torture device."

"All noble ladies are always attended by servants. Are you not of a high noble house?" Abal placed the gloves, undergarments, and footwear out beside the dress.

"Me? No, I'm lucky to come from a family that survived the Upheaval with knowledge of a lost technology and managed to turn luck into a modest fortune. Father indulged my independent streak when I first went to university, but when I refused to marry the man chosen for me, he cut me off to fend for myself. I managed to fund my way through my master's degree and most of my doctoral work. I'm not sure if I will be able to support my final studies unless Dr. Banks allows us to write and publish papers about this expedition," Quillion said.

"Perhaps you will allow this humble slave to guide you in the ways of the titled families, Mistress," Abal said. "You possess a mentor in the outside world who is well respected for a foreigner. This grants you a status denied to many foreign ladies and offers you a protection not offered to the wives of most emirs. I will guide you as best I can and serve as your companion as my master allows."

"Thank you, Abal. I didn't expect to find a friend here," Quillion said.

"Come to the bath. I will help you out of those clothes and bathe you as a woman deserves," Abal said.

* * *

MACE AND THEO found themselves sharing a moderate set of rooms. An older servant arranged their belongings and laid out their chosen outfits for the evening upon the beds in the sleeping chamber. The servant waited by the door to the hallway.

"When the young masters are ready, I will lead you to the bathing chambers and help you bathe in preparation to dining with His Islamic Majesty, may Allah bless his reign," the servant said.

"Please give us a few moments," Mace said before whispering to Theo, "Do you think he means to bathe us?"

"Yes, *moye serdce*, I do believe he means he will be the one washing our bodies and making us presentable for the state dinner tonight. Doc warned us about dealing with the different traditions. We can always send him to guard the door while we bathe each other," Theo said.

"I prefer handling things ourselves," Mace said. "I don't think we'll find much in the way of privacy either here or out in the field. The servants helping us is different from what's available out in the field back home."

Mace and Theo signaled the servant their readiness for the bath. They followed the man down the hallway to an antechamber where benches lined the walls. On the bench closest to the door was a pile of towels.

"The young masters will undress here. Leave your clothes for the staff to wash and press for you. Once you are ready, we shall pass into the first of the bathing chambers," the servant said.

Mace stole a nervous glance at Theo before moving into the room close to the far door. They began stripping off until the both stood naked and waiting on the servant. The older man took up several of the towels from the stack and led them into the next chamber. The room beyond filled with steam, and the walls and floor were slick with condensation. Mace was self-conscious of being naked around a stranger, but he was glad Dr. Banks made him remove his tattoo. He tensed for a moment when a hand landed on his shoulder until he realized the hand belonged to Theo. The servant appeared out of the steam and wrapped a towel around each of their waists, and both men flinched when he brushed their manhood as though judging size. He directed them to sit on benches along the edge of the room.

"This room will open your pores and help with the cleansing. I will return in a few moments to take you to the next chamber," the servant said.

Mace and Theo attempted to relax in the steam room, but perceived something off. Turning his back to the door, Mace cupped his hands before him and released his Emerald magic. The steam swirling in his cupped hands went from foggy white to emerald green to sickly ochre.

Theo stared at Mace trying to figure out what was going on. Theo started to slump. Mace spread his hands and Emerald magic flashed through the room, neutralizing the drug in the steam. He touched Theo to cleanse the narcotic from his lover's system.

"We aren't safe here, Theo. The drug was meant to render us either unconscious or pliable enough to be overpowered," Mace said.

"What do we do when the servant comes back and finds us still functional?"

* * *

IN THE HIDDEN CORRIDOR, the bathing attendant met with his co-conspirators.

"The drugs in the steam should soon have them so relaxed they will be easy to subdue. Once you have them bound, deliver them to the captain of the palace guards. They should make suitable replacements for the whores the guards wore out."

Unseen by the conspirators, another servant slipped away to alert the true master of the palace.

* * *

THE SERVANT RETURNED a few moments later surprised to find the two young men still aware of their surroundings. The old servant recovered, urging them into the next room where marble tubs stood filled with warm water. A second servant stood beside one of the tubs to assist in bathing the young gentlemen. Behind them, the door closed with the sound of locking bolts. With caution, Mace and Theo climbed into the tubs and let the servants begin to bathe them. Theo sensed part of a compound in the water, which would leave them defenseless.

Accidently knocking over the table of oils and cleansing tools gave him a chance to lower the temperature of the water below the effective zone of the compound. The servants cleaned up the mess and replaced the supplies before setting to work bathing both men. A sudden snapping sound echoed in the chamber before the master of the baths fell, his head twisted at an awkward angle. Mace and Theo scrambled from their tubs as the other servant dropped to his knees, begging the towering stranger who had entered the room.

"P-p-please, Ancient One, spare my insignificant life," begged the servant.

"The mortals in this palace received instructions to give the archaeologist's party every courtesy with no harm to come to them. Yet, I find you and your associates attempting to prepare these young men to be entertainment for the barracks," said the figure in the shadows.

"Our instructions came from another dark servant, who said the young men of the party lacked your protection, Ancient One," the servant said.

"This is my palace. Who dares to countermand my orders?" the monster said, stepping into the light.

He was breathtaking in his beauty, and both Mace and Theo gasped at his figure. The man stood almost seven feet tall and was sculpted muscle. His skin was like porcelain, setting off his dark hair and eyes. Garbed in only a loincloth and sandals, the man appeared to be a gladiator or some other ancient warrior. Only the elongated canine teeth marred his beautiful visage.

"I asked you a question, child of Seth. Who dares to countermand the orders of Dungi, Prince of Baghdad?" The monster reached for the cowering servant.

"The orders came from Lord Bellabarisruk, through a messenger from the Duke of Damascus. Who are we to deny the commands of a primordial, Ancient One?"

"Servants in my house. I do not serve the Lord of Bel-Kino. My sire is Bellabarisruk's equal and my loyalty is to the Lord of all Vampires, who is also coming here. These men and the rest of the archaeologist's party are under Lord Slayer's protection," Dungi said. "Go and tell the rest of the servants involved in this plot how they raised my ire and I will cull the staff of this palace."

"Yes, Ancient One." The servant rose and fled the baths.

Dungi turned his attention to Mace and Theo. The men found towels and wrapped them around their waists for a form of modesty. Both kept their magic ready, tingling beneath their skin.

"I am Dungi, first gifted of Parlathán the Cursed, second gifted of Sharru-Kino, King of El-Abel. I am the lord of this palace and city on behalf of Lord Slayer," Dungi said. "Who are you?"

"I'm Macejah Puap and this is Theophisus Polzin. We're graduate students assigned to Dr. Jeremiah Banks' expedition to find El-Abel." Mace said.

"Such an honor to meet you despite the circumstances. Rare is the scholar visiting the wasteland the so-called caliphs made of my city." Dungi nodded his head to the pair. "Come, let's return to your rooms and make sure proper guards and servants are sent to attend you."

"Thank you for saving us from whatever they planned to do with us, Ancient One," Mace said.

"You may call me Dungi. Only craven servants who forget their place call me Ancient One. No scholars visit to converse with me anymore; the last one visited a century ago if not longer," Dungi said, leading the guys back to their suite. "Long ago, Father Cain bound me to the palace district of Baghdad. I receive reports of the changes in the world from the servants and the rare vampire who travels through my territory, but I long to learn stories from other lands."

"We would be honored to share our knowledge of our homelands." Theo's accent grew thick with nerves being around this stranger. "We hope you will share your history with our mentor, Dr. Banks, or with us."

"You come from the lands of the Slavs. Do you possess news of my sister in the gift, Celina Dyta?" Dungi asked.

"The Dark Crone of the North?" Theo was puzzled why someone would ask after a creature out of folklore. "There are many stories about Celina Dyta, but you ask for news. There is one tale from the early days of the current empire about a hundred and thirty years ago. Tsar Michael's rule was threatened by the Dark Crone and summoned the best hunters in the world. According to the tale, she was destroyed along with all the hunters."

"A shame. Once she was a mighty and wise warrior before our sire Parlathán passed his Cain cursed gift to her. He warped her fierce spirit with the gift."

"Forgive us our ignorance of your kind. Our information only says a vampire named Bellabarisruk seeks to prevent Dr. Banks and Prof. Di Vargas from finding El-Abel or Enoch. They are struggling to figure out if they're looking for one city or two," Mace said.

"They search for two locations if they seek both El-Abel and Enoch, although calling Enoch a city is overstating the place's importance. Enoch never amounted to more than a collection of hovels. They seek in vain. Both suffered destruction when the mage lord Noah brought down the Flood upon El-Abel. Several of my fleeing brethren told me the tale at the time. Father Cain bound me to this place long before Nineveh waged war on El-Abel. My binding was punishment for being a child of Parlathán from before his curse. I must not keep you from the dinner with the mortal who dreams of ruling these lands. Return here afterward, and I will trade stories with you."

"Would you meet with Dr. Banks and Prof. Di Vargas? They're the ones who seek the knowledge you hold."

"I will consider speaking with them. Now I must go and punish those who would disobey my commands."

The ancient vampire left Mace and Theo to dress for the state dinner they guessed others expected them not to attend. Mace pulled Theo close, stripping away both their towels so they pressed against each other's naked flesh. Their arms wrapped around each other and they kissed with a passion and tried to bury their fears. Mace broke their kiss long enough to whisper in Theo's ear.

"Make love to me before we leave this room again."

"And you to me as well, *moye serdce*. Let us be complete." Theo drew Mace to the bed.

INTERLUDE: RICHARD
ATTEMPTS TO CATCH UP

Richard, Azim, and Fahim raced their camels across the distance from the camp of the Brotherhood to Damascus, hoping to catch up to Dr. Banks' expedition before the Westerners left for Baghdad. As the dawn approached, Richard made a gesture. His strange, sparkling Ebony magic formed a portal, which he reached into, and he pulled forth a dark cloak similar to the one Database wore in public. When the fabric was free and the portal was dismissed, Richard wrapped the cloak around him as the first light of dawn broke over the horizon. Though covered, the first rays of the dawn hurt Richard like hell; discovering the trick to creating the portal and the storage pocket several years ago made a difference in his life.

Dawn remained the only time he feared the touch of the sun. A strange connection existed between the sun and the magic, which coursed through him, enhancing his Ruby magic. No matter how many Ebony mages he encountered working magic, never did he find one whose magic sparkled as his did. Other mages' Ebony magic absorbed light, but his produced light. Did the answer to his strange question hide in El-Abel? Cain often alluded to his curse being a blending of Ebony,

Silver, and Emerald magic. Had some other color of magic been absorbed as well? When the group reached the outskirts of Damascus in the late afternoon, they met another member of the Brotherhood of the Crimson Hand.

"Master of Darkness, your agents of the night sent word. Dr. Banks and his party left for Baghdad last night under escort from the caliph's forces," the man said. "They also report the remainder of Imam Abd-El-Basir was dispatched for their rebellion."

"Thank you for the report. We'll need faster transport than these camels to catch up with Dr. Banks' party. Any sightings of Bellabarisruk?"

"No, Master. So far, we've only tracked a few of the primordial's lower-level agents and the imam's forces allied to Barghest and a dark faction of his clan. You should be aware, Master, the palace of Baghdad is the domain of one of Barghest's first gifted."

"Yes, Dungi of Baghdad. He sent a servant to pledge his fealty when he learned of my ascension to Cain's place as Lord of Vampires. I'm not concerned about the undead of Baghdad. What concerns me are the mortals with power in the palace. How quick can the transport to Baghdad be arranged?"

"Transport will be ready when the sun sets, Master. Let me escort you to the safe house where your associates are waiting for the evening to come, before dealing with your mounts and arranging transportation."

"Whatever funds you raise from the sale of the camels and equipment are to be split between Azim and Fahim, as these animals came from their camp. Adam FitzCaine will reimburse your group for the costs of transporting the five of us to Baghdad."

"The costs are the Brotherhood's to bear, Master. Come this way and rest in the safety of the Brotherhood."

The man led Richard and his party into an area of the outer slums of Damascus, a section of the city still recovering from the devastation, which rained down on the place in the early twenty-first century. The war following the Upheaval of 2092 only added to the damage before the city, along with the former state of Syria, surrendered to Israeli forces in 2115. Over time the new state of Greater Israel began rebuilding the ruined region, but slums exist in the most prosperous places and Damascus was far from prosperous. The administrative center, including the vast library, received the most reconstruction financing. A few hotels sprouted up to serve diplomats and a few scholars were allowed travel permits. The Orthodox/Conservative Alliance, which ruled Greater Israel, gave priority to places in Israel and Egypt over the other territories. Damascus only rose to their attention when the new American nations chose to establish consulates in the city for dealing with the caliphate. At this point, the only actual consulate with finished construction belonged to the Federal Union of North America, but rumors mentioned the Republic of Texas looking for a suitable neighborhood as the location for theirs.

Richard came out of his thoughts when his camel came to an abrupt stop. He glanced around to find the various properties in the area under repair. The agent of the Brotherhood assisted in getting the camels to kneel, allowing the riders to dismount. Azim and Fahim gathered their belongings and followed Richard inside the apartment complex, in front of which the trio stopped. Richard's vampiric senses led him to the apartment where his associates waited out the day. He stopped in front of the apartment, barred from knocking on the door by the presence of immense faith. With a glance, he directed Azim to knock for them. The young assassin knocked and answered the challenge in a rapid exchange in a dialect of Arabic Richard couldn't follow despite the gift of languages inherited along with his curse. The door opened, and Richard glimpsed a man kneeling on a prayer rug facing the direction of Mecca. Beyond, he sensed Database and Armand in another room but prevented from leaving by the same reason Richard couldn't enter.

"Azim, defend Fahim, I fear we've walked into a trap. This holy man came after this faction offered my associates shelter from the approaching daylight. He prevents me from entering and them from leaving." Richard explained. "This will be messy at best."

"Allow me to eliminate the imam, Master," Azim said.

"Master of Darkness, may I speak to the imam before we resort to violent solutions?" Fahim asked. "Perhaps he will listen to a logical argument."

"Go ahead, Fahim, but do not enter the room."

Fahim nodded and stepped in front of the doorway. He knelt to face the imam on an equal level. Richard and Azim guarded from opposite ends of the corridor making sure no other renegades arrived. Fahim began a rapid conversation in the same strange Arabic dialect. Richard extended his senses as far as possible, searching for the living and undead opponents. The search revealed the apartment complex empty save for his party and the imam. The scenario didn't sit well with Richard, and understanding dawned.

"Fahim, tell him his allies left him to be a sacrifice to the devil they chose to serve," Richard hissed. "He's not headed to heaven."

"Master, he showed me the detonator for the explosives in the building," Fahim said. "He believes this is Allah's will, blessed be His name."

"His God isn't involved." Richard moved into the doorway, standing over the kneeling figure of Fahim. "Azim, take Fahim and leave. Find someplace safe, and we will locate you after the sun sets."

Azim nodded and grabbed Fahim's wrist, dragging his friend away from the door and to his feet once he put distance between them and Richard. The Lord of the Vampires braced against the outside of the doorframe and let his strange Ebony magic flow into the walls defining the area of the imam's faith barrier.

"Let's test your faith, holy man. I do not believe you possess the power to resist me," Richard said as his magic squeezed the whole bubble of confidence surrounding the man. "The advantage is mine, old man. Detonate those explosives, I'll survive, whereas you must trust Allah will claim your soul and reward you in heaven. Is the going rate of martyrdom still seventy-two virgins, or did they change the number? All the others abandoned you to die alone trying to kill a target who can't die."

Chapter 28

THE MEMBERS of the expedition gathered in the antechamber outside the caliph's state dining room. Each dressed in clothes of the finest materials and proper cuts for an audience with Islamic royalty. The cassock worn by Bishop Fabbri was a dark velvet, episcopal-purple, ankle-length vest with elaborate silver embroidery in the pattern of mixed stags and fleur-de-lis over black pants and shirt. His only visible jewelry was his silver and amethyst ring of rank. The two young monks wore the traditional hooded black robes and leather sandals of the Order of St. Hubert.

Mace and Theo wore the latest fashion from the Republic of Texas. The outfits consisted of loose linen shirts under silk waistcoats topped by velvet mourning coats and leather pants over western boots. The guys completed their apparel with bowler hats topped with brass and glass goggles resting on the brim. However, of the entire group, Quillion captured the most attention. Her outfit consisted of a dress of forest-green silk, leather corset with brass and silver fittings, and black lace fingerless gloves. A black-and-silver lace half-veil suspended from the decorative top hat of forest-green velvet cloaked her eyes. At her throat, a brass, copper-and-silver broach held closed a spray of the same lace as her veil. Her dark hair cascaded around her face to frame the picture of a demure Western lady.

The doors leading into the dining room opened to reveal the lavish ground-level table surrounded by plush pillows. The servants escorted the party members to their places around the table to await the arrival of the caliph. An old noble ambled over to Jeremiah and Juan.

"Wonder of wonders! All praise to Allah. You are as amazing to gaze upon as when you danced for me in my tent during your last expedition, Dr. Banks."

"Excellency, you flatter me. May Allah continue to bless you with excellent health."

The bow Jeremiah executed as he offered his blessing to the nobleman showed deep respect.

"Excellency, allow me to introduce you to the co-leader of my current expedition, Professor Juan Di Vargas of the University of Madrid; Professor, His Excellency Aasif el-Taimur el-Shahin, Emir of Safwãn."

Copying Jeremiah's example, Juan bowed to the noble and offered a blessing on the man's health. The emir listened with excitement to the tales of translated texts and a quest for a lost city. The emir's excitement doubled when he learned the proposed dig site lay in his district. Visions of employment for his people on the location filled his head.

"With the blessings of His Islamic Majesty, I hope to employ some your citizens and your guards as well, Excellency. Do you think this will be possible?"

The old nobleman came close to heart failure with joy at the request.

"Of course, of course, once His Majesty grants his blessing, we can begin negotiating a labor contract."

"I will enjoy haggling with you, Excellency."

The opening of a door at the back of the dining room interrupted Jeremiah before he continued his conversation with the emir. A man dressed in gold-on-gold tones stepped through the door and moved to stand behind the cushions at the head of the table. All around Jeremiah, including the other members of his expedition, bowed at the waist in respect for the newest arrival. Caught by total surprise by the man's piecing emerald eyes, golden blond beard, and lean but powerful physique, Jeremiah stared at a man he thought dead. The man glared back at Jeremiah with searing contempt.

"Is this how the famous archaeologist shows his respect?"

Sketching a bow, Jeremiah straightened and spoke before the caliph granted permission.

"Forgive my lack of courtesy, Your Islamic Majesty. Finding a friend, I thought long dead in such a lofty position of power is a surprise."

"The matter of our friendship is something to be discussed in private at a later time, Dr. Banks. Tonight, you are my guests, so I shall forgive the lapse of courtesy. Please be seated."

The guests settled in at their places around the table. Seated at the right hand of the caliph, Jeremiah found himself in an uncomfortable position. Here was the grad student their field professor sacrificed to the local guards to preserve his excavation. Shame filled him as he remembered trying to find out what became of the young man in the aftermath. The professor blocked every avenue Jeremiah sought to use to find his fellow student. Now here he sat as the caliph. How did poor Jasper St. James become Caliph Makhdoom ibn Pervaiz ibn Sad, Custodian of the Two Holy Mosques and ruler of all Islam?

The servants brought out the first dish of the evening: an appetizer, waraq dawali. Jeremiah's appetite was failing him, and he ate only enough to show appreciation to his host for his hospitality. Beside him,

Juan was enjoying the dish and chatting with Emir Aasif about the man's region of administration. Sparing a glance down the table, Jeremiah found his students eating and conversing with their dinner companions in Pidgin English and Arabic. Before he focused on the others of his party, the caliph caught his attention.

"You brought a bishop and two monks with you, Jeremiah. Rather rude of you to flaunt the rules."

"Jas— Majesty, Bishop Fabbri is the envoy of the Holy Father in Rome and the political watchdog over Professor Di Vargas' half of the expedition. A matter I'm sure your representatives in the Holy Roman Empire will discuss with His Holiness' government."

"Poor Jeremiah Banks, you're at a loss on how to deal with me now. The boy you called Jasper is long dead. Makhdoom took up his shattered life and forged something new out of the wreckage our beloved professor left."

"I tried to stop him, tried to convince him to send me in your place."

"We'll discuss the matter later, Jeremiah. Now tell me, which member of your party will you sacrifice to pursue this quest?"

"You want revenge. You think I'm like our professor, willing to sacrifice the life of an innocent. Take the vengeance you want, Jasper, but I'm the one who will settle the debt."

"The one I want revenge on is beyond my reach, Jeremiah. What I wanted to discover is if the man matched the reputation in the caliphate. The boy you saved spread the tale of how you took his place servicing the emir's guards after his little accident. Now you offer yourself in place of any of your party to appease my wrath. You are everything your reputation claims. Relax, enjoy the meal, and we'll talk more in private after dinner."

The arrival of the soup course prevented Jeremiah from replying to the caliph's comments. The servant placed a bowl of a creamy soup in front of him, and Jeremiah hesitated a moment before taking a spoonful of the soup.

"Frike. I never find the ingredients to make this back home." Jeremiah's excitement caught the attention of several other guests. "This is one of my favorite dishes."

"I think, Dr. Banks, you'll find the menu tonight is a compilation of dishes you enjoyed during your visits to our lands," the caliph said.

"May Allah bless you with a long reign, Majesty."

"Thank you, Dr. Banks."

Water glasses refilled, soup dishes cleared, and conversations continued around most of the table before the staff served the primary course. The aroma drew Jeremiah's attention before the servant set the plate in front of him. The pungent aromas of turmeric and cardamom filled the nose as the servant placed the plate down at Jeremiah's place.

"Lamb Gheimeh, your chef works miracles, Majesty." Jeremiah turned to Juan before speaking further. "This dish symbolizes luck and fortune for me, Prof. Di Vargas. The morning after this meal was served, I discovered the El-Isin tablets with both El-Isinian and cuneiform on them."

"The dish is served tonight, Dr. Banks, in hopes of bring you luck on your quest to discover El-Abel," the caliph said.

Once everyone enjoyed their fill of the primary course, the servants whisked dishes away and refilled empty glasses. Somewhere the majordomo sent a signal, and servants brought the desert course to the table. The dish set before each guest was unfamiliar to Jeremiah. The caliph took delight in the archaeologist's puzzled expression.

"My dessert chef was born near blessed Mecca, and this is one of his specialties. The dish is called halawet el-riz. It is a cheese, rice, and cream dish," the caliph said.

The room filled with the sound of spoons clinking against dishes as the dinner guests tucked into the new dessert. The caliph allowed Jeremiah to enjoy most of the rich and savory dessert before leaning over to whisper in his ear. "We'll continue our discussion about your expedition in my private chambers. I think I'll put your reputation and offer of self-sacrifice to the test."

VAMPIRE INTERLUDE: POWERS BEHIND THE THRONE

After dinner, the caliph excused himself from his guests and left the gathering. In a hallway about halfway back to his quarters, a hand reached out of the shadows and pulled the caliph into a shadowed alcove. A sharp pain followed by knee-melting ecstasy revealed the presence of the master he served, Grand Duke Omar Ghazi, the Vampire Lord of Baghdad. The Bel-Kino clan member found him during the brutal gang rape his professor consigned him to in his attempt to retain his dig site. At the time, Omar served as his maker's enforcer over the province of An Nasiriyah in Southern Iraq. The monster decided to rescue the battered student and nurse him back to health. Offended by the boy's Christian name, Omar renamed him Makhdoom and arranged for his adoption by Emir Dayyan ibn Zidan, the mortal administrator of the province. Ill fortune befell the emir a few years before Makhdoom secured the holy throne of the caliphate and the emir sold his daughter Abal to his rival as part of the settlement of his debt. When Ghazi released his royal servant, Makhdoom staggered from the blood loss but managed to keep his feet under him.

"This palace hosts a danger to our master's plan, Your Majesty."

"Master, I cannot turn away foreign envoys."

"The archaeologist and his party aren't the danger, which worries me. Somewhere in this palace is another of my kind, an elder with vast age. This elder I suspect decimated my network of spies and servants within the palace. This unknown vampire is the danger we must deal with before Lord Bellabarisruk arrives."

"When I seized the palace from the last caliph, he said I might rule the caliphate, but I would never rule within these wall, as this place belongs to Dungi ibn Parlathán."

"A Barghest dwells within these walls. I'll exterminate the vermin myself."

"Master, allow me to remove this threat from the palace."

"Unless this ghoul allowed you to find him, you wouldn't stand a chance, my pet."

The light in the hallway flickered, drawing their attention. A hulking figure stood in the corridor before the pair.

"I choose to grace you with my presence, Bel-Kino lackey. I am Dungi, first gifted of Parlathán the Cursed."

Dungi stepped into the light revealing his god-like perfection. Grand Duke Omar tossed the caliph aside before confronting the older vampire.

"How hideous did you appear in life to achieve such perfection of form, Barghest scum?"

"My appearance didn't alter from my mortal life, worm. I received the gift from Parlathán before he and the others of our clan pissed off Father Cain and received his current curse. Because I didn't raise my hand against my grandfather, Sharru-Kino, the curse passed over me. Instead, Father Cain bound me here to be the guardian of this palace and those who rule here when they prove worthy."

"So, you find my candidates worthy?"

"As long as I'm not disturbed and those under my protection are unmolested, I do not care what mortal sits on whatever they wish to call the throne. Your current puppet hasn't acted against my interests, but you do, little Bel-Kino. Your agents here ignored my warning not to touch any of the mortals of the archaeological expedition, but they moved against the young scholars despite my commands."

"They acted on my orders and those of Lord Bellabarisruk. The caliphate is my territory to rule as grand duke on behalf of the Bel-Kino clan."

"Did you arrange for your control over so much territory with Lord Slayer? Did you pledge loyalty to the successor of Father Cain?"

"The upstart doesn't deserve my loyalty. Bellabarisruk is my Lord, and he confirmed my control of this territory."

"Sorry to learn of your disloyalty, Omar Ghazi. Dungi, would you earn your freedom from Cain's curse?" Richard said, stepping out from a room off the hallway.

"I await your command, Lord Slayer," Dungi said.

"Kill this piece of filth for me, and I lift Cain's curse."

"My lord asks for your head, upstart," Omar screamed.

"He's welcome to come and try. I grow tired of dealing with his minions."

Sparkling Ebony magic flared around both Richard and the caliph, removing them from the field of combat. They reappeared in the throne room. Richard sprawled across the throne, leaving the caliph staring at him in confusion.

"Forgive me for usurping the throne, but I figure you don't sit here when your master is around. Time for a chat, Majesty, but first, let me introduce myself or, better yet, let my vizier do the honors. Armand!"

"How may I be of service, My Lord?" Armand appeared beside the throne.

"Perform your function and introduce me to this petitioner."

"Of course, My Lord. Welcome petitioner to the court of His Unholiness, Richard St. Martin, and Lord of all Vampires. Who comes to petition, My Lord?"

"I am Makhdoom ibn Pervaiz ibn Sad, Custodian of the Two Holy Mosques and Caliph of Baghdad."

"What is your real name?" Richard asked. "You're not a Muslim by birth."

"Before my rebirth, they called me Jasper St. James," the caliph said.

"Well, Jasper, let's talk about how you can assist Dr. Banks and his party."

"You are not master here, nor are you my master."

"Oh, I disagree with you on those points, Jasper. Dungi will finish your master. The closer one's gift is to the source the stronger the vampire. Dungi is the fourth tier of the gift counting from Cain, while your master is at least two levels lower by my estimation."

"What of you? My master calls you upstart and a fraud. Where do you fall on this tier of vampires?"

"Why, I'm the top of the food chain. In my mortal days, I slew Cain the first vampire and, as per the story in the Torah, received his curse direct from God."

"Now I understand why they call you a fraud. No mortal possesses the power to kill a vampire of Cain's age and power."

"I once thought the same thing, Jasper. However, from my chat with Cain and the journals he left, I learned he tired of his existence and allowed me to kill him. So here we are: Lord of all Vampires and Caliph of all Islam."

"This still doesn't make you master here."

Dungi walked into the throne room as the caliph made his declaration. He tossed an object across the room to bounce and roll to a stop at the caliph's feet. The man gazed down on the severed head of the vampire who was once his savior and master. As he stared in shock, the last remains of his master became dust.

"Well, with Omar Ghazi now dust, I think I'm the master of this place and all within," Richard said.

Three more figures emerged from the shadows behind the throne as the caliph trembled in the presence of at least three elder vampires who opposed his former master. Richard appeared before the startled ruler.

"Now, Jasper, we're discussing how you can help Dr. Banks' expedition. Part of your assistance begins by placing these two young men into the archaeologist party."

"I will do no such thing. Helping you opposes Lord Bellabarisruk and the plans of my master."

"Ah, of course Omar bound you to his course. When did you start drinking his blood?"

"When he rescued me from the emir's guards ten years ago."

"Withdrawal is a brutal process and can prove fatal, Majesty. The bond must break or transfer to another. Dr. Banks needs to be on his way to find El-Abel, so delaying him while purging this addiction is not an option. Dungi, this is your territory, so I give this mortal to you to assist in ruling in my name."

"I cannot bind him or give him the gift, Lord Slayer. Doing so would bind me in Father Cain's curse on Parlathán and his bloodline."

"I promised to free you from Cain's curse, which binds you to this palace. Perhaps I can break the one, which binds you to the bloodline of your cursed maker. The removal of both curses will be painful, Dungi."

"I will endure the pain, Lord Slayer."

PART IV

In the Ruins of El-Abel

Chapter 29

Two days after the formal state dinner with the caliph, Jeremiah and the company packed up their baggage and checked on the field equipment. Stepping into the entrance hall, Jeremiah encountered one of the caliph's advisors and two young men.

"Dr. Banks, His Islamic Majesty requests you include these two young students in your party. They are undergraduates in archaeology at the University of Baghdad."

"The truth is my hands are full with three graduate students. An active dig site is no place for students as young as these two are."

"His Islamic Majesty made my instructions clear, Dr. Banks. In anticipation of your refusal, His Excellency makes this offer for you to reconsider."

Behind the official, two sets of guards appeared, holding the struggling forms of Brothers Colum and Tobias. Both showed signs their struggles started earlier. The fabric of their cassocks bore rips in several places and Tobias sported the beginnings of a spectacular shiner. Blood trickled down Colum's face from his nose and a split lip.

The air temperature around Jeremiah began to drop for a moment until he clamped down on his anger. He focused on the two young men before him, ignoring the struggling monks.

"What are your names, and why are you joining my expedition?"

"Excellency, I am Fahim, and this is my blood brother Azim. We are the Islamic counterparts to the monks. We are assigned to assist and protect you on behalf of our elders." Fahim held Azim's tattooed palm up for Jeremiah to examine.

"The monks and Bishop Fabbri will be held here as assurance against your behavior in the field, Dr. Banks," the official said.

"No, all my party travels with me, or the caliph can explain to His Holiness and the President of the Republic why after his assurances underlings disrupted my expedition. I'll include these two in my party, not on your insistence, but because they are honest with me."

"Release the monks into Dr. Banks' custody," the official ordered. "I'm glad we agree, Dr. Banks."

"Tell His Islamic Majesty this for me: I pity the man you've become, Jasper."

Jeremiah turned on his heel and stormed outside, pausing only long enough to lower his tinted goggles over his eyes and to put on his Stetson. Outside he found his baggage and equipment loading on a massive sand train. Around the flatcars and boxcars, workers under the direction of Mace, Theo, and Quillion stacked crates of supplies and tied down the half-tracks and fodder for the herd of camels. Four gleaming brass-and-steel passenger cars hitched behind the massive engine, and a coal car made up the center section of the train. Behind him, Jeremiah became aware of Colum, Tobias, and the two new additions to his party. A quick survey of the scene located Juan emerging from one of the passenger cars followed by Bishop Fabbri.

He turned and found Colum and Tobias squinting in the bright sunlight reflecting off the sands surrounding this side of the palace.

"Board the train and clean up. Find your gear and put on your goggles before you suffer snow blindness. While inside, show our newest members where they can bunk. When the crew finishes loading everything and we're underway, the whole expedition team will gather and discuss what's going on."

The two battered monks proceeded down to the train and gave brief introductions to Prof. Di Vargas and Bishop Fabbri of the two new members of the team. Further down the length of the train, Jeremiah double-checked his students' work. Quillion's voice carried across the grounds. She berated one of the guards as he stood holding a whip poised to beat a fallen woman. This morning, Quillion was dressed more like Theo or Mace, in leather pants, heavy leather knee-length boots, and a loose linen shirt under a leather vest. A Stetson crowned her head, adding its shade to the dark-lensed goggles on her face. At her waist was strapped a heavy pistol, a canteen, and a pouch, which he guessed held her extra ammo. The woman on the ground wore an outfit that belonged in the harem, not out in the desert. Theo was making his way down the length of the train towards Quillion, but with a quick hand sign, Jeremiah sent him back to overseeing the loading of equipment.

As he drew closer, he caught Quillion's angry words to the guard. Outraged by the callous treatment the young woman on the ground received, Quillion was drawing closer to insulting the man's heritage when Jeremiah intervened.

"What is going on here, Ms. Post? I remember giving you directions to oversee the loading of the fragile equipment. Why do I find you arguing with this guard and why is this woman on the ground?"

Choosing to answer Dr. Banks' last question first, Quillion switched from Arabic to English.

"Because this oaf decided to shove her to the ground for being in his way, Dr. Banks. He thinks he can do anything he wants to her because she's a slave to Emir Dhakir ibn Mahaz."

"What did I tell you about the status of slaves, Ms. Post? He is within his rights to do to her whatever he chooses so long as the emir doesn't object."

Quillion retained the sense to realize she bordered on crossing a line with her mentor and blushed as she stared at her boots. Jeremiah caught the flash of gold fire in her eye and guessed she wouldn't give up anytime soon. He sighed and turned his attention back to the guard hauling the slave girl to her feet. The girl trembled with fear.

"How much is the emir asking for this slave?"

"Doctor, what are you doing?"

"Trying to save us from a headache in the future; besides you're without a proper chaperone."

While Jeremiah sought to drive his point home to his student as he argued with the guardsman, an old nobleman approached the group. The slave girl, who appeared scared when the guard grabbed her, became terrified at the appearance of the noble. The guard bowed at the waist in respect for the noble.

"Excellency, the Westerner requests the purchase price for Abal."

"Fascinating, I didn't realize Westerners owned slaves, Dr. Banks."

"Excellency, the Texan Republic and the Confederacy both permit slavery. I seek a companion for my student, Ms. Post. I understand Abal served her in the palace, and I fear she grew attached."

"This slave is a valued member of my household, Dr. Banks. I couldn't part with her. Perhaps another girl would serve your purpose."

"I suppose we can delay a few days to find a suitable girl in the slave markets. I must speak with the caliph to receive permission to delay. How embarrassing after spending so many hours convincing him to let us leave so soon."

"Well, in the interest of not bothering His Majesty with such a trifling matter, suppose I sell her to you for a million daric."

"For such a price, I may buy a hundred slaves, Excellency." Jeremiah gestured for the guard to bring the girl closer. "Before I give you a counter offer, let me examine her condition."

Before anyone reacted, Jeremiah reached out and stripped away the girl's outfit. He picked up Quillion grinding her teeth as she bit back her anger. The girl, for her part, stood still with her hands at her side. Jeremiah walked around her as though examining a camel. Her back marred with whip scars and a horrid slave tattoo design. She was beautiful otherwise, and her bearing suggested a high background. Jeremiah commanded she open her mouth to examine her teeth. With a shrug, he tossed her clothes back to her.

"Taking into consideration the damage to her back from the lash and the hideous slave tattoo, I can offer you a hundred thousand Republican red backs."

"Such a small counter offer is insulting, Dr. Banks."

"Apologies, Excellency, but the tattoo you marked her with cannot be altered with ease considering the artist did the work before the first wounds healed. The price you ask is high enough one would think her royalty fallen on hard times. I'll raise my offer to two hundred thousand Republican red backs, Excellency."

"She is the daughter of a fellow emir who fell into debt. I took her as part of the man's payment of his debt."

"How long ago did she become your slave, Excellency?"

"Two and a half years, Dr. Banks."

"Is she trained in the giving of pleasure, or is she only used to sate the lusts of your guards?"

"She remains untouched by men in those ways. She may be a slave, but she is still an emir's daughter."

"Two hundred and fifty thousand Republican red backs, my final offer." Jeremiah responded more for Quillion than for the emir. He wanted her to understand limits existed.

"This is worse than haggling in a bazaar, but she's yours, Dr. Banks."

"Thank you, Excellency. May Allah bless you with many sons." Jeremiah bowed to the emir and Quillion followed his lead. "Ms. Post, please take Abal aboard and settle her in quarters before returning to your tasks."

"Yes, Dr. Banks. Come, Abal."

Quillion led the frightened slave girl away from the group of men. Jeremiah arranged for the emir to collect the payment for the slave girl. With the matter settled, he returned to overseeing the final loading of the equipment. With the loading completed, Jeremiah went forward to the locomotive where he talked with the engineer about plotting their course to the dig site. Soon the enormous engine built up the head of steam needed to leave and pulled away from the palace depot. Jeremiah headed to the private carriage reserved for Juan and himself. The carriage contained two sleeping compartments and a small washroom, and the central portion of the carriage doubled as a sitting room or converted into a private dining room. The next carriage divided into several sleeping compartments housing Bishop Fabbri, Brothers Colum and Tobias, the two new arrivals, Mace, and Theo. The third carriage contained one private cabin, which Quillion and Abal claimed; the rest of the carriage held dining space and a kitchen. The final passenger car configured as a salon and observation car.

With a sigh of relief, Jeremiah claimed one of the plush chairs and hooked a footstool over to prop up his booted feet. He pulled off his Stetson and his goggles and set them beside his seat. Juan handed him a glass of ice water before claiming the seat opposite his lover. Juan remained dressed in his standard suit style.

"I hoped to find you wearing one of the new outfits from Damascus. You need to start wearing the boots to break them in and adjust to their weight."

"Such casual attire as you favor is foreign to me, Jeremiah. Remember this expedition is my first time going out in the field, and I guess the researcher in me is rebelling against getting dirty."

"All those layers only serve to trap heat, Juan. An old-world suit can't handle the rigors of the field. Once those dress shoes fill with sand and chafe your feet, walking becomes painful. Without your goggles, the brim of a bowler doesn't protect your eyes from the glare of the sun."

"But what about this train?"

"The train goes back to the caliph once we unload our equipment from the cars at the dig site. I offered you the chance to stay back in Damascus, Juan, and you chose to stay with me. We've finished your half of this expedition; now we're into my areas of expertise."

Juan heaved himself out of the chair and headed to the sleeping compartment at the end of the carriage. The new outfits sat in his travel chest. He unbuttoned his suit coat and started to remove his tie and collar. Only the slight creak of Jeremiah's last, few steps warned him of his lover's approach. He found himself wrapped in his lover's arms, but things other than Jeremiah pressed into him.

"I love being held by you, my beautiful boy, but I'm not sure I'm comfortable being hugged by a gun, a canteen, and other items I can't identify."

Jeremiah laughed in his ear before releasing him. The sound of creaking leather and the solid thump of a heavy object on the floor gave Juan a hint that Jeremiah's gun belt now rested on the floor. Warmth and love returned as Jeremiah embraced him once again.

"Is this better, *mi corazón*?"

"Much better, beautiful boy."

Nimble fingers slipped the pin holding the cravat around Juan's neck free and into the pocket of the suit jacket. A slight tug and the jacket eased away from his shoulders and down his arms. A bit of a cool breeze stirred as Jeremiah moved to hang up the jacket before he returned to his place behind Juan. Like he was examining a delicate artifact, Jeremiah's dexterous fingers unfastened first the shirt's cuffs before taking a slow and teasing course down the shirtfront opening buttons. A couple of swift tugs and the shirt pulled free from the suit pants and whisked away. Those nimble fingers returned, teasing Juan's nipples into firm peaks beneath his undershirt before they tugged the garment free from his body. Now the only thing Juan wore above the waist was the cravat.

"Do you trust me, *paliá psychí*?"

"Old soul and in Greek no less. Your gift for languages never ceases to amaze me, Miah."

"Hmm, I don't think anyone ever called me by the back half of my given name."

"Do you like it, my love?"

"Yes, I do, but you didn't answer my question, Juan."

"I trust you."

"I'm glad."

The cravat left Juan's neck with a whisper of silk fabric. The material returned to cover his eyes and tightened behind his head.

"Let me choose your outfit and dress you for the field."

"Go ahead; I trust the car is locked off from the rest of the train."

"Unless an emergency arises, we won't be disturbed. Now no more talking, Professor."

Juan started to protest only to find the second piece of fabric stuffed in his mouth and a third piece used to tie the gag in place. Jeremiah's fingers traced their way down his face and across the areas of his neck, which always made him moan. The muffled sound of his moan turned him on. Once before did Jeremiah take this much control of their activities. The Texan gave the impression he preferred to take the submissive role when they made love. The display of dominance displayed a different side of the quiet archaeologist. The fingers returned to tugging on his erect nipples, drawing deeper moans out of Juan. In his trousers, Juan's cock grew harder in wanton desire. The fingers brushed a breath over the tips of his chest hair, making Juan shiver despite the sweltering heat.

"Brace yourself on the doorframe."

Those whispered words proved the only warning Juan received before Jeremiah's presence at his back vanished. Pressure on the back of his right knee forced the joint to bend and lift. His hands shot out to grip the frame of the door for balance as Jeremiah pulled off his dress shoes. The shivers returned as his pant leg rose up to allow his lover to unfasten the garter holding his sock up. Soon the sock disappeared, and the process repeated with his left foot. Barefoot, naked to the waist, blindfolded, and gagged, Juan wondered what the redhead planned to do next. Pressure and a wet heat against the fly of his trousers answered his unspoken question. His underwear grew damp as his prick began to leak and his moans deepened.

Jeremiah sat back on his heels and grinned as Juan's cries of passion changed to whimpers of desperation when he removed his mouth from the older man's trapped genitals. The view looking up at Juan's fur-covered chest almost broke Jeremiah's resolve to tease the man with extended foreplay. Reaching up, he ran a finger over the length of Juan's fabric-covered cock, which drew a moan of ecstasy and caused a slight thrusting of Juan's hips from the gesture. With deft hands, Jeremiah unfastened and removed Juan's belt. Moving behind the professor, he pulled the man's hands behind him and bound them with the leather strap. He pressed himself into his lover's back as he reached around and popped the buttons on Juan's fly. No longer held in place, the suit pants slid down Juan's legs to pool at his ankles. Jeremiah put his foot on the left side of the pants and instructed Juan to remove his foot from the pant leg. He pulled the material away as Juan put down his foot and they repeated the action with the right side. Now Juan stood in only his boxers, which strained to contain his erection.

Holding Juan by the waist, Jeremiah turned him around to face the sitting room of the carriage. Once again, he knelt before the older man, only this time he pressed his face against Juan's crotch. Juan was biting down hard on the material in his mouth to keep from blowing his load in his boxers. Warm breath brushed over his damp underwear, and those hands slid up the back of his legs towards his ass. The hands reached the bottom hem of his boxers and tugged them down, baring hidden flesh. His cock ached for release, but Jeremiah stopped pulling an inch from freeing the last of the trapped appendage. Now, his lover's tongue ran from the top hem of his boxers along the length of his cock to the base. The tongue traced its way along one side of his cock back to the fabric holding the head. Slithering across to the other side and back to the base triggered enough of a muscle flex to pop the trapped head free and into Jeremiah's waiting mouth. The sensation of Jeremiah swallowing his cock to the root sent him past all control. His load blasted from his cock and into his lover's throat. Jeremiah's throat milked Juan's cock dry as he swallowed his lover's orgasm.

Chapter 30

In her private coach, Quillion attempted to find clothing to fit Abal from her wardrobe. The slave girl tried to convince her the rags she wore proved sufficient for a person of her insignificant station.

"Nonsense, those rags aren't fit for cleaning. We'll find something in my wardrobe for you to wear for now. Once things settle down some, we can rummage through the supplies and find some fabric to fashion you something more traditional."

"Mistress, please, should I appear in Western clothes without permission, my new master is within his rights to beat me. I do not wish to upset him so soon after becoming his property."

"Dr. Banks won't beat you for wearing clothes, Abal. He gave me instructions to attend to you and clothes are part of the process. Go clean yourself up while I find you something to wear." Quillion pushed the girl in the direction of the washroom. The girl was a stunning beauty if you ignored the scarred and tattooed back. Quillion admired the full curves of the natural hourglass figure as Abal discarded the remains of her tattered garments. Turning back to rummage through her garments, a knock on the door to her compartment interrupted Quill. A few short strides carried her to the door, which she unlocked and opened to find Mace standing on the platform between the train cars. In his hands, he held a bulging bag of colorful fabric.

"I witnessed what went down and realized your friend didn't pack anything for the trip. I convinced one of the servants to find her some clothes." Mace handed over the bag. "I hope her style of clothing helps her be comfortable with us."

"Thank you, Mace. Abal will appreciate this." Quill turned to go back inside but stopped. "Do you think your magic might heal old scars?"

"Not heal them, but it would make them fade so they're less noticeable. I'll need Abal's permission, Quill."

"Truth is, I think we'll need Dr. Bank's permission since he's her master."

"He's in his private coach with the professor, so we should wait until dinner to ask him."

"Thank you again, Mace."

"You're welcome, Quill."

The door closed behind Quillion, and Mace returned to his compartment in the center carriage. Quillion emptied the contents of the bag in her sleeping compartment and spread them out on her bed. Silk in many beautiful colors flowed out, pooling like a liquid rainbow on her bed. Abal emerged from the washroom wrapped in a towel. The slave girl stopped short at the sight of the silk garments on Quillion's bed.

"Mistress, I'm not worthy of such garments."

"Nonsense, Abal. The garments are yours. Dress, and we will find a place to store the rest of your clothes afterwards."

"Allah blesses you, Mistress."

"Save your blessings for those who earned them. Mr. Puap arranged with the palace servants to bring these for you."

"I shall thank Mr. Puap when given a chance."

Abal took up one of the garments, discarded the towel, and put on the outfit. She displayed herself to Quillion as she dressed, knowing the Western woman found her desirable. In spite of the horrible scars on her back, Abal remained beautiful, and she was often in demand to please the caliph's wives when they stayed in the harem.

"Should you wish, Mistress, I'm skilled in bringing pleasure to women."

A blush colored Quillion's cheeks at being caught staring at the slave girl. Waving her hand in a dismissing gesture, she sent Abal to the other sleeping compartment in their carriage with her new garments. Wise beyond her years, Abal departed to the opposite end of the car to give her mistress time to recover from her embarrassment.

* * *

A MASSIVE JOLT rocked the entire length of the train as the enormous locomotive lurched into motion, pulling away from the palace station. Dark clouds of coal smoke billowed from the smokestack and the trained powered away on treads whose original design moved the first tanks across the battlefields of Europe. The expedition now headed off toward the unknown.

* * *

AFTER THE SUNSET, the sand train reduced speed, allowing the staff to work in the kitchen and prepare dinner for the expedition and the engineering crews. A bell sounded when dinner was ready, and the members of the party made their way to the dining car, seating themselves at the long table the staff arranged for this first dinner. Unsure of precedence, the staff seated those with titles at one end of the table and arranged the rest in the remaining seats. Working from the list provided by the palace staff, they seated Ambassador Banks at the head of the table with Bishop Fabbri to his right and Professor Di Vargas to his left. On Bishop Fabbri's side of the table, they seated Quillion, Tobias, and Colum with Fahim at the foot. Next to the professor, they seated Mace, Theo, and Azim. Dinner was a simple fare of lamb stew with rice and vegetables, served with a choice of water or fruit juice. A moment of silence settled over the group before Jeremiah stood, taking up his water glass.

"A toast to our quest for answers to hidden questions."

The clinking of glasses followed the toast as Jeremiah resumed his seat. Only the rattle of forks and spoons against the dishes disturbed the silence around the table. Any conversation was limited to questions and answers about settling into life aboard the train. After the staff cleared the dessert course and left, Jeremiah tapped his glass for attention.

"We need to discuss several items before we begin planning divisions of labor for the dig. Allow me to introduce the two new members of our group: Azim and Fahim."

"Don't you mean three new members, Dr. Banks? Are we not including Quillion's companion Abal as part of the team?"

"Thank you for the reminder, Mr. Puap. Yes, Abal counts as a member of the team once we deal with the slave tattoo on her back and those horrid scars. For now, I believe Azim and Fahim's sponsor is someone other than His Majesty the Caliph."

"We are sent to protect you and assist you while you operate in Muslim lands. The Brotherhood serves as a counterpoint to the Cult of Cain.

My brother Azim will serve as your bodyguard, Dr. Banks, while I assist you with research and dealing with the locals."

"A kind offer, Fahim, and I will test your research skills to their limits and beyond. As for dealing with the locals, I deal with the regional emir."

"Forgive me, Dr. Banks, but by the locals, I meant those who walk the night seeking to feed on the living."

"We are well trained in dealing with the undead. How many did you slay in combat, little sage?"

"Tobias, be silent and let the lad speak of what they can offer to this project."

"Sorry, Your Excellency."

"Our only encounter with vampires is our meeting and traveling with the Master of Darkness and his companions to reach Baghdad. He recruited us to assist you in protecting this expedition from the members of the Bel-Kino clan and their master, Lord Bellabarisruk."

"They are no help to us, Dr. Banks."

"Tobias, sit down. Lord Hunter sent them, so they must be worth something to this project."

"Study them, Colum. At best, they are apprentices. Azim may possess the bloody palm tattoo of a full assassin, but how many kills has he made? Do you need another research assistant, Dr. Banks? Three students travel with you to learn your craft."

"Tobias, I never turn away a student who is willing to learn and work hard. As for learning the level of Azim's skills, take him to the last box car on the train. The car is half empty, so you can spar and test his skills."

"Doc, this is beyond weird. Are all your expeditions like this?"

"No, Theo, this is the strangest expedition yet for me and I'm including the one where my fellow grad student was turned over to the local guards as a sex toy and ended up becoming caliph many years later."

"Dr. Banks, perhaps we should discuss the more rational parts of the expedition. Will we be continuing your dig at El-Isin?"

"No, Quillion, we're headed to El-Kino to start a fresh search and excavation. Part of my choice of sites is so you three will gain the experience of working a virgin site. Once we arrive, we will grid out the site and choose four random squares and section those squares. Afterwards we will draw straws and each pick a square to survey, catalog, and excavate."

"One question, Doc."

"Go ahead, Mace."

"What's with the change to addressing us by our first names? You said you kept things formal to make sure people respect us."

"And I will continue to do so, Mace, when we're on the site or with outsiders among us. Since on this train the only outsiders are the staff and crew, I thought to relax the formalities a bit, which is why I didn't reprimand you or Theo for calling me Doc."

* * *

AFTER TWO HOURS of reviewing maps and making some rough notes, everyone returned to their train car to settle in for the evening. In the bachelors' car, Mace and Theo cornered Brother Colum with additional questions regarding the two vampire-hunting orders.

"Hold up, Colum, we need some clarification on some of the things Dr. Banks skimmed over."

"Would you be referring to the weird supernatural aspects, Mr. Puap?"

"Yes, we're trying to understand the threat posed by vampires coming after us."

"Understandable, since you've met one of the oldest vampires around. Yes, Tobias and I are aware you met with Dungi of Baghdad. The caliph isn't pleased to be under his control, which is why his men acted rougher than they needed when they tried to use us as hostages to add the two Arabs."

"Sorry, we didn't know about that. Mostly we want more information about the Cult of Cain and Brotherhood of the Crimson Hand. Aren't you a member of the Order of St. Hubert?"

"This will be a long discussion. Let us return to the dining car so we can talk in comfort."

The young monk led the two graduate students back to the other train car. Further down the bachelors' car, Brother Tobias talked with Azim and Fahim to arrange a sparring session in the boxcar.

Chapter 31

Several nights later, Jeremiah was finishing a sparring session with Brother Tobias in the near-empty boxcar. A strange sound filtered in over the steady hum of the sand train and drew Jeremiah to unfasten the lock on the loading door, which slid open to reveal the moonlit desert. Over the crest of a sand dune lumbered a pair of tortoise-shaped machines. Mounted on top of each craft was a gun platform carrying a .50 caliber Gatling gun. The glint of moonlight off the goggles of one gunner was the only warning they received before both guns opened fire to strafe the side of the train. A hand pulled Jeremiah out of the open doorway as rounds bounced from the armored sides of the car.

"Go forward and tell the engineer to put on more speed, Dr. Banks."

Brother Tobias shoved Jeremiah towards the exit to the next car. Staggered by the shove, Jeremiah stumbled to the door leading to the platform above the couplings. Bracing himself to pull the door, Jeremiah spotted the panel of speaking tubes, which connected to all the cars. He grabbed and yanked the tube for the engine, triggering the call alarm.

"En-engine," came the tinny sound of a panicked voice.

"Dr. Banks here. We're under attack by raiders. Put on more speed."

"The engineer's been hit. I think he's d-d-dead."

"Who is this?"

"Junior Engine Steward Robinson, sir."

With a silent curse, Jeremiah forced himself to remain calm. "Robinson, where's the rest of the crew?"

"Dunno, sir. Engineer Samuels was alone at the controls when I arrived to attend to crew needs."

"Robinson, close and bolt the door to the engine. Lock yourself in and don't let anyone in until I signal."

"Yes, sir."

After slotting the tube back in place, Jeremiah pulled a second one, triggering the tone in the private car he shared with Juan.

"Di Vargas."

Jeremiah detected the trace of worry in Juan's voice.

"Juan, this is Jeremiah. The train is under attack by raiders. I want you to move everyone into cover in the car Mace and Theo are sharing. Stay in the central aisle and keep your heads down."

"Miah, where are you?"

"Safe for now, Juan. Please make sure everyone is safe."

"The crew isn't answering calls."

"Juan, please gets to Mace and Theo, find Quillion, and make sure everyone is safe. Send Colum forward to secure the engine."

"I will. Stay safe."

Turning back to face the interior of the boxcar, Jeremiah waved the monk standing near the open door over to him. Tobias slid the door shut before crossing over to Jeremiah.

"The engineer is dead and the crew is missing, except a junior steward. Can you reach the crew quarters?"

"I can. You should go to a place of safety with the professor and your students. I will grab Colum on my way to find the crew."

"I sent Colum forward to secure the engine. Grab Azim and secure the crew section before it's too late."

INTERLUDE: VAMPIRES BATTLE FOR THE TRAIN - CLAN BEL-KINO VS. CLAN SALAQUA

"Our agent reports the expedition departed this morning aboard the sultan's sand train. Their destination is the ruins of El-Isin, My Lord."

"Did you manage to place a spy aboard the train?"

"Yes, My Lord. We encountered some difficulties, because Lord Slayer freed Dungi of his ancient curses. We lost control of the palace and the grand duke is dead."

"Once we eliminate the archaeologist and his team, I'll deal with Lord Slayer and Dungi. No mortal will step foot in El-Abel."

"All will be as you command Lord Bellabarisruk."

"Report to me when the mortals are destroyed."

* * *

"My captain, we received a report the archaeologist and his team departed this morning aboard the sand train," Shadow said.

"And our member working as one of the train's crew, my Handsome Shadow?"

"He reports Dr. Banks waited until the train was out into the desert before ordering a change of course from El-Isin to coordinates which correspond those we obtained as the location for El-Kino."

"As Lord Hunter suspected, Dr. Banks wishes a fresh site."

"What's in El-Kino that isn't in El-Isin, Captain?"

"A map to lost El-Ishtar, Enoch, and El-Abel, my Shadow."

"Our spy also reports a Bel-Kino agent mixed into the crew. Should we eliminate him?"

"No, the Bel-Kino thinks we lack knowledge of their little band of sand pirates. Fools, to think the Queen of Pirates fails to attend to all who apply themselves to her trade. Let their agent draw their forces to the train at these coordinates. We eliminate the threat to Lord Hunter's plans and remind the Bel-Kino piracy is the domain of the Salaqua."

"I'll send the instructions and make the preparations to eliminate the Bel-Kino's band of adventurers."

"We want them to attack the train first, Shadow. Let them be distracted and let us discover what the archaeologist and his party can do. Rumors say his party contains members of both the Cult of Cain and the Brotherhood of the Crimson Hand."

"We confirmed three members of the Order of St. Hubert in the party, the bishop who acts for the upstart in Rome, and two monks, Captain."

"Shall we attack by land or sky, Captain?"

"By land, my Shadow. Let us keep our flying ability secret until we need to extract the archaeologist and his team on Lord Hunter's command."

"Is Lord Hunter what he claims, Captain?"

"You met him, John Shadow. Is he less than what he claims? Father Cain is dead and Richard St. Martin is our Lord in his place. Respect him and never cross him or final death will claim you before you blink."

"Aye, Captain."

* * *

The lead units of the Bel-Kino crested the dune on the port side of the enormous sand train. When they spotted the open cargo door on the last car and the figure silhouetted within, their gunners squeezed the triggers on the .50 caliber Gatling guns. The target ducked, and the armored door slammed back into place.

"They're aware we're coming. Did our guy on the crew do his job?"

"He reported the mortals changed course for some other location. By now he's eliminating members of the crew."

"How heavy is the armor on this beast?"

"The train belongs to the caliph. What do you think? Dig out the rocket launchers. The other teams should be closing in on the engine and the starboard flank."

"Movement spotted heading along the roof of the fourth car going towards the engine."

"Take the target out. Bet he's one of the cultists."

The Gatling gun began chewing through rounds, strafing the roofline of the train in pursuit of the person attempting to reach the engine. The lumbering sand tanks kept up the chase, closing the distance.

"Rocket launcher ready."

"Target the treads on the fourth car. We can jam up the rest of the train and board her."

"Located a target on the platform between the fourth and fifth cars."

"Take the target out."

The guns swiveled and cut loose on the gap between cars, where the bullets met a wall of ice and deflected.

"Where the fuck did a mage come from?"

"Who cares? Hit the car with the damn rocket."

As the vampire gunner lined up the rocket launcher's sights on the train, an explosion lit up the night sky from the far side of the train. Following the blast, high caliber rounds impacted the gunner's nest on top of the tank, forcing him to duck and lose his lock on his target. Before he regained his position, a wave of sand rippled below the two tanks of his team. The tanks flipped, exposing the weaker armor of the underside to the approaching enemy raiders. Explosive rounds pounded into the vulnerable fuel tanks, and the two tanks exploded, incinerating the vampires and mortals inside.

* * *

From the wheelhouse of a cargo vessel converted into a sand carrier, Handsome John Shadow studied the lead elements of the Salaqua attack disrupting the Bel-Kino forces. He commanded from the cargo ship instead of from one of the dune buggies by order of Laverna Salacia.

"The doctor recruited a Sapphire and an Emerald mage for his expedition, Captain Shadow."

Shadow adjusted his spyglass to focus on the figure standing in the gap between cars.

"By the build and the red hair, my guess is the archaeologist is the mysterious Sapphire mage. Direct our teams to focus on the Bel-Kino headed for the engine. The bulk of their force is at the front of the train."

"Head-on is a strategy, which under normal conditions is suicidal. The engine and its support cars are armed and fortified with armor around a foot thick."

"Yes, but between our agent and the Bel-Kino spy, the crew is either unconscious or dead."

"The Bel-Kino may turn a few for cannon fodder, Captain."

"Not their style to gift servants. No, if we take out their tanks, the cultists or the Brotherhood will eliminate the Bel-Kino agent."

"Captain Shadow, a report from our starboard flank scouts. They located the enemy sand carrier three kilometers east of train and closing at thirty kilometers per hour."

"Message to all flanking units converge on enemy carrier and cripple her. Helmsman bring us to a bearing to catch the Bel-Kino a kilometer aft of the train."

"Aye, Captain, coming about and increasing speed to intercept one kilometer aft of train."

"Sound the call to battle stations."

The klaxon sounded, summoning mortal and vampire hands to their stations. The cargo containers on the deck slid aside to reveal three 57 mm Mark 110s. The combination diesel and steam engines coughed out a plume of smoke as they pushed the lumbering vessel across the sands. As the Salaqua vessel plowed through dunes as she once plowed through waves, the roar of the primary guns mounted on the train caught the crew's attention.

"Sounds like someone managed to reach the train's weapons, Captain."

"The archaeologist and his team possess more resources than our sources conveyed to us. I wish the man luck in his endeavor. Now let's show the Bel-Kino why they shouldn't mess with piracy."

Chapter 32

Staggering under the combination of explosions and the movement of the train, Jeremiah crossed to the platform between Quillion's car and the bachelors' car. The door to the bachelors' car flew open to reveal Mace headed his way.

"Get down," Jeremiah shouted.

The unknown attackers opened fire on the space between the cars, and Jeremiah froze the moist evening air into a shield to deflect the bullets. Mace knelt on the platform and, with concentrated effort, caused the sand to ripple away from the train. The Emerald magic raced away into the desert, spreading to become a larger wave, which flipped one of the enemy tanks. Before anything further happened, Jeremiah shoved Mace back into the bachelors' car and followed on his heels. He glanced around the car for Juan and found him pressing a cloth against Bishop Fabbri's neck. Theo, Quillion, Fahim, and Abad huddled in the center of the car. Jeremiah crept across the car to Juan and the bishop's side.

"What happened to you, Father Fabbri?"

"A vampire attacked me when I went to check on the crew. Brother Tobias and the Arab boy saved me."

"I want you to stay here. For now, this car is the safest until Brother Colum secures the engine."

"Doc, shouldn't we be pushing forward to help take the weapons so we can defend the train from these raiders?"

"Colum, Tobias, and Azim are the only ones trained to take on vampires, Mace. We're better off staying out of their way and out of the line of fire."

The group settled in to ride out the siege of the train, hoping the three young men proved enough to secure their safety.

* * *

BROTHER COLUM KEPT close against the roof of each car he crossed on his way to the engine. His dark cassock made him one more shadow in the night. Ahead of him, a figure rose from between the next cars he needed to cross. Training drilled into his body since boyhood kicked in and a blade of silver and wood dropped into his right hand. The figure turned, and moonlight illuminated his pale flesh and sharp fangs. The throwing knife left Colum's hand as he surged forward with a second weapon in his left hand. His target clawed at its face before crumbling into dust as the dual poison of silver and wood ended the thing's existence. Colum hurled himself across the void between cars, continuing his journey forward. He must not fail, Jeremiah was counting on him to secure the engine and keep them moving forward. Blessed Savior, his thoughts are sinful and his lust immoral in this age of pious struggle. Colum prayed the Lord would guide him while running. As he planted his foot for the next leap, a hand reached up from the gap and grasped his ankle, yanking him off balance. The warrior monk pitched forward, plunging towards the platforms below. The fingers of his right hand managed to grasp the ladder's top rung, leaving him suspended between the grip on his ankle and his precarious hold on the ladder to safety.

"Let go, little monk, and your death will be swift; struggle and your death will be painful and slow."

Colum lashed backward with his second knife, hoping to force the being gripping his ankle let go. A hiss of pain greeted his effort, but the creature yanked and ripped his fingers away from the ladder. The vampire, who gripped Colum's ankle, misjudged his pull and the pair fell backward into the car. The monk tried to roll with the momentum but collided with the bulk of his assailant. He swung his blade again, trying to drive back his opponent. A knee blocked his swing, and Colum found himself pinned facedown beneath the weight of his attacker.

"I love the flavor of the religious. I can't wait to drink you, dry little monk."

The monster's weight pressed down on Colum and lodged the creature's cock in the valley of the monk's ass. Struggle as he might, Colum couldn't dislodge the vampire, and the fiend's hot breath caressed his throat.

"Would you like me to fuck you, little monk? Should I add a little extra thrill to the ecstasy you're about to experience?"

Pain pierced Colum's throat before he answered as the vampire's fangs sank into the exposed flesh. The hard cock rubbing between his ass cheeks drove the monk's focus from his mind as the lulling effects of vampiric ecstasy flooded his bloodstream. A searing pain tore Colum out of the dull space where his mind had wandered off to as the vampire fed. The monster's weight vanished as a bone-chilling cold filled the car.

"Someone missed the don't-touch-the-monk memo. Which clan did I miss sending Lord Hunter's message?"

The unfamiliar Italian-accented baritone voice cut through the fog in Colum's mind. Who was here to save him? Colum rolled on his back groping for another silver dagger. Over his prone body stood the fashion model, the one serving as Lord Hunter's chief advisor. The dark-haired man moved towards the creature hanging limp on the wall, slowing long enough to snatch the silver blade from Colum's hand. The blade flashed in the dim light of the car as he plunged the knife between the creature's ribs and into the heart. The monster howled in pain before turning to ash and dust. In two strides, the Italian stood over Colum, before dropping to his knees beside the wounded monk. The Italian lifted Colum and pressed the monk against his broad chest. With a sigh, the monk lost consciousness.

* * *

FURTHER BACK ALONG THE TRAIN, Tobias and Azim came to the crew compartment and the scene of a massacre. Blood covered most of the car; several bodies lay torn to pieces, while others lay limp in their bunks. Against one wall a figure twitched in agony from the broken chair leg jammed in its ribs. The young Arab assassin moved towards the impaled figure, discovering the head porter. Pain-filled pools of blackness stared at Azim, and the oversized canine teeth revealed the man's true nature.

"This one is a recent convert and not far removed from the ancients. Wood only slows him down but won't kill him."

"Because the person who rammed the chair leg through him missed his heart but lodged in his spine, Azim. Finish the monster off; we need to catch up to Colum."

A quick flash of silver ended the struggling vampire, and Azim flicked the gore from the blade of his janbiya before tucking the knife away. Following behind Tobias, Azim studied the detached mannerisms as the monk moved towards his objective.

"Four members of the crew are unaccounted for by my count. Dr. Banks mentioned one of the junior porters is locked in the engine, but I find no signs of the other four juniors."

"They are all young boys, and several of the cars contain narrow maintenance passages. Perhaps they hid away."

"We'll check the compartments as we go."

After brief checks of the remaining compartments, Tobias and Azim reached the engine where they jumped to the platform and signaled the junior porter inside.

"I'm Brother Tobias. Dr. Banks sent me to assist Brother Colum with the engine."

"You're the first person to contact me since Dr. Banks made me seal off the engine. I'm not to open the engine to anyone without the doctor's clearance."

"Call back to the passenger cars and tell the doctor Brother Tobias and Azim are ready to take control."

Tobias crouched to present a limited target to any remaining raiders. Azim crouched in a similar position on the opposite platform. He caught a faint murmur on the other side of the thick steel door. After a few minutes, the locks disengaged and the door swung inwards. The pair slipped inside the engine and came face-to-face with the frightened junior porter.

"Dr. Banks says he sent you and I should follow your instructions."

"Close and bolt the door. No one gets in until we reach our destination. Can the defensive positions be reached from elsewhere?"

"No, sir, only from within the engine. You go down those two tiny side passages."

"Azim, call back and ask Mace and Theo to come to the engine. We need them to man the weapons. Now, boy, explain the controls to me."

"Sir, I'm only a porter. All I do is serve the engineer and the gunners their coffee or meals."

Tobias stifled a sigh and tried to familiarize the controls. Not for the first time did he curse his lack of Arabic training. With Colum missing, Tobias had to rely on Azim to translate the controls.

"Dr. Banks is sending the students forward to assist us. Colum is unconscious after a vampire's attack. Why aren't you working the break lever to slow us down?"

"Because I never learned Arabic. Which is the break lever?"

* * *

CARRYING the unconscious monk in his arms, Armand walked back along the cars to the first passenger compartment. The presence of living beings inside forced him to halt on the platform outside the door. He kicked at the door to attract attention from those within. The redheaded doctor opened the compartment door and faced the unknown man holding Colum.

"Take the monk, Dr. Banks, and tend to his wounds," Armand shouted over the wind howling between the cars.

Jeremiah reached out and took possession of Colum's limp body, cradling him close to his chest. The stranger leapt up and caught the edge of the roof, vanishing into the night. Stepping back into the car with his burden, he almost collided with Juan.

"Give him here, Miah. Let me care for him. The boys will need you in the engine room."

The train rocked and its forward momentum slowed.

"I think the boys managed to figure out the engine controls."

Explosions rocked the car, followed by internal shifting as the train's weapons system returned fire.

"From the sounds of things, they mastered the defenses as well. Something bit, Colum. The bite is similar to the one of Father Fabbri's neck. Put him in our bed for now, Juan."

"He's running a fever; can you cool him down with your magic?"

"Let him settle, and I'll do what I can for him. I'm curious about the man who brought him back here and vanished."

* * *

THE SAND TRAIN slowed as Brother Tobias and Azim mastered the controls and did their best to bring the beast to heel. The engine hissed and sizzled as the speed reduced before the train halted on the desert basin's edge that Dr. Banks believed contained the ruins of El-Kino. In the forward section of the engine, Mace and Theo stood down the weapons before making their way back to the control room.

"Theo, go inform Dr. Banks we're stopped on the outskirts of a ruined city. Azim will make sure you don't run into anything on the way back." Brother Tobias paused, letting Theo and Azim exit the engine.

"Do you want something from me, Brother Tobias?" Mace asked.

"Yes, Mace. I need you to remove my cult tattoo as you did for Brother Colum. The original plan didn't call for me to venture out here with the expedition."

"Sure, where is the tattoo located?"

The monk turned his back to Mace and unfastened his cassock, allowing the garment to slip from his shoulders to gather around his waist. From where his neck and shoulders met, crimson ink formed the design of a bloody crucifix with a figure drawn in black ink biting into the neck of the doomed man. The image descended Tobias' muscular back to vanish below his belted cassock.

"Impressive ink, Brother Tobias. How far down does the art go?"

"The image stops about an inch above my ass."

"Why was Colum's cult tattoo only a crucifix on his left pectoral and not something like yours?"

"We trained under different instructors and our disciplines are designed to complement each other rather than duplicating skillsets."

"You will experience a tingling sensation across your skin as my magic helps your body absorb the ink. You may experience a spontaneous orgasm considering the size of your tattoo."

Calloused hands traced Emerald magic across Tobias' back, causing the monk to shiver and quake with a pleasure he denied himself. The discipline he followed recommended celibacy and he forced himself into total denial of physical pleasure. Mace's touch was the most intimate he experienced since before taking his vows. Between the power of the magic and the sensations of Mace's touch, Tobias was overwhelmed and he leaned back into Mace to enhance the experience.

"Hmph, Brother Colum isn't the only one denying himself what he wants. How long since you allowed anyone to touch your flesh, Tobias?"

"Five years. My instructor took me to her bed for a night of pleasure, so I experienced what I must leave behind. When our night was over, she locked my manhood away in a chastity cage. Only she or the head of the Cult can remove the cage."

The tingling of magic stopped, but the rough play of Mace's calloused fingers continued tracing down Tobias' chest to brush over his rock-hard nipples. The monk shuddered and his ass involuntarily pressed back against the solid cock in Mace's trousers. Mace withdrew his hands from the monk's body and stepped back, leaving Tobias off-balance for a moment.

"Don't deny all the pleasures of the flesh, Brother Tobias. Such denial often proves unhealthy."

"Some vows we all must keep, Macejah."

An explosion off the portside of the train ended any further conversation, as Mace hurled himself down the passage to the weapons system and Tobias lunged for the engine controls. Azim and Theo crashed back into the engine as a hail of bullets pelted the sides of the train.

* * *

COLUM AWOKE from a fever dream to the strange sensation of being cold on one side of his body and warm on the other. He dreamed of Jeremiah and Juan cradling him between them while he slept and awoke to discover his dream a reality. His head lay on Juan's burly chest, while his back and ass pressed against Jeremiah's solid build. Their arms reached across him to hold each other. The heat radiated from Juan, while Jeremiah siphoned heat away. Could he slip out of their bed without waking them, because he didn't belong between them?

"You're thinking out loud this morning, little monk. Are you recovered from yesterday's attack? Miah, you're freezing pour Colum to death."

"W-what? Oh, sorry I drifted off while breaking his fever."

Colum's backside began to warm up as Jeremiah ceased using magic. However, instead of either man getting up, they snuggled in tighter, squeezing Colum between them.

"Juan and I discussed some things last night while you battled the fever brought on by blood loss. We decided to add you to our relationship, if you want to be with us both."

"You don't need to answer right away, little monk. The offer is open whenever you wish to accept or decline. Miah and I can wait for you to decide."

Colum lifted his head from Juan's chest and kissed the older man, before rolling over to kiss Jeremiah.

"You offer something I want. I fear what accepting your love will bring down on me from my superiors in the Order and the Cult, but I want to be with you both."

The two lovers moved apart enough to position Colum flat on his back, and they both kissed him and stroked his body. Colum lost himself in the sensations of the two men's hairy bodies rubbing against his smooth skin. The tickling of Juan's full beard contrasted to the scratchiness of Jeremiah's stubble caused him to giggle and squirm. Two solid cocks pressed into his hips, exciting him as he reached down to caress them both. Colum thought about the many decisions he needed to make regarding these two unique men or at least he tried to before their attention to his body sent his mind off to another space. He didn't come back to himself until after his third orgasm. These men amazed him with their skills; using only body contact and touch, they brought him to three hands-free climaxes. Holy Cain, what will actual sex be like if they can do this to him with their hands? He would wait to find out. The whistle of the communications tube sounded and Jeremiah broke contact to answer. While Jeremiah talked to the person on the other end of the tube, Juan pulled Colum close against his chest.

"I want you to promise me something, little monk."

"What do you ask of me, Juan?"

"Protect Miah with every skill you possess. He won't think about safety once he's working. The sands and what's buried beneath them call to him with a strength neither of us can match."

"I'm sworn to protect him at all costs, Juan. Do you fear a danger I'm unaware of?"

Jeremiah returned before Juan answered. He glanced at his lovers and sighed a moment before the train lurched forward, knocking him off his feet.

* * *

BROTHER TOBIAS FOUGHT to ramp the engine back up to full speed to prevent their attackers from closing and boarding. They needed speed to protect the vulnerable passenger cars.

"Azim, where can we take the train so our attackers cannot flank us?"

"I am unfamiliar with this region of the deep desert."

"Steer thirty degrees to port; the engineer once mentioned a canyon, which runs almost to the coast. The walls are steep and the canyon narrow." The young porter pointed off into the distance.

Tobias yanked on the levers, steering the roaring behemoth towards the shelter of the canyon.

"They concentrate their attack on the rear of the train, Tobias. What is in the caboose?"

"No, clue, Azim. Boy, what is in the caboose?"

"I can't say, sir. Beyond the passenger cars, I was off-limits to all but the most senior porters."

"Azim, can the engine's weapons be operated by one man?"

"The weapons area possesses a central command station, which might command all the weapons. Why?"

"Move Mace to the central command, then take Theo and pick up Dr. Banks on your way back to the caboose. We need to find out if the car contains a weapons system to defend the rear of the train."

Azim went forward and helped Mace shift to the central command and figure out how to operate all the weapons. Theo followed Azim as he started back along the length of the train. They stopped in the passenger car, where they found Colum, Juan, and Jeremiah all scrambling to throw on clothes.

"We altered course, why?"

"To port is a canyon, which offers protection for the sides of the train, Dr. Banks."

"We must reach El-Kino; the emir's soldiers will repel the raiders."

"Should we stay on course for El-Kino, the raiders chance of scoring a hit on one of the couplings increases. The canyon offers us the best option for mounting a prolonged defense, provided the caboose hosts a defense system similar to the engine's."

Colum attempted joining his brother monk, but collapsed, still weak from his earlier blood loss and light-headed from his blissful orgasm.

"Doc, we need you to come with us in case any of the senior porters are holed up in the caboose. They will recognize your authority."

"I can't leave Colum like this."

"Miah, he's safe here with me. Go protect the train and the expedition."

"Juan..."

A new barrage of bullets assaulted the train, forcing everyone to the floor of the car. Jeremiah, Azim, and Theo crawled along the floor to the door leading to the next car. The train rocked as Mace returned fire with the engine's heavy cannon. The trio rose and began their mad dash for the caboose. In the last half-empty boxcar, Jeremiah halted the group.

"We must be cautious entering the caboose; a few of the senior porters remain unaccounted. Azim, lead. Theo and I will cover you with magic."

Azim crept to the platform connecting to the caboose. He carried the curved silver dagger of the Brotherhood. He sprang across the gap between cars and edged to the side of the caboose door. With a practiced eye, he scanned the lock for signs of forced entry. On the opposite platform, Dr. Banks and Theo crouched on opposite sides. Azim turned the latch and shoved the door open with all his strength. He dropped and rolled into the car as the door swung shut behind him. Years of training brought him up into a defensive crouch facing the interior of the caboose. Azim found himself staring up along the length of a silver longsword into the brown eyes of Richard St. Martin. Behind the vampire, Azim discerned two shrouded figures occupying a pair of bunks.

"Master of Darkness, you must hide yourself and your companions. Dr. Banks and the Russian student will enter at any moment."

"Why are you here, son of the desert?"

"We came to man the weapons system and defend the rear of the train from the raiders, Master."

"I will man the weapons. Go and take the archaeologist and his student back to the safety of the center of the train. My companions will awake soon, and this compartment will not be safe for mortals."

The door to the caboose started to open, and Azim turned and hurled his weight against portal.

"Stay back, Dr. Banks, the senior porter agrees to man the weapons, but he suffers from the hunger for blood. This is not a safe place for you or Theo. I will be out as soon as I secure the porter into the command chair."

"Be careful, Azim. We will wait for you in the boxcar."

"Go and carry out my will, son of the desert."

"I obey, Master of Darkness."

Azim returned to the boxcar and assured Dr. Banks and Theo that the senior porter would defend the rear of the train until the dawn caught up to him. The trio returned to the passenger cars where Fahim, Quillion, and Abal served them a light meal made in haste. Theo took three meal packets forward to serve Tobias, Mace, and the young porter. Jeremiah checked in on Juan and Colum and found the young monk curled up asleep with his head resting on Juan's chest. Colum wore one of Jeremiah's shirts, which draped across the smooth curves of his ass. The older man read from the journal of Richard St. Martin.

"Poor Colum used up more energy than he thought; added to the blood loss from being attacked, he crashed right after you headed for the caboose."

"A rushed healing and a major orgasm will also leave one somewhat sleepy. How's Father Fabbri holding up?"

"Better than he lets on. Are we on a different course, Miah?"

"Yes, because of the raiders, Brother Tobias shifted the course into a narrow valley to protect the sides of the train."

"Will we still arrive at El-Kino?"

"I can't determine where we'll come out."

The interior of the car grew dark as they entered into the valley.

"I think we may end up at El-Abel. In the passages from various accounts of the city, St. Martin included a passage from a book called the Gospel of Cain. The passage includes a description of a battle between the forces of El-Abel and those of a mage-lord named Noah."

"Are we discussing the Noah of the Flood story?"

"The passage includes the mention of a flood decimating the city following Noah's defeat at the hand of Cain."

"Read the passage to me."

"Father Cain wandered for five hundred years after the creation of the last of his grandchildren. He visited many lands seeking knowledge and looking for ways to break the curse. After eight hundred years of wandering, Cain grew tired and found a cave overlooking his city of El-Abel. In the cave, Cain melded with the earth and entered into languor. Father Cain's languor was disturbed by the rising use of magic in ways unknown to him. Venturing out of his cave, he found vast armies marching on the forces of El-Abel and her allied cities. Monstrous creatures led an army commanded by a mage gifted with Ebony magic. Despite the distance, magic revealed the mage as descended from his brother Seth. Along with his children and grandchildren, a group of Silver mages assisted with leading the armies of El-Abel and her allies.

Surprise came more from seeing Silver mages allied with his chosen than from the monsters in the army they opposed. Cain raced from his cave to go to the aid of his city and children, arriving as the leading forces of the armies clashed. Magic flew, claws shredded flesh, the arrows found vulnerable targets, and blood flowed across the plain. The mortals of both armies died by the hundreds. Cain, his children, and grandchildren tore through the ranks of the shape-shifting creatures to reach the mages controlling the enemy army.

For hours, we combated our foes until Cain alone entered the command ranks of the enemy. Fear spread as mages fell beneath his claws and teeth. Cain reached the commander and his last guards with their silver-tipped weapons.

Father Cain spoke to the commander, saying, "You cannot escape the fate I laid upon the children of my brother Seth, little mage. Your death will be by my hands." And the commander replied, saying, "I recognize you, Cain, son of Adam, and I do not fear you. I am Noah, Mage-Lord of Nineveh. You cannot pass this wall of silver." Cain spoke to Noah saying, "Foolish mortal, those little weapons and the children who wield them are no match for me. I am first among the immortals." Father Cain commanded the mage-lord's guards, saying, "Lay down your weapons." The army of the mage obeyed while the mage stood his ground. Next, Cain demanded of the Mage-Lord Noah, "Come and kneel before me, child of Seth." Noah of Nineveh did not move.

Responding to Father Cain's command, "I made myself proof against commands, vampire. Should you wish to slay me, you must come to me." Father Cain seized Noah before he registered his movements and sank his fangs into his neck, drinking him of his life essence. Cain reeled for a moment as Noah's powers poured into him, but recovered as his blood flowed over Cain's tongue. The beating of Noah's heart slowed, and Father Cain took heed of a different pounding sound. Dropping Noah's corpse, Cain turned to discover a giant wall of water and debris sweeping down the valley towards El-Abel. Cain melded with the earth as the Flood poured down on the armies below and slammed into the massive walls of the city.

Forty days passed before the waters receded enough for Cain to rise. The beautiful city lay in ruins, and Cain found no trace of his children. We, his grandchildren found him and ask what we should do. Father Cain told us to scatter across the face of the earth and to live in secret among mortals. He granted each of us permission to create three children of our own. As the eldest among my siblings I asked him, "What of you, Grandfather? Where shall you go?" And Father Cain replied, saying, "I shall continue my wanderings or perhaps I shall join with the earth and let a new age come to find me. Guard your siblings and your children, Bellabarisruk."

Gospel of Cain, 50: 1-48

* * *

JEREMIAH SAT IN SILENCE, letting the new information stew in his mind. Outside, the rattle of gunfire from the raiders died away, leaving them only the sounds of the moving train. Did this valley lead to El-Abel?

"You're lost in your thoughts, Dr. Banks," Juan's deep voice rumbled.

"I'm pondering a lot of new variables, Prof. Di Vargas. Lack of support from the emir's guards to protect the site being a top problem."

"You prepared to dig at El-Kino, but El-Abel poses a different set of problems."

"Yes, the unknown always does. Tackling the outpost at El-Kino carried certain dangers, but El-Abel is a city some people don't want us to reach and others do want us to reach. Despite using this journal, we lack important information about what to expect."

"We need to gather with the rest of our team and discuss what information is in our possession and what we lack."

VAMPIRE INTERLUDE:
PRIMORDIAL FURY

The captain of the raider vessel attacking the expedition's train collided with the bulkhead before he realized Lord Bellabarisruk's landed a blow. Bones snapped and dark ichor spewed from his mouth as bone fragments punctured his lungs. Dark energies swirled around the primordial's hands as his fury rose.

"The pathetic mortals should be dead by this point, not headed on a direct course for El-Abel. Your incompetence disgusts me, Captain. These raiders of yours drive our quarry straight towards Father Cain's city. Tell me why I shouldn't grant you an actual death?"

"Kill me if you please, Lord Bellabarisruk." The captain choked on the ichor from his lungs. "My final death won't change the fact those mortals received aid from the Salaqua clan. Battling them drove the train towards El-Abel and depleted our forces. We will need to break off our attack soon to avoid the sunrise."

"Take the captain below and feed him. Order what is needed to protect us from the sun and further attacks by the Salaqua. I'll be in my cabin."

The primordial swept from the command deck heading for his cabin. His fury at being thwarted by members of another clan radiated through the vessel. Once in his quarters, Bellabarisruk removed the silk covering a diamond the size of a fist polished smooth. He chanted a short phrase over the diamond in the language Dr. Banks called El-Isinian. Above the sphere, Laverna Salacia's image formed.

"What do you want, Bellabarisruk?"

"I seek to understand why your clan aids the mortals seeking Father Cain's city, Laverna Salacia."

"Simple answer. Lord Slayer commanded my assistance, and I obeyed his command."

"A primordial obeys the commands of a tyro, who claims he slew Father Cain."

"Age isn't everything, Bellabarisruk. When you meet him, you will discover the truth of his claim of killing Grandfather. In a face-to-face encounter with Lord Slayer, you can't deny he wields Cain's powers and more. My mortal agents report sightings of him wandering about in daylight. Tread with care when you challenge his plans."

The image over Bellabarisruk's diamond wavered as Laverna Salacia lowered the silk covering on her stone, before firming once more.

"A word of advice, Lord of the Bel-Kino. Remove your clan out of the raiding business. Piracy in all its forms is my domain."

The pirate queen's image vanished as she dropped the silk cover over the ruby in her office. Striding from her office, she stepped out on deck and glanced up at the dirigible attached to her ship. For the Salaqua, breaking the laws against flying machines proved an easy task. Of course, the gigantic blimp didn't keep the ship aloft alone. Below, in nooks adjacent to the engine room, a pair of Amethyst mages worked their air magic to keep the ship airborne over the caliphate's southern desert. Lord Slayer commanded she be ready to whisk the archaeologist and his party to safety. The Salaqua stood prepared to answer Lord Slayer's call.

Chapter 33

The train passed out of the canyon into a sand-choked basin and groaned to a halt of escaping steam and grinding gears. Jeremiah gathered all the survivors together to organize and plan. Mace and Brother Colum reported the engine able to produce power for the train, but without repairs, moving the train was impossible. The young porter, Mr. Johnson, found the food and water supplies in order. Brother Colum and Azim struggled for a few days, but managed to power up the radio and relay their location to the caliph's agents in the region. While waiting for the arrival of the local emir's men, the group set about creating a camp near the train and exploring the area for potential excavation sites. Over the next few days, Jeremiah, Mace, Theo, and Quillion surveyed and established a grid pattern over the entire site. The four archaeologists took painstaking efforts to create a map of the area before removing the first trowel of sand. Once they established the datum point at the southwest corner of the entire map, they divided each grid into its own set of sub-grids. Based on their hand-drawn map, Dr. Banks chose the centermost sub-grid of the central grid of the site.

"Why do you want to dig this grid, Doc?"

"The location is the center of the central square, Mr. Puap. Based on the findings from El-Isin, the spot is the location of a carved stone with a map of the region."

"You're betting this stone map isn't damaged and reveals if this is El-Abel, Enoch, or another outpost, aren't you, Dr. Banks?"

"Yes, Ms. Post, I am hoping the map isn't damaged. We'll meet in the mornings for instructions and joint excavations; in the afternoons, we will work in shifts, rotating between excavating, photographing, and cataloging to prevent heat stroke. After dinner, we'll review the day's findings and discuss."

* * *

TWO WEEKS into their scaled-back excavations, Jeremiah assigned smaller sub-grids to each of students to work in the afternoon. They took turns at each site working as excavator, photographer, and cataloger. Jeremiah continued to work the central site, with Juan and Brother Colum assisting him. On occasion, either Azim or Brother Tobias would take Juan's place, allowing him to work in shade beneath the mess tent to catalog all the finds. At the beginning of the third week, the emir and his men arrived. Jeremiah spent time organizing the workers into shifts and establishing a schedule with the guard commanders regarding patrols. The arrival of the laborers and the guards freed Juan from working out in the field and allowed him to focus on organizing the catalog and translation notes with Fahim's assistance.

A few days after the arrival of the local emir and his men, Juan sat in the mess tent trying to organize his research notes and the rough translations Jeremiah made from some of the fragments discovered so far. Most of the shards proved to be trade goods from other city-states within the Sumerian territories. A few of the discoveries promised hints, which tied into his research. Father Fabbri puttered in the cooking area of the tent with the help of the five surviving junior porters to prepare meals for the team. Fahim worked across the table from Juan, making clean copies of Mace and Theo's notes for Jeremiah to review.

"Professor, what does Mr. Puap mean when he writes, 'found the city's largest crap pile'?"

"I believe Mr. Puap's test site proved part of the city's sewer system. My guess would be he found the spot where the city deposited its waste."

"Oh, I guess I understand the reason for all the foul language in his report."

"Perhaps you should let Mr. Puap clean up his notes for Dr. Banks' review, Fahim. Why don't you sit over here and I'll show you some of the comparisons Dr. Banks and I are working on?"

Fahim took a seat next to the Spaniard and glanced at the artifacts sitting next to several note cards in Dr. Banks' precise handwriting. Many of the cards held rough translations of the cuneiform inscriptions. Two different-colored cards contained writing with a flowing style in a language he couldn't read.

"What do these cards say, Professor? I cannot read the language."

"Oh, those are my notes in my native Spanish. This one is about the piece of a tablet Ms. Post found a few days ago, which we think is a letter from one governor to another."

"Why is this significant, Professor?"

"Well, the governor of Ubaid mentions a small oasis town called Enoch."

"Enoch is the place you believe is the first city in the Jewish Torah."

"Yes, according to tradition, Enoch is the first city of man, built by Cain after his banishment. The evidence suggests the people of Enoch became caravan raiders, and the governor of Ubaid asked for something from the governor of El-Kino. We're unable to figure out what he's asking for because the next section of the tablet is broken off."

"Do you still think Enoch and El-Abel might be the same place, Professor?"

"No, I agree with Dr. Banks, we're dealing with two distinct locations. I suspect from my recent research and the evidence found here that Enoch was a mere village scrambling to make a living by trading."

"Do you think any of their descendants are part of the raiders who attacked us on the way here, Professor?"

"Brothers Colum and Tobias both think vampires attacked us trying to stop us from discovering El-Abel. What does Azim think?"

"Azim is certain one of the groups wanted to destroy the expedition. He's not sure what the other group was doing."

"Well, let's consider the other strange fragment Mr. Polzin found. This piece talks about the outpost of El-Ishtar, the taxes owed to El-Abel, and how the payment is in the form of young men and women of the city."

"I think a society ruled by vampires would pay their taxes in the form of living people, a blood tax of some sort."

"I believe you discovered the meaning of some of the glyphs Dr. Banks is struggling with translating, Fahim."

In the distance, a voice called out and all the local workers not out on the dig site went into the tent Jeremiah reserved to hold their prayer rugs. The Muezzin's voice called out the appropriate prayers for the hour in a deep rich voice. Out on the site, Jeremiah waited while his workers faced Mecca and prayed. With the patience of a Catholic saint, Dr. Banks waited for the time for prayer to end. A growing certainty within him said the goal of his work in this quadrant was within his reach. Taking a break while the workers prayed, Jeremiah sipped from his canteen to stay hydrated in the harsh sun of the Iraqi desert.

As the sun moved across the sky, a shaft of light illuminated the far edge and a flash of reflected crimson light caught Jeremiah's eye. He crossed the excavation and knelt close enough to spot the curve of a polished ruby poking above the sands. With his brush, he swept the dirt away from the stone and exposed a star ruby, measuring close to four inches across the long axis. Jeremiah worked his brush around the ruby, cleaning away the sand to reveal a spiral of El-Isinian text. He took out his notebook and entered in the coordinates of the ruby along with a quick sketch of the stone and script. Below his entry, Jeremiah did a rough translation. Dr. Banks worked his way out from the ruby marker as his team of worker's returned.

"Amal, go back to camp and bring the captain of the emir's guards here. Rasheed, go to each of my students and send them here. The rest of you, put away the shovels and take up brushes and baskets. We reached the map I'm seeking, and we must be careful not to damage the stone."

The two men instructed to serve as messengers scrambled up the ladders and raced to deliver their messages. The rest of the workers passed their shovels up and out of the pit and received brushes and baskets to continue working. Not much time passed before an excited shout in Arabic drew Jeremiah to the center of the excavation. The men working the site drew back to allow Dr. Banks to examine their find. A diamond of unusual size flashed in the sun surrounded by the El-Isian script. By the time the captain of the guard, Mace, Theo, and Quillion arrived, an emerald, a sapphire, and an amethyst marker winked in the fading sunlight. The three students and the guard captain descended to the bottom of the pit and stood beside Dr. Banks. In rapid Arabic,

Jeremiah explained the need to post a constant cycle of guards around this part of the site. The captain agreed and left to establish a patrol schedule. Mace, Theo, and Quillion studied the revealed sections of the map while their mentor spoke with the guard commander.

"Mr. Puap, Mr. Polzin, and Ms. Post, tell me your observations about this map."

"Five marked sites, the four outer locations indicated by a gem representing the elemental magic associated with the particular direction. Amethyst denotes Air in the East, Ruby for Fire in the South, Sapphire for Water in the West, and Emerald for Earth in the North. The diamond in the center represents Spirit in some magical circles."

"Excellent, Mr. Puap."

"Each marker is also the location of an outpost: the sapphire marks El-Isin, the amethyst represents El-Kino, and the diamond by its central location denotes El-Abel. The emerald and ruby mark two undiscovered outposts."

"Correct, Ms. Post."

"Based on the texts you provided, this obsidian marker represents Enoch, given its location close to El-Isin. The points on this map prove Enoch and El-Abel are separate cities despite similar descriptions in the textual evidence."

"Outstanding observation, Mr. Polzin. Starting in the morning, we will all work on clearing the sand away from the rest of the map and recording the details. I'll meet with each of you after dinner tonight to review findings from your excavations."

Once his students left to return to either their dig sites or the hut holding artifacts, Jeremiah returned to clearing the map and making notes on what the inscriptions revealed. When the workers found the outer edge of the stone map, Jeremiah's quick scan of the inscription settled his doubts about what city he was excavating.

Chapter 34

A FEW NIGHTS LATER, Jeremiah was reviewing the day's finds in the artifact storage hut when Brother Colum came in looking distraught. Setting down the clay tablet he was examining, Jeremiah focused on his young lover. His eyes were red-rimmed from crying, his tidy monastic habit was in disarray, and the cords around his waist were a tangled mess. Colum's fingers traced the beads of his rosary in a manner Jeremiah sensed was a nervous habit. What made Jeremiah pause was Colum not fingering his usual oak rosary, but the blood-red jasper rosary, which marked his membership in the Cult of Cain. When Colum realized another person was in the hut, he stopped in his tracks and tried to stuff the rosary away in his robe. Jeremiah pulled out the stool next to his own and urged Colum to sit. Dejected, Colum slumped as he sat, trying to make himself smaller and refusing to meet Jeremiah's eyes. The archaeologist brushed back the cowl from Colum's head to expose the bright-blond hair hidden beneath. He let his fingers caress the soft cheek, and Colum leaned into the touch.

"What's upset you, Colum?"

"Cardinal Joan learned I'm involved in your relationship with Prof. Di

Vargas. She reminded me of my vow not to become involved in your love life. She's ordered me to break off loving you both and didn't take the news well when I informed her Lord Hunter swore me to his service above all other vows."

"What did she say, Colum?"

"She gave me three choices: honor my oath of obedience to her and remain a member of the Cult of Cain, which means giving you and Juan up; leave the Cult and honor my vows as a member of the Order of St. Hubert, by becoming a simple monk; and the last choice is to give up both and hope you and Juan take me into your household."

"And the oath of service to this Lord Hunter doesn't prevent her from issuing this ultimatum?"

"I think she's afraid of what Lord Hunter plans for my future."

"She's afraid he might elevate you to her post or give you what she covets the most. She thinks by becoming our lover any usefulness to the Cult is compromised. We understand becoming an actual member of the Order and honoring the vow of chastity isn't an option. So, your choice is between your oaths to the Cult and hoping Juan and I want you as a third in our relationship."

Colum fumbled the rosary, trying to find comfort, and nodded. Jeremiah caught up Colum's hands and stilled the fingers on the rosary. The blood-red figure of Christ on the cross hung between them, facing Colum and exposing the tiny vial in the back of the cross. Jeremiah lifted the cross to study the flask.

"Does this truly contain the blood of Cain?"

"The vile contains only Lord Hunter's blood, based on witnessing him fill the container. The drop of blood inside before was his as well. Tobias' contains a drop, which is part Cain's and part Lord Hunter's blood. Older pieces are said to exist, which contain only the blood of

Cain since Lord Hunter is said to only be about two centuries old as a vampire."

Colum met Jeremiah's eyes for the first time. "Why do you ask, Jeremiah?"

"Hearing you use my given name makes me think you reached your decision, but I ask because of something I read on a tablet Mace uncovered yesterday. The text suggests Cain's blood holds the key to unlock an ancient secret within the palace. The primary question is whether Cain's blood must be used or if the blood of any vampire would work."

Jeremiah released the cross and Colum's hands, and returned to the tablet he'd been working with before Colum's arrival. Colum reached out and touched Jeremiah's face, turning the older man back towards him. Dark blue eyes locked with bright sapphire eyes as he leaned in to kiss one of the first men to love him. The kiss lingered for a moment, but Jeremiah broke off first to study the younger man's face, looking for a clue.

"My decisions made, Jeremiah. I love you and Juan, and want to be with you both, but until I set aside all my vows, I must restrict myself to protecting you both. First, I must contact Her Eminence and ask for my release from the Cult of Cain. I'm sure with a few words to Bishop Fabbri I can obtain a release from my vows to the Order as well." Tears filled his eyes, which he tried hard to hold back. "When I'm free, I hope you and Juan want me."

"When do you plan to ask my master for release from his service, little vicar?" a voice spoke from the shadows. "He made plans for you, and he expects you to hold up your end of the bargain."

"Who are you?" Jeremiah said, trying to move Colum behind him. "Show yourself."

"I'm called Database by my master Richard St. Martin," said the cloaked figure, which stepped from the shadows.

"What do you want?" Jeremiah demanded.

Colum reached out and laid a hand on Jeremiah's arm. "Don't anger him. He's an ancient vampire and a direct servant of Lord Hunter."

"You are wise beyond your years, young vicar, and we didn't waste our time training you. I came for the tablets and the rough map to the site of El-Abel, Dr. Banks."

"If your master is here, he doesn't need my notes or map to El-Abel. I'm willing to bet Juan came into possession of those journal pages for a reason. Your master wished for someone like him to begin searching for this lost city."

"You are wiser than some in Lord Hunter's inner circle give you credit for, Dr. Banks. Now, why do you say he doesn't need your notes and the map?"

"For one, my notes and the maps are in El-Isinian, so unless your master is fluent, they won't be much assistance to him. Call me paranoid, but I figured one side or the other in the vampire feud would come for them. Ask your master to give me another week before taking over my expedition and I'll give him a precise location to the prize he seeks."

"How can you guarantee your claim, Dr. Banks?"

"Because we're standing in El-Abel. Hazarding a guess, Lord Hunter waited a century or more to discover this city and the location of the palace. Will another week of waiting bother him if I can lock down the actual site of Cain's citadel?"

"I will ask him, Dr. Banks. I will return here tomorrow night with his answer. He will not be pleased with any delay."

"As a sign of my pledge, I offer this clue to the puzzle of El-Abel.

When I completed my city on the sixth day of construction, I offered up a sacrifice of my blood in honor of my brother. Make a similar sacrifice and the seals on my palace will be broken."

"A riddle? Do you possess the answer, Dr. Banks?"

"Not yet, but I suspect the key is in either Lord Hunter's blood or a talisman containing Cain's undiluted blood. The riddle is all I can offer at this time. I think more lies are hidden in the sands."

"I will meet you tomorrow night, Dr. Banks. Perhaps you will discover more."

"Perhaps, I will," Dr. Banks, acknowledged. "Everything depends on what the sands release."

The shadows shifted, and the strange vampire vanished, leaving Colum and Jeremiah alone. Moving with care, Jeremiah locked away the tablets and several reams of notes in a safe at the back of the Quonset hut. He led Colum outside.

"Time for you to return to your tent, my little monk. Until your vows—and I mean all—are resolved, best we don't press the issue."

"We should wait and discuss the possibility with Juan as well. The relationship between the two of you comes before my desires."

The pair separated and returned to their tents unaware of the little vampire observing them from the shadows. Database departed the camp and returned to where Richard waited for his report.

Chapter 35

BASED on his discoveries at El-Isin, Jeremiah set up his compass and surveyor's equipment to determine which grid held the prize. On the page made with his students' assistance, he noted four candidates for searching. In the evening, he worked with Juan reviewing their findings: various historical and religious texts, and the strange diary attributed to Cain.

"Both Cain's journal and the Book of Ham mention the gates of El-Abel across from the canyon, Miah."

Jeremiah laid out the hand-drawn map and marked the closest sub-grid to the canyon's mouth. With a grimace, he placed a straight edge on the drawing from the gorge through the possible placement of the walls and the excavated city center.

"The layout is off. El-Abel differs from El-Isin or any other town of the era. The line from the river valley to the front and into the middle runs from the northwest to the southeast."

"Aside from the pass, does another geological reason exist to design on a different axis?"

"No."

"Why rotate the plans from the standard north/south or east/west? The cardinal points referenced the gods during the period."

"Two possibilities, Juan. The simplest being geography, the chasm is the primary access to this area; the architects considered the position and built facing the natural gateway. The second reason is an outright rebellion against the conventions of honoring directional deities."

"Both apply to this case, I think. Well, Cain revolted against God before and, after being cursed, his builders turned everything forty-five degrees and constructed following the terrain."

"The concept holds merit. Let's hypothesize the planners carried the idea out further when they created the outer settlements. Grab the regional chart for me, Juan."

Jeremiah retrieved his notes on the coordinates for El-Isin, El-Kino, and El-Abel. Once Juan spread the larger map out, Jeremiah circled the three verified locations. After double-checking the measurement from the central marker to both outposts, he made two additional marks designating the positions of the remaining towns. Juan took the pencil and ruler from his lover's hands before making a notation halfway between the northwestern and southwestern ones.

"The location of Enoch."

"Due east from El-Abel on the trade route from Egypt. Explains why Khons and his caravan ended up in the village instead of in El-Isin. A traditional culture confused by a nontraditional one."

Jeremiah flipped back to his excavation diagram and checked a single square along the path across the city. Puzzled, Juan glanced at him.

"The entrance to the palace of Cain."

"The site of your next dig?"

"Yes."

Chapter 36

THE EXCAVATION WORK on the entrance to the palace took days to complete. The team of archaeologists ventured into the labyrinth of passages below the sands. The group separated into two teams, the first lead by Dr. Banks and the second followed Professor Di Vargas. Despite taking precautions, Jeremiah suffered the only accident of the explorers. A section of the floor gave way beneath him and dropped Jeremiah into the chamber below. Lights and the physician furnished by the emir descended into the room to find Jeremiah with his right wrist and elbow cradled against his chest.

Once the doctor splinted the arm, Jeremiah dismissed further treatments and concerns to focus on the wall paintings. Preserved in the sealed chamber for uncounted centuries, the paints retained their vibrant colors. Informed of Jeremiah's accident, Juan and Colum lowered themselves into the room. The trio stood and studied the narrative.

"Let a doctor put a proper cast on your arm, Miah."

"In time, Juan. I want to understand the version presented here. Some parts match the records we read, and others represent a different story."

"Give me an example."

In full teacher mode, Jeremiah started to point with his right hand before the pain stopped him.

"Start at the third row of images from the top, Juan. The tale carved here doesn't follow the biblical version of Cain and Abel. The images represent a different story: one of war between brothers and angels. Please photograph these walls, Juan."

"Is this a true account of the beginning of the vampires?"

"Hard to say. I need time to work through all these strange figures. What or who is the figure surrounded by a golden light, and why does he wield a gold-and-silver knife?"

"What does the golden image represent, Dr. Banks?"

"At a guess, a deity."

"A correct guess, Dr. Banks. Grandfather kept a number of secrets from us, but his war with his god wasn't one of them."

"Who are you?"

A blue-robed figure stepped out of the shadows; his dark skin gleamed in the lamplight. Half his face lay shrouded behind the hood of his garment.

"I am Immertun, first chosen of Nina-Ishtar, Queen and Vizier of El-Abel, the founder of the Kalumtum Clan, who advised the other clans, and the actual guardian of El-Abel."

"He can't be who he claims, Jeremiah. The records of both the Cult and the Order report Immertun's destruction at the hands of Izcacus in the ninth century after Christ."

"Do they say how he destroyed me, little monk? I would enjoy reading the account."

"The records say he consumed the essence of Immertun and took for himself the powers and rank of a primordial."

"He did try to commit Parthalán's sin, but with some help, I escaped with enough life force to seal the wounds he inflicted. The scholars didn't come to hear my tale, little monk. The story they and two others want is the one partly written on these walls."

The sounds of screams, clashing swords, and gunfire interrupted Jeremiah's attempt to ask a question. Quillion's voice echoed into the chamber.

"Get away from them, Ice Bitch."

VAMPIRE INTERLUDE:
GOODBYE MISS BEAUMONT

The tranquility of the evening shattered as the first watchman's scream ended in a gurgle. Gunfire and clashing swords echoed through the night, waking everyone in the camp. Well, the noise woke all those who were not claimed as silent victims of the Bel-Kino raiders. In several tents lay the remains of workers drained of their life essence. Brother Tobias, Azim, and Fahim worked their way through the shadows to the tents occupied by Mace, Theo, and Quillion. The three graduate students plus the slave girl Abad huddled together in the center of Mace and Theo's shelter behind overturned cots, with guns pointed towards the entrances.

Swift action on Quillion's part kept Abad from shooting Azim as he slipped into the tent on the women's side. He bowed to her in thanks.

"We must make our way to the palace to join Brother Colum in protecting Dr. Banks and Prof. Di Vargas."

"How many attackers are there, Azim?"

"The number is unknown at this time, Mistress Post. We fear most of them are vampires with a few mortal guides."

The tent flaps parted, and a figure in jeans and a sweatshirt with a faded logo stepped inside, a silver longsword in his right hand.

"The son of the desert is correct. The Bel-Kino ambushed enough of the guard patrols to slip into the camp undetected. Come with me, and we'll work our way around to the palace."

"Master of Darkness, the Bel-Kino presence means the Primordial Bellabarisruk intends to take the palace and kill the doctor and the professor."

"The primordial is my concern, son of the desert. Lead the others out along the perimeter of the camp to the palace entrance. Once there, join with Brother Colum in defending everyone. Armand and Database are waiting to help you inside."

Azim gave a quick bow before urging the others out into the desert evening.

* * *

At the palace entrance, a small group led by a blonde woman dressed in the latest fashion dispatched the guards before entering. The woman gestured for two of her party to take posts in the niches next to the doors of the palace. The group proceeded towards the hole in the floor where Dr. Banks fell earlier in the day.

"Stay here and make sure no one else passes into the chamber below."

"Yes, My Lord."

The red-robed figure of Bellabarisruk separated from the group and descended into the rooms below.

* * *

The grad students led the way to the palace entry until Brother Tobias stopped them short of entering the complex.

"The enemy is sure to position defenders at the entrance. Azim and I will go first to eliminate the guards."

"Stay put, monk. The two guarding the door beyond are elders of the sixth generation. Database and I will deal with them."

"Armand, let me go deal with them; no point in sending any else to do my dirty work."

"My Lord, our duty is to protect..."

Richard vanished before Armand finished his protest. He reappeared a few moments later to signal the way was clear for them to proceed. The group passed two piles of ash as they made their way towards Dr. Banks and company. As they came around the final corner, the blonde female vampire stepped out to confront them.

"Oh look, the three urchins and one of the annoying monks. Dispose of them and the rest of the trash they brought along."

Four hulking brutes blocked the passage until a shot rang out from Mace's Colt revolver, dropping one of them like a tree. The hole in the monster's forehead gaped for a moment before starting to close, but stopped as the creature crumbled to dust. The remaining three blinked and rushed their opponents. Two silver knives flashed as Tobias and Azim countered the rush and dispatched their opponents. Theo dropped the remaining vampire brute with a shot to the heart. The female vampire moved to grab Mace or Theo, but Quillion blocked her way, eyes blazing with golden light.

"Get away from them, Ice Bitch."

Miss Beaumont turned to strike Quillion, only to catch a blast of Gold magic as the grad student punched her in the jaw. Fueled by divine magic, Quillion's punch snapped Eunice Beaumont's neck and fried her vampire nerves. The former government watchdog hit the ground and crumbled into dust. A moment later, Quillion fainted.

"Azim and Armand take everyone to the chamber at the intersection and stay there. Database, my friend, keep watch here while I descend to confront Bellabarisruk."

Chapter 37

THE RED-ROBED FIGURE of Bellabarisruk floated down the ladder into the story chamber. He turned to find himself face-to-face with a blue-robed doppelganger.

"I-Immer, how is this possible? My agents told me Izcacus destroyed you."

"He tried to commit Parthalán's sin upon me perhaps a century after you made him, Ris."

"How did you survive?"

Before Immertun replied, the Bel-Kino primordial caught sight of Jeremiah, Juan, and Colum, and took a step in their direction. Immertun put a hand on his chest, stopping him.

"The mortals are my guests and under the protection of my hospitality, Ris. Please honor our ancient tradition."

"Hospitality is sacred, and I honor my brother and his guests."

"The few remaining agents I possess informed me of your pursuit of these interesting mortals. Allow me to introduce Dr. Jeremiah Banks, Professor Juan Di Vargas, and Brother Colum. Gentlemen, this is my brother in the Gift, Bellabarisruk the first chosen of Sharru-Kino king of El-Abel."

Another figure descended the ladder behind the group.

"Sorry to interrupt the reunion, although from what I overheard, my vizier Armand will be overjoyed to learn his clan's founder survives."

"Ris, who is this child to speak so in our presence?"

Brother Colum crossed the room and bowed to Richard. "Lord Slayer, on behalf of the Cult of Cain, I welcome you to El-Abel. Should my services be required, I am yours to command."

"Who is this Child of Cain?"

"Richard St. Martin is my name, though many refer to me as Lord Hunter, Lord Slayer, Lord of all Vampires, or the Master of Darkness. I am Cain's successor in the Curse."

"Not according to the story on these walls, Lord Hunter. The vampire you inherited the curse from wasn't the real Cain."

All eyes focused on Jeremiah as he moved closer to the first painted wall. With his good arm, he pointed out the lines of the image supporting his statement.

"The story here differs from the accounts in the major holy books. From what I can make out, this is an account of a war between two heavenly factions. Cain supported one side of the war and Seth supported the other side. Abel attempted to make peace between his brothers, but something went wrong."

"Grandfather did keep lots of secrets from us. Perhaps the three who made us possessed this information. What surprises me is how you didn't know any of this, Immer."

"As you said, Ris, Grandfather kept secrets, although I think he shared some with one of my less-sane great-grandchildren. One from the sixth generation produced a work he called the Gospel of El-Abel. The scroll is in the palace library down the hall from here."

Immertun left the room to retrieve the scroll. The leader of the Bel-Kino turned to face Richard.

"Laverna Salacia gives you high praise, Richard St. Martin."

"Praise from the Queen of Pirates is high praise indeed, Lord Bellabarisruk. She and the elders of your clan speak often of your integrity, courage, and leadership. The Bel-Kino rule well and with wisdom."

"I learned much in my service to the king and from Immertun, whose wisdom is unmatched among our kind. I cannot understand why Grandfather allowed you to destroy him."

"Professor, did you bring the journal with you into the palace?"

"The book is in Colum's satchel, sir."

Colum reached into the satchel and removed the volume in question. He held the book out to Richard, who took it and turned to the back pages.

"Cain tried to stay my hand, but I wanted vengeance more than anything else at the time. One of the notes in his journal contained a set of instructions, which sparked this quest two centuries ago."

"May I read the passage, Richard St. Martin?"

"Be my guests, Lord Bellabarisruk."

"'Under the full moon in the throne room of El-Abel, soak these last pages in blood from one of my grandchildren and reveal the deepest truth.'"

The two vampires stared at each other for a moment before the primordial spoke again.

"The throne room is located on this level on the other side of the library. I think we should leave the mortals behind. The secrets contained in here are meant for you alone. Dr. Banks, you and your party may study this room, but do not venture any further into the ruins of the palace. I will send orders to my clan to help your expedition pack and relocate to the ruins of Enoch. In those ruins are wonders as contradictory as any to be found here."

"What happened during Noah's Flood?"

"A tale for another time, Professor. Should I survive this encounter with Lord Slayer, perhaps he will allow me to come and tell you the tale."

The two vampires departed to make their way to the throne room. Jeremiah turned his attention back to the walls around him. With Colum's assistance, Juan took photographs so they could aid Jeremiah in translating the story of the origin of the vampires.

* * *

On the way to the throne room, Richard and Bellabarisruk stopped in the library and found Immertun pulling out the scroll of the Gospel of El-Abel. Richard watched the interaction between the two primordials and realized they shared a deep affection for each other.

"I almost envy your friendship."

"The ancient civilizations were young when Ris and I first met. I made a fool of myself during our first introduction. I studied Ris as part of the history of my people growing up and idolized him. Imagine the shock when I arrived in El-Abel and the first member of the court I'm introduced to is Bellabarisruk, the first Mage-Lord of Babylon."

"The stunned expression on his face was priceless. The Lady Nina-Ishtar bragged about the eloquence of her first protégé. When she presented him to Father Cain and the court, he stammered like an illiterate peasant."

"Well, I managed to survive the encounter and with Ris' assistance, I survived my trial period in city administration."

"How could I say no to her? The Lady came and asked me to mentor you. She figured my experience would help guide you through the pitfalls I navigated on my own."

"Our story is a long one, Lord Richard, spanning most of history. To us, you are unique, a direct recipient of the original curse or gift."

"I didn't choose to take on the curse. I didn't get a choice. I lost a loved one to vampires and the trail lead to Cain's doorstep. We talked, but in the end, I didn't listen to his advice to leave. I killed him and a dark cloud wrapped around me as a golden voice cursed me to take his place."

"Would you break the curse?"

"One of the entries in Cain's journal mentioned the attempts he made to remove the curse. One even mentioned his encounter with Jesus of Nazareth."

"Yes, we were instructed to make sure no one interfered with the young man's destiny."

"Plus, Father Cain instructed us not to offer the gift to the young fanatic Iscariot. Some of the others felt we were wasting huge talent by not recruiting Judas."

"The only one who thought we lost out was Parlathán."

"Ris, you wanted the Nazarene."

"Well, of course I did. He led a popular movement against the odds of success. What better example of the principles of the Bel-Kino could there be?"

"Be glad you didn't take a bite out of him. Do you remember when one of Astryiah's lot tried to devour the Oracle of Delphi?"

"The bitch went up in flames, like the sun touched her. Calming the oracle down took the priests of Apollo two months."

"Certain magic causes our kind to explode. I remember one of mine almost died feeding from a hedge witch in Ireland."

The trio came to a stop at a set of heavy bronze doors. Richard stepped forward and the doors swung open.

"The last time the doors opened was day before Noah's troops attacked the city. Sharru-Kino and Father Cain are the only ones who could make them open."

Both primordials bowed to Richard.

"We acknowledge Richard St. Martin as the true successor to Cain and Sharru-Kino as Lord of El-Abel."

A voice long unused spoke.

"Welcome, home successor to Cain, Father of Vampires."

Chapter 38

AT AN UNVOICED SIGNAL, **Database** descended into the story chamber and collected Jeremiah, Juan, and Colum. He escorted them to the room where Armand guarded the others. Despite the pages of notes Colum took for him, and several rolls of film taken by Juan, depression settled over Jeremiah. He remained silent as the group returned to the ruins of their camp.

"Pack only your personal belonging and tools; leave everything pertaining to this site behind."

As the hooded vampire spoke, Jeremiah collapsed to his knees in the sand and gave into his despair. Juan and Colum dropped on either side of him and held him while he cried.

"What's wrong with Dr. Banks?"

"Quillion, now isn't the time. Let's go start packing."

"No, Mace, something is wrong with Dr. Banks. He wouldn't abandon all the work done here. Without the artifacts, how does he prove his or Prof. Di Vargas' theories?"

Juan glanced at the two vampires guarding their group, then nodded to Colum. The young monk rose and drew the three graduate students aside.

"The three of you must never speak of El-Abel or the findings here. Once we pack, the expedition moves northwest to the site of Enoch. Once there, we'll work until the season is over."

"But El-Abel is Dr. Banks' life's work. Are you saying he's giving up his research?"

"Yes, Ms. Post. In order to protect those, he cares about, he's giving up his research. He's strong, so forgive his moment of weakness. Juan and I will help him refocus on Enoch and proving Juan's theories."

"We'll do everything we can to assist. The sudden change affects our fieldwork credits."

Jeremiah struggled back to his feet with Juan's assistance.

"Don't worry about your credits, Mr. Puap. I'll see you receive all the fieldwork credits for the work you've done. I'm shaken by losing access to the truth."

The tinkling of bells drew everyone's attention to the arrival of two individuals in colorful clothing. The two vampire companions of Richard St. Martin straightened as the male pirate approached.

"What do you want, Shadow?"

"Relax, Sweet Armand. My Lady Captain wishes words with the archaeologist and the theologian at the request of your master."

"We'll speak with the Lady."

Despite Colum's attempt to stop him, Juan placed himself between the two vampire groups.

"Apologies, My Lady, for the lack of proper hospitality. Our last guests proved a bit rowdy."

A hearty laugh erupted from Laverna Salacia, who waved off the mess of the camp.

"A trifling matter, Prof. Di Vargas. Perhaps we could make use of the caliph's train as the dawn draws near."

"Of course, please follow us, My Lady."

Juan helped Jeremiah to his feet and the group made their way to the private car Juan and Jeremiah shared.

"The caliph was generous to loan you his private train and personal car, Dr. Banks."

"We were graduate students assigned to the same mentor for field work, Captain..."

"Darling Shadow, you didn't give me a proper introduction."

"Apologies, My Captain. Gentlemen and young lady, this is Laverna Salacia, the Queen of Pirates."

"Forgive my directness, Captain Salacia, but you're like Lords Bellabarisruk and Immertun."

"Yes, Dr. Banks, I am what our kind call a primordial, or a member of the third generation of vampires. I am the third chosen of Nina-Ishtar and the last chosen of the nine."

"Your companion mentioned you came with a message from Lord Hunter or Slayer. Sorry, his titles are confusing."

"Understandable, Dr. Banks. Yes, Lord Richard commanded I serve as escort and guardian for your team. My clan is to escort your expedition to Enoch, where you may continue your research."

Jeremiah scowled at the thought of researching and excavating Enoch. The prize of his research lay here in El-Abel. The answers Enoch provided solved questions Juan posed and, out of love, he would dig up half of the caliphate for Juan.

"Captain Salacia, were you here during Noah's Flood?"

"Yes, Dr. Banks, I was. I expected Prof. Di Vargas to ask me about the Flood. I fought beside my brothers and sisters in the gift against the Mage-Lord Noah and the abominations you call shifters."

"Did a river once flow through the valley leading here?"

"A mighty tributary of the Tigris once flowed down the valley and around El-Abel. The war between El-Abel and Nineveh altered the river's course, Professor. For now, let us make sure preparations to depart for Enoch are underway. Pretty Shadow, check on the crews."

"Aye, Captain."

The handsome pirate made for the exit, but found his way blocked by Brother Tobias

"Why does the monk bar the exit?"

"Because, pirate, the sun is about to rise. I doubt the Queen of Pirates wants her first mate transformed into a pile of ash."

"The monk has a point, my Handsome Shadow. Perhaps the little monk would check on the preparations."

Chapter 39

The immense bronze throne on the opposite end of the hall drew Richard forward. The two primordials followed like dutiful attendants, stopping at the base of the throne as their lord ascended to take his place. Once Richard was seated, they bowed in unison before taking their places on either side of the dais. Immertun stood to Richard's right in the place reserved for a vizier, and Bellabarisruk to Richard's left in the place reserved for a general.

"My Lord will find a switch on the right arm of the throne, which opens the Portal of the Moon."

Richard glanced between the two attending vampires, before blinking himself back to reality. He paused for a moment, letting Immertun's words sink in before finding the switch and flipping the position. Above them, the ceiling began to grind and grate as a round section split open, pouring sand to the floor below. Once the sand flow ended, moonlight streamed into the chamber. Richard waved his hand and the sand swirled away to the outer edges of the room. He descended from the throne to stand in the moonlight with the mysterious blank pages from Cain's journal in his hands.

"Under the full moon in the throne room of El-Abel, soak these last pages in blood from one of my grandchildren and reveal the deepest truth. Which of you volunteers your blood?"

"My clan is shattered beyond repair, My Lord. I will be the sacrifice to Father Cain's magic."

"Immer, we can share the burden. I don't wish to lose you a second time."

"Ris, Grandfather's magic says one of his grandchildren. I'm hoping he didn't set this up to drain the chosen grandchild dry. Should final death be the price, better I'm the sacrifice. The Bel-Kino still need you."

Under the moonlight, a faint line of text appeared to Richard.

"After the chosen's blood spills, allow them to drink from the vessel of the curse."

"Don't fear. Final death isn't required, Immertun. Once enough of your blood soaks these pages, you will feed from me."

"An honor beyond measure, My Lord."

"Or a death so painful, bleeding out might be preferable."

With a flick of his wrist, Richard slashed open Immertun's arm from wrist to elbow. Blood splattered the pages as he twisted the primordial's arm to keep the wound from healing. The scent of Immertun's blood caused Richard's fangs to descend and his mouth to water.

"I believe the pages are saturated, Lord Richard."

Immertun sagged in Richard's arms, head rolling back and exposing the carotid artery.

"What remains of my essence is yours, My Lord. Drink your fill."

Richard snapped out of his hunger trance at the mention of self-sacrifice from Immertun. He slashed open his own arm and presented the wound to the primordial.

"Drink of my life as Cain, Father of Vampires, requested."

A grimace of pain shot across Richard's face before the gentle sigh of euphoria escaped his lips as Immertun's fangs sank into his flesh. The sexual high hit a moment later and Richard felt his cock expand to full erection. Bellabarisruk took notice of his expressions.

"This is your first time on the receiving end of a vampire's bite, My Lord. Enjoy the sensations of euphoria and enhanced sexual desire."

With an effort, Richard pulled Immertun away from his arm and sealed the wound shut. The healing and blood loss, along with the fading sexual bliss, left Richard dizzy and off-balance. Immertun moaned and prostrated himself before Richard.

"Immer, get up. He may be Grandfather's successor, but he's not worth such a display of respect."

"He can't help his reaction, Lord Bellabarisruk. As the bite from vampires like yourself bring sexual bliss, so drinking my blood brings obedience and submission. For the next few days, Immertun is bound to my service and will."

"Release Immer from this bond, Lord Richard."

"The effect will wear off in a few days, provided he doesn't drink from me again."

The Lord of Bel-Kino drew his bronze sickle sword to strike at Richard, but found himself at crossed blades with Richard's silver longsword.

"You should know to bring weapons of silver or gold when planning to face a vampire of our ranks, Lord Bellabarisruk."

An emerald spark leapt from the blood-soaked pages exposed to the moonlight and drew their attention from Immertun. Bending down, Richard picked up the pages, and at his touch, they burst into emerald flames. When the magical flames went out, two pages remained. The first page was a map to a location someplace in Central America. On the second page appeared a drawing of a dagger and text in what appeared to be El-Isinian.

* * *

To help keep Jeremiah from moping and brooding over the loss of his work at El-Abel, Juan went to the darkroom on the train and processed the film taken in the story chamber. While he wasn't in his lover's class when translating, Juan could decipher the basics. As the first picture developed, he followed the story. The pictograms began with the creation of Adam and Eve but flowed straight into the birth of their children.

"Odd no Garden, tree, serpent, or expulsion. Were Adam and Eve without sin? Best to discuss this with Miah."

When all the photos were dry, he took them back to the car he shared with his lover. He found Miah and Colum deep in conversation with Lady Laverna Salacia. What had she witnessed in her long existence?

"Oh no, Dr. Banks, the early Bronze Age sailors took risks beyond belief. Uncle Bel-Sharra convinced a group to sail him beyond the Pillars of Hercules because a quest drew him to the west. Our brother in the gift, Howahkan, came from the indigenous peoples of what is now North America."

"One of the primordials is a Native American? But there are no legends of vampires in any of their cultures."

"I'm sorry to interrupt the conversation, Miah, but I developed the photos from the story chamber."

Juan placed the stack of images before Jeremiah. The archaeologist worked through the photographs and scowled.

"This account doesn't match any other I've ever read, Juan. In only the first few lines of this text, Cain gives an entirely new version of the creation. According to his account Adam and Eve didn't get kicked out of the Garden of Eden. Here in his narrative of his, Able, and Seth's births, he adds a twin sister for each them. Plus, on this line he says the war for Heaven occurred after the creation of Adam and Eve instead of before."

"There are stories of Lucifer's fall being caused by his refusal to bow to Adam as God commanded, so this account isn't too off base," Juan said.

"No, the strange part is the rivalry isn't between Cain and Abel, but between Cain and Seth. They went to war against each other over who was righteous. Abel got caught in the middle, trying to make peace."

"You must be reading something wrong, Dr. Banks. Father Cain taught us the rivalry was between Abel and Seth, and how he fell victim to their magic," Laverna Salacia said.

"One account or the other is a fiction. Is the account Cain taught you written down anywhere or an oral account?"

"As far as I can recall, an oral account."

"Well, based on this account, Abel is the first vampire, but he's not the vampire who created your race."

"Did he create Father Cain in an act of revenge?"

"No, according to this, the reverse of the actual Cain and Abel story took place. Abel killed Cain at the altar of the Lord under something called the Silver Banner of Peace. Seems God wanted total victory, not a peaceful settlement of the dispute. The transferrable nature of His curse on Abel came after He convinced another to strike down the monster Abel became."

"You refer to the part where God said whoever killed Cain would take up his curse sevenfold," Colum said.

"Yes, a touch of divine retribution added to a seething mess of twisted hatred."

"So, who is the father of our race if not Cain?" Laverna Salacia asked.

* * *

OVER THE MASSIVE bronze throne of El-Abel, a second moon portal opened and illuminated the seat. A figure appeared seated on the throne and Bellabarisruk gasped as he recognized Cain.

"Greetings, Richard St. Martin and my beloved Immertun."

After a slight pause, the message continued.

"Yes, Lord Hunter, I call you by name. I always knew who my successor would be as the knowledge was imparted when I became what I am. When we met in life, I introduced myself as Cain, son of Adam and Eve, the first murderer and the first of our kind. I am sorry, Immertun. I lied to all of my children. I am not Cain, and I was not the first of our kind."

Bellabarisruk fell to his knees in shock, while Richard stared at the figure before him.

"Down the hall from this chamber is a room containing the true account of the origin of our kind. Immertun can translate the story for you."

"So, who the hell are you if you're not Cain?" Richard demanded.

* * *

AND THE LORD COMMANDED ADAM, "Go and fashion a knife to slay thy son, who is an abomination in my sight. The blade of the knife shall be a cubit in length of pure bronze. Fashion the handle and guard from cedar, and wrap the handle in leather made from a newborn calf. In the pommel, set a ruby the size of the end of your thumb. When this blade is completed, bring it to the Cave of Treasures and leave it at the entrance for three days. On the morning of the fourth day, take the blade from the Cave of Treasures and seek out thy son, the abomination, and slay him.

"A reading from the Gospel of El-Abel, chapter two, verses one through five."

"Miah, are you suggesting Adam is the Father of Vampires?"

"I'm not suggesting, Juan. Here's the same scene in pictographs: Adam forging the knife, leaving the blade in a cave, and using the weapon to slay Abel."

"So, Adam fell victim to Abel's Curse, became the second vampire, and created all other vampires?"

"In a nutshell, yes."

"Dr. Banks, what are these images of Adam attacking a cloud-like figure?"

"Yahweh offered to free Adam from the curse and seat him at his right hand in Heaven, Captain Salacia. Adam refused and turned the gift of naming against Yahweh, before attempting to devour him. Here's the translation:

Your sons, O Adam, are a disappointment to me. Cain the Twister, who crafted beasts from what, was once divine. Abel the Peacemaker, who sought to bring peace where peace was not desired. Seth, the self-righteous, possessed a pride and beauty, which lead to the fall of my beautiful Morning Star. How fitting you should shoulder the Curse unleashed by their actions as penance for your sins against me.

And Adam replied to the Lord, "How fitting I use the gift of naming to rename myself. Henceforth I am Cain, for I now possess his hatred of You O' Lord. Against Yahweh of the Mist, I shall raise up a mighty city to be called El-Abel, in honor of he who sought to bring peace. I continue lost Abel's curse on the House and Lineage of Seth. One last thing I name O' My Lord, before the Curse of Abel consumes me.

What do you name O' man?

I name you, O' My Lord, and I name thee food to sate my hunger.

Therefore, did Adam, now called Cain, feast on upon the essence of Yahweh, the Lord of Hosts. The essence of the Lord struggled against Cain and split. The fragment of the Lord escaped to wander a broken spirit howling in the wilderness.

The Gospel of El-Abel 3:1-11"

EPILOGUE

Two Years Later

THE TROPICAL BREEZE blew between the buildings of the University of Hawai'i, as a man with long, flowing red hair made his way to his office. A smiling older woman opened the door for the man, letting him enter without juggling the stack of books and papers in his arms.

"Welcome back, Professor Banks. Did your class go well?"

"Thank you, Mrs. Pike. Yes, I think the coconuts are actually learning something, but we'll find out once I've read and graded their papers."

Mrs. Pike closed the door with a sigh and glanced fondly at the reverse of the lettering on the glass. Professor Jeremiah Banks, Associate Dean of Archaeology and Taha Baqir Chair of Middle Eastern Archaeology. The older woman recalled the fancy gentleman, who informed her of her selection by the University of Hawai'i to serve as the personal assistant to their new Associate Dean of Archaeology. She still glowed with pride at Jeremiah's professional recovery following the expedition to Enoch. With the publication of his paper on the expedition, he'd flattened his critics. The University of Arizona attempted to seize the credit for the paper, but a strange benefactor intervened and Dr. Banks received a job offer from the University of Hawai'i, which included the purchase of all artifacts relating to Enoch and El-Isin. He accepted without thinking twice and boarded a train for the coast two weeks later after supervising the packing of all the artifacts.

Two months after starting his new position, a new chair was sponsored as a joint venture between the Caliphate of Baghdad and the Holy Roman Empire. At the insistence of the caliph and the Holy Father, the Taha Baqir Chair of Middle Eastern Archaeology was offered to Dr. Banks. After a brief consultation with the dean of the department, Jeremiah accepted the chair and gave his maiden speech as full professor at the Honolulu Theological and Archaeological Conference later in the year. Mrs. Pike couldn't remember seeing Jeremiah blush harder than when Professor and Dean of Theological Archaeology, Juan Di Vargas, pulled the younger man in tight and kissed him in front of the entire staff of the department.

"You settle in, Prof. Banks. I'll bring you something to tide you over until time to prepare for the banquet tonight."

"Bless you, Mrs. Pike. I'm so glad you agreed to transfer out here."

"Well, the young gentleman who offered me the job tossed in a number of healthy incentives. I'm here to get you established and settled in, and then, I can retire to my nice little home on the beach.

"I promised him not to keep you from the beach too long."

* * *

"MASTER, the archaeologist and the religious scholar are settled into their new lives in the Republic of California."

"Thank you, Database. What of the young vicar and those grad students?"

"The young vicar is undergoing further training in preparation to found a new organization, My Lord. As for the graduate students, they are finishing up their doctoral programs and are expected to receive their degrees in the fall."

"I see patronage still greases the wheels."

"Adam's quiet donations and not so subtle blackmail cleared the majority of the roadblocks."

"Adam didn't make those donations or apply the blackmail. I did."

"Master, Adam's name is on the checks to the University of Hawai'i and to the University of Arizona regarding the purchase of the artifacts."

"Of course, his name is on the checks. I don't possess a checking account in my own name, Database. Adam is a front for my activities. Playing him allows me to move about without people fawning all over me."

As he spoke, Richard raised the glamor of Adam over his own visage. When he spoke next, Adam's rich baritone voice carried his words.

"I'm still shocked neither of you figured out this ruse, considering the number of other such personas I adopted over the last two centuries."

"Forgive us, Master, for not seeing past your disguise."

"Apologies, My Lord. I did not suspect your use of magic to craft Adam."

Adam faded away and Richard once more stood before his friends. He gestured them to seats as he sprawled on a couch.

"Did any of the grad students take up the study of ancient Central American cultures?"

"Ms. Post shifted her focus to the Aztec Empire."

"Did the slave girl Abal come back to the Texan Republic with her?"

"Yes, My Lord. Lady Abal received a restoration of her position when her brother; the caliph settled their late father's debt. The best mage-healers removed her tattoo and scars. Our agents report she and Ms. Post are sharing accommodations while the latter finishes her doctoral program."

"Excellent, in time we'll send Azim and Fahim to them with the clues to Adam's knife."

"Master, do you plan to use the knife?"

"No, Database. I wish the knife in my possession to prevent others from using the blade against me. I've grown used to immortality, and I think I'd like to experience the ages to come."

The End

HISTORICAL FIGURES

There are a few academic chairs mentioned briefly in this book, all of which are fictional, although the people for whom they are named are not fictional characters. Other than Juan Di Vargas' Ferdinand II Chair for Biblical Studies, each chair is named for someone who contributed to their field of study. Below is a brief biography of each of these historical figures.

Alessandro Barsanti (1858-1917) was an Italian architect and an early figure in Egyptology. Barsanti discovered the tomb of the Pharaoh Akhenaten in December 1891. He worked for the Egyptian Antiquities Service and oversaw the transfer of the Cairo Museum's collection from the original Giza site to the present location in Cairo.

Jane Dewar Schaberg (1938-2012) served as the Professor of Religious Studies and of Women's Studies at the University of Detroit Mercy from 1977 to 2009. Dr. Schaberg's publications deal with the New Testament, including commentary on the Infancy Narratives, the Gospel of Luke, and on feminist contributions to historical and literary research. Her noted and controversial works include: *The Illegitimacy of Jesus: a Feminist Interpretation of the Infancy Narratives, The*

Resurrection of Mary Magdalene: Legends, Apocrypha and the Christian Testament, and many essays on women's studies.

Dr. Taha Baqir (1912-1984) is considered one of Iraq's most eminent archaeologists. The works he is remembered for include the Akkadian to Arabic translation of the *Epic of Gilgamesh*, his decipherment of Sumero-Akkadian mathematical tablets, his Akkadian law code discoveries, and his excavations at Sumerian sites, such as Shaduppum in Baghdad.

GLOSSARY

Abel: (Multi-color Mage) According to biblical legend, the second-born son of Adam and Eve, murdered by his brother Cain. In vampire legend, Abel cast one of the three spells, which became the Curse and transformed Cain into the original vampire. A multi-colored mage noted as being strongest in Silver magic. Abel's death was revenge for his part in the murder of Cain.

Abel, Book of: A vampire gospel of questionable authority, which some believe contains the real story of the creation of the Curse. Scholars in the vampire clans debate both the authenticity of the text and the identity of the author.

Adam: (Multi-color Mage) According to biblical legend, the first man. In reality, this occasional Gold magic wielder was the first disciple of the minor Sumerian deity, Yahweh. He is the father of Cain, Abel, Seth, and their three sisters.

Aluka: (Hebrew - Leech) Slang term used by ancient vampires for the hangers-on at a vampire court.

Armand: (Vampire, presents as a Sixth-Generation Bel-Kino Clan, is a

Fifth-Generation Kalumtum Clan) Armand was born a peasant in a small village outside of Milan, Italy in the late 15th century. As a young man, he showed an aptitude for studying and fashion, which drew the attention of both the Lorelei and Kalumtum clans. On his way to Milan to try his luck gaining an apprenticeship, a dying elder of the Kalumtum clan took him. This vampire used Armand's youthful strength to recover, and the pair escaped to the court of the Grand Duke of Milan. The elder vizier took Armand on as his apprentice and trained him in the arts of learning and advising the influential. When Armand reached the age of twenty-five, his mentor was given permission by the Grand Duke of Milan to grant him the Gift of Caine. Armand served as an advisor at various courts around Italy until the rise of Mussolini disrupted the power of the vampire courts. The Izcacus clan came hunting for Armand and his mentor seeking to destroy the Kalumtum vampires. Armand and his mentor escaped to the United States and separated to better their chances of avoiding detection. Armand adopted the guise of being of the sixth generation of the royal Bel-Kino clan for many decades until he met Richard St. Martin. To escape actual death at the hand of Lord Hunter, Armand pledged his service to the new Lord of all Vampires. As vizier of the most influential of all vampire courts, Armand helps maintain the fictional difference between Richard's two legendary personas, Lord Hunter and Lord Slayer.

Ashtoreth: (Vampire Clan) A female-dominated clan composed of women from all twelve tribes of Israel took their name from the principle goddess of the Semitic people. Their symbol is a nine-pointed star. The Ashtoreth claim Astryiah, an ancient vampire of Hebrew legend, founded them. The oldest of the clan is the sixth generation elder, Davke-Mot, who received the Gift of Cain around the time of Roman Emperor Augustus. The Jewish revolt against Roman rule from 65-70 of the Common Era (C.E.) destroyed many if not all the eldest members of the clan and their lore.

Astryiah: (Third-Generation Vampire) An Ancient Jewish female vampire. The information is conflicting as to whether she is the third or fourth generation from Cain. Fragmentary evidence discovered in the Dead Sea Scrolls places her in the third generation as a daughter of Nina-Ishtar. Legends credit her as the founder of the Ashtoreth Clan.

Barghest: (Vampire Clan) A twisted and deformed vampire clan. Legends and rumors say the members once possessed remarkable beauty until their third-generation sire Parthalán offended Cain. According to legend, Cain cursed the bloodline to be as twisted and deformed on the outside as they are on the inside. Members of this clan come from amongst the most beautiful, vain, and arrogant mortals. The Barghest version of the Curse comes with a surprise for those few who are twisted and deformed of the body but possess beautiful souls. These individuals suffer a reverse of the curse and become beautiful. This clan established an extensive information network, and its members are legendary in their abilities to keep and collect secrets.

Beauty, House of: (Mortal Hunters) The descendants of Belle or Beauty from the story *Beauty and the Beast*. The members of the House of Beauty are renowned shifter hunters. Led by the Huntress of the House, women dominate the leadership of this family. In the 15th century, a son of the line became the Hunter of the House but died in battle after only a few years as Hunter. In the 21st century, Kieran Samuel Belle-Cooper became the Hunter of the House of Beauty and began a new era in the family history.

Bellabarisruk: (Third-Generation Vampire) A former Chaldean nobleman and Chief of the Magi, who usurped the Babylonian throne. His usurpation brought him to the attention of Sharru-Kino, the second-generation vampire king of El-Abel. Bellabarisruk received the Gift of Cain and transformed into the first vampire of the third generation. He founded the princely Bel-Kino Clan.

Bel-Kino, Clan: (Vampire Clan) Founded by Bellabarisruk sometime after the biblical Flood. These vampires choose only those with proven political leadership skills. They rule over the various clans of vampires in a given city, county, province, or country depending on their age, skills, and power. Regardless of how much territory they control, the leader's title is Grand Duke or Grand Duchess and addressed as Your Grace.

Cain: (Multi-colored Mage, First Vampire) According to biblical legend, the first-born son of Adam and Eve, the murderer of his brother Abel. In vampire legend and lore, Cain is the first vampire. Based on myths and legends, Cain farmed the lands of the first family's valley and, using Emerald magic, served as a healer. The Book of Abel, a vampiric gospel of questionable authority, says Cain attempted to stop a duel between his brothers Abel and Seth but fell victim to their deadliest spells. These spells added to Cain's life-giving and preserving Emerald magic, forming the transforming basis of the Curse.

Children of Cain: The term used by vampires to describe themselves.

Cult of Cain: (Mortal servants) Developed during Cain's extended stay among the nomads of the Asian steppes. Due to his dark appetites, these people thought of him as Komur Han and gave their third-born sons to his service. After a few centuries, Cain grew bored and moved on, but his cult remained and became influential within the ranks until called to the West to infiltrate the followers of the crucified Christ. They serve as mortal eyes and ears within the most sacred of Mother Church's sites. Members of the Cult of Cain wear a cross with a secret compartment in which is hidden a vial with a single drop of blood inside. According to the sect's traditions, this is the blood of Cain. Those who serve in the Cult of Cain wear the habits of many different monastic orders, such as the Cistercian, Dominican, Franciscan, Hospitaller, Jesuit, and some say the Templars. When the members of the Cult gather for conclaves, they wear blood-red robes tied with a black, silver, and emerald rope belt. Cultists go barefoot and wear a cross of red stone, garnet for the lower-ranked members, or a ruby for the leadership of the order.

Curse, The: The ancient magic, which transformed Cain from human to vampire. The Curse is a deadly combination of Silver, Ebony, and Emerald magic the removal of which requires a multi-colored mage strongest in Gold magic. Yahweh, the God of Adam, offered Cain the salvation of a bright afterlife, but he refused, demanding justice instead. Divine-level Gold magic locked Cain into his state between life and death. The Curse is tied to Cain's blood and can be "gifted" to others by bringing them close to the brink of mortality and letting them drink the blood of one carrying the curse. According to legend, the one to kill Cain would inherit the Curse seven-fold.

Dante's Inferno: A nightclub in the city of Boston opened in 2118 by Adam FitzCaine as neutral territory for inter-clan or inter-species business negotiations. The nightclub occupies ten of the upper floors of the old Prudential Insurance building. Guests enter the first circle on the top floor and work their way down by upgrading their membership or earning an invitation to the next level. The Inferno is a sex club catering to all fetishes and desires. The ninth circle reserved for Grand Dukes, Pack Alphas, and mortal leaders. The tenth floor is Mr. FitzCaine's private domain.

Database: (Fifth-Generation Vampire, Barghest Clan) Born a slave in ancient Egypt, Database was born with a spinal deformity, which left him twisted and in pain. He served in the dark temple of the god Anubis, where he caught the attention of the fourth-generation Barghest, high priest of Anubis. His village temple sold him to the central temple of Anubis where he expected death. Instead of serving as a sacrifice at the age of eighteen, he received the Gift of Cain. Because of his beautiful soul, his twisted and scarred body underwent the reverse version of the Barghest curse, transforming him into a good-looking young man. He escaped his sire's lair before the elder enslaved him anew. He spent the first four millennia of his unlife hiding from his sire and collecting the secrets of mortals, vampires, shifters, and mages alike. He became the first vampire to encounter the Richard St. Martin after the hunter slew Cain. He is privy to all St. Martin's secrets, including those hidden from his counterpart, Armand.

Dyta, Celina: (Fourth-Generation Vampire, Barghest Clan) This ancient vampire is one of the most dangerous and capable of her generation. Parthalán forced the Curse on the young warrior queen of the tribal ancestors of the Polish people. Her physical beauty warped when the curse on Parthalán's bloodline unleashed the darkness within her soul. The once-mighty warrior queen became a twisted and horrifying hag. She began an actual terror campaign earning the appellation the Crone of the North. Some believe she is the fact behind the stories of Baba Yaga and other ancient evil crones. Sometime in the late medieval period, Celina Dyta slipped into languor and the terror ended. Rumors about her return sprang up in the mid-twentieth century when the Soviet bloc collapsed. Confirmation of her return came in the late twenty-first century when the second Russian Empire rose to power in Eastern Europe. The new Czar of all the Russias ordered her hunted down and destroyed. Her destruction is unconfirmed despite the rumors claiming both Einar Frost and Richard St. Martin as chasing her.

El-Abel: According to vampire legends, the City of Cain located south of Ur along the coast of the Persian Gulf. Cain alone ruled the city for many mortal generations until he became lonely and granted his gift to five of his ministers. While Cain was away visiting a vassal king, two of the five chosen tried to seize the rule of El-Abel for themselves. Cain returned and reclaimed his government, destroyed his rebellious children, and passed control of El-Abel on to his three remaining children. The biblical Flood wiped El-Abel from the map.

El-Abel, the Gospel of: A text written by Adam following the destruction of his son, Cain, and his acceptance of the Curse. This hidden gospel details his final encounter with God and how the Curse became the gift for vampire society. The text contains the means to bring about the end of all vampires and the location of the knife Adam used to slay Cain.

Enoch: In the holy books of the Children of Seth, this is the name of given to the City of Cain, named for Cain's firstborn son. The same chapter of Genesis also denotes a lineage of Cain created by biblical authors at the direction of Seth.

Eve: (Multi-color Mage) By biblical tradition, the first woman, wife of Adam and mother of Cain, Abel, and Seth. In ancient Hebrew writings, Eve is Yahweh's second attempt at making a female companion for Adam. In actuality, she is the first woman disciple of the minor Sumerian god, Yahweh.

FitzCaine, Adam: (Suspected Vampire) The owner of the infamous nightclub Dante's Inferno in the city of Boston. Some proclaim Adam FitzCaine to be a vampire of incredible power, but his generation is unknown. Passing FitzCaine's tests earn supplicants the right to bring their petition before the court of Richard St. Martin for adjudication. He remains unaffiliated with any of the clans, and his nightclub is neutral territory. Vampires of almost all clans are welcome as long as they play by the rules and can afford the membership fees.

Frost, Einar: (Mortal Hunter, created by Phetra H. Novak) Einar Frost is a hunter like his father and his grandfather before him; hunting is in his blood. Born and raised in Sweden, Einar grew up in in the frozen wilderness hunting shifters from the time he was old enough to walk and carry a gun. Vampires are rare, but both his father and grandfather learned the methods of sending these monsters to their final death and passed this knowledge on to Einar. Nothing else matters to Frost but the hunt. In the Scandinavian region, the Frosts rival the fame of the ancient House of Beauty in kills of shifters. The changes over the last decades of the twenty-first century brought Frost many opportunities to expand his hunting territory, which brought him to the attention of the fifth-generation Bel-Kino Grand Duke of St. Petersburg. Frost resents the intrusion of the famous hunter Richard St. Martin into what he claims as his territory. The Czar did not need to invite help to remove the ancient Barghest vampire, Celina Dyta, The Crone of the North. Frost is human and proud. He inherited a legacy to live up to, and he doesn't plan to fuck up.

Genesis, Book of: In the holy books of the Children of Seth, this book contains the stories of the creation through the enslavement of the children of Israel in Egypt. Among these stories are the story of Cain and Abel and the story of Seth. Under Seth's direction, the biblical scribes created the moralistic tales about the first family with the goal of portraying Seth as the biblical hero.

Gift of Cain, The: Term used by vampires to describe the transformation from mortal life to undead life as a vampire.

Grand Duke/Duchess: Vampire ruler of a given territory in the form of a city, county, state, or nation. The Bel-Kino clan provides most of these lords, but some are from other clans. The Grand Duchess of Hollywood is a member of the Lorelei Clan.

Ham, Book of: A non-canonical lost book of the Old Testament attributed to Ham, a son of Noah. Passages in this text purport to describe events leading to the Flood, life on the ark, and in the early days after the end of the Flood.

Howahkan: (Multi-colored Mage, Third-Generation Vampire) In the legends of the early peoples of North America, he was a medicine man of immense power. He wished only to protect his people. Some legends say the Maker gave him the power, for the stories tell of him glowing with golden light whenever he faced down threats to the people. Some of the later legends claim he miscast a spell and summoned a demon by accident, while others claim he cast the spell with the purpose of summoning the monster. Whatever the case may be, Howahkan found himself face-to-face with the second-generation vampire Bel-Sarra, who chose to grant him the Gift of Cain. As Howahkan underwent the change, his Gold magic worked one last transformation on him, leaving him and the males of his bloodline with the ability to sire children with mortal women. Perhaps this was the Maker's answer to his prayers to protect his people, for children born of such unions possess the strength of their vampire fathers plus the ability to detect vampires. Howahkan's voice can charm the most savage of beasts, including a shifter in frenzy. Many of the clan he founded possess this power in varying degrees. Howahkan and his clan are sensitive to sunlight and operate only in the deepest shadows, and they use the Sioux word for shadow, Ohanzee, as their name.

Hubert of Liege, Saint: (Mortal Catholic Priest and Hunter) This eighth-century bishop was canonized as the Patron Saint of Hunters because of his ability to detect vampires and shifters. His profound holiness kept vampires at bay and forced shape-shifters back into human form in the height of their frenzy. His relics are reported to possess the ability to cure rabies and the diseases brought by the bite of wild animals. His feast day is November 3.

Immertun: (Third-Generation Vampire) A gentle scholar-priest of the sect of the Babylonian goddess Ishtar, Immertun's teaching and kind nature attracted the attention of Nina-Ishtar, the second-generation vampire vizier and consort to Sharru-Kino of El-Abel. Depending on the list, he is the second or third created of the third generation. He discovered a method of controlling the beastly nature of vampirism. He founded the scholarly clan Kalumtum, few of whom survive today. Izcacus, who devoured him, taking his power and generation, caught him in the deep sleep of languor.

Izcacus: (Third-Generation Vampire, once Fourth-Generation) Born in Hungary soon after the Magyar invasions of the late ninth century to a Frankish mother and a Magyar warrior. He grew up to become a fierce warrior and a mighty pagan priest. His prowess as both warrior and priest drew the attention of Bellabarisruk, who gave him the Gift of Cain in the early tenth century. Izcacus chaffed under the yoke of Bellabarisruk's rule and sought his freedom. Using his magic and the magic of his fellow shamans, Izcacus broke the controlling bond created by the drinking of his sire's blood. Seeking a way to make himself his sire's equal, Izcacus discovered the resting place of the third-generation scholar vampire, Immertun, and traveled to the location. He drank Immertun dry, destroying the ancient vampire and taking his rank and power among the third generation. Returning to his native Hungary, Izcacus gave the Gift of Cain to many of his fellow priests founding the clan, which preserves the ancient shamanistic traditions and carries his name.

Izcacus: (Vampire Clan) Ruled by a council of warrior-shamans of the fourth generation who choose the strongest warriors or the holiest shaman as candidates for membership, this clan prizes and preserves shamanic traditional magic. They are fierce opponents to the scholarly traditions of the Kalumtum clan. Their legends claim their clan founder destroyed Kalumtum to gain his power and position. They will go out of their way to kill a member of the Kalumtum clan regardless of the sanctions, which will fall on them if the grand duke of the territory learns what they did. Members of the Izcacus clan take on the role of a guardian spirit to a shaman and guide him and his tribe. When a shaman comes close to the end of his days, his guardian spirit will offer him the Gift of Cain so he might join the ancestors and take over guiding the tribe. They made some incursion into Native American and First Nation cultures until the Ohanzee clan and their semi-mortal children the Keme-Nawhaw became aware of and removed them.

Kalumtum: (Vampire Clan) This clan founded by Immertun as a council of scholar-priest to act as advisors to the grand dukes and grand duchesses of the vampire world all but disappeared following the destruction of their founder. Most of the survivors hide in the ranks of the Bel-Kino clan. If any elders above the sixth generation remain active, they remain well hidden.

Khons: (Fourth-Generation Vampire, Barghest Clan) This ancient Egyptian vampire started as a high priest to the god Anubis where he transformed many slaves and sacrifices to Anubis into vampires. He is the creator of Database, the fifth-generation spymaster of Richard St.

Martin. Khons' physical form is so weathered and wrinkled he appears mummified and, by the time of Rameses XII's reign came, he was to be worshiped as a mummy god.

Lamasthu: (Third-Generation Vampire) Ancient Babylon demon-goddess. Her name means daughter of Heaven. The second-generation vampire general, Bel-Sharra, created the demon-goddess as his consort. Husbands dragged adulteress wives to the goddess' temple when they found them pregnant by other men. The bastard children ripped from the mother's womb became sacrifices to her. Lamasthu chose six women from those brought to her altar as her handmaidens and granted them the Gift of Cain.

Lamasthu: (Vampire Clan) Since ancient Babylon, this clan accepts only females, beginning with their founder and her six handmaidens. Each new member is a woman with a child deemed illegitimate under patriarchal laws and force aborted or sacrificed after birth. Many of the members "died" of blood loss due to the procedure or during childbirth. Members of this clan serve as midwives, nurses, doctors, paramedics, nannies, or other positions, which bring them into contact with their chosen prey or a possible convert.

Languor: The term used by vampires to describe long periods of inactivity by many ancients. The majority of the primordials are thought to be in this state. In some circles, the awakening of certain elder vampires is thought to herald the return of the primordials.

Laverna Salacia: (Third-Generation Vampire) The Vampire Queen of Pirates, Laverna Salacia received the Gift of Cain from Nina-Ishtar the Queen of Vampires somewhere around 5000 B.C.E. (Before Common Era). Only the pirate queen understands how she came to the attention of the daughter of Cain and she keeps the tale to herself. She was born somewhere in Italy and grew up a street urchin and thief. Laverna Salacia took to the sea early in her immortal life and became the inspiration for many of the dark tales of spirits who lure sailors to their doom. Her fame or infamy inspired the legends of two Roman

Goddesses; Laverna, Goddess of Thieves and Cheats, although she is quite honorable in her dealings and her word is her bond. As Salacia, she is worshiped as the Goddess of wide-open seas and as Neptune's wife. Laverna Salacia is left-handed, and many of her earliest chosen share this trait. Priests of Laverna honor her by pouring libations on her altar with their left hand. This primordial founded the Salaqua (Salt Water) clan after the destruction of Rome during the reign of Nero. The clan, both vampire and human thralls, took to the sea full-time to escape the wrath of Cain for over expanding. Most encounters with Laverna Salacia take place aboard her flagship, which always carries the name *Sunniva Mare* (Sun-gifted Sea). The current version is the former *USN Freedom*, a littoral combat ship.

Lord Hunter: Both mortal rulers and vampire grand dukes gave this title to Richard St. Martin. Ancient vampire prophecy says this person will one day destroy Cain and become the new lord of the vampires. Lord Hunter is the title by which Armand administers justice at Richard's court. Adam FitzCaine runs Dante's Inferno as a neutral territory under the protection of Lord Hunter.

Lord Slayer: Only vampires use the second of Richard St. Martin's titles, given to him by the Grand Duke of Upstate New York, during Richard's days as a mortal hunter. The grand duke bestowed the title after Richard killed several elders in his quest to discover those responsible for the murder of his fiancée. Under this title, Richard dispenses personal justice on vampires whose acts violate vampire law.

Lorelei: (Fourth-Generation Vampire, Lamasthu Clan) An eighth-century Germanic tribal chieftain's daughter with a golden voice. She is referred to as the Siren of the Rhine because of her beauty and voice lured suitors to her father's territory from as far away as Rome. The outcome of one such encounter ended in disaster for Lorelei. One of her suitors refused her rejection and raped her on the shore of the Rhine. Distressed and disgraced, Lorelei sought to drown herself in the river but was rescued by the third-generation vampire Lamasthu and given the Gift of Cain. Now a vampire, Lorelei sought revenge against the man who destroyed her mortal life. The dark magic of the change made her golden voice a deadly weapon. She sang by the shore as her rapist's ship sailed away and her voice drew the attention of the crew from their duties at a critical moment, and the ship struck the rocks and sank. Her gift allowed her to break the bond between her and Lamasthu, and the two female vampires parted ways. Lorelei traveled and found a young musician whose music blended well with her voice and offered him the Gift of Cain. Together, they founded a sub-clan of vampire artists of all types. Those who found beauty in the world they preserved. The group they founded took Lorelei's name as their own.

Lorelei: (Vampire Sub-Clan) Members of this sub-clan possess gifts in the arts. They are singers, actors, musicians, painters, sculptors, or anyone of the many arts. While many display physical beautiful, not all share the trait. The prime requirement for members of this clan is the ability to appreciate and produce beauty in the arts. Some of those recruited turned out to be frauds in the arts, posers who make up some of the vilest art critics in the business.

Mesu: (Egyptian - son) Used by Khons when referring to Database in particular but also any of the male vampires he's given the Gift of Cain.

Nazaratus: (Fourth-Generation Vampire, Kalumtum Clan, pretending to be Fifth-Generation Bel-Kino) The last elder of his clan, he manages to stay well-hidden and well protected from the Izcacus clan. Born and raised as a Babylonian priest, Nazaratus came to the attention of third-generation vampire Immertun towards the end of his mortal life. According to Greek legend, Nazaratus trained Pythagoras in the divine mysteries. Scholars are uncertain if he was a vampire or if the training was his last act as a mortal. Nazaratus was seeking a pupil in the Italian countryside when Izcacus attacked and destroyed Immertun and began his war on the Kalumtum clan. He adopted the name Pasquale Silvestro and helped establish the court of the Bel-Kino Grand Duke of Milan. As Silvestro, he is the sire and mentor of Armand.

Ohanzee: (Vampire Clan) In the days before the people of North America organized themselves into tribes and nations, Bel-Sarra came seeking a candidate for the Gift of Cain. He found and gifted a young brave called Howahkan (of the mysterious voice in the Sioux language). The majority of the vampires of this clan are Native American or First Nation members. The Ohanzee, from the Sioux word for shadow, are fierce protectors of their peoples and seek to find a way to reconnect with the Maker. Like their founder, members of this clan are sensitive to sunlight and operate from the deepest shadows. Some members also possess Howahkan's ability to calm wild creatures with their voice. They are rivals with the Izcacus and destroy members of the clan on sight. Only on rare occasions does someone of European descent receive the Ohanzee clan's version of the Gift of Cain. Something in Howahkan's relationship with the Maker allowed him to retain the ability to mate with mortals and produce children with some aspects of the gift, like enhanced strength or capacity to commune with spirits. This mating ability is present only in male members of the clan. Because of their undead status, female Ohanzee cannot conceive or carry a mortal child to term. These offspring make efficient vampire hunters, as they can detect the presence of the undead. They formed a secret order crossing tribal identity, as their vampire fathers' clan does. They adopted a name combining the Algonquin word for secret (Keme) with the Winnebago word for wood (Nawhaw). The Keme-Nawhaws are warriors, medicine men, and a few wise women, scattered across the various nations.

Parthalán: (Third-Generation Vampire) Once the bright and shining light of Sharru-Kino's court at El-Abel, Parthalán made the mistake of attempting to kill and consume his sire, Sharru-Kino, in front of Cain. The dark power of the first vampire cursed Parthalán and all his bloodline after him to wear their evil on their bodies. His beauty was deformed and twisted as the darkness in his soul revealed. Parthalán fled the ancient Middle East and was reported appearing in Ireland around the time of the Tuatha Dé Danann. He entered into Irish as a barrow ghost after sightings near the burial mounds of kings and heroes. The Gaels called him a Barghest, he adopted the name for himself, and those he sired took adopted for their clan name. Barghest, as he now called himself, made two trips out of Ireland, one to ancient Egypt, where he chose the high priest of Anubis to become one of his first children. Khons rose to achieve the status of a minor god. Barghest's second trip was to the thick forest of Northern Europe, which became part of Poland. Here he met the young warrior queen Celina Dyta and forced the gift on the beautiful warrior maiden, transforming her into the horrid Crone of the North. Parthalán vanished from vampire records around the sixteenth century, and rumors report him lying in languor beneath an ancient tomb.

Primordials: A term used by vampires and hunters alike to identify the most ancient of vampires; Cain, the lost second-generation Bel-Sarra, Sharru-Kino, Nina-Ishtar, and the original members of the third generation. All these vampires date to before the Flood destroyed El-Abel and command powers understood by few outside their generation. While Izcacus controls the abilities of a primordial, they refuse to acknowledge him among their numbers.

Salaqua: (Latin - Salt Water) Vampire clan founded during the reign of the Roman Emperor Nero. This clan was one of several culled on the order of Cain for expanding to the point of revealing the existence of vampires. Taking their land skills to the sea, the vampires of this clan became pirates. This group is unique in recruiting humans to serve in the family sailing their ships and raiding during the daylight. Some of the daylight crews are aware of the status of the night crews, but most are only temporary and become food sources for the vampires. The Primordial Laverna Salacia commands all pirates, both human and vampire, and does not tolerate other clans attempting to enter the pirate/raider trade.

Sigrún: (Third-Generation Vampire) As a young girl in the frozen north, Sigrún became a slave when a band of warriors from a rival village overran her village. Subjected to the worst treatments, the young slave girl survived until a warrior woman took her from her drunken and abusive master. Sigrún trained hard before being inducted into a band of warrior women called the Valkyrie, where she excelled and flourished, rising to become the band's leader. Only a few years into her leadership, the second-generation vampire Bel-Sarra wandered into the Valkyrie encampment seeking a candidate worthy of the Gift of Cain. He issued a challenge to meet him in combat, which Sigrún accepted. The fight lasted an hour before Sigrún score a lethal blow to her opponent. Bel-Sarra stood before the gathered warriors with Sigrún's sword piercing his body. Before their eyes, the man pulled the sword free and the wound healed. He invited Sigrún to return with him to his homeland to meet his Lord and gain his blessing before he granted her his gift. Sigrún traveled to El-Abel and met Cain, who listened to Bel-Sarra relate the tale of their fight. Cain granted Bel-Sarra's request to give Sigrún the gift. After the warrior woman received the Gift of Cain, Sigrún returned home where she chose her nine strongest women to receive the gift from her. When all recovered from the transformation, they discovered they now shared a bond, which let them borrow fighting techniques from their sisters. In time, after each of the nine earned the right to grant the gift to a chosen circle of nine sisters, they learned this was the gift of the Valkyrie Clan of Vampires.

Sons of Seth: Old vampire term for mortals.

Valkyries: (Vampire Clan) Far to the north the second-generation vampire, Bel-Sarra wandered looking for his third and final candidate for the Gift of Cain. In the frozen wastes of what is now Scandinavia, he found the warrior maiden Sigrún and her band of warrior women, the Valkyries. The warrior women, eager for greater strength to use against the men from rival villages, urged Sigrún to accept the Gift of Cain. When Sigrún returned from receiving the blessing of Cain, Father of Vampires, and the gift from Bel-Sarra, she chose nine of her fiercest warriors to receive the gift from her. The Valkyries select only strong women for membership in the clan. For this clan, the Gift of Cain allows each Valkyrie to share her combat skills with the sisters of her circle. A Valkyrie circle consists of an elder and the nine vampires she created in honor of Sigrún's original group.

ABOUT THE AUTHOR

Kethric Wilcox began writing and publishing as a personal challenge to be creative in a new medium. He was attracted to the LGBT Romance genre after reading several paranormal romances where shape-shifters never faced dangers outside the relationship issues thrown at them by their authors. Thus, was born the shifter hunting House of Beauty on the premise of a twisted fairy tale. What if *Beauty and the Beast* didn't possess the traditional happy ending? Wilcox's Legend of the Silver Hunter trilogy seeks to answer this question. The series asks what happens if a member of this family falls in love with a descendant of the Beast. Can they find a happy ending, or are they doomed to repeat the tale? Born and raised in Massachusetts, Wilcox now lives and works in Little Rock, Arkansas in a house he and his partner renovated. By day, Wilcox is a graphic artist and exhibit designer, and at night, an author of paranormal romances.

The Curse is the first book in Wilcox's new Origin of the Vampires trilogy, which continues in *Lord Hunter* and *Lord Slayer*. This trilogy set in a dystopian future of the Silver Hunter world follows Richard St. Martin's quest to discover the secrets of the vampire race he now leads. Wilcox is also working on the Legacy of the Silver Hunter trilogy (*The Goldilocks Pledge*, *Ruby Wine*, and *Black Snow*.) The Legacy series continues Kieran and Cory's story from the viewpoints of other couples in their lives.

Details about the world of the Silver Hunter can be found on Wilcox's blog at www.kethricwilcox.com.